Fiona M... ...he
UK, but ...er
family be... ...ere
her father wor... She left ... PR career in Lon... to travel
and found herself in Australia where she fell in love with
the country, its people and one person in particular. She
...as since roamed the world working for her own travel
...ublishing company, which she runs with her husband.
...iona lives with her young family in South Australia.

...ead about Fiona or chat to her on the bulletin board via
...er website: www.fionamcintosh.com

...nd out more about Fiona McIntosh and other Orbit
...thors by registering for the free monthly newsletter at
...vw.orbitbooks.net

By Fiona McIntosh

The Quickening
Myrren's Gift
Blood and Memory
Bridge of Souls

Trinity
Betrayal
Revenge
Destiny

Percheron
Odalisque
Emissary
Goddess

FIONA McINTOSH

DESTINY

TRINITY: BOOK THREE

www.orbitbooks.net

ORBIT

First published in Australia in 2002 by Voyager,
HarperCollins*Publishers* Pty Limited
First published in Great Britain in 2006 by Orbit
Reprinted 2007 (twice), 2008, 2009, 2011, 2013

A CIP catalogue record for this book
is available from the British Library.

ISBN 978-1-84149-459-3

Typeset in Garamond Three by Palimpsest Book Production Limited,
Grangemouth, Stirlingshire
Printed and bound in Great Britain by
Clays Ltd, St Ives plc

Just for Ian. Fx

Acknowledgments

And so this tale finally ends and I have loved crafting it. Sincere thanks to all who have followed the series and especially to the countless readers who have taken the time and trouble to contact me. Your enthusiasm for the Trinity trilogy is the best reward for so many hours spent at a lonely keyboard.

There are those whose generous support has been invaluable over the past couple of years, especially authors Sara Douglass and Robin Hobb, as well as my editor Nicola O'Shea at HarperCollins who is a dream to work with. I must also give a nod here to the regular visitors to my website's bulletin board for the late-night laughs, companionship and constant encouragement.

Which leaves my close friends and lovely family to thank, the most deserving of these being Will and Jack who seem to accept this solitary pursuit of their mother's with their usual good grace. Gratitude and love to my heartiest critic and most ardent supporter, Ian.

THE EXOTIC
ISLES

Neame

CIPRES

N
W — E
S

TALLINOR

Caradoon

Kyrakavia

RORK'YEL

Valley of the
Sentients

Caremboche

Brittelbury

Ildagarth

Warbyn

Bebberton

Saddleworth

THE GREAT FOREST

Duntaryn

The Heartwood

Mexford

Fragglesham

Tal

Axon

Minstead

Perswych

Twyfford Cross

Flat Meadows

Brewis

Mallee Marsh

Hatten

Harymon

Arandon

PROLOGUE

Darganoth of the Host walked with the Custodian through the breathtakingly beautiful gardens of the gods. The King's voice was kind. 'Thank you for coming, Lys. I'm sorry we welcome you back to us during such troubling times.'

She did not lift her eyes or smile. Lys walked stiffly beside the King of the gods, her heart heavy. 'My lord, I have failed you.' But she had not come here for forgiveness. She had come to seek the help of her fellow gods and the Elders.

'This is not true, Lys,' he offered gently. 'Come, let us walk through the magnolia valley.'

He took her by the arm and guided her through the small gate which would take them into the cool, fragranced corridor of splendid trees. She allowed herself to be led into the exquisite surrounds which, after so long in the Bleak, might have lifted her spirits. But Lys was distracted; filled with despair.

'Dorgryl tricked me, my lord; fooled like a child I was.' She shook her head sadly.

'He fooled me too, Lys. And now he has tricked us again.' He paused, then added: 'It is for the last time.'

Darganoth inhaled the sweet perfume of his magnolia trees. He was tall and broad with black hair and the brightest of blue eyes with a piercing gaze that could hold one still as no chains could. He is so like his son, Lys noted, with the same flaw of – what was it? Kindness? Weakness? – she knew not what. Still, it saw the King unable to destroy his own brother.

Darganoth interrupted her thoughts in a voice achingly similar to another's. 'We must consider what to do now, not dwell on what is done. We cannot change the past.'

Lys felt slightly reassured by his calm. 'Have the Elders discussed it, my lord?'

But her fragile confidence crumbled with his next words.

'They have. They offer no solution. They assure me that in order to finally deal with Dorgryl, our precious ones may perish.'

Lys stopped. She felt her skin go clammy even though it was cool beneath the canopy of trees.

'No!' The King turned back as Lys fell to her knees. 'You cannot, your majesty. I beg of you, don't desert them now.'

'Lys, we no longer have any choice.'

'What do you think will happen?' she whispered.

'I presume Dorgryl will overwhelm the body he inhabits and we will be forced to interfere against the Law and Quell him once and for all.'

'Murder your own heir,' she said bleakly. 'I thought it could not be done.'

'There is a way,' he said, softly. 'He was always at risk,

Lys. He must pay the ultimate price, but I can ensure it won't be in vain — Dorgryl will die with him.'

'And what of the others, my lord?' Her voice trembled. All this time of patience and watchfulness; centuries of pain for the Paladin; such sacrifice of young souls — Lys could not believe it was all over, and in vain.

Darganoth shook his head; said nothing.

She felt anger rise. Her voice was hard this time, no longer caring for protocol. 'We cannot let these loved ones die. They've given their lives to us, been through so much hurt and despair, with more still to come. I cannot stand by and watch any longer, your majesty. Do you forget who it is I gave to the cause of the Trinity?'

She knew she should never have said it — but it could not be helped, the words could not be taken back. She watched the grief move across her beloved King's face; he too had suffered similar pain. He knew as well as she what it meant to sacrifice a life, a life which he had sired.

He bit back on the words which sprang to his lips; who knew better than he what it was to lose a treasured child.

'I can never forget the lives we have enmeshed in this, Lys, but Dorgryl's escape has changed the complexion of this struggle. With him, my son becomes more powerful than we could have ever dared to dream . . . even in our nightmares.'

'We must *not* forsake Tor and Alyssa, nor their children, your majesty,' she implored.

'Then pray my firstborn is strong enough to withstand Dorgryl,' he took her hand, 'and that Torkyn is stronger still.'

Lys felt shattered. Her King gave her no hope with

these words. In truth they sounded the death knell for the very people she contrived to protect.

Distraught, she took her leave and fled the grove. Beauty had no place in her existence now.

I

An Omen

The grumble of not-so-distant thunder was now ominous. It had been a long ride to get this close to the city but Prime Herek had decided, despite the bleak weather, to push on to reach Tal before the Thirteenth Bell. Apart from the men's desire to be back in the comfort of the castle quarters, he knew the King appreciated the decision made a few hours earlier to ride on through the night. Of them all, he seemed the most eager to get home. Lorys would never say anything to this effect, of course, but Herek understood the sovereign's desire to be reunited with his young Queen. The forced separation of recent weeks due to official duties had fully tested his usually dependable good humour.

Lightning, still just far enough away not to startle the horses, suddenly lit the sky in warning. The column slowed to a walk.

'What do you think?' Lorys asked the Prime, knowing the certain blunt response would not be what he wanted to hear. Herek was a conservative man who would never put the Sovereign, nor the men beneath his command, under unnecessary threat. He had been trained well by the former prime, Kyt Cyrus.

'The storm is coming towards us faster than I anticipated, your highness,' the Prime admitted.

Lorys did not disguise his bitter disappointment. This would mean another night without his beloved Alyssa in his arms. Both men looked up gloomily towards the moon as it slid behind heavy, black clouds, plunging the way ahead into a murky and unwelcome darkness.

Herek knew his proposal would make for an unhappy King this night but it could not be helped; safety had to be his first consideration. 'My lord, I believe we should set up camp now before the rain arrives. I would suggest that this offers more shelter than we would have ahead.' He nodded towards the small ridge nearby which provided a safe and convenient gully.

The thunder rolled threateningly towards them again, much louder this time. When the sky blazed overhead, Lorys capitulated. 'As you see fit, Prime,' he said, disappointment knifing through him.

Herek held up his hand to halt the column of soldiers. Orders were given and dispatched through his captains; within moments the entire Company was busily unsaddling horses and setting camp for the night.

Someone grabbed the reins of his stallion and led it away but Lorys was too preoccupied by his own grim thoughts to even thank the man. Normally he would unsaddle gladly, and wipe down, feed and water the horse himself – he was a King who led by example, far preferring physical prowess and the outdoor life to the paperwork and bureaucratic tasks involved in running his realm – but right now he allowed it all to happen around him as he finally accepted that Alyssa would not be fussing over him and warming his chilled bones tonight. And yet he so badly wanted to hold her again; so badly wanted to look Gyl in the eye and admit that he, King Lorys of Tallinor, was his father; so desperately wanted to roam the halls of his palace again.

It was not like Lorys to feel so insecure, but he had been in this pensive mood since an event earlier that afternoon. The Company had been passing a field where a small group of ravens had gathered, their calls loud and grating. It was not a common sight in Tallinor. The raven was considered the most intelligent species of bird, shrouded in ghoulish mystery and superstition, and the Tallinese tended to be wary of it. It was no surprise to Lorys that the entire party of soldiers had murmured a warding at the birds, invoking the Light to protect them, but even he had been vaguely alarmed when the large birds had suddenly lifted into the air as one, flown past the column and then wheeled back towards them. They had appeared to fly deliberately towards the men, and, being at the front, it was the King who had been in direct range. The birds had flown over and one had been low enough to swoop by the King's head, raking his short hair as it squawked in its horrible voice, unsettling him from his horse.

No man in the Company had dared so much as chuckle at seeing him fall. Even the most simple-minded of men understood such an omen. A collective breath had been drawn by the soldiers and Herek had immediately leapt down beside the King, quick to dispel any superstitious nonsense. Lorys had said nothing in this regard, merely making some jest which had relieved the tension amongst the men. He had remounted and they were quickly on their way, the incident apparently forgotten.

Except it had not been forgotten by the King. He was a spiritual man and this attack by the black birds of evil was seen by him to be a marking – that his life was now haunted by a black shroud. He felt himself touched by death. He did not share this notion with his companions and tried to put it out of his mind, but it lingered, nibbling at his resolve during the long journey until he felt ragged by the weight of its portent.

'King Lorys.' It was the Prime back again, ever attentive.

'Yes?' he replied, snapping himself out of his black thoughts.

'Fires are lit, sire. Perhaps you care to warm yourself? Food is being prepared now.'

'Thank you. Where's Caerys?'

The page was at his side in a second. 'Here, your majesty.'

'I want a rider sent ahead to the palace.'

Lorys watched Herek grimace but knew the Prime would not challenge the King.

Caerys nodded. 'I'll fetch someone immediately. Will you be sending a written message, sire?'

The King blinked; he thought about it a moment. 'No. I'll brief him.'

'At once, sire. I shall fetch a messenger,' Caerys said, turning.

Lorys glanced at Herek again but the Prime's face now betrayed nothing. The soldier stood to attention. 'I'll see to the men, my lord, if you are comfortable now?'

The King nodded. It was clear Herek did not approve of risking the man, or his horse, out in the blackness and the approaching storm just so Lorys could send a message of love back to the Queen. But Lorys needed to reach out to her. After the scene with the ravens, it would be reassuring to have some communication with Alyssa – even if, for the time being, it was one-sided.

The storm had moved in around them more quickly than any had imagined it could. Their only solace was the moon, which broke through the clouds momentarily to provide a watery glow through the drizzle. Now hunched beneath rough shelter, the soldiers worked hard at keeping the flames of their small fires fanned and alive. The horses were skittish and many of the men chose to stand by their precious mounts, stroking and talking to them whilst the worst of the storm raged.

Herek sat by his sovereign and encouraged him to eat. Lorys chewed on some dried meat out of habit more than hunger – there had not been enough time to warm any food. He was glad for the wine though, and drank thirstily to drown his sorrow. As he swallowed the last of his second cup a massive thunderclap sounded directly above. They all turned towards the animals, except the King, whose eyes were fixed absently on a distant single tree he could just pick out in the thin light, bending against the angry wind but still proudly standing atop a small hillock. He had been staring in its direction for a while, keeping his thoughts private and brooding, angry with himself now that he had risked a lone rider out in this weather. He regretted his decision bitterly.

The sudden mighty clap of thunder was accompanied by a bright, thick hand of lightning which illuminated the entire sky for a few moments as it reached a long finger towards the tree.

Only the King witnessed it. The tree was struck by all the fiery anger of the heavens, splitting in two and bursting into flame. The rain which had turned heavy subdued the fire immediately. To Lorys, it felt like his blood had become icy in that moment; clogged frozen in his veins as he watched the violence.

Herek turned back to the King. 'That was close, sire.' He saw Lorys, mouth slightly ajar, staring blankly ahead. The King was clearly shocked. The Prime followed the direction of the King's stare, trying to discover a reason and his eyes locked onto what had his Sovereign's attention. Ahead the tree which had stood so strong and proud, alone on the small hill, was a smashed, smouldering wreck.

He looked back at Lorys, a pit in his stomach. 'Sire,' he said, gently.

'It's the worst of all omens, Herek.' The King's voice was soft, filled with fear.

'My lord . . .' Herek hoped he could break the spell of the ruined tree, devastated by the fingers of the Host. It was true though: to witness the destruction of a tree by the gods was considered the bleakest of all warnings. He tried to think of something comforting to say and found himself without words.

In the end, the King came to his rescue. His voice sounded resigned. 'The gods have spoken to me, Herek. They warned me earlier today with the ravens and now it seems they are reminding me.'

'Please, your highness, I—'

Lorys interrupted whatever his Prime had intended to say. 'It is a sign, Herek.'

Before the Prime could say anything further, the King stood and stepped out from the ridge's shelter towards the blackened tree. He waved away a shocked Caerys who had immediately followed, making it clear his own dark thoughts were company enough. Herek could not allow this. He ran after his King. Lorys moved swiftly but as though in a stupor. He had eyes only for the still-smouldering tree. For some reason he felt he needed to make peace with it — as though it had taken the rebuke from the gods meant for him. Why did he feel like this? All his ghosts joined him on the hill. Was it Nyria's untimely death? Was it marrying Alyssa so suddenly? . . . Or perhaps just the pure guilt of desiring and loving her so much?

Or did it go deeper still? Was it siring the child, Gyl, now a superb young man and yet one he failed every day by not telling him who his father was. Or was it Gynt? Did the execution of Torkyn Gynt still haunt him after all these years? Could he ever atone for the darkest of all sins — allowing a madman like Goth to carry out his grisly work under royal proclamation? So many atrocities perpetrated on good, loyal citizens in his name.

And then he wondered with fresh despair whether a freak occurrence on a windswept, stormy night in Perswych could truly be an omen. He allowed all these thoughts to loose themselves upon him as he ran now towards the tree. He must touch it; feel its death, show his sorrow for its end and his regret for all his questionable decisions.

The King saw the skies lighten, heard the monstrous slam of thunder directly overhead and realised, with a sense of wonder as well as acceptance, that the old adage of lightning never striking twice in the same spot was indeed a fallacy. The hand of the gods reached across the sky, creating daylight in that terrifying second as Prime

Herek watched the deathlight arc once again towards the land and murder his King in the early hours before dawn.

Queen Alyssa hugged a thick shawl about her. It was a very early hour before dawn and she had not slept, unlike her young visitors in comfortable lodgings not far from her own chambers. They were exhausted not only from the walk to Tal, but also by the emotion of the previous night. And why not? She herself was rocked by the revelations. She stood silently by the window watching the storm lash the moors. Alyssa hated storms; always craved their end when the heavy rains would finally break.

The man she had loved for most of her life moved behind her; without the disk of archalyt on her forehead she could sense his power shimmering around him as his arms slid about her waist.

'What did the messenger say?' he asked.

'Poor fellow. I'm surprised they risked sending him out in this weather. Apart from a personal message from Lorys, he told us that the Company will not be returning as planned. The storm is too great. They are camped safely outside Perswych and will depart at first light.'

Tor said nothing immediately but she could feel his relief.

'Then we have this night together,' he whispered into her ear, risking a kiss in her hair.

'What's left of it,' she replied just as softly, turning into his arms. 'Tor, what are we going to do?'

He searched her face; her beautiful face . . . the one he had tried to forget but never quite managed to. 'I must find our other son,' he said firmly, staring deep into her eyes, refusing to allow her to look away.

'And me?'

'Alyssa, I will not make this difficult for you. I promise.'

He hugged her close, understanding her helplessness, feeling it himself too. She was only just recovering from the physical shock of learning a few hours earlier that she was a mother to two grown children. There was no mistaking them: Gidyon virtually identical to his father and his sister, Lauryn, so close in looks to herself that no one, not even the King, could have disputed who the parents were.

And then there was the shock of learning that her first love still lived . . . and she now married to the King. He felt her despair. No son had died in the Heartwood as she had been told by all those she loved. Instead this son, together with his newborn sister, were vanished away at birth to some other world, leaving her in ignorance to suffer years of pain over the boy's death. And now fresh heartache at hearing that another son, weak – almost dead – was secreted away deep in the Forests of Tallinor. Alyssa shook her head with disbelief that any of this could be happening to her. She had two living husbands now – and she loved them both.

It was as though Tor had heard her thoughts and cut through all her confusion to clarify what had to be done. 'Rubyn must be found, Alyssa. We must complete the Trinity.'

'And then what!' She did not mean to sound so churlish.

He shrugged. 'I hope Lys might explain more.'

'I hate that woman.' She watched his discomfort at her words. 'Oh, I know you trust her, Tor, but she brings nothing but sorrow to this life of mine . . . and to everyone she touches.'

'She is as much a victim as we.' He wished he could tell her more but he had given a promise.

'No! Lys is just as bad as Merkhud and Sorrel, manipulating our lives and creating pain. How can you allow her to keep you as her puppet, dancing to her tune?'

'I have no choice, Alyssa. Orlac is free. Our only hope is to face him and we need the Trinity to succeed.'

'Tor, you don't know anything – you only believe what she tells you!'

Alyssa suddenly felt sorry. He looked so beaten.

'I have no one else to trust. Orlac is coming.'

She felt the fight go out of her at his final words. He was right. They were all victims and they could choose to give in or to at least die fighting this god.

'What do you want me to do?' she finally asked of him, wishing his handsome head was not bowed by the same empty despair she felt.

'Look after Gidyon and Lauryn. Keep them safe whilst I go in search of Rubyn. If and when I return with him, we will consider our next move.'

She nodded; said nothing.

Tor finally voiced the question he feared most to ask. 'What about the King?'

'Lorys will be given the truth. He will lay no hand on our children, you can be sure of this, Tor. They have my absolute protection.'

Tor shuddered. Similar words had been said to his parents many years ago by a silver-haired man who had also believed he had a royal authority of safety to offer. His thoughts drifted back to Jhon and Ailsa Gynt. He must see them.

'When will you leave?' she asked.

He glanced towards the window. 'Before dawn . . . soon.' He looked at her, sadness flitting across his face. 'It's best I'm not here when the King returns.'

'How will he believe me if you are not here for him to see for himself?'

'The children are enough proof,' he said flatly.

'I have never told him of our marriage.'

'Keep him in ignorance,' Tor said, bluntly. 'He has enough distress headed his way.'

Alyssa turned back to the window at the sound of an almighty thunderclap. She looked out just in time to see the sky turn almost white as a massive strike of lightning arced menacingly across the land. She saw its jagged pattern disappear behind the moors and would not understand until later that morning the great wave of sadness she suddenly felt pass through her.

With these final theatrics the storm broke and the heavens opened, unleashing a hard and relentless rain which would last for several days, making a setting fit for the great sorrow of Tallinor at the death of its King.

Far away across the seas in the land of Cipres, itself being lashed by torrential rain, another woman looked out from a palace window and made a fearful decision. She was not a queen, but she protected one . . . a young one.

'Why these dreams?' she asked herself. Relentlessly invading her nights – which were sleepless anyway since the death of her beloved Queen Sylven – was a woman's voice. It was a lovely voice which did not frighten her, and yet what she spoke of did.

Hela watched the downpour intensify, finally blanking out views over the manicured gardens and treetops. Why did this dreamspeaker implore her to smuggle the child away from her home? Surely Sarel was coping with enough? Here she was, barely dealing with her own intense grief following her mother's murder, whilst the realm fell into crisis and dignitaries clamoured for the child's immediate coronation; fierce competition was already erupting between the men who sensed they might control the nation as the new Queen's regent until she came of age. Plus, there was a harem to consider for the future and begin assembling, as well as advisers to gather . . . people they could trust with the young mind.

No, it was all too fast.

Sarel was certainly of an age to assume her royal role but Hela knew she could only be a figurehead for a while yet. The young Queen was still too immature and unworldly to make decisions on State matters. Hela shook her head, imagining how Sarel's idyllic childhood would be gone in a flash, replaced with weighty tasks which Sylven had not planned for her beautiful daughter so soon. Hela knew how the former queen had protected Sarel, even from the adoring public, and she had often heard Sylven proclaim privately in her chambers that she would not allow Sarel's special years to be claimed by royal protocol as her own had.

But all of these protestations fell aside as Hela tried to understand the implications of this strange woman's earnest words to flee with the young Queen.

Still more extraordinary, this woman told her to find Torkyn Gynt. He alone would cast the ring of protection around Sarel whilst he dealt with her usurpers. Usurpers? What did she mean? The Regent? Or was there something more sinister in this Dreamspeaker's words.

Hela laid her hands and cheek against the cool of the window and made a pact with herself. If the dream woman spoke to her tonight, she would find the courage to reply rather than just cringe, terrified, hoping she would leave her alone.

The notion of seeing Torkyn Gynt again was enticing. She had admitted to herself many times that if Sylven had not fallen for him so hard, she herself would have made her own moves to win his attention. However, the thought of escaping with Sarel, smuggling her away from all things familiar and travelling into the Kingdom of Tallinor was petrifying.

Hela needed a reason – one she could fully appreciate – and she intended that this Dreamspeaker would provide it, or once and for all leave her alone.

2

Departures

Lys did visit Hela that night and was pleased that the maidservant was finally responsive. So far she had been mute; the conversation so one-sided it sounded ridiculous even to her ears. Until the girl began to ask questions it meant she was not taking to heart anything which Lys was saying. Time was short; she needed Hela to take action immediately. Orlac was about to enter the city, bringing with him the demonic mind of Dorgryl. It was obvious they had designs on Cipres; an ideal place from which to access Tallinor whenever Orlac was ready to make his move.

She knew Dorgryl too well, assumed he would want to play for a while and resume his former debauched habits. It would be novel for him to have a body again and he would indulge it to its fullest. Time was clearly on his side: Tallinor could fall just as easily later as now.

The Prince of the Host might feel differently, of course. In fact, she was counting on Orlac to fight back. Oh, she was happy for any additional time she could win, but her last hope for saving lives curiously relied on Orlac ignoring

Dorgryl's demands. How odd that she found herself on the side of the young god; perhaps they might even find themselves united in the struggle to rid all worlds of Dorgryl.

She pushed these thoughts aside and concentrated on Hela's tentative voice; good, the girl had found the courage to ask a question in her dream.

Who are you?

My name is Lys. I am a friend of Tor.

Why do you visit me in my dreams?

It is the only way I can reach you, Hela.

What do you want of me?

I have already told you. I need you to get Sarel away from Cipres.

What are we running from? Surely she is safest in her own country?

Under normal circumstances she is. But right now, Hela, there is evil headed into Cipres. Evil's name is Orlac. He intends to snatch the throne of Cipres.

Hela smirked in her dream. *We don't have kings in Cipres, Lys, we only have queens. How can he hope to rule?*

He will rule by giving Cipres the new Queen it needs, craves . . . but it won't be Sarel.

How can you know this? She sounded angry now.

Because I know him. He is clever, interminably patient and he is fuelled by a terrible hatred. Hela, I want you to listen to me now . . . I have a story to tell you. Will you hear me out?

Yes, came the firm reply.

Lys told the maidservant the tale from ancient times, bringing her up to date with Tor's escape to Tallinor and why he had had to run away and not return to the site of Sylven's death. It took some time to relay this and when she finally finished, there was silence.

She pushed Hela. *Do you believe this story?*

I believe in Tor. I knew there had to be a reason why he didn't come back. Everyone said he was involved in the killing but I never accepted this.

You like him, don't you?

I defy any woman to say differently.

Lys laughed. It was a lovely warm sound in Hela's dream and she joined the Dreamspeaker in her mirth before the woman spoke again, seriously.

Tor is the only one with the knowledge to fight Orlac.

So why are you here talking to me and not helping Tor fight this Orlac?

Because Orlac is almost at the gates of the city and I am responsible for his arrival, shall we say. I want to restore order to the world he invades. If something should happen to Sarel by his hand, then I will not be able to right things. She must be protected whilst the fight between Orlac and Tor is dealt with. I promise you, Hela, if you cooperate we will return her to her rightful throne, but first we must keep her life whole.

And Tor will be able to do this?

Tor and his supporters, yes. I believe Sarel is much better off amongst the Tallinese than with her own kind right now. Cipres is not safe for her. Lys held her breath.

I shall do as you ask.

The Dreamspeaker felt relief flood through her. One step at a time, and this was the first in the right direction, the first step towards keeping everyone she could safe from the threat of Orlac and, moreso, the evil Dorgryl.

When must I leave? It will not be easy.

You must make your preparations immediately. You have access to Sarel and, most importantly, you have her trust. Use that now and get her away from this place. Take only what you can

*carry. Jewels and gowns are not necessary. Wear peasant clothes
but carry money. Pay for passage across the seas and when you
reach Caradoon, look for a woman there called Eryna – she runs
a brothel. She will help you. You must tell her you are a friend
of Tor. You can tell her the truth and your secret will be safe.*

How will I find Tor? Hela asked.

*He will be making his way into the Great Forest – I know
this means nothing to you but all will be plain when you reach
Tallinor. The Heartwood, within the Forest, is a sacred place
– it is where you will find him. Right now Tor is back at the
palace in Tal.*

With the Queen he loves?

You know about that?

*Before she died – that same morning in fact – Sylven
mentioned something to me about a proclamation that King Lorys
had married a beautiful, young civilian. She remarked that this
woman was Tor's former lover.*

Oh, she is far more than that, Hela. Alyssa is Tor's wife.

Tor took his leave of the Queen and their children just
prior to daybreak. It was the hardest of partings. Gidyon
was stoic but Lauryn's face betrayed her feelings; they both
understood the need to remain at the palace whilst their
father completed this journey to find their brother. They
had learned the incredible news of their brother's existence while huddled over tea and honeycakes in their
mother's rooms. Sallementro and Saxon had rejoined them
and even Gyl, in better humour, was permitted to join
this intimate gathering.

There had been silence when Tor told Sorrel's tale.

It was Gidyon who gathered his thoughts first. 'So do we
presume that Lauryn, Rubyn and myself form the Trinity?'

Tor nodded. 'It is my belief that once we find Rubyn, yes, we will have assembled the Trinity.'

Lauryn looked alarmed. 'But what is expected of us?' She gazed at the Queen as she said this.

Alyssa shrugged slightly, a faint smile playing around her lips. 'When you start to hear a woman speaking in your dreams, then you'll know more.'

'You mean Lys? This woman who speaks to Father and Sax?'

It was Tor who nodded. 'And Cloot, Sallementro, Arabella, Solyana, Figgis . . . all of the Paladin. I agree with the Queen, Lys will probably advise what is required of the Trinity.' He ignored Alyssa's slight scowl at his formality. Considering they had only recently kissed so tenderly, it did seem a fatuous pretence, but she understood the need for his caution.

Lauryn's eyes narrowed. 'Does she speak to you, your highness?'

'Please, Lauryn . . . I would like it if you called me Mother.' Alyssa looked hopefully at her daughter. Even though she was a queen and used to giving orders, it was a difficult request to ask of someone who was still very much a stranger to her. 'No, Lys has never spoken to me,' the Queen answered, brushing the crumbs of her light meal from her gown. 'I don't know why this is so but I have given up wondering over it.'

Gyl's patience was wearing thin. He had made a silent promise that he would try very hard this morning to find a level of understanding; one which was generous enough to cope with all these strange stories and concepts. He clamped his jaw tight for fear of saying something he might regret and yet all of this was so far-fetched. And now the conversation was drifting into banality. An old woman had died on this very seat before him just hours ago – where the corpse had disappeared to remained a mystery and although her death had set off some frantic decisions, here they all were sipping tea, munching honeycakes, politely talking about strangers being allowed to call his mother, 'Mother'!

Gyl's eyes inevitably strayed back to Lauryn; he was angry with her. How could she be his sister . . . half-sister, that is – or was it stepsister? What ludicrous series of events had led to this? Mind you, he had to admit it, she was worth all this frustration. What a beauty – and to think this was the girl he had met on that terrible day on the road to Axon. She had been heavier then, he thought, and dripping in mud so the beautiful face was shielded from him. She was deliberately avoiding his gaze now, he knew this. That boded well – if she had not found him attractive, she would have been able to stare straight back at him. As for the brother – his stepbrother he conceded with slight bitterness – he did not give much away; held his thoughts close and yet seemed fairly at ease with the supposed strangers around him.

Gyl's own thoughts turned outward again, back to the gathering which seemed, finally, to be on the move. The man, Gynt, was pulling himself to his feet, his incredibly blue eyes always glancing back to the Queen. Gyl imagined these two people together, and their love which had produced three children – real children; not like him, an orphan welcomed into the palace. His mouth tasted suddenly sour. He must not start to think like this. The King would be home shortly – any hour in fact – and all would be put right.

He stood too, glad for the movement. 'Can I organise an escort for you, Physic Gynt?'

Tor smiled at the old title; he had not heard it in so long. It was not hard to see that the young man, not that much older than his own children, was struggling to cope with what had presented itself at his door last night. Tor could not blame him – all sentients, but especially Tor and the Paladin, lived with the strangeness of their lives, accepted each new curiosity for what it was and rarely thought to analyse it. Young Gyl over there would be trying to rationalise everything and yet it was not possible – none of this was rational. Gyl must learn to accept that now, and it was to be hoped that his mother, the Queen, might help him to achieve the level of understanding he would require as Under Prime to assist rather than fight them.

'Thank you, Gyl, but I shall be fine.'

The soldier nodded curtly. 'Then if you'll all excuse me, I must do my rounds. If I can be of any help, please don't hesitate to seek me out.' Gyl cringed inwardly at how hideously polite and restrained he sounded. He could not help but cast another glance *her* way. Lauryn was looking at the floor, but a brief smile flitted across her mouth. She felt embarrassed for him. So be it. He bent and kissed his mother's hand.

'Your majesty,' he said, not looking at her. 'I shall contact you immediately your husband, the King, returns. Try and rest, Mother.' He felt pleased with himself that in one brief phrase he had managed to remind everyone in the room – including the Queen – of who she was, to whom she belonged and to whom loyalties must lie. He closed the door behind him.

Alyssa leapt straight in. 'Gyl will be finding this extraordinarily difficult. I hope you will all forgive his gruff manner. Saxon, perhaps you should . . .'

Saxon nodded. 'I'll speak with him,' he said. Saxon walked over to Tor and hugged him hard. 'Send us word,' he said. 'Use Cloot if necessary, and his wretched question-and-answer system.'

Tor grinned. 'Look after everyone, Sax.'

The Kloek nodded formally. 'You have my word. The Light guide you safely, Tor.' He followed Gyl's footsteps out of the Queen's chambers.

Alyssa caught Sallementro's eye. 'Sal, my son and daughter would probably appreciate a bath, fresh clothes, a look around the palace. The King will be back soon and I will want to present them later in the day. Would you help?'

'Of course,' the musician replied, a brief bow to his Sovereign. 'It would be a pleasure to take you two under my wing.' He smiled kindly at Gidyon and Lauryn. 'Let's make a start by heading down to the castle baths.'

Tor did not wait for his son to cross the room. He beat him to it, pulling the boy close. 'I shall be back soon, I promise, with your brother.' *Stay close to Lauryn; she'll need your strength. Get to know Gyl.*

'Figgis?' Gidyon said quietly.

'He'll journey straight here, I'm sure. He won't wish to be separated from you now or ever,' Tor replied. 'Look out for him.' He looked towards Lauryn who appeared remarkably composed.

She stepped up and he held her close, whispering, 'Back soon, I give you my word. I need you to be brave now. Get to know your mother a little more,' he said smiling.

She's very nervous about you both, he pressed into her mind.
That won him a short grin from Lauryn.

Stay close to Gidyon; he'll need your strength, he added as
he pulled apart from her.

She mentioned what had been niggling at the edges of
her mind. 'Father, how will you know who Rubyn is? I
mean, are you counting on him bearing a strong likeness
to us?'

'I hadn't thought beyond finding a young man in the
Heartwood, to be honest.'

'How about the stones?' Gidyon suggested.

Tor frowned. 'How do we know he would have one?'

Gidyon could only just remember a conversation with
Sorrel. 'I think it was when we were preparing to leave
with Sorrel – this is all a bit hazy I have to admit – we
demanded she prove we were sister and brother. She
achieved this through the stones which we both had on
us and had both cherished since childhood. She told us
how you'd given her the three stones when she fled with
us from the Heartwood.'

Tor nodded and Lauryn picked up the story, frowning
as she strained to recall that conversation.

'You're right, Gidyon . . . I can remember that too,
and I think I'm right in saying that when you asked Sorrel
where the third was, she said not to worry, it was in a
very safe place.'

They both looked back at their father. He was beaming.
'Clever old girl she was. She must have left the third stone
with Rubyn. She wouldn't have known what they're for
– as I don't – but perhaps she thought it might protect
him. This is excellent news. You must both keep them
very safe . . . we are yet to find out their purpose.'

Gidyon suddenly looked sheepish. 'Um . . . I have to admit something.'

Eyes turned to him and lingered on his discomfort.

He cleared his throat, his eyes searching his father's face for understanding. 'When I left Yseul we had both just survived a traumatic experience.' As he paused Tor looked towards Alyssa's puzzled face and shook his head just enough to tell her this was not the time to go into it.

The look was not lost on Lauryn. She enlightened her mother. 'Yseul is Gidyon's friend.' She loaded the word 'friend' with all sorts of meanings.

He squirmed a little more, glaring at Lauryn. 'Er . . . yes she is. Anyway, it was a difficult time for us and . . .' Awkwardly, he looked again at his father before taking another deep breath. 'Well, I wanted to give her something from me . . . of me . . . and I gave her my stone.' He did his best to ignore the audible gasp from his father. 'I told her I was lending her my stone and that I would find her and collect it one day.'

Tor was shocked. 'What was in your head, son?' he asked quietly as he tried to assess the loss of one of the Stones of Ordolt – what it might mean to their success or failure.

His softly spoken rebuke was enough to crumple Gidyon's already fragile confidence. Gidyon ran his hand through his hair, totally crestfallen as he searched for a suitable answer. It was his mother who came swiftly to his rescue.

'Tor, don't you dare use that accusatory tone. Gidyon has been ripped out of everything familiar and deposited back here with a group of strange people he has to trust

– even accept as family. A meaningless, harmless looking stone, supposedly left with him by his parents, has no significance to him other than the sentimental value it represented in his life.'

Tor was about to say something but the Queen refused him any opportunity.

'No! He is not to blame in this. I can't imagine what the traumatic incident is that Gidyon's referring to but I expect to learn it soon. This Yseul will presumably keep it safe will she not, Gidyon?' Her son nodded, eyes turned to the floor. 'Then there's nothing lost, Tor. To her it's a harmless stone as well, with sentimental value, given to her by someone I am assuming means something to her.'

Now she saw her son's colour rise. So Gidyon had wasted no time finding a young woman upon whom to work his charm. My, my, she thought, I wonder who he takes after. She looked back at Tor, her expression forbidding him to take this matter any further. 'The stone is safe, Tor. Where does she live?'

'A place called Brittelbury,' Gidyon replied, grateful for his mother's support. Watching her now take command he appreciated her for the Queen she was. He liked her like this; had hated seeing her so filled with despair and grief the previous night. His father had told him she was a formidable person. He could believe it now.

'Well, that's several days' ride west of here. *If you don't say something nice right now, Torkyn Gynt, I shall spend the rest of my time in your absence telling the children every embarrassing tale I can think of about you including that time you—*

Alyssa was not permitted to finish outlining which of the humiliating tales she would start with.

'It's all right, Gidyon. Really. Your mother is right and

I'm sorry to have doubted you. You were not to know
about the Stones of Ordolt and I'm as much in the dark
about them as you, so let's think about getting the stone
back.' He turned his blue gaze towards Alyssa. *Thank you.
I'd forgotten how very beautiful and desirable you are when
you're cross.*

She felt a little lightheaded when he turned that look
on her. 'Well,' the Queen said brightly, trying to lighten
the pang of separation she was trying to convince herself
was being felt only by the children. 'Why don't you two
go on with Sallementro and I'll see your father on his
way?' *Please let me have just another minute on my own with
him*, she begged silently. 'I'll find you both afterwards and
we can spend some time together.' *Please . . . oh please.
Just once more in his arms and then I shall give him up*, she
promised herself.

Sallementro and the younger Gynts departed with one
final searching look at their father. Tor felt a searing grief
at leaving them, recalling his own father's anxiety when
he had finally ridden away from Flat Meadows so full of
the desire for adventure. Tor wondered how he would find
the reserves of courage required for what was ahead of
them all. He put that aside as the door closed and he felt
Alyssa's eyes turn towards him.

'I must go,' he said, reflexively, but made no move.

'I know.'

'Will you be all right?'

'With Gidyon and Lauryn?'

He nodded.

'Of course. I intend to spend every spare minute catching
up on all that I've been denied with them. They are wary
of me. That's hard.' She said the final words wistfully.

'They will fall hopelessly in love with you as I did . . . as I still am.' He did not mean to say it but the words had a life of their own, rushing out and serving no other purpose than to foil the Queen's resolve.

'Oh, Tor, why does this happen to us?' Alyssa could not wait another moment.

She stepped into his embrace. He kissed her hair and stroked her cheek as she hugged him harder, loving the familiar feel of his tall, broad body.

'We must not risk this, Alyssa. I . . . I must stop touching you like this. It's dangerous . . . and embarrassing,' he said looking down at himself, trying to lighten her despair. He was pleased to see the ghost of a smile come to her face at the mention of his discomfort. 'I can sense Gyl's fury when I merely look at you — and if he could see this!' he said and tilted her face so he could kiss her lips.

She pulled away finally. 'Gyl will not know how it feels until he experiences his first love,' she said.

'Well, if I'm not mistaken it was happening in front of our noses!'

She loved to see that broad smile which touched his eyes; made the blue spark brighter, if that was possible.

'No . . . not Lauryn. Surely not?' she said, enjoying the intrigue.

'Mark my words,' Tor said. 'I'd bet on it being confirmed with a kiss or more by the time I return,' he added, eyebrows arching theatrically.

Alyssa laughed. 'Ten sovereigns that you're wrong.'

'I don't have ten sovereigns,' he replied, 'but I'd be happy to take that bet.'

Their laughter was short-lived.

'Let's not prolong this pain,' Tor suggested. 'I love you, Alyssa but you are no longer mine to love. We must remember who you are now.'

'Can you forgive him, Tor?'

'You may recall I already did . . . years ago.'

'No, I mean for this . . . for loving me?'

I already did . . . years ago, he whispered into her mind.

She felt the sting of tears. So Tor knew as much as she had suspected – even as he went to his death – that Lorys had had designs on her.

'He loves me so much, Tor. I'm good for him too. I can change the way he looks at things. I can help him to be a better King. But I'm so torn.'

He kissed her mouth to stop her talking. 'Don't be. You have responsibilities now. I understand why he loves you because I do too. I forgive him and I forgive you for loving him. It is our children who matter now, Alyssa. Help him to grasp their importance. I believe the time has come for our King to learn everything. Tell him all you know. Make him understand the need to help us achieve our ends . . . or Tallinor will die and so will its people. That's your task now.'

Tor took from his pocket the disk of archalyt he hated and with her pained nod of authority he pressed it back against her forehead where it adhered. She hated the sudden absence of his magic and spirit surrounding her. Alyssa felt the loss keenly.

Then he bent and kissed her hand very tenderly. 'I take my leave, your highness.'

As he did so, she sadly touched his soft, beautiful hair in reply, permitting his departure.

* * *

Despite the sickening feeling of having to leave Alyssa once more, Tor was relieved to be gone from the palace again – and from all of its reminders. He could still taste her on his lips, smell her perfume on himself, and he realised with deep regret that he may never do so again. With the King back at Tal, he would not have such intimate access to the Queen again. And, he decided with a sigh, that was as it should be. His children were safe; she would now protect them with her own life if necessary. He must journey back to the Heartwood and find the boy, Rubyn. It lifted his spirits to think of the other son and he felt happy when Cloot finally showed himself at the tops of the trees.

How is she?

Unnervingly beautiful.

Well, she was always that, Tor. Will she be all right with Gidyon and Lauryn?

She's already in love with them, though it will take longer for them to accept the Queen of Tallinor as their long lost mother than it did for them to accept me as their father.

Possibly, the bird conceded. *I presume Saxon remains?*

Yes, he will stick close to Alyssa now.

Tor's exceptionally fine hearing picked up the sound of a horse galloping towards them. *Alone?* he asked, knowing Cloot could hear just as well and see far more easily from his treetop perch than he himself could from the ground.

Solitary rider travelling at breakneck speed. Must be urgent news for the palace.

Tor moved to the side of the dusty road. At this speed the rider would hardly have a chance to swerve; he took the precaution of getting well out of the horse's path. The rider was upon them in seconds. He did not so much as glance his way but Tor noticed his teeth were clamped together in grim concentration – and were those tears streaming down his face or just the rain?

Cloot landed silently on his shoulder.

He's moving so fast his eyes are watering, Tor commented.

Did you notice the stallion? It had the King's personal insignia on it. Rather regal for a messenger don't you think?

I can't say I noticed but then you have a knack of spotting these things, Cloot. If a bird could shrug, Cloot would have.

Tor considered the import of this rider. *Must be very urgent for him to have clearance to travel so dangerously fast. Saxon told me the Shield lives by a very strict code of rules. Riding like the wind is only permitted in hunts, competitions, emergencies and war, I believe.*

He might simply have been enjoying the chance to let such a fine horse have the rein – it's not often a messenger would have such an opportunity.

Yes . . . you're probably right. The King is due back any hour, apparently, and I don't want to go back there to be honest.

He imagined the King's return and how his Queen would be waiting on the steps to throw her arms around him and welcome him home with some alarming news.

Except Alyssa never did get the chance to speak to Lorys again.

3

Tallinor Grieves

Orlac would never be comfortable with Dorgryl sharing his head but he had begun to get used to it during the walk from the hillsides of Neame towards the capital. They had been walking for five days now and, he had to admit, Dorgryl's expansive views were entertaining at least. His uncle had managed to make him laugh out loud several times, though they both agreed that in company this might have the effect of making him seem quite mad. But for now, travelling through the picturesque country-side of Cipres, he could almost say he was enjoying himself, and as long as Dorgryl continued to fuel his need for vengeance and leave the rest of his body alone, he was content for the time being.

Cipres needs a new queen, Dorgryl suddenly said.

How about a new king?

It is a matriarchal society . . . always has been.

Is there no heiress?

Not that I'm aware of.

Then I presume we shall supply her.

Correct.

How?

Leave that to me.

And why will they accept her?

Because they are frightened and distracted and best, they are grieving.

Why would that make them accept a stranger?

You just walk, boy, and let me think now.

Orlac shrugged. He was more than happy in his own silence and he was glad of the fact that Dorgryl could not touch his private thoughts. They remained his own and a good thing too. Suddenly he felt obsessed with the need to know a woman. He had been alive for centuries and apart from that brief time of childhood he had spent the whole time fighting – pitting his wits and magics against others. This wonderful freedom – if you could call it that with another god's spirit roaming one's mind – was seductive. Dorgryl had spoken to him about the pleasures of life and Orlac realised how much he had missed. Just this time to walk through beautiful countryside was a treat. Dorgryl would sneer, he knew, and probably suggest that it was nothing in comparison to having a beautiful and compliant woman on her knees, your own hands buried in her hair as she pleasured you. So much to learn and experience.

A milestone at the grass verge told him it was barely a day's walk to the city gates. Orlac smiled. Perhaps the right woman on her knees in front of him was not that far away now. He strode on towards Cipres.

On top of the battlements a soldier on lookout called to Gyl. 'Rider approaching, sir. Very fast.'

Gyl looked out towards the southwest and squinted.

Yes, he could see the rider; his man was right, the horse was at full pelt. As it drew closer he could see the flecks of foam on its flanks.

'The Light strike me! What the hell is that rider doing wearing down the horse like that? I'll have him flogged.'

The soldier next to him added that the horse bore the King's insignia too. This confused Gyl. No simple messenger would wear the personal colours of Lorys. Only the King's Guard was permitted and no member of the Guard would be sent on an errand unless it was of the highest and most urgent importance.

Gyl swore colourfully. 'Bring the messenger directly to me.' A soldier hurried off. 'And someone get that horse seen to before it dies on us,' he ordered.

He and Saxon had spent an hour or so together earlier, sipping a milky concoction which Cook liked to send up for the men on watch in the early hours of the chilled mornings. Moody and still piqued by the previous night's strange activity, he had appreciated the Kloek's company. He regarded Saxon as a father and so it was with good grace that he accepted the older man's counselling. When Saxon explained everything it seemed to make so much more sense and yet every time he tried to wrap his mind around the fact that his mother had lain with a powerful sentient and given birth to triplets who would save the Kingdom of Tallinor from some madman called Orlac — it just seemed like utter claptrap. Hearing that Tor had been executed at this very palace and was now walking around very much alive with clear designs on his mother, the Queen, made the whole story even more flawed. And looking at Saxon as he talked gently of their struggle made it still worse. The Kloek was a Paladin — whatever that meant — as was some dwarf still in the Great Forest and some falcon, no less!

It had taken all of Gyl's resolve to remain seated and listen. But the more the Kloek explained, the more resigned he began to feel. Who could make up such a tale, he asked himself. By the time they parted company, Saxon had exacted a promise that Gyl would keep an open mind and accept that magic existed in their world and when wielded by the right hands — of people like Gynt and like his mother — great good could come of it.

Gyl knew Saxon would not lie and so knew he must put faith in what the Kloek advised. Even the amazing story of Saxon's disfigurement and blindness and of being cured in the Heartwood was too fantastical to imagine, and yet he knew the Kloek expected him to accept it because it was the truth.

Gyl put his troubled thoughts aside as the messenger was virtually carried to where he stood. The man was exhausted and if it were not for the two soldiers holding him upright, he would have surely collapsed onto the flagstones.

The rider made a dazed salute to his Under Prime. 'Sir, I bring baleful tidings.'

Gyl felt the hairs on the back of his neck rise. This man was indeed from the Guard which meant the news was brought directly from the King.

'Speak,' he commanded.

The breathless man did not have a chance to reply. They were interrupted by the Queen's arrival on the battlements. Saxon followed.

'I saw this man ride in. He bears the King's colours. What news?' Alyssa asked. 'I've been expecting Lorys for hours . . . why is he so late?'

Gyl's eyes flicked to Saxon. The message in that glance said enough.

'Your highness,' Saxon said gently. 'Why don't we—'

'No, Saxon,' she replied. 'I want news from this rider. What is your name?' she asked the trembling man, ignoring all warning glares from her son. Gyl was the man's superior but she was his Queen and that left absolutely no one of higher rank on this rooftop. She would have news of her husband directly from this messenger's lips.

The stricken man was still trying to get his breathing back to normal and he coughed. 'I am Larkham, your majesty,' he said, struggling to get down on one knee and pay her correct respect.

'You may stand, Larkham. I can see you are in great need of rest. Please deliver your news of the King and his arrival.'

Incredibly, the man broke down. No one could believe the tears which consumed him to the point where he could not speak. It was the Queen who went to him and held his hand. Her own eyes were filled with tears now and her face pinched with fear.

'Larkham, where is the King?' she urged, low voiced.

'He . . . he is dead,' was all the man managed to say.

Herek escorted his King but this time took no joy in it. The blackened, ruined body of Lorys was shrouded in sacking and carried in a cart as they made their slow journey into Tal proper. The men travelled in a shocked silence. They had been like this since the King had been impaled by the lightning strike. Lorys had been dead even before he hit the ground, long before his loyal Prime could reach him.

With an enormous effort of will, Herek forced his mind from its confused, horrified state to consider what lay ahead. The bulk of responsibility would fall on his and Gyl's shoulders as the realm would surely spiral into stunned stupefaction, capable of no activity other than grieving at their shocking news. He knew Queen Alyssa would have received the grim tidings by now. How much more punishment could a single person take? He felt his heart ache for Tallinor's beautiful young Queen – it seemed her whole life was destined to be one of grief.

More importantly, the King had died without an heir. Tallinor faced very testing times. Herek was a soldier not a politician, but he quaked at the thought of how the question of sovereignty would be resolved now. As far as he could recall, Tallinor's royal line had always been secured by a single male heir. What in the Light would happen now to their precious Kingdom?

Word had clearly not yet spread. Tal warmly welcomed its soldiers home, hardly glancing at the contents of the cart . . . just another footman perhaps who had passed away. And if they did notice the King's fine stallion at the front, it did not register yet that the horse was rider-less. Many would have presumed the King was arriving separately. The Company approached the palace gates, where it was clear that a far more sombre welcome awaited. Herek took a deep breath and silently asked the Light to guide him through this difficult time.

Queen Alyssa, flanked by the Under Prime, who held her arm protectively, awaited them on the steps of the palace. Herek was quietly relieved to see the Kloek had returned from his wanderings. Saxon stood beside the Queen and would provide much needed support. The entire palace staff had gathered in the bailey and awaited their King in dread silence. Soldiers stood at full attention on the battlements where the colours of Tal flew at half mast. That alone would begin to filter into the minds of the populace and Tal's people would begin to grasp that death had visited and claimed their sovereign.

Dignitaries and courtiers, heads bowed, awaited a little further back on the vast steps and Herek's keen eye roved amongst them, picking up two strangers, standing with the musician, Sallementro. Unlesss his sight deceived him, one looked alarmingly like the physic, Torkyn Gynt — though that was surely fanciful. The other, her head bowed, he could not see in full, but in spite of seeming familiar in that brief glance she was definitely not known to him.

Herek looked back at the Queen. She appeared composed. Her chin held high, a look of defiance on her face as she dared that composure to fail her. It would not; he knew this. Herek recognised that same strength in her stance that he had witnessed many years previously when she had laid eyes on the corpse of another great love of her life. She had not cried then and she would not cry now in public. He admired her courage; was proud of the dignified figure she presented to her people. She would be the reason all of them would find the strength to move on; Alyssa would be the catalyst which might push them through their grief to the future of Tallinor under a new monarch . . . but whom?

The cart he had led rolled to a halt and Herek stepped down from his horse and onto his knee in the presence of his Sovereign. His head held low, he heard her softly approach.

'Your majesty,' he said, angry to hear his voice catch slightly.

She touched his shoulder, bade him rise and then he was looking down at the tiny figure – already a former queen, he realised, as she would never be permitted to rule. Herek looked into sad, fathomless grey-green eyes and somehow conveyed his despair that he had brought his King, her husband, back in such a manner. No words required.

The Under Prime was snapped to attention. People began to weep now around them but Alyssa remained composed.

'At ease, Gyl,' Herek said, glad to hear his voice was more steady now. He must take command of the situation. 'Your highness, may we speak inside?'

She nodded. Bearers rushed out from the palace to lift the body from its cart but several soldiers growled. No one would bear the King's body other than the King's personal Guard. The confused servants looked to their Queen. Herek noted Gyl squeeze his mother's arm gently. She nodded again at the servants who moved away. Gyl left her side to join the Guard. He would be one of those to carry their beloved King to his resting spot, for the time being, in the chapel. With Saxon close by, Queen Alyssa turned and climbed the stairs back into the palace, a grief-stricken retinue of people following.

In her private chambers, she held an audience with Herek whilst Gyl made arrangements in the chapel to lay out the man he did not know was his father. The only other person present was Saxon. Alyssa sat, stiff-backed, and after a tray of drinks had been served – which only Herek gratefully touched – she asked him the question he dreaded.

'Tell me how my husband died?'

The Prime told her everything, spared her no detail in his precise, brief way, from the moment they had spotted the ravens in the field to the second his body had burst momentarily into flame. When he finished speaking the room was enveloped by a frigid silence. No one moved until the Queen finally nodded.

'I saw that hand of lightning, Herek, which you speak of. It lit the entire sky.'

'It was a fearful strike, your majesty.'

'And you say Lorys felt doomed?'

'That's my interpretation, your highness. He spoke of being marked by the gods . . . shrouded. I sense this is why he risked sending a man out into the storm.' Herek cleared his throat. 'I am guessing it was his way of reaching out to you, my Queen.'

Alyssa bit the inside of her cheek. She would not permit herself to break down. She must be strong. People would count on her to show courage in the face of such adversity.

Saxon finally entered the conversation. 'Arrangements must be made, your highness . . . er, for the King's funeral. This is something you might consider entrusting to Gyl.'

He flicked a look towards Herek which suggested he would explain later. 'After last night, your boy could use a chance to flex his authority and demonstrate his abilities.'

A strange, unreadable look flitted across the Queen's face. 'I fear the boy has far more responsibility settling on his shoulders than any of us could possibly imagine,' she said. 'Herek.'

'Your highness?' He was glad they were able to slip into familiar roles and duties, away from that sense of confusion.

'Gather the nobles.'

'As you command, your majesty, but should we not lay our King to rest first . . . if you'll pardon my presumption?'

'The question of succession is best dealt with immediately, Herek. I suspect it is already the main question on everyone's lips.'

There was a soft knock at the door. Gyl entered with the Queen's private aide, Rolynd.

Alyssa mustered a smile. 'Just the people we need.' They bowed. 'Rolynd, I require you to assist Gyl, who will take charge of all proceedings surrounding the funeral, burial and feast for King Lorys.'

She noted Gyl's eyes flash. This was a proud moment for him.

'As you wish, your majesty,' said the dour Rolynd.

'Gyl . . . Rolynd will prepare a full list of neighbouring royalty who will need to be invited to attend. Please make all arrangements for the King to lie in state for the appropriate period of time. In this instance, we will wait for all monarchs who wish to attend to be present before the funeral takes place.'

'I understand,' he said and bowed. 'I will take my leave, then, your majesty and get on with my tasks,' Gyl said.

'Gyl.' He turned back to face his mother, marvelling at her dignity in the face of such grief and turmoil he knew she would be experiencing. 'You will be required to attend a gathering of the nobles.' She looked at Herek, a question on her face.

'Tomorrow, your majesty. I shall have them assembled in the Throne Room by sunrise.'

'Good,' she said.

Gyl was confused but this was not the time to question the Queen. He nodded and departed with Rolynd behind him.

Saxon managed to convey a brief smile towards Alyssa. He was pleased she had given Gyl a prominent role.

'Herek, you need some rest. And I must go and sit with Lorys,' she said, her forlornness profoundly affecting the two men in the room.

'May I accompany you, Alyssa?' Saxon said, forgetting the protocol just for a moment.

'No. This is something I wish to face myself, and I need some time alone with my husband before the arrangements for his embalming begin. You understand.'

'Of course,' Saxon replied. 'Allow me to escort you to the chapel at least?'

She took his hand and stood. Herek was back on one knee.

'You are a good man, Herek. I am grateful to you for all you've done and continue to do. We shall meet tomorrow after sunrise.'

Alyssa, Queen of Tallinor for the last day of her short reign, left her chambers to kiss her husband for the final time.

4

Escape of a Princess

Orlac glimpsed his first view of the Ciprean capital. In spite of the late hour, it remained a beautiful sight with its houses softly glowing in the light of oil lamps whilst blazing torches splendidly lit the breathtaking palace on the cliff.

However, his pleasure was soon interrupted by Dorgryl. *Time for us to claim a throne.*

How do you propose we take over an entire realm?

Ah, that's the messy bit, Dorgryl said. *By force. A few will die – certainly enough for the Cipreans to realise there is absolutely no point in opposing us.*

Messy?

Yes. I shall unleash your powers, boy.

Orlac seethed privately but bit back on his temper. *Surely you mean I shall unleash my powers, Dorgryl?*

Of course. That's what I meant, his uncle replied smoothly. *Come. Let's not dawdle . . . now the fun begins.*

Hela had made careful preparations. Now she had to convince the uncrowned new Queen to listen to this mad tale of hers and agree to flee the city. With Sarel still uncommunicative as she mourned the loss of her mother, all other palace staff left the child entirely in her care. Hela seemed to be the only person Sarel could tolerate. Anyone else interrupting her grief would be met by either fury or cold silence. She had been seen by barely more than three of the palace staff since her mother's death. All her former carers had been left behind at Neame. In fact, she was virtually a stranger to the palace staff who had met her only on rare occasions since her birth, so strong was her mother's desire to protect her.

Sylven had been cremated in the Ciprean fashion. Her ugly death had left her once handsome face scarred with purplish welts, her lips erupted with sores. It had been decided to burn the Queen immediately, and the ceremony was pulled together hastily and performed on the Mound where all previous queens had risen from death to afterlife amongst the swirling smoke of their burning pyres.

Several thousand loyal subjects had gathered to witness the event, all still stunned by the premature death of their Sovereign. Talk had spread that she had been murdered; already whisperings had begun that the deed was connected to the stranger she had publicly humiliated on the last outing of the Silver Maiden. His name was Torkyn Gynt. The grief-stricken had comforted themselves with the thought that at least the succession was safe. A new Queen would be crowned after a suitable period of mourning. Sarel was young but on the few occasions that the Ciprean people had been permitted to share her, they had found her engaging and as seemingly devoted to them as her mother and grandmother before her. The child would be a beauty it was said and the people respected their Queen's wish for her daughter to enjoy childhood –

her time would come soon enough to accept the responsibility of ruling a realm. If only they had known then what would unfold over these next few days, the city fathers would have crowned Sarel on the very day of her mother's burning.

But now Sarel was trying to control the alarm which her mother's closest servant was forcing on her. They were in Sylven's chambers, standing on the same balcony where Torkyn Gynt had once seduced and ultimately won the heart of a Queen.

'Sarel, have you any reason not to trust me?' Hela looked at the girl earnestly.

The new Queen did not return the eye contact; she continued to look out over the city. 'I do not.'

'Then you must heed my warnings. I have never had such a dream before, child. It was as though this woman was real like you and me. She has visited me each night to repeat the same warning that great harm will come to you if we do not flee.'

'I don't understand, Hela. These people loved my mother . . . surely they will love me too.'

'They do. But this Dreamspeaker, Lys, talks of people from foreign lands . . . bad people who wish us ill.'

Now Sarel dragged her stare away from the beautiful cityscape in front of her and rounded on her friend. 'How cowardly, then, of me to flee when Cipres most needs her Queen.'

At this Hela could not help but smile. 'Brave, Sarel. Well said. Your mother would be proud of you. But she would not wish you to throw your life away. She would uphold me in this. Let me get you to safety whilst I still can. Don't you see, you are more of a threat alive. If nothing occurs in Cipres which is untoward, we shall return and you shall be crowned.'

Sarel, though young by Tallinese standards, was verging on what the Cipreans considered womanhood. She turned back to gaze out at the city she loved fiercely. This was her birthright. She understood that her mother had diligently protected her from royal duties and yet she had secretly craved them. She indulged her mother's whim to keep her as innocent as possible but her mother had had little knowledge that she had been studying Ciprean history, laws, affairs of State ferociously. She had even engaged her own pair of advisers, based in Neame but with eyes and ears working for them throughout Cipres, who kept her fully briefed on events, political or otherwise. Sarel had known of Locklyn Gylbyt's call for the Silver Maiden almost as quickly as the rest of the cityfolk had learned it. In fact she had become somewhat infatuated with the notion of the pirate's son for a short while, dwelling on his bravery and wishing she could ask her mother if she could attend the Kiss. But Sarel had known it was pointless to even ask such a thing. She had been in Neame anyway; closeted safely from the public eye; expected to play with dolls and puppies. Her mother had adored her – she knew this – but her mother had read her incorrectly for most of the past few years.

Sarel wanted to reign; had an urgent need to learn and absorb all State matters. She deeply wished she could have lived and worked alongside her mother, as Sylven had her mother. But now her mother was gone, murdered; there would be no opportunity to learn anything from the best teacher of all.

Hela echoed her thoughts. 'Your mother's death is our most urgent warning, Sarel. There is treachery afoot and your safety is paramount now. We have no time to lose. We must leave the palace.'

'This Torkyn Gynt. You trust him?'

'I do . . . yes.'

'I believe I do too,' she said, bringing great relief to Hela. 'I met him at Neame, spent some time in his company. Whilst I believe my mother fell in love with his handsome looks and charm, I too was captivated, but by his intelligence. Those eyes are penetrating, aren't they? Seem to speak volumes whilst guarding so many secrets.'

Hela was taken aback. Sarel, at thirteen summers, had clearly been hiding the adult she had become. The child was speaking like a grown woman. Had she been fooling them all, especially Sylven, all these years? Pretending to be the innocent youngster who enjoyed nothing more than sugared desserts and a game of throw-ball? Hela looked at the young Queen with a new respect.

Sarel grinned. 'I'm not enchanted by him, Hela. He's much too old for me although he is certainly a beautiful man. But I would trust him.'

Hela shook her head slighty, unbalanced by the newly revealed maturity of Sarel. 'Your mother was in love with him, Sarel. She told me this in plain words . . . was even flirting with how she could change Ciprean law to permit her taking a husband.'

At this Sarel's eyes did widen. 'Truly?'

Hela nodded. 'I could hardly believe it either when she told me. Sylven was always able to control her emotions and in all the time I served her, never once did she fall prey to a man's affections, honeyed words, physique. No, no one until Torkyn Gynt had ever roused her passions like this. I do believe she meant to make him Royal Consort.'

'And is this possible?'

'Ancient laws would need to be overturned. I'm no scholar, Sarel. I would not know what such a mighty change in Ciprean philosophy and culture might entail.'

Sarel nodded sadly. 'She should not have died the way she did. I will see to it − if it takes all of my life − that the perpetrator is punished.'

'Then you must protect your life to achieve this. Will you come with me?'

'Give me this night to consider, Hela. I promise to deliver you my decision on the morrow.' She suddenly looked regal. Gone were the childish attire and ribbons she had obviously worn to please her mother. Sarel stood before her, slim and clearly going to be as tall as Sylven one day, and perhaps even more beautiful. In her simple soft blue gown, slim fitting, curving over her high breasts, she looked anything but a child.

Hela nodded, knowing she must find the patience to wait out another night, and bowed to her Queen. 'I shall leave you then, your majesty, to consider.'

As she departed the chambers she almost bumped into a familiar figure; one she detested. Her frustration found a target. 'What are you doing here? No one is permitted in this tower without my permission.'

'The guards gave me access. I would offer my condolences to the Princess,' replied the oily voice.

Its high pitch, effeminate in the way it caressed her ears, had disgusted Hela from the very first time she had heard it. She looked into the cold, almost black eyes, small and ever wary. 'She is no longer a Princess, Goth. She is a Queen now and the Queen insists on privacy to grieve. She has given instructions that only I will attend her for the time being. You will leave and not return until summoned.'

Goth kept his face impassive and nodded once but in truth wished he could wrap his pudgy fingers around the woman's neck and throttle this upstart maid. How dare she address him with such discourtesy. He was, after all, a former adviser to Sylven. The fact that he had murdered her was unfortunate, of course, for now he would need to ingratiate himself with the child. Until recently he had not been aware there was a daughter and had berated himself for not knowing such an important detail, but Queen Sylven had obviously kept the daughter well protected. It was a rare mistake – he would need to be more careful in future. He turned away from the maid, took his leave and was aware that she watched him until he had disappeared from the corridor down the stairs from the private tower.

Goth continued to surprise himself at cheating death. Surely he was running out of lives? He had survived the fall over the crashing water's edge and managed to keep himself beneath the rushing river's surface just long enough to be dragged swiftly out of the keen eyesight of his pursuers. He had hurt himself though, and if not for the few remaining drops of clear arraq in the vial secreted in his clothes, he might not have survived so well. The drug had rejuvenated him and once at full strength he had made his way carefully back to Cipres.

After establishing that Gynt was no longer in the palace, he had simply resumed his former chambers, feigning shock and horror at the news of Sylven's death. No one had seen him leave the city; no one had seen him at Neame. He presumed Gynt and the Kloek had already sailed for Tallinor which meant for the time being he was safe. He had spent the next few days promoting the rumour that Torkyn Gynt was the man responsible for Sylven's murder and, that achieved, he prepared to meet with Sarel and find out more about this new Queen of Cipres. Goth had counted on her refusing all visitors, hence his attempt to take her by surprise. But this toad of a maid was lurking. He hated her; she had not trusted him since he first came to the notice of Sylven and clearly distrusted him now. Well, perhaps she might need to join her former employer, wherever she was now. He would not let a mere servant get in the way of his plans. Goth decided as he left the Queen's tower that if Hela locked horns with him again, she would die.

Orlac entered the royal square of Cipres, attracted by the sounds of many voices raised in agreement with a single speaker. He paid no attention to what the man was saying. It mattered not in the light of what would happen in the next few minutes. It was darkening into evening and the huge square was elegantly lit by torches. Shops as well as eating and drinking houses lined the square, all beautifully presenting their wares. There was no doubt the Cipreans were far from poor. This square alone, with its smooth, graceful architecture made entirely of white polished stone, literally glittered with the wealth of its people. He looked up towards the palace, towering above on a cliff ledge; its pale minarets shot with gold sparkled like jewels against the inky sky.

We should make our presence felt here, Dorgryl suggested.

Orlac agreed with the suggestion. He skirted the edge of the crowd and then began to push through it. His tall, imposing stature helped to part the shoulders of the gathered until he found himself climbing the stairs of the recently erected podium. The speaker turned, slightly confounded by the interruption and nodded to one of the guards nearby to deal with the nuisance.

A burly man broke away from the guards and approached Orlac.

He was polite. 'I shall have to ask you to step down please.'

Kill him, Dorgryl ordered.

Orlac felt the god flare inside him. He hated the sensation of Dorgryl's presence but he knew he must bide his time. For now, they were both on the same side, following the same path. He opened himself to his powers, felt the Colours infuse him and he cast out a trickle. The guard had put a hand up to prevent Orlac proceeding any further and he suddenly burst into flame, a look of shocked surprise crossing his face as he witnessed his own incineration before he collapsed, writhing and burning.

The speaker yelled, the crowd roared its own surprise which instantly turned to terror. How could this happen?

Dorgryl commanded again. *Deal with the speaker*.

Orlac obeyed. The man who had once held the rapt attention of the gathered before this interruption, now won it again, but for a different reason this time. He began to tremble; his body convulsing as a puppet might, when its strings are jerked by the puppeteer. He began to thrash around the podium, screaming in agony.

Orlac did not want to be told what to do next. This was his show, not Dorgryl's and he would take charge. Turning casually towards the stunned audience, with one man dead but still smoking and another flailed to his death, he loosed his Colours – again it was but an arrogant trickle of his power.

People began to scream as blood ran freely from their noses, eyes and ears. Chaos broke out amongst the crowd and bloodied, mostly blinded bodies began to run in all directions. Orlac turned his calm attention towards one end of the square. It seemed a pity to ruin this dignified architecture, but he pushed again with his Colours and at this bidding the area of buildings began to cave in, collapsing swiftly under their own sudden shift in weight. The grinding and groaning of stone, as it bent to Orlac's will, sounded even worse than the shrieking, panicking people it threatened, and it brought back all his memories of when he had begun the destruction of Caremboche all those centuries previous.

Good . . . good, my boy. Are you enjoying yourself? Dorgryl asked, impressed.

He was, and Dorgryl was disappointed when his nephew pulled back the Colours, allowing them to soften to a glow within whilst he surveyed the damage. Dorgryl so badly wanted to touch that well of power, but this was not the time to reveal himself. He relished the day such power would be his. For now, though, he must be the 'guest' and learn more about his host.

The people who had been hurt were lying on the polished stone, crying and begging for help as their blood ran freely. Some had been crushed under the toppling stone of the buildings. Others, not many, had escaped the touch of his Colours but they were in shock, walking from person to person, trying to find their own and seeking help. Why was this happening? What could cause such a thing? they wondered. Orlac noticed a woman fleeing the square; her shapely ankles above jewelled sandals caught his eye. Obviously one he had spared, he thought carelessly, and felt smug that she had escaped his attentions. Perhaps she was pretty? She would certainly help spread the word.

Hela had picked up her long skirts, revealing her jewelled sandals and, not caring that her veils were askew, ran for her life. This was it. This is what Lys had warned her about. There was magic afoot in Cipres and it came accompanied by death. She had not missed the unaccountably tall, impressively handsome young man who had taken the stage and looked calmly around whilst two men died behind him for absolutely no reason. He had reminded her of someone, but that thought had gone the instant everyone about her had begun to bleed.

They must forgo the night's grace she had promised Sarel. She must get the Queen away from Cipres now.

Hela's voice was urgent; her terror causing her to forget whom she addressed. 'Sarel!' She shook the sleeping Queen. 'Sarel! Wake up!'

The young woman opened her eyes, suddenly in shock, her body tensing. 'What's happened?'

'No time. Get up. Move!' commanded her maid and friend. 'It's begun. There is killing in the square. We must flee.'

Hela pulled the dazed woman from her bed, ripping off her nightgown not caring for the chill it caused to the pale, perfect skin. 'Climb into these. Waste no time, Sarel. We leave immediately.'

'Who is it?'

'I don't know – a golden man – but there are people dead in the square for no reason. I saw them with my own eyes, bleeding from their noses, bursting into flame . . . buildings which have stood for centuries, collapsing as one, killing all in their path.'

Hela had not realised she was weeping as she spoke. Now Sarel's eyes were filled with tears and confusion as she tried to make sense of the babble.

'I don't understand,' said the young Queen.

'Neither do I,' Hela admitted, her nervousness betraying her. 'It is magic . . . beyond my comprehension, but you can be sure that the man who wields it is headed here. Now quickly! Put this veil on and we leave.'

Sarel made to open her jewel box by the bed.

'Leave it! I have all we need. Come.' She led the girl through two doors in her mother's chamber to a short landing leading towards the stairs used by the servants. Hela opened one of the many storage cupboards on the landing used to replenish stocks of Sylven's favourite perfume, soaps, bath oils and linens, which Hela alone held the key to. From inside she pulled two dull brown cloth bags.

'This is all we take,' she said. 'Here, Sarel, carry one.'

She ignored the question which she could see coming to the Queen's lips and turned her back on her, taking her hand. Hela left no room for discussion or, indeed, argument. They moved swiftly — just short of running — down the stairs until they had reached the ground floor, which led into a private courtyard.

'Hela, the yard and the walls around it are guarded,' Sarel voiced her thoughts aloud. But of course Hela would already know this.

'I have taken care of it,' Hela whispered. 'The man on duty tonight is a friend. He is sweet on me, you could say,' she added conspiratorially. 'Mind me, Sarel. Say nothing, no matter what I say or you hear. Do you understand?' It was said firmly, as mother to child. She was satisfied to see the young Queen nod behind her veils. 'Come.'

True enough, as they stepped outside, a guard immediately confronted them and then relaxed when he heard Hela's voice.

'Are we safe?' she asked.

'There's some trouble in the square, or so I hear. I know nothing more but if you follow the old road, it should be clear,' he said, grinning wolfishly at the veiled face of Hela. 'Who knocked her up, then?' he added, turning to Sarel.

His blood would have frozen in his veins if he could have seen the chilled expression his new Queen wore beneath her veils. Sarel felt Hela's hand tighten on her arm with reassurance as the maid answered him, a casual tone to her voice belying the tension she surely felt.

'Stupid girl! She's three months gone and showing – no idea who the father is. I fear she is simple in her head and so lies with anyone,' she answered, playfully knocking Sarel's shoulder with her own. 'But her mother is a good friend of my mother's and I feel obliged to do the right thing and get her home before anyone of rank finds out. You know how they are?' Hela winked at him which he caught even behind those dark veils of hers.

He turned again to Sarel. 'You wouldn't give me a quick one, would you?' he asked, tugging at his breeches, '. . . as it doesn't seem to matter much to you.'

This time, it was Hela's turn to freeze. If only he knew to whom he spoke.

'Garth – leave it will you,' she said, forcing her voice to remain light and playful. 'I need to get going with her before it goes completely black out there.'

'You owe me one, Hela. You can pay me in kind on your return.'

'I'll happily pay, Garth. I've always enjoyed you.'

She kissed him lightly on the cheek; a promise of real payment yet to come. Then she grabbed Sarel's arm and pulled her to follow. Sarel was seething.

'Garth, is it? I'll have him hung when this is over!' she hissed.

'Ssh!' Hela cautioned. 'It's because of him we're safe. He changed three guards over so he could be the one on watch at this gate today. He has no rank, no money, so won their places by fighting them. He knows no fear – he's too young. All that matters to him is the feel of a woman's body against his own.'

Sarel did not respond. She felt a bit foolish for reacting so pompously as she realised just what sort of chance Hela was taking: bribing guards with her body, smuggling her Queen from the palace and no doubt prepared to lay down her own life to protect Sarel's. She remained silent. Once they had left the palace behind, walking briskly, Hela stopped and looked around. She made a soft hooting sound, like an owl, with cupped hands. A similar sound answered back and a few moments later a dark shadow emerged. Another man.

'We must follow him, Sarel. You must trust me now and do exactly as I say.'

They approached the man.

'Who is he?' Sarel whispered.

'No friend, that's for sure, but he can be trusted so long as I still owe him a purse.'

'Are we safe?'

'As we can be, hush now,' Hela cautioned. They arrived before him.

'I am Hela,' she said.

He did not so much as flinch. 'The money?' His voice was gravelly. Sarel could read no expression on his face.

'Half now, as agreed,' Hela said firmly, digging into her pocket and producing a purse which she held out. The man took it.

'Follow,' he said, and led them down the side of a hill, not caring if they stumbled. He knew the terrain well and strode ahead, the women trailing at a tentative pace.

'It would be easier without the veils,' Sarel said, hating to state the obvious.

'Until I feel it's safe, I can't reveal you.' She was surprised to hear Sarel laugh.

'Hela. The Cipreans hardly know who I am anyway. My last trip to the capital was two years ago when I was a child, and you saw to it that no one witnessed my arrival this time.'

'All true. But I am taking precautions,' Hela said in a tone which forbade further discussion.

The man of no name or conversation led them to a horse and cart and with no further ceremony, not even a helping hand to climb aboard, he wordlessly took the Queen of Cipres and her brave maidservant to the docks, carefully avoiding the city's centre. If he knew of the wild scenes unfolding therein, he did not share his knowledge. Hela was just glad to know the palace was far enough away that their most dangerous moments had passed. Now it was simply a matter of putting as much distance between Cipres and themselves as possible. She hoped Sarel had a strong constitution – a voyage during this season was destined to be rough.

'Wait,' the man said, leaving them standing on a

deserted wharf. Nearby a small galleon creaked as it rocked gently at its moorings. They could see the ship's name, *The Raven*, painted in gold on her side.

'Time to dispense with the veils now, Sarel. Soon we must become women of Tallinor.' She watched the Queen dutifully obey as she did the same, then bundled up the black veils and pushed them behind some crates.

'There now,' she said, brightly, wondering yet again where and towards what she was taking this precious young woman.

The man had returned. 'Follow.'

They stepped cautiously behind him up the steep gang-plank, trying to steady one another. A few men stared at them as they arrived and Hela was pleased to see Sarel hold her head high, her expression blank. Her haughti-ness was gone; a Queen fleeing her own city had nothing to be arrogant about. They needed these men to help them now and attitude was all important. Hela chanced a brief smile towards one of them but he looked away immedi-ately. Pirates . . . they knew how to keep secrets, not make relationships with anyone unnecessary to their needs. Good, this suited the pair. They would travel in the obscurity she desired.

The man knocked on a door, opened it and gestured for them to go in. He did not join them. Hela nodded at Sarel and they stepped inside. What they saw surprised them. Whatever both had anticipated for a pirate captain's chambers, this was not it. A man stepped out from behind a satin screen, water dripping from his beard. Sarel recoiled slightly at the sight of his destroyed eye.

'Ah, do forgive me ladies.' He pulled a patch down over the offending wound but stepped no closer. 'I was just neatening myself for your arrival.' He smiled and warmth immediately flooded a battle-scarred face.

Now he did take a few steps towards them. 'Allow me to welcome you aboard *The Raven*. I am her captain and your host, Janus Quist.' He bowed carefully.

'You are too kind, Captain Quist,' Hela replied on their behalf, relief coursing through her.

Quist turned to Sarel. 'Your highness,' he said, this time with genuine awe. He bowed once again, deeply.

It was a shocked Hela who responded. 'But . . . how could you know?'

The captain tried to conceal his amusement but it was clearly there on his wind-burnt face. 'Madam, it is my business to know who comes aboard my ship.'

'But I have shielded all knowledge of our identities from everyone. Even the guard back at the palace did not know about her,' she said, looking quickly at her Queen.

'No, but then I have eyes and ears throughout Cipres, through the palace in fact,' he said, without guile. 'Please, sit with me, let us speak over a glass of Neame's finest.'

Hela felt rattled but the pirate was behaving in a most gracious manner towards them. Sarel sat first and then nodded. Suddenly there was a Queen in this chamber.

The captain bowed again. 'We are honoured to help, your majesty. Your mother, Queen Sylven – may the gods guide her to the Light – was a great sovereign and once did me a rare kindness. In helping you, highness, I perhaps can return that gesture.'

'Thank you,' Sarel said. 'Please sit.'

Hela and Quist finally joined her. There was a knock at the door and a willowy young man stepped in with a tray. Quist nodded.

'May I offer you wine, your highness?'

Hela was about to answer out of habit but felt her mouth close at the look from Sarel. The child had grown up. Here now sat a Queen.

'I would be delighted to share a cup with you, Captain Quist,' she said, her tone measured, her words well chosen.

The server stepped forward. Quist gestured for Sarel to take a cup. 'Your majesty, may I introduce my brother-by-marriage, Locklyn . . . Locky. He will be ensuring your safety and comfort aboard *The Raven* for our voyage.'

Sarel's eyes immediately flicked to the dark pair staring down at her. She felt her breath catch but quickly composed herself. 'Are you the same Locklyn who risked the Kiss of the Silver Maiden?'

He blushed. 'I am, your highness.'

'You are brave indeed. I wished very much to have been there to share in your courage,' she said demurely.

Hela was surprised that Sarel even knew of this event.

Quist cleared his throat. 'Locky was fortunate, your highness, to escape with his life.'

'My grievance was validated,' Locky added softly, stepping quickly to offer Hela a cup of the wine.

Sarel's gaze followed him and none of it was lost on the sharp eyes of Hela.

'To close escapes, then,' Quist said raising his cup, humour playing around his far from handsome mouth.

'To close escapes,' they replied, and Sarel smiled over her wine at Locky.

5

The King's Secret

Far away from the Exotic Isles, in Tallinor's south east, a Queen finally grieved over her King. She had carried herself with grace through this most difficult of all days, holding in her tears, fighting back her bitterness, keeping her emotion entirely in check until it was appropriate to loose it. Gyl had wasted no time and already half a dozen messengers were galloping across Tallinor towards the north, south, east and west of the Kingdom, stopping only to pick up fresh horses and ride through the night to their destinations, delivering news of the death of King Lorys. She anticipated all the neighbouring monarchs would be in attendance at the funeral and extra time had been allowed for the Ciprean Queen to respond as she was the furthest afield, yet Alyssa believed the famous Queen Sylven would pay her respects to Lorys and the people of Tallinor. In the meantime, despite his fatigue, Herek had sent out messengers to all the nobles. News of the death was still to filter into the furthest parts of the city but it would spread fast now, spilling into the countryside. She needed the nobility gathered by morning so succession could be decided without delay.

Alyssa had done all that she could. Now the time was hers to be with Lorys, and she was glad that Gyl and Saxon had cleared the chapel to provide that peace for her. Tomorrow this place would be a hive of activity – the King's body would be cleansed and prepared for viewing and the palace would be dressed in full mourning. Poor old Cook would already be stoking up her fires to prepare the funeral feast which Gyl was also masterminding.

Having ticked everything off in her tidy mind, Alyssa finally allowed herself to pull back the purple satin sheet which covered the near-naked body of a man she loved very much. His face was untouched . . . in death it seemed he had found serenity at last, reflected in his peaceful expression. His body, however, told a different story. It was charred and burnt. One particular area on his chest was a ghastly black and shrivelled; all the hair on his strong arms was singed. 'Dead before he hit the ground.' She recalled Herek's powerfully descriptive words. 'He did not suffer. But he knew he would die. Knew he was a marked man.'

Now she understood part of the first messenger's words; a personal communication from the King for her ears only. She recalled how the little man had arrived wet and exhausted having outrun the storm to reach Tal. Alyssa had folded his cold fingers around a cup of steaming broth and urged him to give her his private message from the King.

'Your majesty. His exact words to you are: Forgive me, my love, for leaving you. Find your own people. Free them. Save Tallinor.'

She had looked at the man with curiosity, not comprehending any of it. He too had shrugged, forgetting himself momentarily in the presence of his sovereign.

Her expression had creased in puzzlement. 'That's all he said?'

The messenger nodded. 'He commented to me, your majesty, just before he chose those words, that he had begun to dream. Then he gave me that message; said you would understand.'

'I see, thank you, Hawse. You'd better away to your rest now . . . and thank you, for reaching here under such circumstances. King Lorys will reward you, I'm sure.'

The man had nodded and then left her with her thoughts. What had Lorys meant? It was cryptic. The first part she understood better now. It was as though Lorys had foreseen his own death. But finding her people? That was such an odd thing to say, for her people were of Tal, like his. Free them? None of that made sense to her. Mind you, saving Tallinor was very much on her mind after the heartbreaking arrival of Tor Gynt back into her life. Could Lorys have foreseen Orlac? Unlikely. But then with the mention that he had begun to dream, anything was possible, if that wretched Lys was involved.

Alyssa lifted the purple sheet to his neck so she could gaze on his fine face and no longer look at his damaged chest – the chest she loved to lay her cheek against. The first tear rolled down that same cheek now; it was the start of a torrent she would cry that night as the impact of his death began to penetrate and shatter the shield she had built around herself that day.

She wept hard, silently wiping her tears away until her own linen was as wet as the cheeks she vainly tried to dry.

As her sobs finally eased, she noticed the candles had burned down and several hours had passed while she had clung to her dead husband's body. During this time of intense grief, her thoughts had crystallised – Alyssa was convinced the gods were punishing her. The death of a husband and a child, both of whom had returned from the dark. Then the man she had learned to love deeply and with whom she had begun to build a life now lay before her, dead. It was too much grief for one person to bear. Still, her resolve hardened and she now knew what it was she had to do.

She whispered to the spirit of Lorys, wherever it was. She hoped it had lingered long enough to hear her words.

'You can join Nyria now, my beloved. She awaits you. I am pleased that your hearts can be joined once more. I have loved you deeply – I hope you know this.'

The Queen bent and kissed the cold, already hardened lips of her King.

'May the Light speed and guide you safely,' she said, shrouding his lovely face with purple, the colour of death.

Gyl could remember a similar awful silence around the palace at the time of Queen Nyria's passing. He had been able to escape it all those years ago, following Herek and some of the Shield into the foothills, but not on this occasion. He had responsibilities this time and he would not let his mother down. She was depending on him to bear the burden of almost all the official duties surrounding the King's funeral; thank the Light he had Rolynd to assist him. The man's calm, measured style was a boon when most of the other minds in the palace seemed messy and confused, including his own.

He had loved the King deeply. Somehow Gyl had always wanted to find a way to tell him, explain to him that it was not just the blind love of loyalty. No, he truly loved Lorys for the man he was. Often he had caught the King watching him; sometimes the Sovereign would attend training sessions in the courtyard and applaud him loudly as he regularly beat all the other soldiers. It was – he knew from what his mother had told him – the King's idea to create the new position of Under Prime. Alyssa had explained it was the King's intention for Herek to groom Gyl for the top job.

At this Gyl's chest and sense of pride had swollen immeasurably – he would not let his King down. And following his mother's marriage to the Sovereign he had felt incredibly close to Lorys, loving every opportunity to accompany him on the morning ride across the moors which had been his preference. There had been many occasions when they rode alone; Gyl acting as sole protector. These were his favourite times because he had had the King to himself and they would talk – almost as father and son. Lorys would encourage him to speak of his early childhood and his true mother, Marrien, promising whatever they discussed would be kept between themselves. At other times they had talked about kingship: how to run a realm effectively and to earn the respect and loyalty of a nation's people. Gyl enjoyed the tales of old King Mort and the King's father, Orkyd, and how they had finally won Tallinor through bloody battle.

These rides together had become habit, with Alyssa encouraging Gyl to spend as much time with the King as possible. It had not been hard to do; he had genuinely loved the King's company and their many private moments of shared laughter. He would miss that companionship greatly. All the other subjects had lost a King but Gyl felt the keen loss of a friend – someone he looked up to as one would a father . . . the father he had never had. He had often thought about what it would be like to have a real father and secretly he had decided it would feel very similar to the relationship he enjoyed with Lorys. He would never air such a thought openly, of course . . . not even to the Queen.

Who would he ride with now? Gyl knew he was popular with the soldiers under his command and that he had their loyalty; he also knew he was just as popular with the ladies of the court and he had already manoeuvred his way around a couched marriage proposal from one of the wealthy nobles who could appreciate the benefit of marrying off his daughter to the Under Prime. But Gyl also knew he had no real friend other than the King. He was close to Saxon, but the Kloek had curious ways and there was a remoteness about him which it seemed only his mother could touch. He loved Saxon but in all truth, he had been far closer to Lorys. There was no young woman to call friend either; no one he had ever felt excited enough about, or even close enough to, to consider calling it a loving relationship. If he looked at his life objectively, Gyl had to admit he was something of a loner. Which is why he felt so removed from everyone now; he had no one to turn to other than his mother, and she was deep in her own grief.

Gyl found himself strolling into the private royal gardens. This was a pretty walled garden which the King had built for Alyssa as his marriage gift. She could always count on it as a haven for absolute privacy; whenever he could not find his mother, he would always come to this place and sure enough, the Queen would be reading within the fragrance of her favourite magnolia tree, or writing at her bench amongst the lavenders and herbs she loved so much. He appreciated, perhaps for the first time, the privilege of having access to his mother's place, which no person bar himself, Saxon, Sallementro and the King had permission to enter without royal assent. Gyl had not yet shed a tear over his King . . . this might be the quiet spot where he could sit and think about life without Lorys.

He sat beneath an apple tree and laid his head in his hands. Tears came easily.

'I . . . I'm sorry, I should leave,' came a soft voice he recognised as Lauryn's.

Looking up, towards his mother's favourite rose arbor, he saw Lauryn's pretty face — so similar to Alyssa's — staring back at him, concern written all over it.

She stood and walked around. 'I felt so awkward in the palace. I thought to escape here but this is a private place for you and I'll leave.'

Gyl said nothing but drank in the large grey-green eyes which regarded him.

Lauryn felt uncomfortable with the way he was looking at her. 'Gyl, I'm so very, very sorry about the King. Were you close? I mean . . . I'm guessing that you probably knew him very well with our mother being married to him and all that.' She stopped. She realised she was gabbling; he truly was disarmingly handsome, particularly when the haughty air was dropped and she could see some of his vulnerability. 'Forgive me, Gyl, for interrupting your quiet time.' Lauryn smiled briefly and began to walk away quickly.

'Lauryn,' he called and was glad she turned. 'I could use the company in truth.'

'Are you sure?' She looked doubtful.

He nodded and patted the ground next to him. 'I'd be

grateful if you joined me for a while. Where's your brother?'

Lauryn tentatively sat down on a bench nearby, ignoring his tempting offer to seat herself next to him. 'I'll stay for a few minutes if you wish.' She smiled and he recalled from the first time he met her how delicious she looked when she allowed her smile to sparkle in her eyes. 'Gidyon's gone for a walk. He wishes he could have gone with our father, but I think he already feels great affection for the Queen and wants to comfort her but does not really know how. He's so sensitive.'

'Not like you?'

'I hardly know Gidyon yet we both feel so close to one another. Yes, I think in all honesty I'm probably hardier than him emotionally. I think Gidyon shows his emotions whereas I've learned how to hide them, probably . . . I don't really know.' She shrugged.

Gyl was surprised to feel himself grin. 'Oh, I think you're as tough as one of the wild boars of the forest.'

Lauryn threw a grimace at him. 'Charmed.'

'Well, I only have our first meeting to go on.'

'I was scared, Gyl. You've heard our story – as impossible as it must sound to you, it's all true. I hardly understand it myself.'

He shook his head. 'No one will ever believe it.'

'Yes, I think you're right,' she said. 'But it doesn't make it any less true.'

'Tell me your story, Lauryn.'

'No. You know plenty about me already. How about you tell me about you?'

'All right,' Gyl said, straightening up and closing his eyes to plan where he should begin.

Lauryn felt her throat tighten. What a beautiful man he is, she thought as Gyl began to tell his own story. Not as tall as Gidyon or her father but they both seemed taller than any man she could remember. He had strong shoulders and his body tapered to slim hips. He wore simple clothes and she liked him for that. Even in her short time in the palace she had seen quite a number of people who favoured bright, decorated garments. She wondered whether the King had been one of those. Saxon, and indeed her mother, she was glad to see, favoured simplicity, but then looking like Alyssa one would need no other adornment. Gyl obviously preferred the garb of a simple soldier even though he was Queen's Champion. Nevertheless, for all their simplicity she noticed his clothes were well cut and hung from his body superbly.

'. . . and they found me chained like that the next morning. If it wasn't for Queen Nyria, I'd have probably got myself a boot up the arse for being such a nuisance. Instead, I was put in the care of our mother, Alyssa, who was just a palace servant at that time.'

She nodded, did not want to interrupt him. Lauryn liked hearing his voice. There was a certain wistfulness in it she often felt herself. Gyl was talking about growing up at the palace now and as he did so, she turned her attentions to his face.

He had a square jaw, a straight nose and dark green eyes. It was a symmetrical face framed by dark, slightly curly hair which he chose to wear short – rather than longer and tied back as seemed the fashion in Tal. His most arresting feature was the long lashes outlining his eyes and she wondered how often he had been teased about those by the other soldiers. Small neat teeth could be glimpsed when he laughed, which Lauryn thought must not be all that often any more. It seemed the weight of his title might have pressed down the young, carefree lad he might have been and required him to be more serious.

'You need to laugh more, Gyl.' She had not meant to blurt out her thoughts.

'Pardon me?'

Lauryn was embarrassed but she pressed on. 'You take yourself a little too seriously.'

'Really?' he said, the tone in his voice telling her he was anything but flattered. 'That's very judgemental for someone who has only been in Tal for a little under one day and who knows me hardly at all. What do you know of my life, Lauryn? Or my responsibilities? Has it even occurred to you to imagine how difficult it is to suddenly be told I have half-brothers and a sister and now I share my mother with two . . . no three others?'

Lauryn felt stupid. He was right, of course. 'I just meant if you were a little easier on yourself – not so tense all the time . . .'

'You don't know what I'm like. The only time you've spent with me has been during rather dramatic circumstances.' He stood. 'Now if you'll excuse me, madam, I have a funeral to arrange. My apologies for my loose tongue.'

He strode away, leaving Lauryn mouthing to no one, 'I just meant you have a wondrous smile which would be nice to see.'

Gyl apparently did not hear her and she did not see him again until the following afternoon under greatly changed circumstances.

* * *

Queen Alyssa of Tallinor arrived in the Throne Room of the Tal Palace shortly after sunrise. She was not a bit surprised to see the hall already full of people, and they were familiar faces; almost all of them she could call friends, having won their faith and trust since her marriage to Lorys. They looked tired from the early summons; many appeared shaken with disbelief at the fact that their King, still relatively young in years, lay cold on a marble slab. And if Alyssa was not surprised by their prompt attention to her request, by contrast they were all certainly surprised at this young woman's composure. They had never doubted her loyalty and love for the King, and had anticipated her reaction might be one of hysteria, having lost him so tragically and so soon after her marriage. They had not been prepared to be summoned so swiftly or for her rigid control as she graciously accepted their muted welcome.

She could see Gyl and Herek standing to one side with Saxon in attendance. No one seemed to mind this familiar trio being present and she was grateful for their reassuring nods, although she knew Gyl was confused as to what she was hoping to achieve this morning and she wished she had taken him into her confidence sooner than this.

Alyssa had asked Lauryn and Gidyon to be in attendance and she noted them now at the back of the hall, almost hidden beneath a small archway. They had no idea what they were doing there and were strangers to virtually everyone in the Throne Room. She nodded at them. 'Gentlemen, please, be seated.'

After the noise of chairs scraping on flagstones and the coughs and clearing of throats had settled, Alyssa slowly swept her gaze around the room, deliberately resting on a few. They were the older nobles – harder nuts to crack but most of whom had eventually fallen under her spell. She needed their support now; required their total commitment to her cause.

She spoke clearly, relieved that her voice was steady. 'Thank you for coming at this early hour and under such circumstances. For those of you who wish to hear it from my lips, King Lorys of Tallinor died as a result of a freak lightning strike which claimed his life last night. Prime Herek was with him when it struck and assures me the King died instantly. No pain was suffered.'

Alyssa paused whilst the murmuring of men, so often heard in this throne room, gradually died back. She continued now, felt her hands turn clammy and her chest tighten with the nervous anticipation of what she was about to announce to this gathering. Too late to turn back now. It must be done.

'Tallinese law requires succession by an heir. I have no desire to claim any right of sovereignty as Queen to Lorys.' She noticed relief crossing the faces of many of the older nobles. So, they had come expecting her to change laws. Indeed, she had a greater surprise than that.

'As you all know, King Lorys and Queen Nyria produced no heir and,' she sounded regretful now, 'Lorys and I simply didn't have time.' She hoped it might lighten the grim mood but no one so much as twitched a smile.

And so it was time. Alyssa looked to her right where Rolynd stood with a rolled parchment.

'I am passing around to you a sample of the King's hand. I would ask for three of our senior nobles to please acknowledge that this is indeed the handwriting of King Lorys of Tallinor.'

She felt her shoulders trembling and steeled herself.

She must not fail now. Fresh murmuring broke out as the gathered started to mutter amongst themselves.

Over them she spoke. 'Sir Deen, would you confirm please that this document bears the handwriting of our King Lorys.'

A grey-haired man from the southwest pushed a monocle in front of his eye and scanned the parchment. He studied it, finally looked up and nodded.

'I would bear testimony to that.'

'Thank you, Sir Deen. Sir Gyles – please?'

Another senior man, this time from the north, cast an experienced eye and nodded.

'I have seen the writing of Lorys many times. This is his hand.'

'My thanks, Sir Gyles. Lord Ayers – I would appreciate your confirmation.'

A wealthy noble – by far the most influential – from the far west took the parchment and glanced at it.

'I would gladly swear this is the writing of Lorys.'

It was handed back to Rolynd who walked back to where the Queen stood on the dais. She lifted now from the sleeves of her formal robes, another parchment.

'This parchment was written by King Lorys on the day of our wedding. It is signed by him and myself and witnessed by the King's aide, Koryn, and by Cook.'

Fresh, heated discussion erupted.

Alyssa put her hand in the air to soothe the talk. 'I realise the choice of Cook is unusual but she is known to all of you, loved by all of you and has been at this palace for longer than many of us can remember. As a trusted member of the staff, her signature is an important authority on the authenticity of this document which was read to her by the King. Cook can't read you see, but she listened in the presence of Koryn and myself before signing her name.

'Lord Ayers, you are the most senior noble in this room and you were close to my husband. May I ask you to kindly read this document aloud so all can hear?'

The man strode to the dais and took the parchment proffered by his Queen.

'Your highness, this is most unusual.'

'These are most unusual circumstances, Lord Ayers . . . please,' she said, encouraging him onto the dais so he could face the gathered.

He unrolled the parchment and squinted slightly. 'Well, this is the King's handwriting, all right.' He looked at Alyssa who smiled gently and nodded.

Lord Ayers began to read. 'I, King Lorys of Tallinor, do make this declaration in the presence of my new wife, Queen Alyssandra nee Qyn, Lyle Koryn and Betsy Charlick, trusted members of staff.

'If this is being read to my trusted nobles, it means I have gone to the Light and I must ask you to trust my Queen in her decision to make this public and beg the forgiveness of those to whom it comes as a shock.

'I have kept a terrible secret for the past sixteen years following an indiscretion during my marriage to Queen Nyria. Only two people from the palace knew of it and both Physic Merkhud and Prime Cyrus took this secret with them to their graves. Both helped me to protect it but at my death it is critical I share it with the Kingdom I love and its people whom I have served.'

Alyssa felt the lump form in her throat. She forced it back down; she must cling to her composure just a little longer. Lord Ayers continued once the loud voices of worry had settled down again.

He read: 'I, King Lorys of Tallinor, sired a son to a woman from Auldgate, more recently of Wytton. Our son was born from a solitary, short encounter. I never spoke to nor heard from her again. Physic Merkhud ensured the child was educated and cared for. Upon my death the throne of Tallinor must pass to him as he alone carries the line of Old King Mort.'

Cries broke out in the Throne Room and the voice of Lord Ayers was drowned. Alyssa felt dizzy from her nerves and the anticipation of announcing the new King of Tallinor. Gyl had arrived at her side to help.

Amongst the noise she heard him speaking to her. 'Mother?'

'I'm well, Gyl. A little distracted.' She looked at him intensely now. 'Forgive me, son.'

He did not understand; he held her gaze and tried to work out what she meant by it.

He too was shocked by the revelation and glanced around the room as he wondered which of the young nobles was to be the next King. Lord Ayers had quietened everyone, demanding silence whilst he finish reading this dramatic proclamation from their King. The room hushed.

'The fact that you are reading this in the Throne Room means I have not yet found the courage to declare myself publicly to my son, who walks amongst you – and for that I ask his eternal forgiveness and seek his understanding that I have loved him intensely from a distance, though I never did have the opportunity to tell him so.

'I ask all of the nobles of Tallinor to gather and pledge

their allegiance and support as they crown the new Sovereign of Tallinor, King Gyl of Wytton.'

Shock passed through the Throne Room of the Palace of Tallinor with the same speed and bite as the lightning had through the former King.

It was spoken. Alyssa felt relief flood through her veins as she slid out of Gyl's grip to her knees. 'Hail King Gyl.' She spoke it loud and firm.

Her words were picked up and voices began to chant them in affirmation. People dropped to their knees until there were only three left standing. Herek, as shocked as anyone in the room, only followed Saxon when the Kloek pulled at the soldier's hand, willing him to kneel before his new King.

And now only Gyl remained on his feet, fighting back fear and nausea. Tears pricked but he fought those too and a sense of betrayal and loss enveloped him. The Great Hall was suddenly still and quiet. He looked around it with even more dismay than the Prime had. He felt the glance of his mother and looked down where she knelt.

Knelt! Light! He bent, hardly able to string any coherent thoughts together.

'You knew? Kept this from me?'

She struggled against the terror of perhaps even losing him.

'We wanted to tell you. He was taken before we could.' It sounded pathetic even to her ears.

He felt rage stirring. His father, the King. How many occasions could that man have taken him in his arms and called him son. Gyl, always so in control, felt himself losing his composure. Whether it was by luck or fate, his eyes, searching the room, locked onto the steady grey-green eyes of Lauryn. They snapped him out of his rising temper as he recalled her words. He had heard them; had felt a strange uplifting sensation at hearing her say how nice it would be to see his smile. He did not feel like smiling now but there was something disarming about this woman. A calm countenance washed over him as he stared at those eyes now and she nodded softly towards him. It was an apology for her presumptuousness earlier.

Gyl was suddenly aware that everyone was still kneeling, still waiting. 'Stand, Mother, please I beg you,' he whispered.

Alyssa's eyes now looked up into his and implored him. 'You must accept it first. Affirm your sovereignty, son.'

Gyl immediately looked towards Saxon, whose gaze had also surreptitiously lifted towards his. The Kloek nodded slowly at him.

Now the Throne Room was so devoid of noise the silence itself began to overwhelm the young man whose heart was pounding. He must say something. Everyone awaited his words. He would deal with sorrow and disbelief later. Now it was time to fulfil his destiny.

He did not even clear his throat. His voice was steady and strong, as a sovereign's should be, and he was grateful in that defining few moments that his mind suddenly worked with clarity and the words which came out were well chosen and regal.

'I would ask the King's Mother to stand beside me as I accept the mantle to rule this realm. I bid all of you – loyal citizens of Tallinor – raise yourselves to your feet and affirm with your new Sovereign the commencement of a new era for our Kingdom.' Gyl found his smile, directed it at Lauryn; it was radiant with pride and a sense of destiny.

'The glory of Tallinor!' he called strongly towards his new subjects.

And they echoed it with the same power and pride. 'The glory of Tallinor! Hail, King Gyl of Tallinor.'

6

A New Guest in the Palace

Orlac stood before the gates of the Ciprean palace and marvelled at its grace. He could hear the soldiers gathering in the main courtyard, their superiors barking orders. Word had spread furiously of his frightening arrival but he felt in no hurry and instead was taking great joy in admiring the spires of the palace, his head turned upwards away from the frightened glances of the men.

Finally a man confronted him from behind the gates. Orlac presumed this must be the most senior officer and he lowered his eyes to look upon this person now.

'Who are you?' the man demanded, no courtesies given.

So be it. 'I am Orlac.'

It ment nothing to the man, though fear was written across his face. Orlac imagined he must be wondering when he too would begin to bleed.

'Depart now and you leave with your life,' the soldier said, not so confidently.

'Otherwise?' Orlac asked. He sounded genuinely inquisitive, though there was no spark of goodwill in his expression. Perhaps there was no 'otherwise'. The man blinked, confused. He was rescued by another, far older man who stepped into view now and answered for him.

'Or, we will be forced to kill you,' the new man calmly said.

Orlac stopped himself sneering, summoned the Colours and felt Dorgryl shiver in anticipation of what he might do. Orlac hated the thing inside and promised himself he would learn how to destroy it, but in the meantime he would do everything he could to deny the ghoul within the gratification he sought.

The young god held the soldier's glare as he curiously pressed himself against the bars of the gates where he held for just the barest of moments before miraculously stepping through them. It was as if he had no body at all, reappearing whole and unharmed in front of the two disbelieving senior officers. He watched, amused, as all the soldiers behind them dropped their weapons as one, in awe of the impossible event they had just witnessed.

'I think we've had enough bloodletting for one night, don't you?' Orlac asked of the more senior fellow.

The man was unable to respond. His mouth opened a couple of times but emitted no sound.

Orlac nodded curtly. 'I'm glad you agree.' He pushed past the man but turned again. 'And you are?'

The stunned officer finally found his voice. 'Bensyn.'

'Thank you, Bensyn. Dismiss the men and present yourself and your senior officers within the palace shortly.'

Orlac strode away, pleased that he could feel Dorgryl's disappointment within.

It may not pay to be too subtle, nephew.

I shall make my own decision on how to wield my power, Dorgryl.

The senior god held his tongue.

Inside the palace staff were agog. No man had ever had access to the palace in the way this man now strode confidently through the beautiful halls. Word had spread fast enough that none were willing to risk their lifeblood to stop him yet the staff, including the senior courtiers, gathered to witness his entrance. What else could they do? Cringe in their rooms? Bleed? Or find the courage to look upon this towering, golden man who brought death and destruction to their beautiful city?

Orlac sensed their fear and indecision. He took command. 'All senior palace staff, courtiers, advisers, officials should gather. You!' he said, pointing to a petite young woman with dark hair he found himself attracted to. She bowed but would not meet his eyes.

'Which room did the Queen take audiences in?'

She cleared her throat and looked around at the others.

'Answer me.' Orlac spoke firmly.

'In the Golden Room . . . er sire,' she suggested, then pointed down a corridor.

'Could you lead me to it . . . please?'

She nodded, surprisingly calmly, he thought. Orlac turned towards the main group of people standing bewildered before him.

'Would somebody kindly organise some food and wine. I have been travelling all day.'

He did not linger for any sort of answer, presuming his request would be heeded soon enough and turned to follow the small figure of the woman.

Command, damn you! You are a god. Act like one.

I have no gripe with Cipres, Dorgryl, Orlac replied smoothly. *My revenge is directed at Tallinor alone. I'll ask you not to give me any further orders.*

Or what? Dorgryl asked, his frustration spilling over. There was a nasty edge to his voice. *What can you do to me? Nothing! You are powerless and without me you will spend the rest of your powerless life looking for Gynt or wishing you were dead. That's how miserable I could make life for you.*

Orlac knew this to be true. But he was determined to find a way to rid himself of the insanity living within. They had arrived at what was supposedly the Golden Room and although he wanted to say something cutting in response to Dorgryl, he resisted and instead ignored his uncle in favour of bestowing a smile upon the woman who stood before him. He knew it would rankle Dorgryl if he favoured her. She was attractive too and although he would have preferred a golden-haired partner, she would do for his first night.

'If you'd kindly wait here, sir, I shall see to your food being fetched.' Again the calm, steadying voice. It intrigued him.

'Your name?'

'Juno, sir.'

'Ha! Juno. I was too strong for her.' He winked. His words deliberately intended to confuse. Orlac guessed she would now be wondering what exactly he meant by such a comment. Instead, her face showed no confusion. If anything, he sensed something behind those clear, steady eyes. Something he could not fathom. It certainly was not fear. The woman forced a polite smile and nodded.

'Well, thank you, Juno. I would ask that you prepare a bedroom for me . . .'

'Yes,' she said, turning to make haste on his requests.

'and . . . await me there,' he added, leaving no doubt in her mind this time as to what he meant. He noticed how she froze at his words and read it as fear etching itself across her face. It was true that he had no quarrel with these people. On his way into Cipres he had even entertained fanciful thoughts of being liked; admired even. But as always it was the same. People feared his power – just as they had in centuries previous – and he felt the familiar coldness grab him. What was he thinking? He had always been hated. He was the avenger . . . the destroyer of people and their cities.

Orlac looked tiredly at Juno. 'Go now. Send in the people waiting.'

They filed in slowly, warily. These were people who had never thought they would see a man sitting on the exquisite gold throne, which for eternity had been the seat for a line of women. When the doors were finally closed behind them and the shuffling had stopped, a dread silence descended on the huge room.

Orlac measured the silence. It was built entirely on fear. He addressed them. 'It is regretful that people were hurt today.' One after another they lifted their eyes to meet his as he continued. 'I have no quarrel with the people of Cipres but I must impress on you that you should not attempt to defy me. I am powerful beyond imagination. You have no weapon against me for I have the Power Arts on my side.'

A white-haired man, richly robed, stepped forward.

'You are?' Orlac questioned.

'I am an adviser to our former Queen,' he bowed before adding, 'highest ranking courtier in the palace.'

'What is it you wish to say?'

The man looked grimly around. 'I speak for all gathered. We know your name but not who you are, why you are here, why you killed one hundred and forty-three of our citizens today with a further eighty, perhaps more, almost certainly still to die from your attentions. What is it you want of us?'

Orlac, about to respond, felt suddenly nauseous. The chamber seemed to spin and the oil lamps gave off light that flickered into and out of darkness as whatever it was that was truly him was pushed aside and trampled upon. He was not ready for this; had no inclination that it was even possible. He was as shocked as the people looked when the answer came, for it was not he who spoke, but Dorgryl.

'Your throne is what I want,' replied the deep voice.

People recoiled instantly; not just from the outrageous claim but more so from the change in the stranger's voice. It was chilling.

Dorgryl continued whilst Orlac felt he was drowning within himself. 'Your Queen is dead. Obey me, good people, and we shall rule fairly.'

The people gathered found their voices, overcoming their fright at this man and protesting loudly at what he was suggesting.

Dorgryl smiled, showing Orlac's perfect teeth, even allowing the smile to touch Orlac's large, strangely violet eyes and blinked his long, beautiful dark lashes. 'For if you do not obey, I will level your city; I will murder all of your people . . . whole families – mothers, fathers, brothers, sisters, grandparents, even babes in arms will die horribly . . . and I shall do it so slowly that each of you will suffer the most grotesque finale of pain and humiliation. Cipres will cease to exist. It will be dust. Forgotten – as will its people.'

The white-haired man looked ashen. 'Why would you do this?' was all he could numbly force his voice to ask.

'Because I can!' Dorgryl bellowed, his voice reaching way beyond the confines of the room. 'I am a Prince. I should have been a King. I will rule!' His tone disconcertingly fell back to its normal level but was no less intimidating. 'Perhaps I might sweeten this deal between us. I grant you a concession. You require a Queen and I shall provide her. I shall rule through her. Accept this or die . . . it's really quite simple.'

People began to look around at one another. They were too terrified to say anything directly to him but he could read the confusion and he loved it. Loved feeling Orlac squirming beneath him, around him, demanding to claim his body back. Well, he could wait. A good lesson was being learned not only by the Cipreans but by his young host tonight.

A figure in black slithered from the fringe of the gathered. A gaunt fellow with a face to terrify children presented himself, bowing low. Dorgryl considered him. He did not appear as cowed as the others. One eye twitched erratically due to a pronounced tic on one side of his face; the rest of his face looked as though it had been mauled by leprosy. Dorgryl found himself momentarily fascinated by the horror of the face in front of him.

'And who might you be?' he finally asked, his interest piqued.

The voice was effeminate. 'I am Almyd Goth, sire. Also an adviser to the former Queen. I wonder, could I beg a word?'

Dorgryl looked around at the expectant faces, filled with fear. Hold that fear, good folk, he thought to himself, and obey me. He felt Orlac attempting to claw back his mind again. He was strong and Dorgryl would have to be extremely wary of that strength which had stood Orlac in such stead during his battles with the Paladin. The boy was also powerful with magic way beyond his own but he was inexperienced, used to wielding only one particular form of it — killing the Paladin. Mind you, it was taking all of Dorgryl's concentration to keep Orlac's power at bay.

Everyone was waiting. 'Dismissed until I summon you,' he commanded. 'You,' he looked at Goth. 'Remain.' He watched the people, now even more confused and wary, shuffling to get away from him as fast as they could.

He noted Goth's satisfied look and the sneer he threw towards the other adviser, but Dorgryl ignored the fellow in front of him for now. Instead he spoke with Orlac whilst the people dispersed. *You may have your body back now but remember how this feels and don't ever forget I can do it to you any time I please.*

Dorgryl gave Orlac no chance to respond. He reduced himself in a second to the shimmering red presence as Orlac felt his body become his again. It slumped and he felt behind himself for the throne. Light! He felt weakened. The man, Goth, was talking to him. For a moment he could not hear what he said; could only watch his lips move.

'Are you sure I cannot get you something?' Goth repeated.

Orlac pushed the dizziness back. *There will be a reckoning* he growled at Dorgryl who did not respond but he sensed his uncle shimmer brightly momentarily as though in a flash of anger.

The room was empty, save for himself and Goth. Orlac deliberately took another few moments to find his composure. The man sensibly remained still and silent.

'What is it you wish to say to me?' Orlac finally said. He gave no explanation for his odd behaviour.

Goth felt unbalanced. He was used to being able to fathom almost every situation. His agile mind and ability to rapidly respond to ever-changing situations meant he could assemble, dismantle and rework a plan in moments. Goth knew he had an uncanny ability to see events from almost any perspective, which was why, he believed, he continued to escape retribution. There was only one situation for which his brilliant and subtle mind had not been able to find an answer and that was the continuing good health and vitality of Torkyn Gynt. He had personally watched him die; watched his body break and take its last gasp before death consumed it. He had absolutely no explanation for his return to life, if indeed he had left it. But now he had another compelling problem to pick at. Orlac. Where had he come from? Why was this throne so important to him? . . . Why this realm and not Tallinor, for example? Goth had felt chilled — a rare sensation — when the golden man's voice had suddenly changed to that deep, detached one.

He, who felt no fear of anyone, had at that moment experienced an awe of something he suspected was so much more powerful and clever than him that he was frightened. The stupid people in the room had muttered between themselves about how to fight this enemy. How ludicrous! Had they not seen the dead and dying in the square? Had they not heard the terrifying tale of this man stepping through iron gates? . . . More than that, *dissolving* through those gates! Soldiers had thrown down their weapons in submission. There was no fighting a man like this . . . if he was a man, for which mortal possessed magical powers such as this?

He looked now at the intensely violet eyes which were regarding him. Orlac was brilliantly handsome. Opposite in colouring but similar in stature, he reminded Goth of Torkyn Gynt, of all hateful people. Probably that uncanny height and those broadest of shoulders, he told himself. And that damn wide, bright smile!

Orlac was waiting; he seemed vaguely amused by the long pause.

'My apologies, sire.' Goth bent low again. 'I quite lost myself there. Your arrival has frightened us all.'

'The Cipreans have nothing further to fear from me,' Orlac said quietly.

Goth showed his surprise. 'But you killed so many of them! How can they not fear you?' He could not help the words spilling out and he braced himself for a painful response.

'It had to be so,' the golden-haired man replied.

'What is it you want, sire? Perhaps I can be of some service?'

Orlac was genuinely amused. 'I don't think so, royal adviser. What I want you cannot give me.'

Goth decided to push his luck. It had held this far and he had nothing to lose, perhaps everything to gain by ingratiating himself with this powerful individual. 'I may surprise you.'

'What I want,' Orlac said with deliberation, 'is Tallinor razed, its people dead and a man called Torkyn Gynt on his knees paying homage to me!' His voice had increased in volume but it was cold.

Goth hardly noticed, such was his shock at what the man had just said. He trembled with the thrill of those words.

He found himself on his knees now, wanting to pay his own homage to this empowered man who lusted for the same vengeance as he. Oh kindred soul, he wanted to cry out loud. Instead he clasped his hands together with glee in front of Orlac. 'My lord, I can indeed help you with what you desire so much. I am Tallinese; I was formerly the Chief Inquisitor of the Kingdom and there is no man on this Land I would rather see on his knees awaiting your pleasure and his pain than Torkyn Gynt whom I know and despise with every ounce of my blood.'

It was Orlac's turn to feel surprised. 'Know him? By sight?'

'Sight! Ha!' Goth almost forgot himself. 'He is my enemy. I nearly killed him but I failed, sire. The Queen died of the poison instead.' Before he knew it the whole story was out of his mouth and laid bare in front of Orlac.

'You murdered her?'

Goth felt nervous and looked around to check no Ciprean had slid into the room and heard his confession. He nodded and was not surprised to hear Orlac laugh again; this time he seemed hugely amused.

'But it is Gynt you seek to kill?' Orlac asked once his humour had settled.

'With all my heart. And his woman. Her name is Alyssa. And all of his supporters – too many to mention now, my lord. I would like to see all of them dead, including his King whom I have heard recently married Alyssa and made her Queen of Tallinor. I hope I'll live to see his Kingdom in ruin and count him dead amongst it.'

'You have a lot of hate inside you, Goth,' Orlac observed.

'I have my reasons, my lord, which is why I will serve you blindly, faithfully and to the exclusion of all other interest, for you desire what I seek.'

Orlac paused to consider this strange fellow. How

uncanny that this man and he should harbour such depth of hate for the same individual . . . the same Kingdom. He wondered why but then cast that question aside. He really did not care. It was the man's passion he was impressed by. There was no question this Goth was sincere; his eyes told Orlac this was a man with no remorse, no empathy with others.

'How can you help me?' the god asked, curious to hear the fellow's ideas.

'In many ways, my lord. I know Tallinor; I know the collective mind of its people and how it works. I know the King and his failings. I know Torkyn Gynt and his companions by sight. I can lead you to those who would support, protect or hide him.'

Goth could have gone on but felt he had said enough. He saw the golden man nodding thoughtfully, considering what he had said.

'And what do you wish in return for such loyal service?'

'In return? Why nothing, my great lord. I wish only to serve. Perhaps a nice plot of land on the hills around Cipres. Or you might throw some of the spoils of Tallinor my way. You may even care to give me status, sire, in your new dynasty for Cipres. I presume you will continue to rule here after your needs have been met in Tallinor. You may consider allowing me to rule Tallinor as your proxy?' Goth was warming to his theme now and even began to strut around, waving his hand for emphasis. 'From the ruins of Tallinor we can build a new Kingdom, my lord. Your Kingdom, which you can adjoin with Cipres. I will run it for you. And why indeed stop at Tallinor? With your powers and my knowledge of the region, we can acquire other realms.'

Orlac chuckled at Goth's grand plan. 'Is there anything else you may want?'

Goth became still. 'Yes, sire. I wish to be present at the killing of Torkyn Gynt but I ask that first he watch his beloved Alyssa be disembowelled, beheaded and quartered. And I wish to be her executioner. I want to look in her eyes and be the last person she sees when the light dies in them, my lord.'

It seemed to Orlac that this man thought along similar lines as Dorgryl. His uncle had already suggested they track down and destroy every family member and friend to Gynt. It would keep him wary and defensive, Dorgryl had counselled, and never in a position to attack. Orlac had seen the sense in this and now here was this strange fellow suggesting a similar plan. Perhaps he could be of some use.

Goth pushed his advantage. 'Sire, in order to help you, first I must know your plan for Cipres.'

'Plan? Simply to rule.'

'How?'

'What do you mean how, Goth? You heard me tell that creaky old man that we would rule through a woman and at least honour their way.'

'So you will rule through Princess Sarel?' Goth asked, trying to understand and knowing he was risking the wrath of the powerful man in front of him.

It was Orlac's turn to look puzzled. 'I have no specific woman in mind yet.'

Goth pushed on nervously. 'So you may kill the Queen and install another?'

'There is no Queen, Goth. You irritate me now. You killed her, remember?'

Goth believed he could feel his own blood chill. 'No, my lord,' he said carefully. 'I killed Queen Sylven. I am talking about the Princess . . . the soon to be crowned Queen Sarel.'

Orlac sat upright and regarded Goth – he had been taken by surprise and was unsure what to make of this news.

Dorgryl, who had been listening carefully to this exchange, broke his own silence. *She must be found and killed. She is too dangerous.*

Why killed? Orlac asked, deep down knowing the answer.

As long as there is an heir, the people will not rest. There will always be those – many in fact – who will want their rightful Queen on the throne. And whilst you're off wreaking havoc on Tallinor, you don't want an uprising here. Waste no time, Dorgryl growled.

For all the young god's immense powers, the elder god decided his nephew was spineless. When the time was right he would overpower him for good but that was some while away yet – he must wait until he had the full measure of his host's extensive magics and strengths. He must know that before he could make any decisive moves.

Goth cleared his throat uncomfortably. He noticed that Orlac did a lot of staring into nothing. The pauses in the man's conversation unsettled the former chief inquisitor. It was as though Orlac's attention was entirely diverted; that he was seeing something else, talking to someone else.

Orlac came out of whatever reverie he had been in and looked down upon Goth.

'Where is the Princess?'

Goth was relieved to be talking again and released from the disarming silence. 'Presumably in her chambers. No one has seen her much since her mother's death at Neame and the girl's arrival in the city. She has a maidservant who is rather,' he carefully chose an appropriate phrase, 'over-protective.' It was the right choice he decided and just stopped short of smirking. Perhaps he could get Hela thrown out of the palace as well. Better still, killed or, wait, even more satisfying . . . delivered to him as a slave.

Orlac's voice disturbed his flight of fancy. 'I want the girl summoned. I instruct you to personally find her and bring her to me.'

'Now, your highness?' Goth was not quite sure when this golden man had become a sovereign but he felt it was the right amount of respect to show to this person.

Orlac ignored the title. 'Did you think, perhaps, I meant tomorrow?'

Goth felt his colour rise immediately. It was not often he could be caught out like this. 'No, sire. I presumed you meant right now.'

'Then why are you still here?' Orlac asked, a subtle change in his tone suggesting something of a threat.

Goth snapped into a bow. 'At once, sire.' He left the chamber immediately in search of Sarel.

After a lengthy and extensive search of every room, every nook and cranny of the palace with dozens of people involved in the orchestrated hunt, Goth found himself once again standing in front of Orlac. This time, however, he felt a lot less confident.

He bowed low. 'My lord. She has disappeared.' Brevity was best, he decided.

'Would escaped be a better word?'

Goth found the courage to look into those violet eyes.

'Perhaps, sire. I have no idea. She was not under any constraint. I'm guessing now that she may have been alerted to your arrival in the city and took flight.'

'Perhaps,' the god conceded, suddenly tired. 'I want her found and returned to the palace. You, Goth, will track her down.'

Dorgryl whispered. *She will have fled to Tallinor.*

To Gynt?

I couldn't say but you can be sure it's Tallinese soil which beckons. It would be the safest place to flee to . . . and the largest to get lost in. The only other places around here are tiny islands.

Goth felt a finger of doubt poke at him and again the silence was unnerving. 'She may already be on a ship, sire,' he offered.

'Then chase her. This is your first duty for me and if you succeed you will be richly rewarded, in the manner you wish. Don't fail me, Almyd Goth.'

'I will not let you down, my lord. May I have some men?'

'Take what you want. Leave immediately. I suggest you head for Tallinor first.'

Goth bowed, ecstatic. Back to Tallinor and with armed men behind him. Could it get any better?

'Try not to bumble and kill another Queen of Cipres,' Orlac added as Goth made his departure. 'I wish her returned alive.' That would annoy Dorgryl, he thought, and smiled.

7

Decision

Alyssa's face betrayed the pain filling her heart as she revealed her plan to Gyl. They were alone in what had been Lorys's chambers. How sad, she thought, that someone so vital, so alive just days ago, was now being referred to as the 'old King', as if he had been in his dotage.

'You would leave me now,' Gyl asked, 'when I need your counsel more than ever?'

She took his hand but felt none of the affection returned. 'You know as much about running a kingdom as I do, son. Very little.' She hoped he might smile but Gyl's expression remained solemn. She pressed on, her words spilling out quickly as she found good reasons to justify her sudden departure. 'Those rides out on the moors with your father weren't for nought. Much would have been discussed without you understanding why. I have ensured the loyalty of the nobility; you have their un-wavering support and you can rely on the three I singled out to advise you well. Can I add that you must know you possess qualities which already lend themselves superbly to leadership. Change the title from Prime to King – the job is much the same. Lorys believed firmly in you; was so very proud of you, and I too feel bitter that you were cheated from hearing this by his own mouth. He died in sadness, I'm sure, because of it.'

Alyssa desperately wished those were not tears in the King's eyes, yet knew full well her wish was in vain. 'Don't weep, son. You were loved. You are still loved.'

He snatched his hand from his mother to push away the hateful tears of weakness. Gyl was angry; would not tolerate more tears. He had shed enough of them over a man he loved – the now-dead father he had never known was his own. His pain spilled out. 'How could you not share such a knowledge with me!'

It was an accusation. Alyssa remained calm. 'I knew it would cause pain. We wanted to find the right time.'

'Well, standing in front of the entire nobility was not it, Mother!' he yelled now.

'I realise as much,' Alyssa responded, her voice suddenly hard. 'Who knows, it might even be that the untimely death of my husband pushed my hand.' Alyssa could not help the sarcasm which spilled into her words. Perhaps Gyl was forgetting that she had been a Queen earlier today and was due some respect. He might also be overlooking the fact that he was not the only one grieving for a beloved King.

He answered with a similar and surprising sharpness she had not encountered before, his normally soft grey eyes now glinting with anger. 'And yet I see that no amount of grief over your new husband stops you chasing after your former lover like some whore!'

His cruel words punched Alyssa more effectively than

any physical blow. 'Sire,' she said firmly, remembering her new place and his elevated one. 'Perhaps it is best I take my leave.'

Gyl swung around. She knew he was upset. He had been forced to absorb a number of shocks these past two days but she would not permit him to speak to her with such disrespect, king or not. Alyssa was not tall – Gyl seemed to tower above her yet her eyes held a cold fury her son did not recall having seen before. He had not meant to say what he did, could hardly believe he had uttered such a dreadful denouncement to his mother.

She was offering him a precise but angry curtsy and he grabbed her before she could make an exit. 'Madam, I demand a better explanation than you have given me.' It was deliberately worded to remind her of his new status and it was not lost on her.

'Careful, Gyl, you wouldn't want the King's Mother sporting bruises now would you?' She looked down at where his fingers pinched into her slender arm.

He let go as if stung and felt the anger diminish instantly into the sorrow it hoped to hide. 'Damn you! I'm sorry for what I just said. I have no right. Mother . . . give me a reason!'

Alyssa felt the two days of pressure and tension explode out of her. She was tired of being regal and dignified; weary from having to control her emotions and be strong for others. With every minute she lingered here in loneliness and grief, Torkyn Gynt was taking several steps further from her and towards her boy, Rubyn; towards trying to save the Kingdom this man in front of her took for granted.

She screamed her response at him and liked it when

he stepped back, confused by her sudden vehemence. 'You would not believe a word I told you because you are deaf to my voice, blind to what I have seen; ignorant of my life before you came into it!'

Gyl was shocked. His mother was always so controlled. He had pushed her too far.

'Then tell me again,' he shouted back at her, glad now that they were in the chambers of his father which were discreet, unguarded. No one would hear this exchange, except the dog, Drake. 'Forgive me my cruel mouth and tell me everything you know and what I must understand!'

The dog had pricked his ears at their loud voices and walked over to lick Alyssa's hand. The simple action of concern from the animal seemed to quell her rage but Gyl noticed she was breathing hard, working at staying calm. Alyssa laid her small hand on Drake's big head and spoke gently to him. The hound padded back to its favourite spot and flopped down. Gyl wondered if Drake understood his beloved master would not be returning to this room. It was a poignant reminder that his father's death and the subsequent grief touched more than just his own heart. He knew he needed to start acting like a king and that began right here and now with his father's widow.

With no haughtiness now, he addressed her. 'Please, Mother. Forgive me for what I just said. It was a bold and inaccurate suggestion. Talk to me. I promise to be open-minded. Tell me everything.'

And so Alyssa swallowed her pride and told him of her life before she came to the palace and all that she knew of the impending danger facing Tallinor. They sat down on the window seat overlooking the frantic activity below in the castle's main courtyard in preparation for the coronation, and Gyl heard a story like no other he had heard before.

Gidyon and Lauryn had chosen to escape the tension which the King's death and subsequent revelation of his heir had created in and around the palace. The kindly stablemaster had offered them horses and they had leapt at the opportunity to get out into the calm of the moors behind the castle. They rode in silence for a while, deep in their own thoughts, but when they slowed the horses to a walk, it felt necessary to share what was on their minds.

Lauryn broke the silence first. 'What do you think about Gyl as King?'

'I hardly know anything about him to make comment. He seems determined not to be too friendly to me so I've just tried to stay out of his way.' Gidyon shrugged. 'I really can't say, though I thought you'd struck up some sort of friendship?'

'Well, yes, we had for a minute. Then I mucked it all up suggesting he might loosen his braces.'

Gidyon looked at her, puzzled.

'You know,' she responded. 'He's so tightly wound. And yet, Saxon says Gyl has always been the sunniest of people – I can believe it when he smiles.'

Gidyon nodded, resisting the urge to tease her that her interest in the King-in-waiting seemed more than just casual. 'I think we must allow him a little time. I've been thinking about everything that has happened to him in just the last two days. Can you remember how we felt when we learned we were brother and sister?'

Lauryn shook her head. 'I can't remember anything very clearly before we arrived in this world.'

'That's true. It is all blurry for me too, but I think we were both shocked and angry at being cheated. I know when I was on the road trying to reach the Heartwood, I began to feel real grief that we had been kept apart and that I'd spent most of my life so lonely, so bereft of a family to love and to love me back.'

Lauryn pushed him gently. 'You're such a softie, Gid. I didn't feel any of that,' but her sly smile told him she was tricking him. 'No, you're right of course. Gyl, I gather, was an orphan and it was our mother who built a life for him at the palace. Did you know he was left by his own mother, tied to the palace gates?'

Gidyon looked surprised. 'No.'

'It's true. He was abandoned as a child . . . mother goes off to die from some fever or other. He's never known his father but he gets on with his life with this new woman at the palace and then a few years later, he's suddenly introduced to us. Meet your step-siblings . . . they come from another world!'

Gidyon shook his head, a wry smile on his face. 'It gets worse though, doesn't it? Saxon told me that Gyl worshipped the King. So it's understandable that his death would have a profound effect on him. And then to learn that the King is really his father . . .' Gidyon sentence trailed off but Lauryn finished it for him.

'. . . and that he's the heir to the throne. One minute you're a soldier, the next a king. And I'll tell you this, he's got another shock coming. How long do you think our mother will remain at the palace twiddling her fingers and playing King's Mother?'

He looked at Lauryn's glinting green eyes. Mischief was in them. 'You think she'll follow our father?'

'Of course I do! Could you not feel it between them? It was like the way the air gets just before a storm. You know how your hair begins to stand up and it all goes very still and thick?'

He nodded.

'Just imagine it, Gidyon. She has believed him dead all these years and now she learns he's very alive. They were married – don't forget that. They were deeply in love with one another when he was executed. I would guess they still are!'

Lauryn's eyes glittered with the romantic vision of her parents, and her brother could not help but smile.

'I'll grant you they make a good-looking couple,' he replied, and ducked when she threw a playful punch this time.

'Good-looking! Are you mad? They're glorious. Yargo was right, our father is deadly handsome and the Queen—'

'King's Mother,' Gidyon corrected, deliberately goading her.

'Alyssa, then, is just about the most beautiful woman I think I have ever laid eyes on.'

'Are you saying that because everyone thinks you look so like her?' he replied, grinning widely now.

Lauryn looked exasperated. Her brother was not going to allow her to enjoy the fantasy of her parents.

Gidyon pulled a face. 'Oh come on, I'm only teasing. I think they're wonderful together and I suppose I could get my head chopped off or be burned at the stake for saying something treacherous like this but I'm pleased the King is dead. Perhaps our parents can be together. I presume they kept their marriage secret?'

'I don't know but I'd wager our mother won't waste much time departing the palace.'

'It won't win her any friends, if she does leave now,' Gidyon said gloomily.

'Considering what's at stake, and if Orlac does appear as our father predicts, then I'm not sure she would care much about whose feathers she ruffled. Only the two of them seem to know what is going on anyway. I hope she explains more to Gyl, though. He needs to understand, then he may lend his support.'

'You like him, don't you?'

Lauryn took a moment to answer him. 'I cannot admit that he has made himself easy to like, but Sallementro and Saxon have both told me that he can be brilliantly charming and eloquent. He's the best soldier in the Company, the most eligible bachelor in Tal . . .'

Gidyon's smile widened. 'Well, I can see you've done your homework.'

'Don't tease me. I would like to know him better but I've offended him twice and I'm not sure, now that he's King, he would bother with me.'

'Don't be too sure of it. Remember who you look like.'

'Do I really?'

'Lauryn, you're the image of our mother.'

Embarrassed by his earnest compliment she changed the subject. 'When is the coronation, anyway?'

Gidyon stroked his horse's mane. 'Saxon says it will happen fast. Most likely within the Eighthday. They will invite all surrounding sovereigns, I gather.'

'Well, if our mother does not stay, I suppose we'll be here together at least.'

He looked towards his sister sheepishly. 'Ah. There is something I need to talk to you about.'

Lauryn had dreaded it; already sensed he might announce something like this. 'No, Gidyon, you cannot do this.'

'I have to.'

'Why can't you wait a few days?'

'Did you see the look on his face when he learned I'd given the stone away? No. I must travel to Brittelbury immediately and get it back.'

'Then I'm coming with you.' Lauryn stopped her horse's slow progress, anticipating an argument.

Gidyon followed suit but did not reply immediately. He allowed the pause to lengthen into a silence. Then finally he spoke quietly. 'You know I won't take you. It could be dangerous.'

Her temper flared. 'So everyone is leaving me?'

Gidyon shrugged gently. 'Someone needs to represent the family at the King's coronation . . . and you're the only one he'll probably tolerate by day's end if your hunch is right.' He moved his horse closer and took her hand. 'I promise not to leave you for long. I'll ride as fast as I can and return immediately.'

'No, you won't,' she said sulkily. 'That girl is there and you may even fall for her.'

'Too late . . . already have.' He grinned, and kicked his horse into a gallop, laughing as he heard his sister shriek her frustration.

They sat in a frigid silence after Alyssa had finished her story.

At last he spoke. 'You and Torkyn Gynt are married.' It was a statement, not a question.

'We are. I watched him die, as did countless others, including your father and her majesty, Queen Nyria. Saxon even helped shroud his corpse in muslin.'

'Mother, this is madness. How can he be alive then?' Gyl worked hard at keeping ridicule from his voice. He had promised her he would remain open-minded.

'Magic, son. He and I are both sentient. My powers are no longer open to me because of this archalyt disk,' she said, pointing to her forehead, 'but his talents are vast. I'm not convinced that even Tor understands the breadth of his own magical skills. There is no one to match him.'

'Other than this Orlac you speak of, who is coming to raze Tallinor and wreak havoc . . . killing us all, I presume.' He did not succeed in covering the scorn in his voice.

Alyssa did not overreact. 'You say that so casually, Gyl. I can only presume you do not believe a word I have told you of Orlac. Understand that he is a god. Tor has already seen a vision of him escaping his enchanted prison. Saxon and Sallementro were two of his keepers whom he has already triumphed over, which is why they are here now, re-forming the Paladin in Tallinor, to fight the final battle.'

'You truly believe this?' Gyl looked deeply into his mother's solemn eyes.

'It is happening now, my son. You have to believe it too if you are going to save your Kingdom and your people. He will kill everyone. Not even a child will be spared his wrath. If you don't trust me, everyone will perish.'

Gyl sighed and stood. He stared out once again into

the courtyard, his hands resting on his hips as he considered all that he had heard these past two hours. Some of it was shocking . . . most of it too incredible to believe and yet his mother was convincing. He had had no idea how much pain and anguish she herself had suffered at the hands of Goth. The man had been at the palace well before Gyl's time but he had heard plenty of stories about the former chief inquisitor. She could not have fabricated such a complex, compelling tale of heartache and suffering; or such immense magics that would restore a man's sight and limbs and indeed bring a man back from death. Why would Alyssa, his own mother, lie to him? She had to be telling the truth.

'What must I do?' he said finally.

Alyssa's expression relaxed. 'Understand why I must leave. I am not chasing Tor. I am going to find my son. My task is to assemble the Trinity, our only hope against this fearsome god.'

'And the Trinity is Gidyon, Lauryn and Rubyn . . . this is what you believe?'

She nodded. 'If they are not, we are lost.'

'And what can they do to fight him, these three inexperienced "warriors" from another world?' Oh dear, he could hear the cynicism cutting into his words.

His mother shrugged. If she heard it, she was not showing it. 'We must learn more about them. They are surely empowered, but I've only known them as long as you have. Their true magics and strengths are yet to be revealed.'

'So tell me how your running off to this Heartwood achieves anything?'

'I must find Rubyn. I told you, I watched Goth kick

at the leaves covering a dead baby boy in the forest where they captured me.'

Gyl nodded sombrely. It was an horrific tale.

'I cannot push that image from my mind. It visits me every day and has tormented my soul since the moment I saw what I believed to be my dead child. I will lay that vision to rest if I find this child . . . can you understand this?'

He nodded again.

'There is more,' she said, in a business-like tone. 'You must remain alert, Gyl. Every soldier should be training hard and put on battle stand-by. I have no idea what Orlac will do or when, but you must be ready for anything. Extra food and provisions should be stockpiled. You must make plans with your captains for the safety of your people. Set up more effective communication routes throughout the Kingdom. I don't believe they are efficient enough to withstand whatever attack he may launch. Use this time wisely; do not waste it, son.

'Gather your nobles and tell them in the plainest language that Tallinor is under threat. They will not believe you but you must convince them that the Kingdom must be prepared for any eventuality. Use the excuse that as a soldier you can see that the realm is not protected appropriately and that you wish to make changes. You are a new King, they will anticipate all sorts of new laws as well as a whole new approach. Handle it carefully but firmly. They will respect your strength and follow you.'

Gyl looked aghast at all these suggestions. She was not unlike a battle commander herself, firing off instructions. Could this really be that gentle, funny, almost girlish mother of his?

He nodded. 'All right. I will take all the precautions you suggest. And then we shall see.' He must do this much for her or make mockery of all her warnings. 'Will you wait until after the coronation to leave? No one will believe it if you are not here for it,' he added hopefully.

'I cannot. I must make haste immediately. I will think of something for you to say.'

'I see.' He did not see but he realised his mother was far more determined than he initially appreciated and guessed that she had made her mind up even before the revelation of his bloodline – perhaps even as soon as she learned of the King's passing.

'And Tallinor is safe until this Themesius person you spoke of falls?' Gyl worked hard at making this sound very reasonable and as though he fully believed it.

'Tallinor is no longer safe.'

His expression creased in puzzlement. 'Why?'

She turned sad green eyes towards him. 'Themesius has already fallen. Orlac is free.'

8

Orlac's Lover

Orlac stared at the woman called Juno who stood before him. His leisurely bath and massage from two extremely nervous women had brought him great pleasure. Even their jittery silence did not spoil their careful, exquisite ministrations. Orlac felt extraordinarily relaxed as he sat in his suite of magnificent rooms.

Juno was fully robed.

'I thought I mentioned I would like you naked when I arrived,' he said, no trace of threat in his voice.

'My lord,' she bowed low, once again. 'My grandmother always said I possessed a special talent. I am something of a seer, you might say.'

'Really?' he replied, stepping closer and wondering what this could possibly have to do with his wanting to feel her skin against his.

Juno hurried on, resisting the temptation to step backwards at his advance. 'Yes, indeed. When I met you, my lord, I could sense straight away that your taste stretched beyond my plain looks.'

'Oh come now, Juno. You do yourself a disservice,' he

said, and meant it too, for she was lovely. A little too angular perhaps, possibly not enough flesh on those bones, but nonetheless, an attractive woman. He took another casual step forward.

'Thank you for the compliment, my lord, but may I be so presumptuous as to present you with something more in keeping with your taste for this very special first night of yours in our palace?'

He liked Juno's defiance. She was intelligent too. He could see it in those dark and depthless eyes of hers which seemed to possess wisdom beyond the years of the young woman before him.

'I knew a Juno once,' he said, startling her with this change in direction of their conversation.

The woman watched him carefully. 'Oh?'

'Mmm, yes – may I?' Orlac asked pointing towards a small table where wine had been laid out.

'Oh, of course. Allow me,' she said, cautious but moving to pour him a glass. 'You said you were hungry, my lord. May I summon the food we have prepared?'

'Is it poisoned?' He displayed his brilliantly broad, white smile.

'No, sire. We would not do such a thing.'

'I jest with you. I would know anyway,' he said, sitting and leaning back in his chair.

'You look tired,' Juno admitted, despite her discomfort at being in the room with him. She moved to pull a cord which would sound a bell outside the chamber.

'I am. But not too tired for what I have promised myself this night.' He stretched languidly and was glad to see she did not flinch.

Orlac watched her let two servants into the room who nervously approached his table.

'May we lay out your supper, sire?' one of them asked, a tremble in her voice giving away her anxiety at being so close to this murderer of Cipreans.

'Thank you. Juno?' She arrived at his side. 'You must convey to the palace household that they are not to be afraid of me. I will not harm anyone who obeys me.'

Juno nodded and then dismissed the servants, who left quietly.

'Please eat, my lord.'

'Won't you join me?'

'I shall sit with you, if you like.'

He gestured to a chair opposite.

'You were saying that you knew a Juno once, my lord?' she asked carefully.

'That's right,' he replied, eyes scanning the array of delectable dishes as he hungrily chewed on some cheese. He spoke but seemed distracted by his need for food. 'She was old, ancient in fact. I rather liked her, though. Her hair was silvered grey, not at all lush and shiny like yours. Her face was wrinkled and spotted; her voice croaky.' He took another heaped ladle from a dish he was enjoying. 'But apart from sharing the same name, the only similarity I see with you is in the eyes. Hers were rheumy, turning white with the affliction of blindness, but there is something there,' he continued and then lost his thread of thought. 'This supper is delightful, thank you.'

Juno inclined her head. 'We have a wonderful young chef at the palace. His name is Ryk Savyl and he is descended from the famous culinary family of Ildagarth.' She watched Orlac's eyebrows raise in acknowledgement.

'Well, your Ryk possesses a rare talent. Please convey my appreciation of this meal to him.'

She nodded once again. He was charming. Not at all how she remembered him from when she did battle in her mind to keep his powers at bay. She cast a silent thank you to the Heartwood for returning her in this particular era of her life. Orlac had never known her as a young woman. He only remembered the Esian crone. Clever Lys. Did she know Juno might have to face him so closely again?

'You seem far away?' she heard him ask, which brought her thoughts back to the present and the dangerous pathway she now trod.

'My apologies. It sounded like you were describing my grandmother earlier. It made me think of her.'

He swallowed some wine, violet eyes sparkling above the goblet. 'The one who called you a seer?'

She nodded.

'And you were about to tell me how you have used this talent tonight, I believe,' he said, dabbing at his lips with a napkin.

'This is true, sire. I have taken the liberty of selecting someone whom I believe might please you greatly.'

'Why do you believe that you would not?'

Once again, the politeness and charm of the previous moments had almost made her overlook the god with whom she was dealing. She must not forget again. His mind was razor sharp; it moved swiftly and adeptly and she was not prepared for this direct question.

'Why . . . I, well, I mentioned to you that I have the "sense", as the old ones say. And when I met you I saw the woman in my mind's eye who might make a perfect match for you, my lord. We wish to please you, not vex you.'

He surprised her by laughing. 'I'm not sure whether to be insulted by you, Juno. So tell me about my ideal companion?'

'Actually, my lord, the woman I wish to present now is not your own idea of perfection but she will be a wonderful bedmate for you tonight.' She knew she should never have spoken of anyone other than the woman she had chosen. It was a mistake.

Orlac was intrigued. He drained his cup. 'Oh? Tell me what your mind's eye saw would be my idea of the perfect woman.'

Juno felt her colour rise. The woman she did see was almost the opposite of the woman chosen for him. What a fool. Her nervousness had made her mouth loose.

'Come, don't be coy now, Juno. It is clear you do not wish to spend the night with me, so I would hear about whom it is your skills would scry out for me.'

She knew she must answer him. 'Well, sire, in truth I see the opposite of me. I see a woman who is golden-haired like yourself, my lord, but not tall like you – petite in fact; slim, delicately boned. I believe I noticed her eyes were a greyish green, like the sea on a stormy day.'

'Go on,' he encouraged, listening carefully but not looking at Juno.

Juno did not want to continue but Orlac was intimidating in his suddenly quiet demeanour. 'Er . . . I saw she possessed high cheekbones, my lord. Her complexion is creamy; though there are a few freckles around her nose which crinkles when she smiles – she has a beautiful smile and is quick to use it, as she is her temper, I believe.'

She watched the dazzling smile break across his face now. It was curious that she had never appreciated how incredibly beautiful he was during all of those centuries they did battle in the Bleak. Perhaps as the very ancient Juno the Esian – descended from a distinguished line of famous seers of Esia – fighting to save a world, she did not notice such trivial things.

'Then I must say you are the most talented of seers. This woman in your head sounds irresistible to me.' He stood, again abruptly changing the conversation. 'Why don't you introduce me to the woman who is going to make this first night in Cipres memorable?'

Juno felt her entire body relax with the relief that she had diverted his attention from herself. She wondered what she would have done had Orlac insisted she be the one he chose to bed tonight. As she bowed to him carefully, she reminded herself this was only for this one night that she had wriggled out of such duty. She would have to survive many more before the individual she waited for – the one Lys said was coming – actually arrived.

She stepped beyond the chamber, her heart still slowing from relief, and motioned to a cloaked figure who had waited patiently in a small room to be called. The person stood, her face shrouded by the hood.

'It is time,' Juno said.

The stranger nodded and followed her back into the chamber where Orlac had been. They noticed he had walked out onto the balcony to enjoy the night air. The city looked particularly beautiful beneath the full moon. He had removed his shirt and stood arms stretched wide to the silver light; his body like a perfect piece of

sculpture; the muscles superbly outlined on the broad
framework of his flawless torso.

Juno caught her breath. Here stood a god. Proud,
defiant, magnificent. Only she truly understood the
terror of his powers and the darkness of the mind which
fuelled a hatred. She hoped he would not hurt the girl.
This one beside her had readily agreed to the task
though, had begged for it in fact. Whilst Orlac had
privately met with the hateful Goth, Juno had given
orders to make up these rooms and then personally made
a hasty visit to the most sophisticated and expensive
brothel in the city to choose a woman. She knew what
she wanted and she had found this woman. And yet Juno
had nearly decided against awarding her this special duty
for there was something about the young woman's
arrogance, coupled with her desperation to be the one,
which almost put Juno off. Mind you, there were few
others who put up their hand. Too many had heard what
had occurred in the square. No amount of gold could
tempt most – there were always a few, though, for whom
money talked loudly, but the chosen one needed to be
special. And Juno knew a poor performance tonight
might incur wrath towards the Cipreans tomorrow. No,
this woman had the confidence needed to face him. She
had seemed uninterested in the purse on offer and showed
no fear when she learned the identity of her mate. Even
now there seemed no anxiety as she stood here awaiting
his pleasure.

Juno had told her to come naked, sheathed only in
the satin cloak provided. The woman had not batted an
eyelid at the suggestion; in fact Juno believed she saw
a smile twitch at the corner of the whore's mouth. This

one was experienced; would know how to pleasure Orlac and satisfy him.

Enough procrastination. She cleared her throat and he lowered his arms, turned slowly towards them. Juno cast a wish to the gods that she had chosen well. She reached for the thin cord at the woman's neck and pulled on the bow which held the cloak together. It slipped from her shoulders soundlessly revealing the naked woman. She was tall and voluptuous with perfectly proportioned limbs and full high breasts. The woman whose head had been bowed now threw it back defiantly and a mass of raven hair fell around her. Dark eyes regarded the god while a full mouth turned up at the corners in a sensuous smile. She was exotic and arresting with a certain mystery, accentuated by the curious pale blue disk which glinted in the moonlight at her forehead.

Orlac drew a breath. She was ravishing and he could imagine this one on her knees pleasuring him as Dorgryl had promised. In fact he felt the pulse of the intruder within – a red shimmer – as it entertained a similar thought.

Juno felt relief course through her for the second time that night. The choice was perfect.

'My lord, Orlac, may I present Xantia.'

9
The Pursuit Begins

Goth had wasted no time since his audience with Orlac.
He had been given freedom to assemble two dozen or
so men and money was plentiful in his purse from the
royal coffers. He told the soldiers that, at Orlac's
bidding, he was leading a raiding party into Tallinor to
track down the killer of their Queen Sylven. More than
enough men volunteered their services and he was
careful to take one of the officers who would command
these soldiers.

He explained that someone had left the palace in a
hurry — a servant called Hela — who had information
leading to the Queen's murderer, a man called Torkyn
Gynt. Some of the men knew Hela and he noticed their
look of surprise at the mention of her name. He quickly
quashed any doubts they had, suggesting that it was she
who had first encouraged the Queen to meet with this
Tallinese physic. It did not help that one of the officers
expressed his shock, saying that he knew Hela very well
and that she was the most loyal of all of her majesty's
confidantes. Goth swiftly laid his most damning

accusation, announcing that Hela had captured the Princess Sarel and had taken her prisoner with her into Tallinor to meet up with Gynt, holding the heir to the throne of Cipres to ransom. He was making it up as he went along, his mind sliding this way and that around every objection – if only he had known that Hela was indeed fleeing to the safety of Torkyn Gynt it would have amused him.

When questioned about the fearful stranger he reassured the men that Orlac had every intention of putting Sarel on her rightful throne and that he was their only hope against the conspiracy which had been uncovered – that Tallinor had designs on Cipres. Killing the Queen and imprisoning her heir was the first step towards the Tallinese success. He was rather pleased with himself that all of this fakery had been contrived as he stood there in front of these men. His fabrication was thin: Orlac had killed so many. When further objections ensued, he reminded them of what they were dealing with – magic beyond understanding; powers they could not fight. Better to have him on their side, he reasoned, as he played on the Cipreans' shock for their dead Queen and now their stolen Queen. He knew he was clutching at straws and needed more time to come up with a better rationale for them, but he had his own pressing mission and that was to track down the heir to the throne. Beyond that task he envisioned unimaginable riches but mostly power, which was what he craved more than anything.

The men were readied; they would begin to sweep the city for news – any clues at all which might lead to Sarel's whereabouts.

A man was dragged up in front of Goth. He had been

beaten badly and was favouring one side of his body. The soldiers who held him upright threw the man down in front of Goth.

'He knows, sir,' one of the soldiers said.

Goth gestured for the injured man to be lifted up again. When he faced him, he could see his lips were so badly wounded, they were almost shredded. Someone had either worked him over very well in anger or the man was too courageous for his own good.

'If you have information on the maid, Hela, it is best you tell us now,' Goth said in a pleasant voice.

The man spat the blood running freely into his mouth at Goth's face. The former chief inquisitor did not react predictably. Instead, he pulled his horrible sneer-like smile and motioned for silence.

'Who knows this man?'

A soldier stepped forward. 'I do, sir. His name is Garth; a good man, just a lowly guard.'

'I see,' Goth said, turning back to the soldiers who held the man. 'What makes you think he knows something?'

'He was boasting at the guardhouse that Hela owed him a roll between the sheets because of a favour, sir.'

'Ah, good.' Goth returned his attention to the soldier who knew Garth and whispered something to him. The man nodded and disappeared with another soldier.

'At ease, men,' Goth said, 'we have a little while to wait.'

Puzzled, the men dropped their cargo to the dust, where Garth now lay in silence, bleeding.

A short time later the soldiers returned; this time they carried a child with them; a little girl of around six or so summers. She was crying. The mother had come

too and was wailing. Both men looked uncomfortable
and frightened.

'Get him up,' Goth said and watched Garth being
heaved back to his shaky feet.

Garth immediately recognised his sister and his niece.
The woman was screaming at her brother and the child's
crying grew louder. Goth could not help but enjoy this
pathetic scene. He wished he had a branding iron handy
because this so reminded him of the good old days in
Tallinor.

He finally spoke above the din. 'Now, Garth. As you
can see, I care not for your suffering – as indeed neither
do you, it seems. But if you do not tell me what you
know of Hela's disappearance, then I will cut off the finger
of your sister's child here and I will continue to cut off
fingers until she is left with two stumps at the ends of
her arms.'

He could sense the horror of the men around him at
such a suggestion. Cowards, he thought. The Cipreans,
like the Tallinese, had grown soft. He continued. 'And
then I will start on her toes, Garth. But you can save her
becoming a cripple and no amount of pain if you offer up
immediately what you know. It's really very simple.' He
even tried to grin although his twitch had become
extremely pronounced and frequent now . . . it always did
when he was excited like this.

Garth hung his head. Goth counted silently to five and
then grabbed the child. In a flash he had removed a
wicked-looking knife from a pocket. The girl was
screaming so loudly he wanted to thrust it straight into
her heart but he resisted. Men closed around him
murmuring angrily.

'Back off, you men,' he warned. 'I have Orlac's authority here and you would do well to show your respect. He will not look upon you with any favour for interfering with the safe return of her majesty, Queen Sarel.'

That seemed to have the desired effect.

'Garth?' he called and was pleased to see the man had the decency to look at him.

'What's it to be? Finger or information?' The little girl was just whimpering now and her mother was chalk-white, staring at her brother and continuing a stream of desperate cajoling to get him to deliver the information.

Goth was not prepared to be patient. He wasted no further time. Garth would need to be reminded that Goth never made empty threats. He bent the child's tiny hand across his own thigh and without further warning had sliced off the smallest finger of her left hand. The scream meanwhile sliced through the heart of every man around and several retched.

The mother shrieked and fainted, as did the child finally, which was a mercy. Goth returned his cold stare to Garth, as he handed the man his niece's finger.

'A memento for you,' he said.

Garth broke down and told him everything. In moments they had the story of Hela's strange departure from the palace with a cloaked friend. Garth explained she was a maid who was pregnant with no idea of the father and that Hela was taking her home to prevent tongue-wagging and a cloud hanging over a good family.

Goth laughed. 'And you never saw this friend?'

Garth watched his shocked sister and her screaming, bleeding daughter being led away. 'No. I believed Hela. She had no reason to lie but I did have her followed for her behaviour was strange. She met a man and my only information is that she and this companion were taken aboard a ship.' All of this was said haltingly and with difficulty but Goth held his patience.

'And the ship's name is?'

'*The Raven*. It belongs to a Captain Quist of Caradoon.'

Goth was pleased. He recognised the name from his time in Caradoon; knew the pirate's formidable reputation as running the most successful ship in the archipelago. Now they had a path to follow.

'Thank you, Garth,' he said before slashing the blade of his knife across the guard's throat. The man died quickly and quietly. Orders had already been given to a paid mercenary by Goth to rid Cipres of Garth's sister and niece. The mercenary was, in fact, waiting for their return home now to finish Goth's ugly work.

Goth wiped at splatters of Garth's blood. 'Get rid of his body – and I want a ship readied immediately. We are bound for the Kingdom of Tallinor.'

Soldiers unhappily but obediently snapped to his command.

Goth turned away, satisfied. But next time he headed into Tallinor, he vowed, it would be with an army and the sorcerer, Orlac, for protection. He would see Torkyn Gynt's severed head sewn onto the body of Alyssandra Qyn's and he would burn the single corpse and scatter its ashes to the very corners of the Kingdom and he would then assist his new master in razing it to the ground.

10

New Journeys

Gidyon was told he would find his mother with the King. Making his way up the beautifully sculpted stone staircase to the royal chambers he felt the Link slicing open, cool and sharp in his mind.

Figgis! It had to be. *Where are you?*

In the bailey. They will not permit me to enter the palace . . . good afternoon, by the way.

Gidyon grinned. *Good afternoon, my friend. Stay there. It is too complicated to explain why. I'll be with you shortly.*

No hurry. I've spent several centuries in wait for you.

Gidyon had arrived at the chambers which were now permanently guarded. He announced himself and it seemed they were expecting him. He was led by one of Gyl's men into the room where he found his mother sitting straight-backed, perhaps a little tense, speaking quietly with the King. They both turned at his arrival. Alyssa beamed, whilst Gyl nodded. Gidyon bowed out of respect for both.

'Forgive me for interrupting you,' he began.

'No, it's good to see you, Gidyon. I am sorry you meet

us all under such troubled circumstances,' the King said.
'It feels like just a moment ago we were strangers, then
brothers . . . now King and subject. It's all very confusing.'
His mouth stretched into a lazy smile and Gidyon knew
exactly what Lauryn had meant about it changing Gyl's
demeanour. He must try harder to get to know this man.

He dragged his hand through dark hair and returned
the smile. 'I think we may have got off to a difficult start.'

'But no fault of yours,' the King said, gesturing towards
a chair for Gidyon. 'Can I offer you wine? . . . Mother?'

'I'll have an ale,' she said and Gidyon was puzzled that
both she and the King laughed. The sound seemed to
release the pervading tension.

'Gidyon?'

'Same as her majesty,' he said, shrugging.

And so mugs of ale and Gyl's wine were delivered
together with savoury wafers and before Gidyon knew it,
he was relaxing in the company of the King and feeling
a lot easier about the decision he had reached.

How much longer do you suppose? a voice asked in his
mind.

He jumped and his ale spilled on his hand. The others
in the room noticed it and shot him puzzled looks. Alyssa's
expression suddenly relaxed into comprehension.

'Once you get used to it, that won't happen again,' she
said, wryly.

'Used to what?' Gyl asked, putting his wine down.

'To the voice in his head,' she replied.

Gyl turned to his mother, gently exasperated.
'Whatever are you talking about?'

'Let Gidyon explain,' she said, relaxing back into her
chair.

The King looked towards his stepbrother.

'Er . . . well, it's Figgis, you see. He's arrived at the palace and anxious for us to be on our way.'

Gyl nodded, not understanding a word of this but humouring his mother. 'I see. And Figgis is who?'

'My Paladin.'

'Ah good, I've heard this word before. You are bonded. Am I right?'

'Yes. As Sallementro and Saxon are bonded to our mother.'

The King nodded once again, a somewhat fixed grin on his face. 'And the connection between him and the ale on your hand is?'

The question hung between them as Gidyon looked from the King to his mother and back again, before answering. He felt suddenly foolish. 'Figgis spoke to me and I wasn't expecting it.'

'Ah, now you're losing me you see, brother.'

Alyssa knew she must come to the rescue though she had been amused these past moments watching Gidyon's increasing discomfort and Gyl's very best attempt to sympathise with all this magical stuff unravelling.

'Gyl,' she said, and he turned to her. 'Figgis can link with Gidyon. This means he can talk to Gidyon over a distance by communicating directly into his mind.'

The King stood and waved his arm theatrically. 'Well, why didn't you say that beforehand? That makes all the sense in the world to me now.'

It was time to rein him in. 'Listen to me. Tor and I spent years speaking to one another in this manner without meeting. We both lived in separate villages, you see,' she said, remembering those early, wonderful days. 'I fell in love with him through the Link. We can all speak with those we are bonded to through the Link and I suspect without the archalyt I could communicate with Gidyon, Lauryn, Tor, Saxon, Sallementro and possibly a number of others connected through the Heartwood.'

Gyl noticed she was no longer smiling; there was an intensity gleaming in those green eyes which he had learned over the years meant: I make no jest.

'And whom do *you* speak to like this?' He was intrigued, imagining how powerful such a skill could be on the battlefield or even simplified as a communication tool for his men.

Gidyon realised the King was talking to him again. 'My father, Lauryn, Figgis . . . so far.'

'It is a talent I wish I had,' Gyl replied, meaning it. 'You said you were leaving us?'

His switch of subjects caught Gidyon by surprise. He was glad the cup of ale was already to his lips. Being able to take a draught and swallow it earned him a fraction of time to think.

'Yes. That is why I came to you. I wished to say thank you for your hospitality,' he directed this towards the King and then glanced towards his mother. 'I must find Yseul and my stone.'

She nodded. Had expected as much. 'And Lauryn?'

Once again Gidyon looked to the King. 'I am hopeful your hospitality will extend longer for her.'

'She is most welcome to remain as guest in the palace for as long as she wishes. I am very happy for her to stay. It will be rather nice to have some family around for my coronation ceremony.' Despite the stab at her, he avoided his mother's gaze.

Gidyon immediately looked at Alyssa. 'Lauryn was right, then. You are leaving?' He did not miss the King's face darken at this.

'I must,' she said, flicking a glance towards her royal son. 'Gyl understands. He just has to make the people understand.'

'How do you propose they will accept that yesterday's Queen of Tallinor . . . my own mother, the woman married to the King who died just days ago, is not present for the coronation . . . what possible excuse can you come up with, Mother?'

Gidyon realised he had reopened a wound. 'I'm sorry, I—'

Alyssa did not permit him to finish. 'It's all right. Gyl is correct, I am putting him in a very difficult situation but Gyl has accepted my reasoning.'

'Rubyn?' Gidyon tactfully did not add the name of the other person he believed she would seek.

She nodded. 'And so, Gyl, I am proposing that we use the excuse that your mother is so traumatised by the death of the King that I have taken ill and you have seen fit to send me to a convent to recuperate.'

Gyl snorted his derision. 'And you think all the courtiers will accept that, after you stood in the Great Hall like some sort of imperious ruler, composed and dignified, beautiful and serene . . . not sick and sobbing—'

His mother refused him the chance to continue his tirade. 'Gyl, every married man in this city will know there is no benchmark for a woman's emotions, particularly someone who has had to face what I did. You forget I am not pretending this, son. I am not acting out a piece of theatre. I am living it. Your father has died and I did carry myself stoically earlier and it took every ounce of my strength to do it. It is not contrived . . . . it is who I am. And now I am asking you to lie for me. They will accept it because you say so and because they know how much I love you and would under any other circumstances be there for your coronation. No one will question you, son. You will tell them I have been sent away to regain my sanity if you must . . . but you will spin the tale and ensure it is credible.'

Alyssa watched her son, the new King, nod his agreement, and she took his hand and squeezed it. It was a private moment between them and Gidyon felt embarrassed to be sharing it. She is amazing, he thought, and then realised she was speaking to him now.

'I shall leave today. You say Lauryn knew?'

'She guessed you would want to help find our brother. She is not happy about my decision.'

Gyl moved towards the window. 'Well, I for one shall be delighted to have her sit with me as my private guest at the coronation feast. I promise she will not be allowed to be lonely. There are sovereigns and officials travelling from far and wide. In fact I received confirmation today that a Ciprean delegation will be joining us.'

'Light! They won't make it here in time, surely?' Alyssa said.

The King shrugged. He suddenly reminded her of that small bright boy with no cares or worries of just a few years ago. 'We shall wait. Another few days will not matter and I am honoured they are joining us.'

Gidyon stepped towards his mother. He bowed, rather wishing he was able to hug her but feeling that might be unseemly, their having only met so recently. It must have been written on his face, however, for Alyssa, after taking his hand, pulled him close. Gidyon was amazed at how tiny she really was and how fragile she felt in his arms.

Alyssa desperately wished she could link with Gidyon, offer him something special and private from mother to son. Instead she said: 'May the Light guide you, my son, and bring you back to me swiftly and safely.'

Gidyon bent to kiss her hand and felt a thrill as she touched his bowed head, burying her hand in his thick dark hair. He hoped his voice would not choke now. 'I shall return with my stone urgently, your majesty,' he added quickly. 'Your light will be my beacon.'

Alyssa felt herself filled with love for this young man. She did not trust herself to say another word to him at this moment and was relieved when he moved away to speak with the King.

'Thank you for taking care of Lauryn, your highness.' He bowed.

Gyl saluted Gidyon in the Tallinese way. 'It is no effort. She makes fine company. I promise you she is safe here. Travel safely in the Light. I'll instruct my stableman to give you Tully. She's a sweet-tempered mare who will gallop all day if you ask her to.'

'Your highness, there is no need . . .' Gidyon began to say, but he was touched by the King's offer. After his conversation with Lauryn he knew how hard it must be for Gyl to be acting so reasonably in such strange and challenging circumstances.

Gyl smiled and once again Gidyon was reminded of Lauryn's comment. 'Nonsense. I insist. It's the least we can do for people we're counting on to save our world.'

Neither the King's Mother nor his stepbrother could be sure that he offered this last comment without irony.

Alyssa made haste. She could hardly wait to depart now that the worst was over – her farewells to her children. Farewelling Lauryn, strangely, had been the hardest of all. The young woman had remained composed but Alyssa sensed there was something of desperation in their final embrace. In truth they were still strangers and yet connected so strongly that Lauryn, though not surprised to hear her mother's news, felt bereft: in a matter of two days she had been deserted by her father, brother and now her mother.

'Still,' the King's Mother had added a little too brightly, 'Gyl is determined to ensure you enjoy your introduction to courtly life at Tallinor.'

Lauryn looked confused at this.

Alyssa pressed on. 'He intends you to be his companion during the coronation. Oh Lauryn, you will meet several of the surrounding realms' sovereigns and so many colourful and influential people. Your next few days will be so lively and busy, you will hardly notice us gone.'

Even Alyssa could hear the hollowness of her words.

'May I not come with you?' Lauryn asked in earnest.

'No, child.' She gave no further explanation and Lauryn had not added any more to her argument. 'You will be our family's representative at Gyl's coronation. I'll tell you something now, Lauryn, which you may surely sneer at, but I believe Gyl needs you more than anyone right now.'

'Me?' Lauryn wanted to laugh at such a suggestion.

Alyssa's face remained grave. She nodded. 'I mean it. Gyl has lost someone incredibly important in his life.

Lorys . . .' She hesitated as she heard that name from her lips again. 'The King was more important to Gyl than even I had imagined and the series of shocks he has been hit with this Eighthday is taking its toll.'

'I don't see how I can help,' Lauryn shrugged.

'No, I'm not explaining myself well,' Alyssa admitted, taking her daughter's hand. 'You are a complete stranger to him. That means you won't judge him nor do you come with any pre-knowledge of court gossip and whisperings. You may well prove to be a good friend to Gyl, who, like his father, can be a bit of a loner. I sense he already likes you very much and feels badly that he did not do more for you at your first meeting.' Alyssa saw Lauryn's smile twitch at the corners of her mouth. 'I suspect you'll be just what Gyl needs around him. Far more companion than I could be right now,' she said. 'So will you do this for me, Lauryn? Will you be Gyl's friend?'

'Of course. You and Father, and even Gidyon, at least feel useful rushing off and doing what you have to do . . .' She wanted to say more but her mother's look stopped her.

'And you will do more good than you can imagine by remaining here. In fact,' she said, arching her eyebrows, 'from a distance you could pass as me!'

They shared a laugh. Alyssa was so used to her closest friends being men, surrounded as she had been by Lorys, Gyl, Saxon, Sallementro and even Herek to a lesser extent, that she had forgotten the grand fun it could be to laugh with a female companion.

But right now she had to leave. The page had already carried down her small bag of belongings. Where she was headed, Alyssa knew she needed no fancy gowns nor satin slippers. She also knew Saxon would be waiting some-what impatiently with the horses.

It was as if Lauryn had read her thoughts. 'Will Saxon go with you?'

'Yes, we are bonded. He is compelled, if I travel, to travel with me.'

'And Sallementro?'

'Will remain. He is required to sing at the coronation.'

'As your Paladin, is he not compelled in the same way?'

A slight frown creased Alyssa's brow. 'Yes, it's an inter-esting question. I asked Tor a similar one before he left and he believes that one of each of our Paladin is more strongly bound to us than the other.' She shrugged. 'It's a reasonable guess.'

There was nothing more to say. 'Time for you to leave, I suppose,' Lauryn said, trying not to sound sad.

'We will find him and reunite our three children,' Alyssa replied, hugging her daughter close. 'I shall miss you before I even get to know you, but I will think about you the whole time I'm gone.'

'Me too.'

Alyssa shook her head, her grey-green eyes glittering. 'No, Lauryn. I think you'll have plenty to occupy your mind in my absence. Oh Light! We are of a size perhaps . . . you must take whichever gown you care to from my wardrobe. I'll instruct Rolynd and my dresser, Tilly, before I leave. You have your choice – be sure you look utterly gorgeous at all the festivities!'

Lauryn realised her mother looked like a young girl when she acted so flirtatiously and could not help but grin.

'Pale blue or softest green will do you justice. Take whatever you want.'

And with those carefree parting words, the King's Mother, formerly and rather briefly the Queen of Tallinor, departed her exquisite chambers overlooking the beautiful walled garden which Lorys had built for her. She would never see either again.

II

Enlightenment

Orlac sat on his balcony and stared out across the immaculate gardens of the Ciprean palace. It was the early hours of the morning and the city was still. He sipped an exquisite sweetened wine made from grapes grown on the foothills of Neame whilst his other hand restlessly twirled the tassel on a parchment which had been delivered to the palace shortly before his own arrival. He had been fortunate to open it and had answered it immediately. He presumed his response would have already arrived. He looked now at the unique tassel which marked it as a regal document. The rich crimson of the interwoven satin threads matched the colour of the now-broken royal seal of Tallinor, the Kingdom from where this missive emanated. The special invitation suited his plans perfectly. He looked forward to leaving with some urgency.

He hoped that by now Goth would have already tracked down the Ciprean Princess who had outwitted all of them . . . or at least that the one in black with the pocked, twitching face would be very close to having her in his clutches. Orlac believed the young woman who would be

Queen was no longer any threat to him. With that consideration aside, he could concentrate on what really mattered to him.

A soft and sleepy moan from behind him, one which only his superior hearing might pick up, disturbed his thoughts. He turned at the sound and cast a glance over the naked woman sprawled in his bed. They had been inseparable since their first meeting although Orlac knew it was nothing akin to love or even companionship. He was not sure he even liked this woman. However, there was something compelling about Xantia. Her ferocity and passion in his bed more than made up for any lack of affection for him or indeed vice versa. And yet she seemed determined to be with him. He knew she did not love him but he felt her eyes burn with something when she turned those dark looks towards him.

Right now he felt sated. It had only been a week and yet he felt he had made up for a lifetime of erotic need during that short period since he had been introduced to this mysterious woman. She was beautiful – there was no mistaking that. And it seemed there was nothing she would not do to ensure his pleasure, but he sensed cruelty there.

Once, in her ardour, she had bitten him. The pain was intense and at the time tempered only by his need to reach his own climax, but now even several days later the bruise and soreness of that bite lingered on his otherwise flawless skin. Xantia was a ruthless woman, he decided. Despite his inexperience with females he sensed that Xantia was no ordinary woman. She spoke to him about power and revenge. At first he believed she had somehow stumbled onto his own dark thoughts and needs but quickly realised these were her own burning desires.

She was a woman scorned. She was a woman who held a hatred for the Tallinese way of life — its hypocrisy as she called it — and how she wished she could kill the King who supported it. When Xantia spoke of her sentient abilities and how her powers had been separated from her, he had been surprised. He pressed her for more information and learned about the archalyt and the Academie at Caremboche. Orlac knew one touch to her forehead and he could release that clumsily attached gem which stifled her power . . . not just yet though, he would wait.

But now this document in his hand perhaps changed everything. It seemed Xantia's desires had been answered and although she never would have the pleasure of killing Lorys, King of Tallinor, it seemed the gods had seen fit to do it themselves in answer to her prayers. He smiled. Tallinor would be easy for the taking now. A new King to be crowned. Perfect.

Dorgryl's mind unexpectedly touched his. Orlac squirmed. The older god had been silent for a day or more. In their most recent argument Orlac had banished him from his presence, hating his uncle for joining in with his sexual activities. There were moments when Orlac was not sure whether it was he or Dorgryl moving above Xantia and making her moan. His fury had worked. Dorgryl had retreated, giving his nephew the space he demanded for his own private pleasures. The senior god's whining that he too needed the release of a woman's touch did not wash with Orlac. His nephew had ranted that he would go so far as to kill himself if Dorgryl did not withdraw. That did not suit Dorgryl, of course, and his nephew understood this. His uncle's plans would be fatally injured if he did not have the body of a god in which to seek retribution from his brother, Darganoth. He could enter a mortal, but that would be a hollow victory for he sought a far loftier body to inhabit. As a god, his pride demanded a god's body for his own. And only the most superior of the gods' bodies would appease him now. He wanted his brother's body. He would be King of the Host.

Orlac turned back from Xantia to resume his view across the city.

Congratulations. I think you have found our Queen, nephew, Dorgryl offered.

Orlac sighed. He would have to talk to him. *What do you mean?*

Just that she's perfect as your puppet. It solves the problem for the Cipreans. You can keep your promise and give them a queen. She'll do anything you ask . . . already does, in fact, I see.

Orlac ignored this last comment. *Yes, the same thought had occurred to me.*

The plot thickens, though. He heard his uncle chuckle in his head. *You do not know who Xantia is, of course.*

Should I?

Well, you were a little busy overthrowing that stupid group of Paladin but I was paying attention.

Are you going to enlighten me?

You'll really enjoy this, Dorgryl said. Orlac could picture him licking his lips. *Xantia, as she has explained, is a former member of the Academie at Caremboche. She's told you all about that place and what it stood for so I need not go over that.*

Orlac hated the self-importance of Dorgryl. The senior god relished every opportunity to tell a story, particularly if only he was privy to its details. He pushed back the wave of despair he felt at having this thing inside him.

Go on.

Guess who her best friend used to be at the Academie?

I'm afraid my mind is blank. You'll have to tell me. He tried to keep the impatient edge from his voice. He realised this could be an important tale and he would have to indulge Dorgryl's need to lengthen its telling.

Her best friend used to be Alyssandra Qyn . . . the one and only Alyssa.

Orlac refused to respond to his uncle with the surprise he had hoped for. *Why 'used to be'?*

Oh, but this is the good bit. The red mist shimmered inside him. *Their initial falling out occurred because of competition for the role of Elder. Completely unimportant to us,* Dorgryl admitted and dismissed that part of his story. *But Xantia's real hate was fired because of competition for a particular man's attentions. I wonder if you can guess who?*

Is this a joke?

I would never jest about something as wonderfully ironic as this. Torkyn Gynt won the heart of Xantia but cast it aside when he rediscovered his beloved Alyssa at Caremboche. And as for that ill-favoured wretch with the gored face . . .

Goth?

Yes, him. Well, he was trying to kill Gynt at the time. Almost got him too but Gynt used a very clever trick to vanish himself and his lover somewhere. I imagine to the Heartwood.

What happened?

I cannot tell you about the Heartwood. I cannot see into it. It is closed to me. Even in the Bleak I could only perceive what happened around it.

Well, what can you tell me, then?

Only this. Both of them failed in their designs on Gynt. Xantia and indeed Goth harbour a great deal of hate for him and Alyssa. We can make very good use of it. Xantia will do anything for you if you dangle the carrot of these two people – of course she believes Gynt is dead. Goth just loves to persecute, maim, kill. Give him men and a free rein, as you recently did, and he will be loyal . . . well, as loyal as such a man could be. His need to end Gynt's life and torture Alyssa is all-consuming.

Orlac considered all of what he just learned. His despised uncle had his uses, he grudgingly admitted. *Where do you suppose Gynt gets his power from?*

The red mist shimmered. *I am not enlightened on this. I would guess, like Xantia and Alyssa, he has the wild magic. He does seem far more powerful than he should be, I grant you. But there is no other form of magic in this world. Only few possess it and it is mostly of such a tame variety, it might only curdle the milk – if you understand me.*

Orlac nodded. *But surely there's more to Gynt than we are giving him credit for. Why, for instance, do the Paladin gather around him?*

This is true and I admire your adept thoughts. It was a rare compliment for Orlac from a thing from which he mostly sensed disdain. His uncle continued. *What else have they got? They are desperate and have locked onto one last-ditch effort, you might say. This Gynt is clearly highly empowered. And they have found him. Merkhud spent several lifetimes seeking someone who might challenge you. It is a vain attempt. But try they must. With the Paladin's strengths and magics he is stronger but it is obvious he is still weak by comparison to you.*

Is it obvious? Is he weak compared to me?

Orlac heard his uncle chuckle. The disdain was back.

All of it made sense to him and yet Orlac finally voiced a small and gnawing thought he had been chewing like old gristle since his mind had first linked with Gynt's. *What if he too is a god?*

This amused Dorgryl enormously. It seemed as though his bellow of laughter must wake Xantia but of course no one could hear inside Orlac's head.

I think you are unduly frightening yourself.

I am not frightened of him.

Apologies, nephew. Let me rephrase that. I think you credit him with far more than he deserves. He is the son of a poor country scribe. I watched him as a lad. He is nothing more than a peasant in guise of some saviour of the Land. Even he doubts himself. A god? Dorgryl's thoughts disintegrated in high amusement once again.

Why not?

How? Dorgryl demanded, irritated now by Orlac's persistence.

The same way I came here?

Why?

To prevent me doing what I intend.

Dorgryl chuckled again. *Well, it's a novel thought, nephew.*

And at those words, the red mist that was Dorgryl shimmered but this time with a chill such as he had not felt in many centuries. Orlac was talking to him but he did not hear. His mind raced. No, surely not? Surely not! The other child? Darganoth was not capable of such a courageous decision. Evagora would never have countenanced such sacrifice.

And then parts of the puzzle began to snap into place.

Orlac was talking again. *Hush, let me think!* Dorgryl spat at his host.

It was Orlac's turn to fall silent, subdued by the vehemence of the rebuke. He waited.

Dorgryl's mind began to examine the facts, not daring to believe the audacious suggestion of his nephew that another god had been sent. And each time he refuted the idea he returned to the same thought: Lys. Her protection of Tor and Alyssa was overwhelming. It was possible. More than possible. Darganoth and Lys had pulled off a masterstroke.

Well, well, was all Orlac heard from the senior god. More silence. More waiting. *An ingenious plan. Congratulations, Lys . . . far, far cleverer than I gave any of the Host credit for.* He tsk-tsked in Orlac's head and even barked a harsh laugh at one point. *A move even I would feel proud of.*

Are you going to explain? Orlac finally asked.

It's brilliant; quite breathtaking in its simplicity if it is true. There was indeed another child I have overlooked. It was not yet born when I was still whole. What if the Host did sacrifice what was arguably its second most precious possession? . . . Perhaps even its most prized since the theft of its heir to the throne of the gods.

Who? Who was this child?

Not a child really; not even an infant as you were. It would have been a newborn. Must have been taken from its mother still steaming, he said, his voice laced with hatred as he tied together the threads unravelling from his mind.

He ignored Orlac, spoke aloud his thoughts as they came flooding now. *Delivered to its mortal parents. By whom I wonder? It couldn't travel alone without a carer.* There was a long pause. And then: *Of course, my old friend, Lys, would surely have done the deed. She delivered the newborn to be doted on within a humble but loving household. He was raised like you as a mortal and remained none the wiser to his identity — other than the possession of curious and immensely powerful magics.*

Dorgryl spoke softly now, mentally ticking off the points in his mind as he recalled the events he had witnessed from the Bleak.

The child was passed off as simply sentient and was well schooled by wary parents to keep his talents to himself to avoid the attentions of Goth and his band of inquisitors. Along comes Merkhud, searching for centuries for this very individual. And he finds the child, now a lad of fifteen or so summers. He contrives to bring the youngster to the palace where he can keep a watch over this enormously precious person. He manipulates the life of the lad until the boy can take it no more and breaks free. Merkhud wisely lets him go but uses other methods of spying on him and all the while is plotting the young man's death for his own ends.

Orlac was lost in the telling of the story. He hardly understood the thread but he grasped some of Dorgryl's mesmerising tale. Certainly his uncle seemed to know where it was headed. He allowed him to continue.

Dorgryl spoke quickly now as he pulled it all together. *Merkhud used Alyssa to bend the young man back to his will. Save her, die yourself. But die he did not. Merkhud had other plans for him. He would live on. But in secrecy. And all the time, the Paladin were gathering around him.*

Orlac could not take much more. The story was hopping around and he could not keep up with it. He lurched out of the seat he had been reclining in and angrily stepped to the balcony to bang his fist down on the palish pink stone from which the beautiful palace was crafted.

Who! he screamed. *Who is Torkyn Gynt?*

Dorgryl's voice was soft again when he spoke; all the swaggering nuances gone from his words as he uttered with no little awe: *He is your brother.*

*   *   *

Juno stood in one of the lesser courtyards of the palace, deep in conversation with a tall, dark-skinned man, Adongo the Moruk. Both were watchful, and they whispered their speech, too cautious to use the Link in case Orlac picked up on the magic.

'He is going to Tallinor,' Juno said.

Adongo checked over his shoulder yet again for signs of anyone nearby. 'How do you know?'

'A parchment arrived. It has the great seal of Tallinor.' She shrugged. 'He told me about it.'

The Moruk's eyes widened. 'He shares a lot with you.'

She nodded. 'He does. It baffles me too. He is making preparations to leave.'

'And?'

'And he asked me to handpick a servant to go with him.'

'Me?'

'Yes. Our child is there. I feel the pull of our bond. Don't you?'

He nodded. 'I had to fight the urge to go into Tallinor first. But something forced me to come to the Palace of Cipres first, after leaving Tor.'

'You did the right thing. You've had time to settle in here and be a familiar face. It will serve our purposes.'

Adongo began to pace. 'How do we know our bonded one is where he goes?'

'We don't.' She dropped her voice even lower. 'But you can keep a close watch on his movements.'

'What have you told him?'

'Only that I have the ideal manservant in mind. You are a Moruk. Your name is Titus and you are well trained. Very discreet.'

Adongo grinned slyly. 'So discreet he does not even recognise me.'

'Well, I didn't either.' Juno returned the smile. 'Go, Adongo, please.'

The Moruk nodded a polite bow. It was a traditional gesture of his tribe. 'I shall be Titus.'

Juno felt relief sweep through her. 'Good. Now make haste. He suspects nothing.'

12

Lauryn's Heart

Alyssa and Saxon pulled their cloaks tighter about them against the rain, glad to have sensible horses who happily moved alongside one another at a demure walk. It was muddy underfoot and the Kloek was not taking any chances of being thrown.

Queen no longer, he reminded himself, glancing at the petite figure in her deliberately nondescript clothes. She had moved from the role of royal back to civilian with ease. Alyssa was never one for vanities and this quality helped her now as she cast away her immediate past and rebuilt yet another identity for herself as a travelling noblewoman, her private bodyguard in tow. He noticed a new shine in those soft grey-green eyes and he hoped it was not for Tor, worried that this splendid and courageous young woman might be about to get her heart broken yet again. He pushed the thought to one side – it was not his business and Alyssa would be quick to remind him of this. She maintained this journey was necessary because of her passionate need to find her son.

'I wish I could link with him,' she suddenly said into

their comfortable silence. Her voice sounded just a little too wistful for his liking.

'With Rubyn?' He hoped she might agree.

'I meant Tor,' she replied, a little self-consciously.

Perhaps it was time to counsel her. 'Alyssa, it could be unwise—'

He was not allowed to finish his sentence. 'Don't, Sax. That he is alive fills my heart to bursting. I feel more fortunate than I deserve. This is about finding Rubyn and bringing our three children together. It is not about Tor and myself. Our affections for one another have nothing to do with this.'

He took a chance. 'Nevertheless, may I suggest caution.'

She threw him a stern glance of admonishment. 'No, you may not, Kloek.' It was a flash of the Queen she briefly had been. 'You forget he is still my husband but that does not mean I rush back to his bed.'

Alyssa could be fierce when her temper was inflamed. He wished he had not fired it so early in their journey. Now they would travel in an uncomfortable silence.

'I had forgotten that, your majesty,' he said, hoping the formality might remind her that he did respect her.

Her pinched expression relaxed. It softened into a ghost of a smile. 'Call me Alyssa now. Sorry, Saxon. I feel very jumpy. Husbands dying, husbands returning from the dead, sons coming back from the dead, children I didn't know I had presenting themselves . . . and perhaps another heart hurt when it should have been avoided.'

'Gyl?' he asked gently.

She nodded. 'He is in much pain.'

'He has all the raw stuff to make a good King,' Saxon assured her.

'But who will guide him? He has no one, and now even I have deserted him.'

'Gyl will make his own way, I'm sure. He will surprise all of us.'

'You're worse than a doting mother,' she teased.

Saxon shrugged. 'He will make a fine ruler for Tallinor. Let's not ignore the fact that Old King Mort's blood runs in his veins.'

She smiled. 'Gyl is fortunate that we all place such faith in him.' She bit her lip. 'I hope he will look after Lauryn.'

'King he may be these days, but barring Herek there is no finer soldier in all of Tallinor than Gyl. There is certainly no finer swordsman. She is safer with him than here with us.'

She arched her eyebrows. 'You were so merciless with him in the practice yards. Always telling him how terrible he was.'

The Kloek spat. 'No good swelling a young lad's head with notions of grandeur, Alyssa. You were too soft on the lad. Someone had to be the grouchy man about his life.'

He noticed the wistful expression cross her face once again. Had he said the wrong thing?

'Yes, I deeply regret withholding the information of his birthright from him but Lorys insisted. He could have achieved so much with Gyl over the years.'

'What's done is done. Now,' he said, deciding to put an end to any grim thoughts, 'let us see what these sturdy mares can do for us. The Heartwood calls.'

An organised chaos had gripped Tal as it prepared to crown its new King. News of Gyl's birthright had raced around the realm and was welcomed with great enthusiasm. It was understandable. Gyl was a popular man in the city, especially with the local gentry who had daughters of marriageable age. Being the Under Prime had taken him around the Kingdom several times in his career already and that meant he was a familiar and well-liked face within its far reaching districts. He was someone the realm knew and that immeasurably softened the anxiety of having a new ruler, particularly as they knew him to be a just and courageous man.

The household staff moved like worker bees in their dedication, whilst the head of the household kept up a steady stream of instructions. The palace was stripped, cleaned and refreshed from top to bottom. Everything, from the palace silver to the King's Guards' armour, was polished to gleaming. Cook's team swarmed around the kitchens and whole wings of the castle were reopened, aired and brought back to life. A seemingly unending convoy of carts and wagons brought enormous bunches of herbs and lavenders to restuff beds and strew across the floors of all the guest chambers which would be packed to brimful within a day or two. In fact Gyl had already been advised that his first royal guests were due to arrive by nightfall. Animals were slaughtered, gutted, skinned, plucked, boiled, or hung.

Lauryn felt a little useless amidst the frenzy of industry. She did not know how to go about offering her help because everyone was just too busy — it seemed rude to interrupt them. And so she found herself this day strolling around the grounds somewhat aimlessly until she noticed Rolynd trying to entice old Drake deeper into one of the tiny courtyards where she could see preparations were underway to bath the King's hound. There was a team of page-boys ready to do the deed but none were game enough to begin. These days, apart from Alyssa and Gyl, Rolynd was the only other person Drake genuinely liked – everyone else he simply tolerated. But it seemed that not even for Rolynd was the dog going to subject himself to the insufferable humiliation of a bath. Too long in the tooth to be tricked or even bribed, the huge hound sat very still, as if rooted to the ground where he sat, and regarded his enemy.

Lauryn only caught sight of this merry theatre because one of the older pages, who obviously had many other tasks to perform on his list of today's duties, became impatient and rather bravely approached the dog with a length of rope. Drake, famous for his enormous bark, let rip with one of his best which sent all the other younger pages scuttling backwards, rather swiftly followed by their elder.

Rolynd shook his head and then noticed Lauryn standing nearby, her amusement evident. 'My lady, may I introduce you to Tallinor's most stubborn and indeed most grubby royal hound, Drake.'

She laughed. 'Whom does he belong to?'

Rolynd sighed. 'King Lorys, may the Light shine upon him. But this dog is exceptionally fond of your mother. She had a genuine way with this beast. He is Gyl's dog now. They are inseparable, but the King has given very strict instructions that the hound is to be bathed. It only happens for coronations so I would imagine this is his first – and hopefully last – ever bath.'

Lauryn was now truly amused and walked towards the dog, still laughing. 'Does he have to?'

'King's orders.'

'Well then, Drake,' she said, hands on hips, 'let's blame the King and not these nice young lads here.'

Rolynd was astounded to see the huge dog stand up and wag his tail at the young woman. She grinned and beckoned him to her and, as if he were her own pup, he came to her call and allowed her to pet and cuddle him.

'My lady. You have a way with animals just like your mother.'

She smiled. 'Can I help you in this task?'

'But you'll get all wet and muddy.'

'Oh please, Rolynd. Give me two minutes and I'll change and you can dismiss the pages. I can do this for Drake without any help.'

With his mouth still open in surprise, Rolynd watched the young woman lift her skirts and run back into the palace. The dog sat down again and eyed them balefully. The palace secretary shook his head.

'Dismissed boys. Get on with your other duties.'

They did not require a second telling and had dispersed within seconds. Drake growled for good measure as they left.

Rolynd scolded him and was still berating the dog, albeit rather gently, when Lauryn reappeared kitted out in a man's loose shirt and breeches she had pulled in tight to her waist with a length of leather.

'I borrowed these old clothes,' she said gleefully. 'Come on, Drake. You'll love us for making you all clean and then I shall comb you until your coat gleams.'

Whether the dog understood her or not he obediently crossed to the horse trough where Lauryn began scooping up water with a large pot and pouring it over him.

It was not a pleasant time for Drake but he submitted

to her ministrations with calm and good grace. Even the soaping and the rinsing he accepted with only the slightest show of indignation. Rolynd listened to the constant soft stream of chatter coming from Lauryn as she spoke gently to the dog of how all the itches would be gone and the burrs which poked him as he slept would be combed out. Her tone soothed the secretary as much as the hound, which is probably why he didn't notice the King strolling into the courtyard.

Gyl stopped with amazement at this scene and then, not wishing to interrupt its progress, he leaned against one of the walls and watched Lauryn. She looked exactly as he remembered his mother when she had lived a more carefree life. Lauryn's golden hair, which she had unsuccessfully tried to pull into a hurried plait had worked itself loose and now strands, glinting in the midday sun, were hanging down her face which glowed with her efforts. She was altogether lovely. He too admired her gentle talk to the animal and he was reminded of that day when he had first met her. She had found Bryx for him and yet Bryx was not a horse who came to anyone. She obviously spoke the language of animals. And that day she had been covered in mud and now here she was dressed like a man and completely indifferent to the normal vanities of women. As he was thinking how gorgeous she looked in her simple garb with her hair flying around her, Drake decided he had had enough and stood up to shake himself. He did this with particular care to not only expertly drench the unsuspecting Rolynd but to shower his carer with as much water as possible. Lauryn screamed throughout the ordeal and then began to laugh at Rolynd and then at herself.

Drake trotted off, longing to roll in the dust but Gyl was too fast, knowing precisely what dogs like to do when their coats are damp. He grabbed the hound, laughing as he did so. This was the first moment that either Rolynd or Lauryn had realised the King was present. As one they bowed, looking rather ridiculous in their wet clothes.

When Lauryn stood up, she looked self-conscious. And well you might, the King thought, unable to drag his stare from the now suddenly transparent white shirt which clung to her breasts rather splendidly.

Gyl cleared his throat. 'I presume this is the fashion where you come from?'

She followed his gaze and then shrieked, horrified at her indiscretion and desperately trying to cover herself. 'Excuse me, your majesty. I . . . er . . . I must change my clothes.' She did not bother with a bow but fled into the palace, cheeks burning, no longer from her labours but from her sense of humiliation.

Rolynd said nothing but his look told Gyl he should not have embarrassed his mother's daughter in such a manner. Gyl had far too much respect for the old secretary to ignore the warning in that carefully expressionless face.

'Sorry, Rolynd. She's too easy to tease.'

'No apology due me, your highness, though might I mention that the girl is feeling intensely lonely.'

Gyl considered this. 'Have I made it worse?'

'No, sire. I think she just wishes to help and be a part of palace life. She just wants to fit in . . . like most of us.'

The King nodded. 'I must make it up to her.'

Later that day, as Lauryn stared out of her window

towards the moors to where she imagined Brittelbury might be, wishing desperately she could have gone with Gidyon, she heard a tap on the door. Behind it she found a page with a message from the King requesting her to join him for a ride that afternoon. She assumed it was with a party and grudgingly gave her acceptance. She did not particularly want to see the King today again – her cheeks still burned each time she remembered her nakedness – but at least amongst a group she could avoid him. Also it gave her something to do and meant another few hours of loneliness had been killed.

After the morning's debacle, Lauryn took care with her preparations. Rolynd had filled her wardrobe with dozens of garments she would probably never wear but he had eased her discomfort with the news that her mother had insisted she have a full range of clothes to wear during her stay at the palace.

At the appropriate hour she presented herself in the main courtyard and was surprised to find herself greeted by a single horse and its handler.

'Where are the others?' she said.

'They've gone ahead, my lady,' he demurred, helping her onto her horse. 'Her name's Firefly. She's really a very gentle beast to ride once you get to know her. I might add, my lady, she can be just a little feisty for new riders but you'll soon get her measure.'

'Thank you. How do I find my way to the rest of the party?' she asked, seething at the affront of being specifically invited and then left behind.

'I shall lead you, my lady. It's not far.'

They headed towards the back of the palace in silence with Lauryn too furious to even make polite small talk.

She could see a few soldiers ahead standing around with a couple of horses, but there were no finely dressed men ready for a genteel ride – nor women for that matter. How rude of the King.

'What is your name?' she finally said to the man who held the reins.

'Barkly, my lady.'

'Well, Barkly, I do not wish to ride this afternoon. Take me back.' She hated the haughty tone in her voice but it was either that or rage.

Barkly hesitated. He was only yards away now from the other men.

'But, my lady. The King—'

'The King is not here, I see. He will not miss me,' she said loftily, unable to drag herself back to a level of politeness for the poor, rather red-faced man standing below her.

She became aware of a third person approaching behind on a horse, but she ignored them. 'I wish to return to the palace immediately.' It was a command now.

Lauryn saw Barkly's eyes flick beyond her which she interpreted in her irritation as a lack of respect for her wishes. That combined with her anger at being treated with disdain by the King fired something in her. She pulled at the reins to release Barkly's hold. Lauryn decided she would find her own way back to the stables if she had to. Her sudden movement and Barkly's equally strong grip on the mare meant the horse's mouth took the impact and, in her pain, Firefly bucked and then in an instant was galloping. Lauryn screamed. She was competent in the saddle but was no expert and a startled horse was definitely beyond her riding skills. The horse suited her name very well . . . it felt like she was flying.

Lauryn could hear the sound of hooves behind her and begged for them to catch up before Firefly entered the small copse she seemed doggedly targeted towards. Too late — they crashed into the branches of trees which whipped at her. She let go of the reins to protect her face, feeling her hair grabbed and ripped.

The rider behind must have caught up and as Firefly lurched to a halt, Lauryn lost her seat and fell hard to the ground. She saw stars as she regained her wits a minute or so later, opening her eyes to look into the concerned face of the King.

'Hush, don't move. Do you hurt anywhere, Lauryn?'

There were other faces. All anxious. It was rather nice to have the attention of all these men. 'I hurt everywhere,' she croaked and unhappily accepted the King's help to sit up.

'Take it slowly, my lady. Please don't injure yourself further,' Gyl said gently. It was a lovely voice. But she had been so angry with him, hadn't she? Lauryn frowned, thinking back to why that had been. And then it all returned to her as the fuzziness in her head cleared. Her back and ribs hurt.

'You left me alone,' she said. At some given signal she did not catch, the men began to disperse. 'Where's everyone going?'

Gyl's mouth tweaked with the beginnings of a grin. 'I thought you may appreciate some privacy. Can you stand, my lady?'

With an effort she could.

'Nothing broken then?' he asked, his face still showing traces of how scared he had been that she had sustained a real injury.

'No. Just plenty of bruises I'm sure,' she admitted, feeling very sore and sorry for herself. 'I must look a fright,' she added, noticing her hair torn once again from its neat plait.

'You look as gorgeous as you did this afternoon. Sadly, you chose not to wear that delightful damp blouse again,' he said, battling to keep the grin now from his face.

She looked at him, realising he still had his arms around her from helping her up and somehow, looking up into that boyish, handsome face, she found her sense of humour. Her amusement through her aches and groans was genuine, laced with relief that her perceived humiliation had been an overreaction. 'I'm so sorry about that. I am still burning with embarrassment.'

He helped her over to a tree and encouraged her to sit down again. 'Don't be. Most women in the court would gladly give an arm or a leg – both in fact – to look as good as you did this afternoon, even without the water effect.'

Lauryn covered her face with her hands. She wasn't sure now if she was still embarrassed by the event or by his unexpected flattery. 'Oh, please don't let's talk about it any more – I'm so ashamed.'

He gave a full throaty laugh. 'I'm afraid I shall never be able to forget it. Shall probably dream about it for years to come.' He changed the subject. 'Why did you kick your horse into a gallop by the way?'

'I didn't,' she admitted, forlornly. 'I was so angry at you for deserting me I decided I would refuse to be led to where the party was and when that Barkly fellow did not turn the horse around, I thought I'd find my own way. It seems I startled Firefly.'

'What party?'

'Hmmm?' she said, trying to tuck the loose hair back into some order. It didn't work.

'The party,' he repeated. 'I'm wondering which party do you speak of?'

She gave up on the hair and began to realise she had made another mistake. 'Oh, I just assumed your invitation meant a group of us were heading out for an afternoon ride.'

'Why?'

'Why what, sire?' she said, now unnerved by the steady green gaze. He was sitting close enough that his knees touched hers. Why was her heart suddenly racing?

He rephrased his question. 'Why would you assume we were to travel in a party?'

'Why not?' she retorted defensively, noticing the short cut of his hair and how the ends seemed tipped in gold. They were much too close for her comfort.

He laughed at her evasiveness and took her hand. She stared at the large hands which held hers and noticed how carefully he took care of them, for a soldier. Mind you, they were suited for the King he now was. The nails were clipped short and filed smooth with perfect half moons at the cuticle. They were scrupulously clean. She shocked herself with the powerful urge to feel those hands on her. Lauryn immediately dragged her eyes away from the offending hands and back to the green gaze.

'Pardon?' she asked, suddenly, thrown by the vision of him caressing her through her water-drenched blouse. She shook her head to rid her mind of it.

The King smiled. It was a wicked and knowing look. 'I didn't say anything. Your hand feels suddenly moist, Lauryn. Are you all right?'

She snatched it away, rubbing it on her skirt. 'I'm fine. Perhaps we should go,' she said, eyes darting around in case someone had glimpsed them together. All at once they seemed to be sitting so close their heads almost touched.

'Are you really fine?' The gentle concern was back in the voice of the King.

'I am, I promise. I was winded and I'm sure I'll sport some superb bruises but otherwise, I feel well. Shall we go?'

She made to stand but the wretched beautiful hand had hers in its clutch again.

'If you are well, then I would be honoured if you would continue with the ride and the picnic I had planned.'

'Picnic?' she said, feeling and sounding like a pet parrot she had seen at the palace in a gilded cage. She promised herself she would not repeat nor make him repeat another word.

'Yes, our picnic. Yours and mine.'

'I don't understand.'

'Well, I invited you to join me for a ride this afternoon. I thought we could take a quiet picnic together and I could make use of your sound advice and practise using my smile again.'

'Oh, Gyl, I didn't mean it . . .'

His grin faltered and the vulnerability was back. She found it rather endearing now. 'I know. I know. But you're right. These past weeks . . . well, I feel as though some sort of grim countenance has fallen upon me as catastrophic news blended with strange news. I really have forgotten what it is to smile but you reminded me. I'm grateful. So . . . will you join me?'

She looked around, confused. 'You mean just us?'

'That's all it ever was going to be. Those men are my guards. They were waiting for me as I went to check on something. You arrived and obviously decided I was not in attendance. But I promise you, I was there all along and simply went ahead to see to some kingly decisions,' he said with faked importance. They shared a smile. He nodded at the men. 'They will keep watch but at a discreet distance. We'll be essentially travelling alone, but not far, I promise.'

And with that, he lifted her hand and kissed it. It was so soft and so fleeting she had trouble convincing herself it had happened at all.

With no self-consciousness for what he had just done, the King stood, helped her to her feet and walked her towards Firefly, all the time one hand guiding her. His touch she felt burning through her clothes all the way to her skin which was now tingling.

Later, they sat beside a very small brook and shared a simple, delicious meal. They had talked at length during the ride, allowing the horses to set their own comfortable pace. Gyl had already decided that Lauryn was not up to anything swift that afternoon and deliberately permitted Bryx to stroll. They shared many laughs over trivial matters and Gyl noticed that Lauryn was a clever mimic . . . already, in the brief time she had been in the palace, she could produce hilarious impersonations of Koryn and Cook. And once again he chuckled and she cringed over the afternoon's episode, and then he promised her he would never refer to it again. Inwardly, Gyl knew the vision would haunt him daily and he would not be able to rest until he felt her body against his.

As they had drifted into a companionable silence he began to wonder whether there was anything wrong with his desire for this woman. She was not his sister after all. Her birth mother was his adopted mother in truth and neither had been raised together as kin. As far as he was concerned she was a needy young stranger who had come into his life in the most unexpected way. She had intrigued him from the moment they met and she intrigued him even more now.

As they sat by the brook the mood deepened into something more sombre as Gyl began to speak about his father. In a short time Lauryn felt she almost knew the man through Gyl's keen eyes and soldier's attention to detail.

'He loved your mother deeply, you know,' he said.

'I gather. How do you feel about my father?'

He appreciated her directness. 'I wish he'd never come but then I would never have met you.' Gyl could not meet her eyes as he said this. 'I am trying to keep an open mind about all that he apparently stands for. But Lauryn,' he chanced taking her hand again, 'I may be the King of Tallinor but I am still a simple soldier at heart. I deal with what my eyes can see and my ears can hear. All this talk of magic and angry gods and . . . you appearing from some different world to save this world – well it all befuddles me.'

She squeezed his hand. 'I do understand. I hardly know what I'm doing here myself. Save the world? Ha! How? But Gyl, look at me.' He did. Lauryn cast and aged herself by fifty years or so. She watched the horror come across his face as he shrank back from the touch of her gnarled fingers. Then just as fast she snapped the glamour off and she was Lauryn again.

There was no amusement in her face when she said: 'How do you suppose that happens if there is no magic in this world?'

The King was clearly shocked. 'What else?'

'What else can I do? Lots. I have no idea of the limitations of this power. Remember the man you found lying by the tree not far from where we thought Sorrel died?' He nodded. 'I did that. And I did it by pushing out with my mind . . . no hands, no weapon . . . just my powers.' He shook his head, half with disbelief and half with dread understanding. She continued. 'And the lad you were looking for? Well, I think I broke several of his limbs when I cast out with my mind and threw him high into the air. He landed heavily.' She looked sheepish but Gyl could not laugh.

'I don't know what to say,' he admitted.

'There is nothing to say. I feel as clueless as you but I trust my father. He has brought us back to do something. You must trust him too. If you care about me, if you care about our mother . . . Light Gyl! . . . if you care about Tallinor, we have to trust that Tor and Alyssa know things we do not.'

'What should I do?'

'Don't be sceptical any more. Be open to suggestion. Allow yourself that magic is here and around us and that it can be used for good but there is a darker side and I believe that's what we face now.'

He nodded. 'My mother . . . our mother counselled me along the same lines before she left. I gave her my word I would make preparations for extra security in the Kingdom.'

'Don't hesitate. Something bad is coming. My father

was forced to confront it before we came to Tal. Not here in Tallinor but somewhere else. This god's intention is to destroy all of us and to raze Tallinor.'

'How do I know who my enemy is?'

'You don't,' she said. 'None of us do. But my father will recognise him. For now, we must trust those who know more than us, who have been preparing longer.'

Lauryn looked towards the sun setting behind the hills. She sighed. 'It's getting late.'

'Yes,' he admitted, making no move to leave. 'Lauryn, will you stay close over the next few days? I could use a friend around the place. This whole coronation business is daunting.'

'Of course I will. It would be an honour. You're going to be a brilliant King for Tallinor. I know it. And all the nobles will want to marry you off to their daughters.'

He pulled a face. 'I know this. That's why I'm asking you to remain close.'

'To put them off?' She laughed, amused by his sudden anxiety.

'No,' he said very deliberately. 'Not to put them off. To let them know my heart is spoken for.'

It was as though a mighty wind had rushed through her and sucked all her breath away as it passed. She swallowed, trying to breathe, trying to find a voice . . . *any* sound.

He met her eyes. 'I'm not sure where that notion came from but I'm glad that it is out and in the open between us. Have I disturbed you by saying it?'

She shook her head, still unable to utter a sound. A random thought passed through her mind; an echo from the past. *She would catch herself a fine man one day. He would*

be strong and witty and a leader amongst men. They would be
madly in love and he would never want any other but her.

Here was such a man. She could not deny that in the
past few hours she had felt herself drawn deeper and deeper
into his life. She would be lying if she did not admit that
she was captivated by him and would be jealous of any
other woman who held his desires. It would be folly to
suggest – as tentative as it was – that it was not the
strongest of desires she was feeling towards this man. And
here he was boldly speaking her thoughts back to her.

'Please say something,' he said, quietly, looking at her
hand in his.

Lauryn swallowed again and hoped her voice could be
found. 'I will stay close, sire. I will show all of Tallinor
that our hearts are spoken for . . . by each other.'

He looked back at her then, his eyes literally sparkling
in the dying pink light of dusk. 'May I kiss you, my lady?'

'What are you waiting for, your majesty?' she said,
pulling him fiercely towards her and no longer caring for
prying eyes.

13

The Coronation Feast

The Ciprean party made its way majestically through the fabulously ornate gates of Tal. Orlac's heart leapt as they entered the city. What would he do? Unleash his powers and start the killing rampage now?

The red mist which was Dorgryl could imagine his thoughts. *I've been thinking*, the elder god said, the familiar slyness in his voice.

I wish you wouldn't, Orlac snapped, wanting to be left alone.

Dorgryl continued as though his nephew had not responded. *I believe you should wait. Don't reveal anything yet.*

I've waited too many centuries already.

Nevertheless. Orlac could tell his uncle was deliberately choosing his words; keeping his normally voluble thoughts to a minimum. He was obviously serious in his intent to convince Orlac of something. *Stick to what we promised. Wait until we know where Gynt is. To exact maximum retribution you should take some time to learn something of today's Tallinor. After all, you have waited this long . . . and you have all the time in the world to ensure your vengeance is pure and perfect.*

Oh, he is good, Orlac thought. Very good. And for one of those rare times they agreed on something. Orlac felt his uncle was airing sound advice: he would find out more about this King and his court. It would make the dismantling of it all the more fun when the time came.

So we continue in these roles, he finally said.

For a while, yes, Dorgryl responded. *Just look at the welcome awaiting you, my regent.* And Orlac heard the senior god's deep chuckle.

It was amusing. There were dozens and dozens of courtly people awaiting his carriage on the grand steps of the Tal palace. They were all bowing or curtsying as they watched his party draw close. Trumpets blasted and guards, uniformed in the brilliant Tallinese red, stood to stiff attention.

And in their midst, Orlac noticed, stood a young man. He was not especially tall but was broad and handsome in a rugged sort of way. He was dressed simply as one would expect a soldier might but his dark clothes were a perfect cut and hung well from his square shoulders. He wore a sword at his side and the crimson of Tallinor fluttered around him in the shape of a cloak. His bearing was regal. Without question this was the new King – the Bastard of Wytton – whom they had come to witness being crowned.

I presume this is the famous Gyl. Dorgryl echoed his thoughts as their own carriage halted. *But just who is that delectable creature next to him?*

Orlac's gaze shifted and locked intently on a young woman with golden hair and greyish-green eyes the colour of the sea on a stormy day. Her cheekbones were set high, chiselling the creamy complexion of her skin. The god's breath caught in his chest. The woman was strikingly beautiful and he knew in that instant he wanted her; she was perfect to his eyes.

They await you, nudged Dorgryl in his mind.

Orlac tried to gather his thoughts but they were scattered by the dazzling smile on the face of the young woman who seemed to be directing all that warmth at him as he stepped from his carriage. There were several soft exclamations from many women on the stairs that afternoon as, unbeknown to them, a god entered their lives. His height alone was enough to turn heads but the exclamations came from women whose hearts began to beat harder at the beauty of the foreign dignitary who elegantly bowed towards the King of Tallinor. Orlac heard none of them; paid no heed to their sounds. His attention, though seemingly directed towards the King, was actually riveted on one pair of eyes only. She dipped them from his gaze as she bowed once again.

And then Gyl of Wytton was striding towards him. He was smiling broadly and making noises of welcome. 'Your rider came ahead. I'm sorry to hear of your Queen's illness but extremely glad she sent her Regent. You are most welcome to the Kingdom of Tallinor,' Gyl said, extending a hand.

Orlac took it. 'I feel privileged to be amongst you and sincerely thank you for this rousing welcome on behalf of Cipres. I am Regent Sylc.' He smiled at the name he had taken. It had only just occurred to him to use it. In the old language of Cipres, not much used now, the word meant thief. He liked the irony. The King was speaking again.

'I trust her majesty's ailment is only minor?' Gyl enquired out of politeness.

'Yes, sire. Our Queen should be well within a day or two but we did not wish to delay your coronation, nor to miss it. Please accept the Queen's apologies for not being here and her commiserations on the untimely death of your father. By all the accounts we heard in Cipres, he was an excellent man.' Orlac felt the twitch of amusement from Dorgryl at this exchange.

'Thank you. He was,' Gyl said, not wanting to discuss his father with the stranger. 'Come now,' he continued, 'let us show you your chambers and your servants can unpack and settle you in for a wonderful few days as our honoured guest.'

Orlac smiled, his eyes flicking to the woman standing not so far away. He was not mistaken; surely this was the woman that Juno spoke of. Juno had not lied; she was indeed a seer. Those were certainly freckles on the girl's face and now that he could see her smiling, her nose crinkled as it did in Juno's vision. He would make this woman his.

The Cipreans were the last of the royal guests to arrive and the palace was now brimful of people in all wings except the chambers at the top of the west tower which remained dusty and unused. Lorys had left instructions many years previous that they were not to be reopened during his reign. The housekeeper had enquired of the new King whether these chambers should now be unlocked and cleaned out but Gyl had shaken his head, deferring to his father's sentimental wishes. They were not essential to this event; they could make do without them and anyway, which guest would want to climb to the very top of the tower after a night's feasting? Merkhud's rooms and their secrets remained untouched.

The coronation itself had gone smoothly; the weather had turned on a picture-perfect spring afternoon and Tal's populace, swelled by thousands for the event, had begun a long week of celebrations in which the violet shroud was replaced by the Tallinese crimson edged in coronation gold and almost fanatical decoration had appeared in every nook and cranny of the capital to mark the occasion.

Inside the palace, the coronation feast was underway and Cook's team had surpassed themselves with course after sumptuous course – the rare sea lamprey a particular highlight. And in between each special dish Sallementro would take the floor and sing for the guests, his superb voice winning acclaim amongst the visiting royalty, many of whom suggested he might care to visit their realms and sing within their palaces. The King of Briavel – to the far east of the Kingdom of Tallinor – was especially insistent. The bard was more flattered than he would admit to but knew in his heart he could not leave Tallinor with the threat of Orlac hanging over it.

The god was thoroughly enjoying himself, finding his seat positioned not far from the King and near enough to the Lady Lauryn – as she was introduced – to speak with her. So far the entertainment and banqueting had ensured their conversation was brief and polite but he hoped that might change, now that the evening had reached the point when softer ballads would be sung. A natural break between the savoury and sweet courses had occurred and people were allowed to settle back and talk uninterrupted for a while.

Orlac found himself engaged in a tedious and lengthy conversation with a dignitary from one of the kingdoms to the far east of Tallinor. He was barely listening and certainly not paying attention. Even Dorgryl's comments interested him more.

His uncle shimmered. *She is spoken for, I'd suggest, or at least her heart speaks to someone in this room.*

How can you know this?

I notice things. I observe people.

She has hardly taken her attention from me.

Dorgryl laughed. *Perhaps, but watch how her eyes stray every few moments towards the King; see how her lips purse because he is not paying her attention. I would be most surprised if those two are not lovers.*

Orlac felt a painful spike of jealousy. He knew he had no right to and yet his desire for this woman had become overwhelmingly proprietorial. He tried to ignore his uncle's sly voice and managed to extricate himself from the attentions of the eastern dignitary.

'Lady Lauryn,' he said, flashing a brilliant smile. 'Do you hail from Tal itself?'

'No, Regent Sylc. I have only been here a short while.'

'Oh? Where is home?' he asked, determined to hold her attention.

Lauryn felt distracted and just a bit irritated. As much as she was enjoying all the pomp and ceremony, the fabulous gowns and amazing food, most of which she had never tasted before, she was also in the grip of jealousy.

Across from her, Gyl was engaged in animated conversation with the most gorgeous young woman from some far away realm. Lauryn had established that this woman was a Princess, set to inherit a wealthy throne. The King

and Queen seemed very intent on encouraging their
daughter's time with the King of Tallinor. Lauryn watched
with loathing as the olive-skinned Princess dipped her
dark eyes to show off her long lashes at some little jest
of Gyl's.

She heard the Regent of Cipres clear his throat, and
refocused her thoughts. The man was paying her a great
deal of attention and she could feel the weight of glares
from other women in the room who would have given
their eye teeth to be so close to this exceptionally handsome man.

'Er, my family is from a rural part of the Kingdom. A
small village, Mallee Marsh, not far from Flat Meadows,'
she said, knowing the man would never have heard of it.

Gynt's home! Dorgryl was just short of spluttering.

Orlac kept his face steady but his ears too had pricked
at the mention of this sleepy village. 'You know we had
a visitor in Cipres not long ago who hailed from that very
place. How odd that you should mention it.'

Lauryn was rescued from the direction of Sylc's
thoughts by a familiar laugh and then a not-so-familiar
yet instantly unlikable giggle. Gyl and the princess were
sharing another intimate joke it seemed. Lauryn could not
stand it another moment.

'Regent Sylc, would you be kind enough to excuse me
just for a short while.'

Orlac stood and effected a brief bow. 'Of course.' He
did not fail to notice the high spots of colour on her
cheeks.

Lauryn fled the hall, half in anger, the rest in plain
hurt. Outside she dragged in the air of the crisp night
and calmed herself. Candles sitting in painted paper

lanterns threw glowing colours around the courtyard in which she found herself, but she paid scant attention to the prettiness surrounding her or to the air fragranced by the different perfumes of the candles.

What had happened between her and Gyl? Had that been a declaration of love, spoken only two days ago and sealed with a kiss? Several kisses, in fact, including a long and memorable one that had left her breathless and weak-kneed. And during that kiss she had indeed given her heart over to this man. And now here he was flirting outrageously with that girl. It was bad enough that he had already danced with several eligible women and been involved in lighthearted conversations with at least half a dozen others.

Once they had been seated, Lauryn felt sure he would pay her more attention but he had not even made eye contact with her. She felt the sting of tears but refused them, fought them back. Instead the anger took over from the sorrow.

'Ah now, why are you here, beautiful girl, and not amongst the festivities?'

It was Cook. On her way to rouse up another shift of kitchen workers, who were being rotated throughout this day and night of festivity. 'I came around here for just a quiet moment and an ale,' she said, holding up a cup to show Lauryn. 'You know your mother is very partial to the stuff but only Gyl and I were permitted to know this,' Cook said, tapping her enormous and rather red nose.

Against her mood, Lauryn smiled. 'Is that right?'

'Oh yes, it was our secret. Your mother likes to have a large mug daily . . . says it keeps her regular.'

Now Lauryn laughed. 'May I taste it?'

Cook thrust the enormous mug towards her.

Lauryn sipped and pulled a face. 'Ugh! I think I prefer Tallinese wine.'

The large woman sat down on a bench nearby. 'Ah well, you may get a taste for it if you stay with us long enough. I love your mother, Lauryn. I wish she hadn't left.'

'Me too.'

'So what's got you all sad?'

'Oh I'm fine, just needed some air.'

'You not only look like Alyssandra Qyn but you act like her, and in being so similar you can no more hide your emotions from your face than she can. What's making you sad, my girl?' The beefy woman took another long draught and then eyed her steadily.

'It's Gyl,' she blurted, not really meaning to.

'Oh that silly boy. Don't let him upset you so,' she said, waving one enormous hand towards Lauryn. 'I've known him since he was a stripling. On the day he arrived he won the heart of two of Tallinor's most important women.'

'Oh?'

'The Light strike me if I lie to you. Queen Nyria was quite taken by him on first meeting and then your mother, bless her, loved him as if he were her own son. I saw him tonight, my lady. He's flirting isn't he?'

Lauryn nodded.

'Yes, Cook's right. I always am. Well, child, flirt back. You're not exactly the ugliest woman in the room tonight are you? Have you noticed how many men watch you?'

This time all Lauryn could do was shake her head. She genuinely had not noticed anything along these lines. She was still reeling from Gyl's first fleeting kiss; the notion that anyone could fall in love with her or even desire her seemed remote. The suggestion that many men ogled her was laughable and yet Cook seemed earnest.

'And what about that dashing Regent from Cipres? Oh he's got all my serving lasses' hearts a-flutter. They can't stop talking about his golden hair and violet eyes; his perfect white smile and broad chest. I have to admit, he looks like a god.'

'Yes, he is extremely handsome.'

'Well, he only has eyes for you, my dear, and I would suggest you take advantage of that. Perhaps achieve a little jealousy of your own.' Cook drained her mug noisily. 'Well, I must get back to my steaming kitchen, my lady. We have the sweet pies and treats to be brought out next – I'm very proud of our marzipan fancies.' And then she bustled off, with a wave to Lauryn.

Lauryn smiled to herself. Cook was right. If she was going to win Gyl's attention back, she would not achieve it staring at him like some sad lap-dog. Regent Sylc was showing an uncanny interest in her and what was the harm in returning that interest? None at all, she decided, as she straightened her pale green gown which set off her eyes perfectly.

When she returned to her place, Regent Sylc stood politely once again and without so much as a glance towards Gyl, Lauryn took her seat and immediately fell into conversation with the man from Cipres. The night wore on and their talk became more intimate. At one stage he passed across a piece of candied fruit which had been rolled in sugar. No one, not even the King of Tallinor, missed Lauryn taking the Regent's outstretched hand and somewhat seductively placing her mouth around the fruit he held, her lips just touching his elegant fingers which he then put into his own mouth to lick off the sugar which still clung to them. And when Sylc asked Lauryn if she cared to join in one of the dances, she readily accepted, making a small jest that he was so tall he might have to hold her off the ground.

They danced several times and not once did Sylc take his violet eyes from her sea-green ones. She held his rapt attention and surprised even herself by how much she enjoyed his attentions. Sylc was devastatingly handsome, a witty and intelligent companion, and his mannerisms were as elegant and fine as his garments, which were tailored from the purest cream silk and dark velvet – a fine catch for any woman.

Lauryn realised several pleasant hours had passed. She was pleased that she had managed to put the King to one side for this evening and enjoy the company of this splendid man who seemed to have no hankering to share himself around, which made her the envy of most of the eligible women in the room, if not all of them. She had cast a surreptitious glance Gyl's way only once since her return and found him glaring at her. In reply Lauryn doubled her attentions to the Regent. Gyl would learn tonight that her heartstrings were not to be plucked and then left unplayed. She liked the vision she had conjured and laughed coquettishly at something Sylc whispered in her ear, infuriating the King.

Gyl seethed. He felt like drawing his sword and running the Regent through. How dare he monopolise Lauryn in this manner – and their whisperings, laughter and flirtatious activities were not going unnoticed. This was humiliating, to say the least. He could have sworn Lauryn had felt the same way about him on the day of their ride and picnic. There was no doubting the affection in *that* kiss. Nay, it was not affection – it was much more than that. He had felt her desires – and, dare he say, her love – being returned in that long and passionate embrace.

Gyl had made love to many women in his time; far more than he cared to admit to. He had broken hearts too, but in truth he had never made any promises to these women. Their own desires had forced them to believe that he would be true to them; that, in lying together, they had reached some pact, some agreement of commitment. But not so. Gyl was a known flirt – he readily admitted it himself and he was happy to carry that dubious honour. His mother had made it painfully clear in recent times that he was never to promise himself to any woman without consulting her. It had made him laugh whenever she put her hands on her hips and threatened him with terrible punishment. Now he understood. She had known he would be king one day, knew he must make an excellent marriage – for the girl he chose was destined to be a queen.

But his mother need not have worried. Gyl felt remote from women. As much as he enjoyed their company and the exploration and touch of their soft mouths on his skin, not once had he felt any connection of love. Herek had once spoken of chemistry. The Prime had admitted it was old man Merkhud, a former physic to King Lorys, and his father before him, who had said that until the humours were right between two people, then the love would never happen. Until that point, it was all lust and heated desires.

What Herek said had made sense to the young Gyl and so he comforted himself with the notion of chemistry when he found himself wondering why no girl could ever touch his heart. And then in a blink this one had . . . dripping with mud and answering him back – in a manner just short of insolent – she had sparked something in him. And then again in his mother's private garden, she had fired him up and he had been so taken by the surprise of his feelings he had walked out on her and almost set off an argument between them. He recalled how he had searched her out in the Throne Room when the shocking news of the heir to Lorys was revealed and it was her calm flowing out to him across the room which had steadied his nerve. Every flick of her golden hair, every casual glance of those gorgeous green eyes, every feisty riposte or gentle grin just hammered another nail of love for Lauryn into his heart – and he had known her such a short time! This must surely be the chemistry of which old man Merkhud had spoken, for Gyl could not help himself. There was no remedy for this powerful feeling; no drug which could alleviate the exquisite pain it brought now to his heart to see her so much as smiling at another.

He would not be able to take it much longer, her continued ignorance of him and her attentiveness to the Ciprean. Gyl had not exactly taken an instant dislike to the man, but within a few hours of his arrival he had loathed the very name Sylc because it was on the lips of every woman in the palace.

As Gyl churned his grumpy thoughts, Cook entered the hall to take some well-deserved applause as the last course was served with sweet wines, bringing with her a crown made from sugar crystal. It was transparent as glass and had been painted with luminous colours to look as if it were made of jewels. It was exquisite. She beamed as her staff presented it to their King, who graciously accepted it and made a toast to the finest head of kitchen Tallinor had ever been fortunate enough to enjoy. Cook bowed low and when she stood, her eyes – ever expressive – cast a severe glance towards the Princess, now once again seated close by him. Her face clouded into the look of reproach which had become very familiar to him over his years of growing up and stealing hot biscuits from her kitchen.

Could that be it?

Could it be that Lauryn was cross with him for favouring the Princess? Well, he had to be courteous to all of his guests, did he not? And perhaps she did not grasp how politically important it was for him to curry favour with all of the monarchs feasting at his table tonight.

He needed to ensure a smooth transition from Lorys to himself as King. He could not risk falling out of favour so early in the piece. Snubbing a Princess was a sure way to disgruntle a King, and risk alienating important and strategic neighbours. But Lauryn would not be thinking along these political lines, he realised. She would be feeling scorned perhaps and no doubt hurt by his inattention. It was true – he had deliberately avoided her gaze. But he needed to tell her that it was the only way he could keep his eyes, filled with unspoken desires, off her. It took all his willpower not to sneak a foot beneath the table to touch hers; or whisper something only she could hear. All he wanted to do was wrap her in his arms and kiss her all night long – but not tonight. Tonight he had to play the role of King for all the realms on show at the palace.

Gyl felt sickened by the realisation that she had interpreted his activities tonight as a cooling of his desires for her. It was so far from the truth. He would marry her here and now if only he could. There, it was out! Spoken aloud in his mind, it could not be taken back. He wanted Lauryn for his wife. He needed Lauryn . . . her strength, her courage, her love. He suddenly could not care less if his mother approved or disapproved. He thought she would hardly consider it the wisest choice but that would not deter him. He was King after all. He would marry whom he pleased.

How could he put things right? Tomorrow he would find a way. First thing in the morning, he would send a messenger to her chambers requesting a meeting.

14

Sylc the Thief

As the coronation feast and its entertainment drew to a close, Orlac kissed Lauryn's hand and then held her gaze steadily. His strangely violet eyes – an almost impossible colour – said all that he needed to. She felt her throat go dry. The message which he conveyed in this look was unmistakable, even to a maiden.

'Thank you for this evening,' she said. She felt her cheeks burning.

'I feel the pleasure was all mine,' he offered graciously, not yet letting go of the hand he had so recently kissed. She could feel his cool skin against hers. What was happening here? 'In fact I believe I may have been too greedy tonight . . . perhaps I have kept you from the other guests,' he added.

Lauryn could not help it; the truth was she felt immensely flattered. When she had set out to teach Gyl a lesson earlier in the evening, she had had no idea that her flirtations might lead her to where she now found herself. She had to admit, in spite of deliberately provoking it for her own ends, that she had genuinely enjoyed Regent Sylc's dashing company. Everything about him was cultured and sophisticated; any other woman would be falling into his arms. And yet there was something about the intensity of his interest in her; something curious about him she could not quite put her finger on. She felt sure her time spent with him this night had achieved her original goal — she could feel Gyl's wrath and that was satisfying. But now she had the Ciprean all but tumbling her into bed. And what scared her more than anything this night was that his intentions did not shock her. In fact, she would have to show considerable willpower to resist him.

She decided to tell the truth, perhaps naively hoping it would help to work things out. 'Actually, you have been something of a saviour tonight. I don't know many of these people . . . none, in fact. The King — well, he is a friend — but he has been otherwise engaged.'

'I noticed,' he said, betraying no expression.

'Yes . . . well, your company tonight has been extremely welcome and I have enjoyed myself.' She hoped that might bring a gracious close to the evening's proceedings and knew her inexperience with men was now glaring.

Orlac's gaze intensified. In spite of the dozens of people milling around and saying their goodnights, Lauryn felt there was suddenly no one else in the room but the pair of them. It was as though the Regent had pulled her with him into some sort of private cocoon. She felt a sense of breathlessness within the powerful hold he suddenly had over her.

In her distraction, she tried to pinpoint what it was that bothered her about him. Staring into the curiously coloured eyes she was reminded for just an instant of her father. An odd comparison perhaps, but he too had eyes of such intense colour that if you had not looked upon them with your own, you would not have been able to picture their vibrancy nor, she believed, could one expect to see them ever repeated in any other face. Her father's were of a colour to remark upon, and so was the colour of Sylc's — a dark and yet somehow brilliant violet.

And in that moment of wonder she saw something in Sylc she had seen briefly in her own father. It was not merely the colour of the eyes which was similar — it was their vulnerability. There was a sorrow lurking behind those bright eyes, that brilliant smile and the smooth manners. The same sort of hurt she had seen in her father. His grief was over her mother — or so she thought — and she tried to imagine what had caused the same haunted look in Regent Sylc.

She faltered, drew back her hand, and the spell was broken. She was aware of all the people in the hall again, and particularly aware of a pair of royal eyes burning into the back of her head. It was time to make her exit.

'I bid you farewell, Regent.' She made a move to leave.

'Not farewell I hope, Lady Lauryn, just goodnight perhaps.'

She nodded, smiled demurely and departed the hall as fast as she could, relief flooding through her.

In his chambers, as a small fire burned cheerily to warm the cool rooms, Orlac paced. He felt disturbed enough to unleash his powers now and bring this whole castle down around King Gyl of Wytton. The girl had unnerved him. What was it about her which tugged so strongly at him? Juno's insight was keen. How had she phrased it? *Your own idea of perfect* – that's right – and then she had gone on to describe none other than the Lady Lauryn, surely? Her description of *petite, almost fragile looking* fitted perfectly . . . he ticked off all the other points in his head, even the comment about her temper. He had noticed she was quick to fire, especially when she had felt slighted by the King and excused herself. Orlac was now certain Juno had seen a vision of this woman.

It was meant to be, then.

He had not realised he had been airing his thoughts aloud and nearly cursed himself when Dorgryl joined his thoughts as though continuing a conversation.

Well claim her, then.

Orlac scowled. *Throw her over my back and ride off into the night with her – is that what you mean?*

Something like that. His uncle waited. When Orlac offered no further resistance but plonked himself heavily into a chair, he continued. *It's perfect, boy! Think about this. You had in mind razing Tallinor to the ground, when in fact you can be far more subtle and disable the Tallinese King by stealing the object of his desires. I do so enjoy sophisticated intrigue. To humble a proud man by so insightful a move as taking what he most wants is so much more brilliant than just beating him on the field, so to speak.*

What makes you think he'll care a hoot?

Oh, I think he will. I think our King of Tallinor has set his heart on making Lauryn his Queen. I believe he will give chase and we can lead him and his soldiers a merry dance. We can belittle him and humiliate him and if it still pleases, we let you go about systematically destroying the Kingdom behind his back.

He paused, giving Orlac time to think about this.

You mean literally steal her?

Well, I don't believe she'll leave willingly.

I want her.

More than Tallinor?

It was a clever shift. Orlac felt trapped. No, he could not say he wanted her more than the demise of Tallinor, but if he was honest, Tallinor's destruction did not intrigue him as much as this woman.

No. Tallinor can wait. My desires cannot.

Then she shall be yours, nephew. We can take her back to Cipres and you can make her the slave to your every desire, if you so choose.

What of Xantia?

What of Xantia! She is a pawn . . . nothing more. But she is cruel too; she will enjoy the intrigue as much as you.

Orlac's thoughts refocused. *There's something about Lauryn,* the god mused. *Irrespective of how much I desire her, there is another factor I can't pinpoint.*

I think I can, his uncle said, the slyness back in his voice.

Tell me.

The deep chuckle made him feel anger and the Colours within him pulsed.

Steady, boy. I will tell you what I suspect. He laughed again and Orlac hated him. *I'm guessing now because I have no proof other than what I can see through your eyes. You have never seen Alyssa Qyn but let me assure you that the Lady Lauryn you wish for yourself is the spitting image of Gynt's Alyssa.*

You lie!

I have nothing to gain by lying to you on this. It was when you kissed her hand, and looked deep into her eyes. He sensed

Orlac was about to fly into a rage. *Wait! Now listen to me. Lauryn mentioned Flat Meadows. Even you picked that up. I suspect that she could be the daughter of Torkyn Gynt and Alyssa Qyn. I can't confirm it but I know he has children and that they have returned to Tallinor. Lauryn resembles Alyssa too much not to be related.*

My niece! Orlac roared.

Hush . . . let's not wake the palace. I too need convincing. Call for a messenger now. Where is that servant of ours?

Orlac walked to the door and pulled it open. Outside, a man, clearly from the Exotic Isles, wearing the colourful costume of the nomadic tribes, bowed low. 'How may I serve, Regent Sylc?'

'Ah, Titus, fetch a palace page immediately.'

'At once, sir,' Adongo said, bowing low again.

Orlac closed the door and waited.

Where did you find him? Dorgryl asked, thinking of the dark man outside.

He was amongst the palace servants. Juno picked him for me; said he was discreet and obedient. Perfect for this trip.

He looks at us strangely — as though he knows something.

You imagine things, Dorgryl.

There was a soft knock and Orlac admitted a young page, still rubbing the sleep from his eyes. Fortunately he had the presence of mind to bow, despite his fatigue.

'Sir, my name is Ypek, I am a messenger. How can I help you?'

'I wish you to take a message to the Lady Lauryn's rooms.'

'Yes, sir. Shall I wait outside whilst you write it?'

'No, that won't be necessary.'

Orlac moved to a very beautiful carved desk and picked

up a quill. He dipped it into the inkpot and appeared to scrawl something on a parchment. Then he looked up, a puzzled expression on his face.

'The Lady Lauryn . . . what is her family name? I wish to address her correctly.'

The lad was caught unexpectedly and found himself halfway through a yawn when the Ciprean made this query. He quickly composed himself. 'Her family name is Gynt, sir.'

'Ah good, as I thought,' Orlac said, amazed at how angry he suddenly felt.

And rising on the crest of that anger was a red mist which overtook Orlac without warning. Suddenly it was Dorgryl's voice which spoke.

'Come here, boy.'

Ypek obediently walked over to the Regent and felt the cold, hard blade puncture his throat. He died without even the chance to cry out his surprise.

Dorgryl disappeared and Orlac was left panting and breathless from the sensation but also from his own rage.

Wrap him in the rug before his blood stains the room, Dorgryl commanded.

In a silent fury, Orlac bent and rolled the corpse as instructed. Then he stood and breathed deeply before speaking. *If you ever do that again, Dorgryl, I will end my life. I will not give you this warning again. You will be forced to live within a mortal's body for eternity — I'm sure that would only marginally improve on life in the Bleak. Hear my words, and heed them.*

Now Dorgryl sounded sulky. *Well, you wouldn't have done it, and the messenger would have become a liability.*

What does it matter? I don't care how many come after us.

They can die at one push of my mind. Don't interfere again.

Orlac opened the door. Once again Adongo bowed as his orders were given. 'I want three horses saddled. We leave immediately.'

Adongo showed nothing on his face. 'Your belongings, sir . . . . the rest of our staff – should I stir them?'

'No, I wish to leave immediately. Our stuff can be brought with the rest of our people who can leave tomorrow. I will meet you in the bailey.'

'May I ask about the need for a third horse?'

'No, you may not – go about your business.'

'At once, sir.'

Lauryn heard the tap at her door. She felt relieved. At last. Gyl had come and they could straighten out their gripes. She knew once he kissed her she would forgive everything and surely he could not hold a grudge when he discovered it was only his love she sought. She pulled on a silken robe, smiling that her night attire was rather sheer, which Gyl would find more than just amusing. Lauryn opened the door a crack and was shocked to see Sylc standing by it.

'Regent! It is late . . . you cannot visit me now.'

'I must talk with you. Please.'

Orlac was still burning with the anger of Dorgryl's recent killing of the lad and the discovery of who this woman was – it made little difference to his need, of course, he still wanted her . . . and he was suddenly in no mood to be resisted.

'No sir, I cannot permit you to enter my room at this hour. What would people think?'

She looked deliciously tousled from her bed but clearly

she had not slept . . . perhaps had even been hoping for a late-night visitor and with regret Orlac realised it was not he she had hoped might come calling. He melted through the door and appeared behind her. She noticed him disappear from her limited gaze through the crack in the door and opened it further to see where he could have got to.

'Lauryn,' he called.

She swung around in shock, slamming the door closed in her movement. 'How . . . how in the Light did you do that?' Her face was pale and scared now.

'Things are not always as they seem,' he said, sagely. 'I have come for you.'

'Come for me? What are you talking about? . . . How did you get into my room?'

'Magic,' he said, and used a spike of it now, directed towards her.

She collapsed and he caught her before she hit the floor unconscious. He smiled as he threw her over his shoulder, recalling his conversation with Dorgryl, who was mercifully silent throughout these proceedings. And then he flung open her wardrobe and grabbed a few items, including a stout pair of boots, which he tossed into a cloth bag and also shouldered.

He pushed with his Colours and Lauryn, still slung, a dead weight, became invisible. Orlac left her room and made his way from the southern tower towards the bailey. He encountered only two guards during this journey as the palace slept, and claimed to their expected enquiry that he was peckish. The guards said he'd always find something simmering in the pot in Cook's kitchen. He thanked them and moved swiftly on, trying not to give the appearance of being burdened.

Outside, Adongo waited with three horses.

'Take this bag and tie it onto one,' Orlac said, slinging Lauryn's bag towards his man.

Adongo deftly caught it. He could feel the thrum of magic but could not work out what was going on. He could also feel Lauryn's presence close. Was she in trouble? He did not want to leave her but he had no idea what his master had in mind tonight, and the nagging feeling that Lauryn was somehow with him would not leave. He spent the next few moments trying to absorb his sense of her being nearby. How could this be? She was sleeping in her chambers. But he could not linger. Adongo made the decision that for the purposes of his disguise he must go along with his master's wishes for now. If he found they were travelling too far from Lauryn this night, he would contrive a way to make his escape and get back to her.

She did not know him yet – had not even made eye contact, but he was now bonded to her and would not leave her side if he could help it.

With Juno's help he had manipulated himself into the service of Orlac. It was unnerving to be in his presence again but Juno had warned him of this and he had taken care not to show anything in his face. She, fortunately, had come back in a youthful form and thus unrecognisable to Orlac, but Adongo had returned with the same appearance and so with Juno's assistance they had set about changing it.

His long hair had been shaved. Now his darkish skin was oiled, his head shiny. And he had grown a moustache and beard, both kept trimmed short, but the transformation was so dramatic that even he could not recognise himself. It was no Moruk chieftain staring back at him from the glass. Juno had giggled, warning that they could not use magic around Orlac; he would sense it in an instant. This would do. He would never recognise the Fifth of the Paladin.

And Orlac had not. Nor had Dorgryl, who was infinitely more suspicious. Adongo had passed the test and been accepted as Titus, who was now climbing onto the back of his horse. He had not seen Orlac throw an invisible burden across the back of the third horse, but he did think it strange that his master insisted on attaching the reins of the spare horse to his own, rather than his servant's.

At the guardhouse, Orlac turned on the charm. 'Can't sleep. I've got my man with me . . . thought we'd go into Tal and see what action is afoot.' He winked.

'Is that why you need the third horse?' the guard said, smiling.

'Well, you never know your luck,' Orlac played along, flashing a grin. 'Actually, I thought if I picked up some gifts for the ladies of the court of Cipres at your famous night markets, I might need help carrying them back to the palace.'

'It won't be enough. Women always want more, sir,' the guard replied, shaking his head. 'Enjoy yourself.'

'We will,' Orlac said over his shoulder as he cast one last glance towards the palace. 'Sleep tight, King Gyl,' he offered silently. 'I shall enjoy taunting you before I erase your Kingdom from this world.'

It was later – at dawn – several hours' ride from the capital and deep into the countryside of Tallinor's northwest, that

Orlac cast aside the invisibility glamour and revealed the body of Lauryn slumped across the third horse.

Adongo's sound of despair escaped him before he could prevent it.

Orlac seemed unperturbed, gracefully dismounting and then coming around his horse to lock stares with the man from the Exotic Isles.

'I'm afraid I shall have to kill you, Titus, now that you know my secret.'

Adongo knelt. He had to react swiftly now and somehow keep Lauryn safe. Finally he understood the strange sensation that she was near he had carried with him all these hours.

'My lord, you are the one!' he cried.

'What?' asked Orlac, faintly amused.

'I saw you in a dream. I watched you descend from the heavens and alight in this world. I was told I was to be your servant . . . that I must follow you.'

Orlac felt himself chill at the man's words. 'Who told you this?'

Adongo had to be very careful now. 'I did not see who spoke. But I saw you. That's why I came to Cipres to find you, my lord. I had no choice. We Moruks are spiritual people and my destiny was shaped. I had to find you and be your servant. I have been waiting for a sign of your powers. And now you have revealed them, I am in awe of you. You do not have to kill me. I am already enslaved to you and will do your bidding obediently.'

I told you he watched us knowingly. He could be useful, Dorgryl whispered.

I thought you didn't appreciate witnesses.

Well, when she wakes up, there's going to be a lot of

commotion, I can assure you. He can help. Let him win her trust and then through him we can make her cooperate . . . as far as Cipres anyway. He can even promise to help her escape but all the while have our ear.

You never fail to surprise me, Dorgryl.

I have my uses, the elder god said.

'Stand,' Orlac commanded.

Adongo felt the relief loosen his tensed body. Orlac had accepted him. He arranged his expression to one of awe and supplication. Now he must protect Lauryn as best he could. It would not be easy for her. It did not take much to conclude that she now faced an emotional and probably physical challenge which she must survive. He must guide her through both challenges and help her heal both types of scar until the true One came for her.

As he humbly stood to meet the violet gaze of the god, he took a risk and cast out strongly towards the Heartwood . . . where Torkyn Gynt would hear his plea for help. He prayed the Heartwood, with its special magics, might somehow cloak his message.

Dorgryl shimmered. *What was that!*

I sensed it but could not make out the content, Orlac admitted. He addressed his manservant. *You are sentient?*

I am, oh great one. I cast out my thanks to the gods who watch over me and brought me to you. He knew it meant certain death if Orlac did not accept his story.

'Never do that again or I will kill you.'

Adongo bowed, covering his smile. *No, we will kill you, Orlac,* he thought. 'Humblest of apologies, my lord.'

They heard Lauryn groan loudly as she sat up, terrified. Her terror snapped to anger as her memory brought back what had happened.

'You'll not get away with this, Sylc.'

Orlac laughed. 'I already have.'

'The King will follow . . . and he will kill you.'

'Well . . . he may try.'

She dropped from her horse to her feet, feeling the tempting surge of Colours but pushing them back. Her father had once advised her not to strike out with her powers until she knew exactly what she was dealing with. She took his advice now. She would bide her time and for now would allow her anger to do the talking.

'Whatever it is that you want, I'll not give it. Not ever. You might as well kill me now.'

King Gyl had just received the grave news that the Lady Lauryn was not answering her door because she was no longer in her room. Nor was Regent Sylc . . . but they had found the body of the messenger, Ypek, his throat slashed, his corpse rolled in a carpet on the floor of Sylc's room.

'Search the grounds! And bring me the guard who allowed Regent Sylc to depart the palace during the night.'

Gyl felt his own throat close. The first official day of his reign was destined to be a bad one.

And so it was.

15

Goth's Blade

Goth was feeling inspired. Being back on Tallinese soil
with a dozen or more armed men behind him gave a sense
of the old days when he had led raids into villages and
struck the fear of torture and reprisals into the sentient
ones. It was different now, of course, but he felt the old
thrill of the chase and it rejuvenated him as no drug could.

He could almost smell Sarel and her bitch maid. With
Garth's information it had not taken long to establish that
a ship called *The Raven* had left the Ciprean harbour under
cloak of night on the same evening the royal and her servant
had fled the palace. He presumed that as they were on foot
they carried very little in the way of belongings. He also
assumed they were well-pursed for their journey.

Goth dug back into his mind and it did not let him
down. He recalled that Quist had married a whore; made
her a brothel owner. She was young – originally from
Hatten – and had turned the tavern and its brothel into
the most successful operation of its kind in the northern
region of the Kingdom. Quist was regarded by the
Caradoons – and it seemed the Cipreans were of the same

opinion – as an honourable pirate, if there could be such a thing. It was Quist's much admired brother-by-marriage who had risked the Kiss of the Silver Maiden. How the wheels turn, Goth thought. As he brought more and more of the Quist story together in his mind and paths began to cross, Torkyn Gynt came sharply into focus for him. Gynt and Quist knew each other, or certainly *of* each other. He knew this because it was Gynt who had saved Locklyn Gylbyt from certain death when *The Wasp* sank.

What was the connection here? What was he missing?

Quist had offered the runaway Queen safe passage into Tallinor . . . why? Money might encourage a less well-heeled captain to risk the dangers of pulling out into the famously turbulent and unpredictable waters off the Ciprean mainland at night. He accepted this . . . money talked. But Goth's mind was always one to look beyond the neat answer; the obvious, the most sensible option. Quist was already wealthy. He need not involve himself in such a risky adventure.

What if Quist had not helped Sarel for money? What could his other motives be?

As one of the soldiers handed him the reins of his new horse and they prepared to ride from the harbour into Caradoon proper, he began to ask himself what might encourage a wealthy man to take such unnecessary risk. There was but a single scenario that his clever mind would permit, but it was such a foreign notion that he dismissed it at first. Could loyalty really be the reason? Was a pirate loyal to anything or anyone but himself and his potential booty? And to whom was Quist loyal . . . Sarel? Surely not. The maid? Highly unlikely. Which left only Queen Sylven. Why would Quist feel an obligation to protect Sylven's child? He was not even Ciprean.

Goth could not make the connection and although his mind swerved close, it never would hit on the real reason – which was that Quist was loyal to his wife, Eryn. And that dedication had begun a series of complex, seemingly unrelated events which had eventually led to Hela's explaining everything to the pirate, because she trusted Gynt – and so did Quist, because Eryn did. That was enough to oblige the pirate to help this young woman who pursued Torkyn Gynt and safety.

It mattered little to the former chief inquisitor that he could not find a satisfying answer. For Goth it was simply entertainment . . . something to puzzle at to while away the days of the sea crossing. In truth, all he wanted now was Quist's head rolling in the dirt, and perhaps a clue as to where Sarel might be and who her protectors were in Tallinor. He would not let his new master down; perish the thought of what might occur if he did.

Goth had deliberately plied his companions with liquor, ensuring they were certainly intoxicated, if not drunk, by the time of their arrival at the Caradoon docks. His aim was to ensure their inhibitions would be relaxed; that they might be rougher, less tolerant of reason. He had also craftily steered the conversation during the last hours of the voyage towards scarlet women. The combination of liquor and visions of brothels had achieved the right level of belligerence and aggression together with sexual need. At his encouragement, and with the promise of a hefty pay increase to each soldier, his men fell upon Madame Eryna's tavern, rousing a predominantly sleeping brothel in the very early hours before dawn. It must have been a quiet night's business, for only a few men had stayed the night and their token resistance was quickly beaten back. Eryna's paid bodyguards put up a much better fight, killing three Cipreans and wounding four, but her protectors, seriously outnumbered, soon felt the end of a blade.

Goth allowed the men to have their way. He had told them these were wicked women of Caradoon; outcasts of Tallinese society and of no consequence. The shrieks of the girls pleased Goth no end. He went in search of Sarel, Hela or Quist. He found none of the trio he sought but he did find Quist's woman.

'She's mine,' he warned, licking his rubbery lips, giving the impression of lustful intentions, which was so far from the truth he found it amusing.

All he wanted from this woman was information. He had her gagged, bound and thrown into a storecupboard whilst the Ciprean soldiers did whatever they chose to do with the whores. Much later, in the diffused light of near-dawn, the same men gathered outside the brothel. They were chagrined; many a little disgusted by their own behaviour as the effects of liquor wore off their clouded minds. Nevertheless, Goth, always eloquent, managed to fire up their sense of duty once again and through the haze of their shame, their headaches and fatigue, he reminded them of what they had come here to do and why. His effeminate voice carried through the bracing morning air, explaining that it was every man's duty to rescue his Queen from the Tallinese and prevent her from being thrown into the clutches of the murderous Torkyn Gynt.

He ordered the girls out, and a now-motley group of formerly lovely young women were ushered to stand in front of him, holding their arms around themselves against

the chill. The bruises and cuts they had sustained trying
to fight off the men were now starkly visible in the lightening day; their nightgowns ripped and tattered. Some
of the women wept, others swore at Goth. Many of the
soldiers studied their boots, probably thinking of their
own women back in Cipres . . . even of their own daughters; perhaps eventually justifying their behaviour with
the self-serving notion that the violated women were
whores anyway and so it mattered little.

'Bring out Madame Eryna,' Goth said, loving the sound
of his voice issuing orders again.

They waited as one of the men disappeared into the
brothel, the silence broken only by a few coughs, a groan
or two from girls hurting. It was still too early for many of
the Caradoons to be up and about but a couple of passers-
by stopped, shocked by what they saw. The silence lengthened, interrupted momentarily by the sudden intense shriek
of a small flock of wrens which had been disturbed.

The noise was ominous in the quiet which was then
shattered by the voice of Madame Eryna cursing her captor
in such a vicious manner it brought a genuine shadow of
a smile to Goth's wretched face. He was going to enjoy
this one – there was nothing quite like feistiness to
heighten his enjoyment of a woman's pain.

The girls began to wail as they saw their madam, largely
untouched, thrown to the ground before Goth's feet.

Eryn scrambled to her bare feet, ripping her soft nightgown as she did so but not caring. She spat the dust from
her mouth, ensuring what issued landed neatly on Goth's
boots. No one missed that proud message and somehow
everyone gathered there, including herself, understood she
would pay heavily for such defiance. She held her head

high, eyes blazing as she stared into the warped and ugly face before her.

Goth did not want this woman to steal his show and well understood the seductive power that courage could generate, so he decided to take the lead and allow no further time for his men to find some grudging respect for the prostitute's pride.

'Where is your husband, whore?'

Incredibly, and so unexpectedly, she smiled. Eryn wiped the back of her hand across her face to remove more of the dust. 'I remember you. They call you the Leper, don't they?' she said, ensuring her voice carried.

Goth kept his calm. 'People call me many things.'

'How about the cockless butcher? Have you heard that one? I certainly heard you were no longer a man where it counted. I'm amazed you'd set foot in a brothel. There's nothing for you here, Leper – my girls like whole men . . . real men.'

He felt his anger rise but did not allow it to show on his face, though he could have cursed the tic near his eye which seemed to have intensified.

She laughed now when she saw his affliction. 'Ah, wait . . . I remember another one. Twitching Fu—' Eryn did not finish.

Goth's blow was so fast, so hard, she heard ringing in her ears, and her eyes were suddenly stinging from fresh tears she could hardly feel running down her cheek. She knew instantly serious damage had been done, having felt the sharp pain of fragile bones breaking.

'Stand!' her tormentor shrieked.

Eryn could hear the soft weeping of her girls and she hated these people being able to do this to her. She stood, with a little more difficulty this time, but she refused to give him the satisfaction of showing him how much her face suddenly throbbed.

'Where is your husband?'

'I don't know,' she answered through her pain.

'Oh, I think you do,' Goth responded sweetly this time. 'You might as well tell me and make it easier on yourself and all these once-pretty girls here.'

Eryn looked around; the rays of sunrise, now sharp, highlighted a grim scene. For the first time since being brought outside she noticed the state of ruin her girls were in. Some of them were so battered it would be weeks before they could look after a client again. She tried not to think that far ahead. Concentrate on now, on survival, she told herself. She did remember this man. His name was Goth, which had formerly been a name to strike fear into the sentients of Tallinor, but that was history. She felt sure he had died in the King's prison; but obviously not – for here he was asking her about Janus. Eryn realised now as she gazed around that she was surrounded by Cipreans – the distinctive billowing shirts of the guards; their neatly trimmed beards and moustaches; those swarthy complexions. These were men from the Exotic Isles. So they had come for their Queen. Chasing her down to kill her?

Janus had arrived a day or two earlier and stunned her by bringing home more than his usual booty from the voyage. Two gorgeous women – one young enough to make Locky's heart beat at least three times as fast as it should. Naturally Eryn had taken the women in, but Hela had assured them that she and the Queen would not be safe until they could get to the Great Forest. Eryn had heard the full story of their flight from Cipres from the lips of Sarel's maid and could hardly believe the tale. She liked Hela; recognised a lot of herself in the plucky woman who had sworn to keep the young Queen safe.

Eryn had questioned the older woman as to why they needed to go to the Forest – there was nothing there. Surely they were safer here?

Hela had seemed surprisingly sure when she said: 'Because Torkyn Gynt will protect us.'

At the mention of her lover's name, Eryn's breath had caught in her throat. More careful questions revealed Tor was familiar with both Ciprean women yet not intimate with either. She permitted herself to feel a sense of relief at learning this, though she hated the envy she felt for the olive-skinned exotic beauties who sat across from her. She jealously wondered, just fleetingly, how Tor could resist them . . . her information was that he had bedded virtually every beauty in Tallinor. And then Hela began to relate an extraordinary tale of the former queen's death and Tor's supposed involvement. Hela assured Eryn it was not true and that, in fact, the Queen had been in love with Tor, had hoped to make a special life with him as her consort. Eryn bit back again at the resentment she felt that Tor was loved and desired by so many, including herself. The tale grew more preposterous as Hela spoke of a dreamspeaker; a woman who had told her to flee with Sarel; to find their way to Tor who would protect them from certain death at the hands of a usurper called Orlac. A dozen objections fell from Eryn's mouth at once and yet Hela was resolute. They would go to Tor.

'But how will you find him? We have no idea where he is now,' she had responded, frustrated by the determined set of Hela's face.

'I know where to go,' Locky had piped up. 'I was with Tor and Saxon the last time they headed to the Forest, remember?'

She did remember.

Quist had taken her hand and squeezed it. 'Let the boy take them,' he had said in the unruffled, unfailingly gentle way he had with her.

'Alone?'

Quist had nodded.

'No, I will not permit it, Janus. Locky is a boy.'

She had seen her brother bristle visibly at this and she regretted her choice of words, but she had been worried. This was madness. A Queen from foreign lands on the run in Tallinor, apparently being pursued by some enchanted person who made buildings fall down and people bleed. Ridiculous! More importantly, Locky was swooning over the young Queen and the journey was fraught with dangers because of this.

'You believe all this magical stuff?' she had asked her husband, a tone of exasperation creeping into her voice.

'I keep an open mind, my love,' he had said gently. 'I have seen many strange things in my lifetime and I have learned not to disregard something because it sounds unreasonable or unfathomable.'

Janus had sensed Eryn's famous temper smouldering. He had kissed her hand, which he held in his big, scarred pirate's hands. 'We must help these people, my love. This child's mother was murdered. She was a queen. And now this young woman is the ruling monarch of Cipres. It is our duty to help her whilst others usurp her throne.'

She had known her husband was right. He was usually right about everything. And she had finally nodded.

'Of course we will, but Locky cannot go alone. You must go with him.' And she had eyed him, a dangerous glitter coming into that look Janus Quist knew well. She would not be contradicted nor beaten on this. She had made her compromise to his wishes. Now he must meet her halfway.

'If you can manage a little longer on your own, my dear, then I will gladly escort Queen Sarel and the lady, Hela, to Gynt.'

And so it had happened that the four had left the following daybreak on horseback, Goth and his men hot on their heels, behind by just a day.

Goth's sharp voice brought her out of her recollections.

'I don't wish to have to injure my hands by beating it out of you.'

'I'm sure you don't,' Eryn countered. 'Just get one of your cowardly soldiers to do it for you. I see Cipreans take pleasure in beating women.'

The soldiers did not like this and responded with angry mutters and indignant expressions. Serve them right, she thought. She would offer no information. Beating or not, she would not give up Janus or Locky. These men might look threatening, but it was not as though they would kill her for her silence, surely. If they roughed her up, so be it. She would be strong. She had been strong all her life and she would draw on that strength now if they wanted to hurt her.

The man in black, the Leper, sighed a little theatrically. 'So you will not make this easy for yourself?'

She said nothing, just raised her chin a bit higher. 'Go fuck yourself, Goth,' she cursed, using the sneer she had seen many a sailor use during brawls outside Madame Vylet's in the old days.

He smiled crookedly, but it was more of a smirk. 'Strip and bind her!' he commanded, turning his back on Eryn.

Soldiers, albeit unhappily, leapt to his command and did as instructed, and as they did so, Goth addressed his audience. The sun had risen now and more curious Caradoons had gathered. The Quist family was popular. What could possibly be happening here? Some of the brothel girls – the younger ones – had begun to weep noisily. The elder ones tried to hug and console them but they too were feeling the first real chill of fear for the mistress they knew as Eryna. So far things had only been rough – most of them were sore and used, but that would heal. They feared for their madam. She was a good woman, a generous one, and, they realised now, a brave one. Somehow they sensed that the moment of 'rough' had passed. This man would see to it that the situation spiralled into ugly – dangerous, even. Quist had returned a day or so ago and lovely Locky was back to tease them. A couple of new girls had accompanied them; beautiful, but quiet and wary. They did not speak much to the others and had left almost as quickly as they had arrived. No one had thought much more about them.

What did these men, clearly Ciprean, want with Eryna's husband? Perhaps his pirating had become greedy? Unlikely. They all knew the reputation of Quist was about as high as a man could enjoy in this part of the Kingdom.

The effeminate-sounding man in black held their rapt attention now. He was explaining that he sought the pirate, Quist, for his part in the capture and theft of the new Ciprean Queen, a young woman called Sarel. She was accompanied by a slightly older woman – her maid – named Hela. They all knew he was describing the same women who had been amongst them a day or so ago.

'Who wants to add anything to this story?' he sneered at the women gathered before him.

It was Eryn who shouted back. 'Why would my husband steal this girl you speak of?'

Goth did not look at her, he continued to address the other women – he did so love playing to a crowd. 'I'd like to ask him that question myself. Why would he steal our Queen?'

'She's not your Queen, Goth. You are Tallinese. A murdering, cowardly, cringing, unfaithful dog who deserves nothing from us . . . not even the spit from my mouth which I've already wasted on you.'

Still he did not face her, but imagined the sharp chill of the early morning biting into bare flesh. Eryn was trembling – a combination of cold and anger. She thought of Tor, saw him putting his long, strong arms around both those women and hugging them close – how safe they would feel. She wished she too could feel those arms around her now. Then she thought of her kind and affectionate husband who, she knew, worshipped the very ground she walked upon, and she thought of Locky, the bright boy with the bright future if only he was not in such a headlong rush to get himself killed. And finally she thought of Petyr, her favourite brother, whose life had been cut short because of the attentions of another man like Goth. A man who liked to bully and take out his insecurities and brutal inclinations on powerless people . . . on innocents. As a little girl she had held her new baby brother, Petyr, and loved him at first sight. She had also held his wasted dead body in her arms and that would always be her memory of the brother she had adored.

Something snapped within her as she watched the former
chief inquisitor, now some sort of inquisitor for the
Cipreans, strutting about like a peacock – except this was
a black-garbed one . . . more like a crow. He was sinister
and dark and devious. He brought death.

She would not kowtow to him. She would not reveal
anything about the whereabouts of Janus or Locky or the
women they protected. She would do this for all of them
if it took her life. And if it did, she hoped Torkyn Gynt
– the only man she had ever loved for nothing more than
the man he was – would seek retribution on this death-
monger.

'Do what you will, Leper. Neither my girls nor I have
anything to tell you,' she snarled and felt strengthened
by her own courage.

'Hang her from that tree,' he ordered, pointing to the
one he wanted. 'By her feet.'

Eryn felt all the blood rush to her head. She was disoriented; no longer embarrassed now over her nakedness but
more concerned with the amount of pain the Leper would
inflict. Humiliation was beyond her. Nothing now would
force her to give him the information he sought.

Eryn felt the sun's warmth kiss her bare flesh as the
first hint of summer began to touch this northern land.

On that last wonderful night of carefree affection and
friendship with Tor, he had told her how he had taught
Alyssa not to be afraid – how to escape from her fear and
allow her mind to detach and rush to a safe place she
called The Green. Eryn had not really understood this at
the time but she grasped its meaning now. The menace
of impending pain gave her an insight into what Tor had
meant when he talked about being able to separate the

mind from fear or hurt. She needed to do that now. Eryn did not know how, but she understood that she must remove her spirit from this frightening event and then not matter what the Leper did to her, she could survive it. Perhaps he meant to whip her? Scald her, even . . . she had heard of such torture to extract information.

Feeling dizzy now, she tried to picture something which might carry her away from this, allow her the escape she needed to survive the torment. And in a way she was relieved that it was Quist's face which came to mind rather than Tor's. Tor did not belong to her; she loved him but he would never love her in the way she wanted him to. His heart was spoken for. So, with great fondness, she pictured her pirate's scarred, ugly face and heard that special gentle voice he reserved for her alone. When Janus grinned, his mirth touched his one good eye and made it sparkle. She imagined him smiling at her now.

The Leper was talking and she ignored his presence. She could not hear him very well either because she was making herself listen to Janus and his affectionate words. He was telling her that he was going to take her away for a while, leave the north and sail to some beautiful islands he knew lying west of the mainland, where the purest white sand felt like silk beneath your bare feet and the waters were warm and so clear the fish were visible. A place where oysters gave up their remarkable fat, creamy pearls and he would have them strung and placed about her neck.

Eryn could now hear the lapping of the ocean and the call of sea birds overhead . . . and all the while the soft voice of Janus Quist whispered sweetly to his wife.

The glint of a blade entered her consciousness but she clung to her vision, managed to keep it as real as she could. Ah, so he intended to cut her. An unoriginal torture but so be it. He would slash at her flesh but he would make no impact on her mind because Eryn was swimming with dolphins now and Janus was laughing in the distance as she held their fins and raced through the crystal waters with her friends.

The vision faltered as she heard Goth: '. . . enemies of Cipres must die.'

Did she hear correctly? Did he mean to kill her then? How odd, she had not really considered death as a possibility. She had only accepted torture. It seemed the Leper no longer needed her information; he had been insulted by her – 'a base-born whore' – she could hear him saying.

So she must die in order to give Locky a life and to protect Janus and his royal charge. She knew deep down the Leper would probably have never permitted her life even if she had given up the details he demanded. She sighed with the realisation that it was death now beckoning her so much earlier than she had anticipated.

Janus whispered in her mind. *They call to you, my love*, he said, pointing towards more dolphins. *They want you to ride the waves with them and be for ever safe amongst them.*

If Eryn felt the deep death-slash Goth made across her taut belly, she did not show her shock, but her body did, instantly spilling its slippery contents. She was not aware that Goth had decided to help this process, relishing the opportunity to empty the cavity of all that he could grasp within it.

Soldiers turned away, vomiting. Girls no longer screamed but fell to the dust, pale and unconscious from their own shock. Others held each other and turned away, refusing to give the Leper the awed audience he so desperately wanted.

Goth finished his grisly work, enjoying the steaming wet feel of his fingers and the death they had wrought. He looked up towards the skies at the circling black crows who might later feast at this scene. He smiled at the thought and realised it must have been their arrival which scared the small flock of wrens which had scattered earlier.

This execution was one of his more inspired moves; he had always wanted to kill someone in this manner and had often wondered how long it would take the body – following the shock of being emptied and exposed like this – to die. He estimated that Quist's attractive wife, who tragically had not given the satisfaction of so much as a groan, had but moments left.

Eryn began to feel drowsy.

Janus whispered that she should rest with her friends and she smiled at him. The dolphins took her deeper now; she could feel the seaweed touching her face, ropey and almost warm to the touch.

It's true she was tired. *I didn't tell him, Janus*, she whispered back to her husband's dimming face as the depths of death claimed her.

Eryn's death was mercifully fast on that shiny morning and her friends would later comment that they could almost glimpse a smile on her pretty face. It was a slightly crooked smile, distorted because her face had been so badly broken on that side.

Goth did not have to inflict much damage on one of the youngest girls whom he noticed had suffered some sort of nervous episode following the slaughter of the madam. It turned out she was not one of the prostitutes but a simple serving-girl, who helped out each morning with breakfast and cleaning up the tavern from the previous night's carousing. His sharp eyes had picked her out as the one most likely to spill any potential information, and he was right.

The moment he turned his attention onto her the girl began to shake violently.

'I wish to speak with you,' he said, pointing towards the stricken girl. 'The rest of you men provision yourselves from whatever you can find inside the tavern, then be mounted. We ride shortly.'

Goth motioned to the most senior soldier who approached. 'Leave two men here to guard Quist's wife's body. It is to remain hanging as it is now and to be fully enjoyed by the carrion birds.' He watched the man grimace. 'Have that girl brought over to her mistress.'

She was dragged screaming to cower near Eryn's corpse which was already beginning to attract the attention of flies.

'Shut up!' Goth commanded.

She did from dread but could not stop her terrified whimper.

'If you prefer not to be strung up next to the whore here, you will tell me everything I wish to know. Is that clear?'

She nodded. Her stifled sobs began to excite Goth.

'Were the women we spoke of here?'

The girl nodded but could not look at her captor.

'Good. You see how easy this is?' He continued. 'When did they leave?'

She whispered something and Goth decided he needed to soften her up. She was certainly cooperating but she was too slow. His boot landed viciously in her abdomen and he felt ribs splinter. Good, that should win her prompt attention. The girl collapsed to the dust, landing in the twisted ropes of Eryn's bowel and vomited both from the realisation of what she sat amongst and the pain searing through her body. Vomiting made it hurt more but her small body retched all the same from the dizzying trauma and the smell of Eryn ripening in the sun's warmth.

'Speak up and fast, girl, or you die amongst your mistress's guts,' Goth warned.

Through her gasps she answered him. 'Yesterday. They left at dawn.'

'Who with?'

'Locky and Mr Quist, sir.'

Ah, Goth thought, so Quist continues to offer protection whilst the brother-by-marriage trails alongside. This was interesting.

'Where were they headed?'

'I don't know, sir,' she whimpered, pulling herself away from the slippery mass she kneeled on.

Then she remembered something she had overheard whilst serving food to the guests. She hoped this item might save her life. 'Oh wait . . . I did hear them talking about the Great Forest. It was brief, sir. I serve food. It was all I heard in passing.' Pain overtook her and she could say no more.

Goth was no longer interested in her and stepped away, grimacing at the mess she had made of herself. So they had made tracks for the Great Forest. Why? Who was there to look after them? He pondered this as he rinsed his hands of Eryn in a nearby trough. The only time he had ever had reason to venture into the Great Forest was in his relentless searching for Torkyn Gynt and Alyssa Qyn all those years ago.

The realisation hit him hard.

Gynt? That was it! They were travelling to be with Torkyn Gynt.

This was too good, he thought to himself as he mounted his horse. He would kill them all.

The men looked towards their strange and detestable leader.

'We ride south. To the Great Forest,' he instructed.

16

Gathering at the Heartwood

Tor had not liked sending Cloot away from him again and the falcon had said little in response to his idea, which meant the bird had liked the idea even less. However, he had accepted Tor's quiet reasoning that they needed to know what might be happening up north. If Orlac was approaching from Cipres, then Caradoon was his logical point of arrival.

Just take a look around and fly straight back, Tor had said. *You'll be gone a couple of days. I'll be another two days getting to the Great Forest. I shall wait for you in the Heartwood.*

Cloot had lifted strongly from his shoulder that same night and flown high so quickly that Tor could not even make him out and heard only the one piercing call his friend gave as farewell.

Tor had felt very alone as darkness enveloped him. As long as Cloot had been with him, he had been able to lock away his heartache at leaving Alyssa. Without his friend's reassuring company and ever-wise voice in this head, thoughts of her came crashing back to remind him of what he had given up, once again. Visions of her lying naked in Lorys's arms crowded his bleak thoughts as he trudged closer to the Forest and sanctuary. He did not feel like stopping to rest or eat. He would walk on through the night.

He hoped his two children were safe in Tal; getting to know their mother and familiarising themselves with the ways of the Tallinese. If they were ever to fit into this new life of theirs, this would be a good proving time. Little did he know one was presently sleeping not far from the roadside having galloped across the realm towards a village called Brittelbury, whilst the other was slung across a horse headed north with two gods and her secret Paladin. If he had known, Tor would not have tried to cheer himself with a bright whistle as he walked.

Alyssa and Saxon had stopped for the night, sharing whatever meagre supplies the Kloek had thought to toss into their saddlebags before their hasty departure.

Alyssa was not fond of pears. She had preferred not to eat them ever since that day near Caremboche when she had stolen three of the fruit from an orchard. Not long afterwards she had witnessed Saxon's eyeless, bloodied face calling to her. Just the smell of pears could bring that hideous scene back to her of Kythay charging about the courtyard laying waste to several screaming men, or she would see those two beautiful Fox boys, Milt and Oris, looking at her lovingly and with awe as she attempted to perform the trick called Flight. She had succeeded and they had died saving her life.

She looked away from the pear that Saxon insisted she take.

'You must eat,' he said.

'Have you anything else in that bag?' she asked hopefully.

'I stole two muffins from Cook but was planning to eat those myself later,' he said, eyes glinting wickedly in the glow of their small fire.

'Oh, you wretch, Saxon. Give me one!'

He laughed and handed the small cake to her. She made noises of great satisfaction as she bit into it.

'It's good to see you like this,' he said, eyeing her carefully, not wishing to make too much of it.

'It's great to feel this carefree,' Alyssa admitted. 'Although I shouldn't . . . what with a murderous god on the rampage for us!' She grinned. 'I feel alive again, Sax.'

'Is it him?' He knew he did not have to speak the name Torkyn Gynt.

She nodded. Nibbled more of her cake. 'Partly.' Then she looked up at her friend. She began to vocally tick off what was making her feel so good. 'I like no longer being Queen, to tell the truth. I love the knowledge that I have children. I agree with you – Gyl will make a fine King of Tallinor, given the right support. I'm in wonderment that I am chasing Torkyn Gynt down and that I find myself here with my closest of friends, an ageing Kloek,' she grinned at the face he pulled, 'and I accept that our only way to find freedom from our burden is to face Orlac and not hide from him.'

'Oh, is that all?' he teased.

Alyssa threw the pear at his chest. He caught it deftly and bit into it. The smell of the juice sickened her. She spoke to avoid the nausea and to keep that scene from returning to her head.

'I do feel unbearably happy when perhaps I least should. I'm embarrassed.'

'Don't be. No one around this fire will make judgements on you.'

'Oh no . . . not even if I tell you Tor kissed me?'

Saxon stopped chewing on the fruit. 'Be careful, Alyssa. We all love him, but you have the most to lose in loving him.'

'I know,' she said, dipping her eyes and regretting immediately that she had shared this information.

'You deserve to be together, you two. But I'm fearful of all that we're yet to face before any of us can feel safe.'

'I know,' she said, again, shaping her bag into a pillow and settling down to sleep. She yawned. 'If we ride all day tomorrow, will we catch up with him?'

'I believe so.'

'Good,' she replied, her eyes closed and voice already sounding far away. 'Because I can't wait to throw my arms around him.'

She opened an eye just briefly to enjoy the scowl which crossed her Paladin's face.

It was just a few hours after Cloot had left him that Tor felt the cold slice of the Link rip open suddenly in his head and heard the alarmed voice of Adongo flood his mind with a call for help. It was brief . . . too brief. *Orlac has Lauryn. We head north.*

The Link snapped shut. Tor swung around in the night, latching onto its trace, following it back in a frenzy of his own doubt that he had heard it and his dread fear that it was true. He found nothing. Adongo had shielded. Tor sat down by the roadside, breathing heavily. He heard an owl hoot but not much else stirred in the stillness of the night. The owl made him think of his Paladin and he needed his wise counsel now.

Cloot! Where are you?

I'm with a group of friends. We're celebrating over a feast and there's minstrels and dancing; acrobats and fire eaters . . . where do you think I am? the falcon asked caustically. *Flying to Caradoon as you instructed! I'll be there before dawn.*

Tor was too distressed to even feel the intended sting of his friend's sarcasm. *Turn back.*

Why? Cloot could now hear the fright in Tor's voice.

Orlac is already here.

The bird paused. He knew when to stay quiet. He also knew Tor would elaborate.

Adongo linked a few moments ago. Very briefly. His exact words were: Orlac has Lauryn. We head north.

There was silence for a while and Tor permitted it to lengthen. He hoped the falcon would come back with something reassuring.

So Adongo has already found Lauryn and Orlac's well ahead of us. Already in Tallinor?

Apparently.

And I presume Adongo will not allow you to link?

Correct. He is shielded. Why?

Obvious. If it is Orlac — and one has to assume that Adongo would not claim something as wild as this if he was not sure — then he cannot risk the god tracing the Link to you.

How can he be sure?

That it's Orlac? Very easily. You forget we all fought him for centuries. Unless he is wearing a glamour he will not have changed. And I cannot imagine that he would use tricks . . .

he will want the Tallinese to fear him; he wants us to know he can enter the Kingdom and do exactly as he wishes.

Why does he not recognise Adongo?

Again I'm presuming, but I'd suggest our Moruk has gone to great lengths to disguise his true identity in order to offer protection to Lauryn.

Another thought slammed into place for Tor. *Cloot, if he has Lauryn, that means he has already been to Tal. Perhaps he has laid waste to it. Gidyon, Alyssa . . . !*

Wait! Listen to me. Adongo risked everything to get that message to you. If he was prepared to take that risk, and damage had been wrought on Tal, or your son or the Queen was injured, he would have told you that too — even if it meant his death. No, I believe he has given you, very succinctly, all the information you need.

Why does a god, bent on revenge, determined to raze Tallinor, enter the city and steal a single woman?

Tsk, tsk. You're not thinking, Tor. Who is that woman?

My daughter.

Quite. And what will you do now?

Follow her.

Precisely. I imagine that's what he wants. He is showing you that he can do this. And once her disappearance is discovered, I imagine the King's Guard will swing into action. Perhaps even Gyl himself — who you tell me is sweet on Lauryn — will give chase. Orlac is achieving everything in one subtle move. By stealing Lauryn he draws you out, which is his primary intention. But he also fires the Tallinese military into action plus he unsettles a new King, possibly prompting him to do something reckless and leave his realm exposed. No, Tor, I think it's an inspired move.

Tor was silent; turning over all this information in his mind. *Why Lauryn . . . why not Gidyon?*

Probably because women seem more helpless — not that this one is — but he doesn't know that. Perhaps Gidyon was not around. We don't know the circumstances.

Why not Alyssa?

Because as much as you love Alyssa, your daughter is even more precious. You will do anything to ensure her safety. I imagine he knows this.

How does he know who she is?

I can't answer that. To all of us it's clear that she bears a striking resemblance to her mother, but then Orlac has never seen her mother.

Tor felt the chill grip him. *But Dorgryl has.*

Cloot flew on in silence and Tor did not want to break the Link. *Are you turning back?*

No. I shall press on. I might as well not waste this journey.

Then I'll do the same. I have to get to the Heartwood and find Rubyn. We'll make a decision as soon as you return. Make haste, Cloot.

Fear for Lauryn and uncertainty about his next move drove Tor on; he had walked hard through the night and even broke into a lope as he spotted the first trees of the finger of the Forest towards which he headed.

Arabella met him with one of her affectionate hugs. 'It's good to have you back,' she said, although she could already see from the grim set of his jaw that he brought tidings she did not want to hear.

'Is Solyana here?' he said, pulling free of her hug but deliberately not letting go of her hand yet. As his Paladin, she craved his nearness, and he knew it would be wrong to foist all his grief onto her by being too abrupt or by not allowing her affections.

'No,' the priestess replied. 'I have not seen her in a long time.'

They walked together deeper into the Forest, towards the Heartwood which Tor could feel tugging him closer. He could even hear the singsong excitement of the Flames calling to him.

'So much to tell you,' he said.

'You look thin, tell me as we eat.' She pointed towards a spread of food and they sat beneath one of the wood's great trees and shared a meal.

'Orlac is here,' he said finally.

She stopped her chewing and eyed him. Arabella chose not to interrupt him — it was important for him to tell her all he needed to. 'Go on.' It was almost a whisper.

He told her about Adongo and his brief message, as well as what he and Cloot had surmised. She did react to this, instantly frightened for Lauryn. Arabella also realised that the time of the Paladin was fast approaching — the final battle they all had spoken of for centuries.

The priestess could see that Tor was distracted enough without her adding her fear to the boiling cauldron of his thoughts. 'What do we do?'

'We await Cloot. Decisions will be made once he arrives. Do you know why I've returned now, Arabella?'

She shook her head.

'Tell me about Rubyn.'

Her brow creased and she looked confused. 'Rubyn? Who is this person?'

Tor was surprised. Somehow he had expected her to sigh with relief and tell him everything, but it seemed the Heartwood kept its secrets . . . even from its own sometimes.

'Rubyn is my son.'

Her expression changed to puzzlement. 'I don't understand. Gidyon is your son.'

'That's true, but I've recently been informed that there was a third child born in the Heartwood that day. Alyssa birthed a frail boy – this information was known by no one but Sorrel and I imagine Darmud Coril, but I thought you may have discovered this?'

She shook her head, looking shocked, before wonderment crossed her face. Arabella put down the piece of fruit she was chewing on.

'A third child. The Trinity?'

He nodded. She wept . . . put her arms around him and wept again. He joined her but could not be sure whether his tears were for Rubyn or, more likely, for his lost daughter. Tor told Arabella all that he had learned since he last met her, including the death of Sorrel which she was sad to hear about.

'She was certainly a secretive old girl,' she admitted. 'You knew the husband, of course – it seems they were a pair well matched.'

Tor nodded. 'Their deeds were carried out as they tried to right the wrong of buying a stolen child, keeping his identity secret. Once they learned of his birthright, I imagine they were terrified. I still don't know how old Merkhud – or indeed Sorrel – actually was, but I'd guess at centuries.'

Arabella nodded thoughtfully, recalling the day of Tor's return to the Heartwood bringing his own smashed corpse with him. 'When you left his body to return to your own, he sighed into his death. When I looked at where he lay, he was turned to dust. A soft breeze rustled through the

Heartwood as if divinely sent. It blew the dust away,' she said.

'It was the same with Sorrel. We were holding her hands as she told us of Rubyn but when she slipped into death, she turned to nothing more than a palmful of dust. How many years they must have spent in their tormented search,' he replied.

'And you, Tor?'

He looked at her, a slight shake of his head telling her he did not understand her question.

'Who are you?'

He smiled briefly. 'Who knows?' he said sadly. 'I thought I was the son of a simple village scribe. All I know is that Jhon and Ailsa Gynt are my parents . . . the only parents I've ever known, but who my true birth mother and father are, I have not learned. I don't think I ever will. They perished in a fire. To this day I don't know whether I have sisters or brothers.'

'How did you come to live with the Gynts?'

'A traveller took pity on me. None of the villagers from where I was born could take on another child, and this woman cared for me but she was always on the move and not really in a situation to raise a son. She stopped at an inn in Mallee Marsh and Ailsa Gynt, my mother, could not bear not to give me a home.' He shrugged. It still hurt to think that he was not a true son of Jhon and Ailsa.

'They had no children of their own?'

Tor shook his head. 'My mother was barren. That's part of the reason they agreed so readily. It's strange though,' Tor said, running his fingers through his hair, 'I used to draw pictures of my family. My parents always found it amusing that I drew us as four.'

'A sister I suppose,' Arabella smiled.

'No, an elder brother. He always seemed menacing in my drawings.'

'What do you mean?'

'Oh, it's hard to say. This was so many years ago. I always drew him as though he was remote from the three of us and he looked angry in my pictures.'

'What do you think that means?'

'I don't think about it to be honest. I was a child. Perhaps I desperately wanted company. I really don't know, Arabella.' Tor felt slightly uncomfortable delving back into his past like this. The brother in his pictures used to play on his mind but he had not thought about him in so long; he preferred not to reopen the past in this way.

Arabella obviously sensed it. 'And the woman?'

'You mean the traveller?'

She nodded.

'No one knows. Never heard from her again. I was a little amazed too when I found out that my parents had asked no questions, but I think they so desperately wanted a child that they could put aside all objections to taking someone else's without any formalities.'

'Does it bother you, Tor?'

'No. That's the past.'

'I didn't mean that,' she said, reaching to take his hand. 'I meant does it ever occur to you that there are similarities between Orlac and yourself?'

Tor seemed taken aback. 'I'm not sure I understand you.'

'Well, Orlac was taken from his true parents, as you were.'

'Except mine died in a fire.'

'So you say,' she said, and he ignored the doubt in her words.

'Orlac was stolen, I was given – there are no similarities.'

Arabella could see how defensive Tor had become. She had no desire to upset him and it was obvious to her that Gynt had most certainly considered the parallel paths of himself and the god Orlac. It was also obvious he preferred not to openly discuss it.

She stretched in a deliberate move to show him that she had no intention of pursuing the conversation. Arabella smiled. 'What about Rubyn? How do you find him?'

Tor ran his fingers through his hair and stood to stretch his long legs. 'I've thought of nothing else since I left Tal. I have this strong feeling that Solyana might be his Paladin and that she will know where he is,' he said, leaning back against a tree.

And you would be right, said a familiar voice.

Tor swung to his left and saw the huge wolf, her silver-tipped fur seeming to sparkle in the dappled light of the Heartwood.

'Solyana!' they both said and moved towards her.

'Where?' Tor demanded, unable to contain his excitement.

Wait. Someone approaches, the wolf cautioned.

The Heartwood will not permit entry, Tor said, confidently.

It already has.

Who? Arabella demanded.

Friends, the great wolf replied, her mouth open; it looked like a grin.

* * *

Kythay entered the clearing with Alyssa and Saxon strolling on either side. Each wore a self-satisfied grin and loved the look of bewilderment on Tor's face.

'Look who met us,' Alyssa said, smiling widely. When no one responded, she filled the confused quiet. 'Well, say something!'

Tor found his voice. 'Why?'

'Because I can't stand the silence.'

'No, I mean why are you here?'

She could not tell immediately if he was pleased or unhappy to see her. Perhaps he did not care for her having left their children in the city.

She deliberately avoided explanations. 'Long story. Any chance of some food? Saxon is useless as a travelling companion.'

The Kloek spat in his habitual way but said nothing.

They all stood just a few feet apart staring, waiting for someone to make the first move or something to break through the trance-like spell between the husband and wife. It was Tor who strode forward and clasped Alyssa close. He did not speak, just held her while the others quietly drifted away. Tor could hear Arabella's affectionate welcome for Saxon and his subsequent pleasure at seeing Solyana again. Kythay ambled off into the depths of the Forest, as was his way.

Tor loosened his hold on his wife and held her back so he could look at her lovely face. 'I daren't allow myself the pleasure but I am so, so glad you're here.'

'You look sad.'

'Long story,' he echoed. 'Have something to eat; we need to share it with Saxon too.'

'What's wrong? Not Rubyn?' Alyssa thought her heart would break.

'No, my love. I have not seen him yet, although Solyana knows something. I have news of Orlac.' He did not want to say more and she did not want to hear it now. Instead Tor touched his finger to the pale green disk at her forehead and it dropped to the ground.

I hate that marking you, he whispered across the Link.

I shall never wear it again, she said, loving the feeling of empowerment and her reconnection with the Link and the man she loved.

In saying that you, I presume, have news too? He could sense it within her, desperate to spill out.

She nodded. 'Let's eat,' she said cautiously. 'And then we'll all share our tidings.'

Tor and Arabella sat back and watched Alyssa and Saxon hungrily devour the plentiful remains of their simple meal. Alyssa admitted that food had never tasted quite so good.

Solyana sat patiently by Tor whose hand constantly ruffled or stroked her amazingly thick silver-tipped fur.

A hush finally fell over the group and Alyssa, wishing it were her sitting so close to Tor instead of the wolf, decided she must speak first and tell them the news from Tal. It was suddenly hard to think of Lorys, now that she was in the presence of her one true love, his brilliantly bright cornflower-blue gaze pinioning her. She felt lightheaded. Alyssa cleared her throat and addressed the gathered.

'I'm here because I am no longer Queen of Tallinor.'

Arabella made a sound of shock. Tor did not say anything but she noticed his eyes narrow as he tried to make sense of what she had just said. She continued, hoping the Light would keep her voice strong. She really did not want to cry any more.

'Lorys is dead.' Simplicity was best she decided, as she watched the look of disbelief now cross Tor's face.

'How can this be? How can this have happened?' he asked her. 'Surely not on the road – he was due to arrive back at Tal just hours after I left. You had a messenger to say he was well.'

She nodded gently, showing that she understood all of this to be true but that he did not know the end of the tale. When Tor stopped talking Alyssa paused and composed herself. She was determined not to weep again over the monarch she had loved.

'Not long after you left Tal, another messenger arrived. He had ridden at high speed, almost killing himself and his horse on the muddy road . . .'

Tor suddenly recalled the messenger bearing the royal oriflamme, who had been travelling so incredibly fast in dangerous conditions that he and Cloot had commented upon it.

'I saw that messenger. I thought I noticed tears on his face but could not tell because of the rain.'

'They were tears,' Alyssa confirmed. 'He had ridden to deliver the news that the King of Tallinor had been killed by a freak hand of lightning during the storm.' She could not go on when she saw Tor put his head in his hands.

Saxon mercifully picked up the tale. 'The King died instantly, we were assured by Herek. His body was brought to Tal and was entombed after the traditional laying out.'

Solyana laid her belly to the ground, her head on her paws and Arabella hugged her knees, her forehead touching them, as she began to consider what these tidings meant.

'Alyssa, why are you here then? What do you mean you aren't Queen any more? Who is ruling Tallinor?' Tor asked, confused.

'Tallinor has a new monarch. His name is Gyl of Wytton.'

This caught Tor by surprise. 'Your adopted son?'

She hated the term; had only ever thought of Gyl as her son. 'He was bastard born to the King. I have only known of it since just before our marriage and Lorys and I never had the right opportunity to tell him.'

Tor shook his head. 'So Lorys was unfaithful to Nyria?' It seemed somehow obscene, and yet why he knew not. The Light knew *he* had been unfaithful to his wife many times since their marriage!

She nodded and smiled at his loyalty to Nyria. 'Once apparently. Only Kyt Cyrus – the former Prime whom you have told me so much about – and Merkhud knew of it. The old man apparently ensured protection for Gyl; saw to it he was educated and well cared for. His mother suffered the Green Fever and died when he was very young.'

Tor fitted the jigsaw piece into place in his mind. 'I see now. This is why Gyl was tied to the palace gates . . . his dying mother hoped the royals would take pity on the child.'

Alyssa shrugged. 'Perhaps, although I doubt she would have expected him to be given such privilege. She probably hoped they would find a good home for him – who knows? He was not base-born and I can only guess that in her state it was the best she could think of to do for him. As mother of the King's son, bastard or not, she needed to make sure Gyl had an opportunity to be near his father.'

'How did he take the news?'

'Badly,' Alyssa and Saxon said together.

'He'll cope,' Alyssa followed up. 'Gyl will make a fine King . . . and you're right about the other business, Lauryn and Gyl. I think I owe you a gold piece.' She found a smile, pleased that all the bad news from her end was shared and done with.

'Ah . . . which brings me to my bad news.'

'Lauryn and Gyl?'

'Just Lauryn.'

'I left her just a day or so ago. She was not happy about my leaving but she was safe. What's happened?'

'Not so safe, it seems. She's disappeared.' Before Alyssa or Saxon could speak what was springing to their lips, he added flatly: 'Orlac has her.'

Alyssa was on her feet so fast it shocked everyone. She had Tor's shirtfront in her hands, was dragging at him, desperate to know what he knew of their daughter.

'All I know is that he has taken her and they are headed north.'

'How! How can he already be here?' She felt the bile rise to her throat and her powers surge back through her for the first time in many, many years. Alyssa was frightened she would strike out randomly in her despair.

'He has visited Tal somehow. No one could know who he is except Adongo, Lauryn's Paladin, who is with her – and Cloot and I are assuming that he knows who Orlac is but not the other way around. Adongo's identity has been kept secret from the god – it's the only protection he has for our daughter.'

'Where is he taking her?'

'I don't know.'

'Why aren't you already chasing him?' she demanded, ignoring Saxon's shuffle by her side. It was his way of suggesting she calm down.

'I'm waiting for Cloot to return from the north. He flew to Caradoon to see if he could pick up any news or clues on Orlac's whereabouts.'

'Too late! We are too late, Tor. He's got our girl!' she exclaimed, her resolve crumpling as he took her into his arms.

'He won't hurt her, Alyssa. We'd know if he had. I would feel it, I'm sure. My belief is he will use her as a lure. You didn't bring Gidyon with you?'

'He left for Brittelbury almost as soon as you left Tal. He felt badly about his stone. He's gone after that girl, Yseul.'

'It's too dangerous, our being separated like this,' Tor worried.

'He'll be safe – he said he would return immediately.'

'I hope you're right. Did he meet up with Figgis?'

She nodded. 'They left as soon as Figgis arrived.'

They noticed they were virtually alone. Saxon and Arabella had quietly taken their leave. Only Solyana remained on the edge of the clearing. It seemed she dozed, although Tor knew not to be fooled. The wolf was giving them privacy.

'As soon as Cloot returns, I'm going after Orlac.'

Alyssa nodded. 'We'll both go. I didn't chase after you to be left alone in the Forest.'

He kissed her and she welcomed it, pulling him closer, holding him hard, demanding with her own mouth that their touch be prolonged.

'Does this mean we can be husband and wife again?'
Tor asked, tentatively, as they parted.

'It does.'

The smile which broke from his mouth and sparkled
in his eyes at her two words lifted her spirits enormously.

Together at last, he said across the Link.

Until death breaches us, she replied, and then shivered
at what suddenly sounded like prophetic words.

He arrived in Caradoon as the sun rose. Circling high
overhead his sharp eyesight took in the disturbing scene
below. Cloot did not want to fly any lower. He could
already see who it was who hung upside down and
bloodied between those trees and there was no mistaking
who strutted before her.

The falcon let out a single cry of despair which was
carried away on the wind. For Tor's sake, he found the
courage to descend into the trees and absorb the ugliness
before him. He did not linger.

Cloot left Caradoon immediately; no one had seen him
come and none witnessed his silent, heavy-hearted departure.

The information he brought back to Torkyn Gynt was
all bad.

17

Quist's Stand

Janus Quist was uneasy. The pirate could not pinpoint what was making him feel so edgy, but something was there consuming his thoughts. He had managed to get through the day but he did so through gritted teeth, hardly speaking to the others and grunting his answers to any questions.

It was nearing dusk and they could just see the outline of trees which told them they were almost at the finger of the Great Forest. Neither of the women rode especially well and for that reason Quist kept the pace slightly slower than he would have liked. He thought Hela might object; she had seemed so jittery and desperate to leave the brothel. But once they were on their way – and especially at the moment he announced they had crossed Caradoon's unofficial border and were now officially in Tallinor – she seemed to find a calm. And when Locky had pointed out the dark smudge ahead in the far distance as the finger of the Great Forest – not much more than a murky haze at that stage – Hela had visibly relaxed and her conversation became almost playful. She tried hard, but unsuccessfully, to bring him into their laughter and trivial talk about royal life in Cipres, which Locky seemed to find fascinating.

In truth, Quist would have enjoyed the lighthearted banter if not for this sense of foreboding. There was no reason for it. Their trip south had been uneventful. They had met few people on the road and the weather had been generous as they travelled, even in the evening. There had been no rain to speak of, and no wind, not even the famous biting northerly coming off the mountains. They had lit a fire each evening, eaten well from their plentiful stocks and slept without interruption.

Except on this particular morning, he noted. He ran his mind back through his strange awakening. He had opened his eyes before dawn in fright. He had looked about him, gathering his wits and calming his racing pulse. Quist was traditionally an early riser, but not before the sun had made her daily announcement. He sat up and was glad to see their small party still sleeping soundly, both women huddled close. He found he liked both of them, with a special respect for the maid, who reminded him of his beloved Eryn. She was plucky and pretty as well as courageous – all qualities he admired in his young wife.

Janus rubbed his eyes and then realised it was Eryn who had woken him. It seemed she had been calling to him in his dream. She had sounded afraid. He could just pick from the blur of his memory of the dream that he had reassured her. And then, miraculously, she had been swimming with dolphins whilst he stood on a white sand beach and laughed at her shrieks of enjoyment. That was all he could remember. Although he did think he could recall having watched her slip from his sight for the last time, into the depths of the sea, whilst clinging to the fins of two strong, proud males who raced through the salty waters with ease.

The pirate shook his head clear of his fanciful thoughts. Instead, he imagined Eryn was still fast asleep, and grinned. She hated to rise early and a foul temper could be provoked if she was ever disturbed before sunrise. He knew he would not get back to sleep now he was awake and so did not bother to try. He stood, stretched, and tiptoed around their small camp which they had made for the night. There was a stream nearby and he decided to fetch some water and stoke the embers of the fire in readiness for when the others woke. They had a long day ahead, with a full day's ride that would see them weary and sore but at the fringe of the Forest by twilight. He missed Eryn. It was his intention to deposit these women into the care of Gynt and be back in the saddle by nightfall – if he could find the man that quickly.

Locky was completely soppy over the young woman . . . a Queen no less. And she was just as bad with her coy glances, inviting smiles and that flash of dark eyes. Locky would object loudly at having to leave Sarel and Hela so soon, but Quist knew his mind was made up. The pirate had no intention of tarrying this far south – he was a northern man and, technically, a wanted one on this side of Caradoon. No. He wanted to be back with his wife and close to *The Raven* as soon as possible.

He roused the slumbering trio and made them all a tea from leaves he had gathered. Quist was a constant surprise to people. Anyone who thought him an ignorant man because he was a pirate was foolish indeed. He was educated and had decided against a profession because he had a genuine love of the sea. When his father forbade his passion, he had run away from his home in the far southwest of Tallinor, gradually working his way up the coast. At Kyrakavia he had enjoyed many years of seafaring until the ship he was on had fallen prey to Caradoon pirates.

The pirates had made a bad job of their attack, and this had changed Quist's life. Quist's ship, under an excellent captain, could have easily outrun the pirates, but the captain had turned to fight, successfully capturing the pirate ship and slaying most of her crew. Quist's captain had explained to the young sailor that greed had been the pirates' downfall. It was from his captain's mouth that Quist first heard the revolutionary idea: if one pirate could learn to spare all life on board victim ships; perhaps take only half the goods; and not attack the same ship more than twice in a year, then that captain would be prosperous and perhaps even gain a grudging respect from enemies and authorities. The captain had simply been voicing his long-held thoughts out loud, but his words, coupled with the rush of joy Quist had felt chasing the pirate ship, made him decide instantly that pirating was the life for him.

'Will we make it before night closes in?' Locky asked suddenly, disturbing Quist's recollection.

Quist looked up to see all the horses stopped before him and three pairs of eyes focused on his one good one. 'Sorry . . . my mind was elsewhere.'

'So we noticed,' Hela said, but not unkindly. She smiled at him.

'Um . . . yes, if we push on. Let's get you women into the safety of those trees and—'

Quist did not finish what he was going to say. His voice was arrested by a not-so-distant rumble. The others heard it too.

'What's that?' Sarel asked, looking around to pinpoint its origin.

Everyone listened intently.

'Riders,' Hela and Quist said together.

Quist looked towards Locky, who was already reaching for the knife he had brought along.

'It's them,' Hela said bleakly.

Sarel had gone pale. 'Who?'

'Those who wish you dead. I knew they would come. So now we turn and fight.'

'No!' Quist commanded. 'Locky, take Sarel and Hela and ride like the wind. We don't know who they are but if they are pursuers I will hold them up. I promise you, I will delay them long enough for you to make it into the cover of the Forest. Abandon the horses when you dare and hide.'

'I won't leave you, Janus,' Locky said.

'You'll do as I order,' Quist shouted back. He turned to Hela. 'Get your Queen to safety. Be brave now and ride as fast as your horse will go.'

Sarel looked terrified. 'But I can't ride that fast.'

'You can!' Hela admonished. 'Thank you, Quist. We shall meet again.'

Quist wanted to say that somehow he did not think they would, but instead he said nothing, leapt down from his horse and gave each of the other mounts a hard slap on the rump. Together with his loud bellowing, it had the desired effect. He saw Locky glance back, a look of anger but also concern on his face, but then he too was galloping, urging the trio of horses faster. Quist watched them grimly; he cast a quick prayer to the Light that it would guide them to safety and prevent the women being unseated from their mounts. *Just get to the trees, Locky*, he silently urged, and then turned away from their cloud of dust and took a deep breath.

This was it! This was what the bad feeling had been about all day. He had experienced a premonition of sorts and now he must act to save lives. Quist wanted to re-assure himself that it could just be a group of Tallinese guards on the gallop, but after his bleak mood he felt this was unlikely.

He dug in his saddlebags for the small pouch he had tossed in as an afterthought when he packed. It would be a great help now. Quist also removed the two cutlasses he habitually carried on a journey, be it on land or sea. He was a formidable opponent when wielding these blades and today he intended to take as many with him to his grave as possible.

As he emptied the contents from the pouch in a line across the road, he realised that he was accepting death graciously. It was true. He had no expectation of living through this confrontation and his only intention now was to kill as many of Sarel's pursuers as he could, giving his friends their best chance of survival. He hoped with all his heart that Torkyn Gynt was in the Great Forest; Hela was following a notion from a dream and although Quist understood none of it, he trusted her faith.

And so now as he crouched in the shadows of the road-side, as dusk turned to nightfall and the riders were almost upon him, his thoughts inevitably turned to Eryn. He thought of her happy squeals in his dream as she swam with the dolphins and he hoped that she would miss him.

* * *

In the Heartwood Tor and Alyssa, together with Saxon
and Arabella, awaited the wolf. It was time to learn more
of Rubyn. Impatience surrounded the foursome but they
knew Solyana would not be hurried and she would arrive
soon enough. It was Cloot who disturbed them, adding
to their sense of tension when his sudden flight into the
trees caught their attention before he dropped soundlessly
and exhausted to the middle of the clearing where they
sat. Tor rushed over to pick him up.

Are you—

Just tired. Give me a moment.

'Is he all right?' Alyssa asked, voicing everyone's
concern.

'He's exhausted. We should let him rest,' Tor answered.

No, the falcon replied, breathing deeply and slumping
against Tor's chest. *I must deliver deeply distressing news.*

Tor felt the hair stand up on the back of his neck and
arms. Cloot was not theatrical in this manner. For him to
voice such an opinion made Tor frightened for what they
were all about to learn.

He touched his finger to his lips to stop the others'
questions. 'Cloot has bad news to share.'

They all fell silent.

Tell me, Tor said, softly.

Goth was at Caradoon, paying a visit to Madame Eryna's.

Tor did not want to hear any more; knew he must and
clenched his jaw in anticipation of what was coming.

*He's chasing Sarel, now Queen of Cipres. I'm guessing she
has made some sort of daring escape from Orlac. It appears Goth
now deals in death for our enemy.*

Tor could see the concern written on the faces of his
friends and he nodded slightly to let them know he would

deliver news soon. He must allow Cloot to tell it as he chose.

Go on, he encouraged.

Goth lingered at the brothel long enough to do his usual dirty style of work and ask questions. He and his men are headed this way.

Wait, Tor said. He quickly filled the others in on what had been revealed. It all meant little to Alyssa and Arabella but Saxon reacted, rubbing his face with his hands in fear for the young Queen.

Tell me the rest, Tor said to his falcon.

I'm sorry, Tor, to bring this news.

Tor stroked Cloot. *I know, but you are our eyes and ears – you must tell it now.*

He heard his bird mentally sigh and knew this would be the last moment of peace in his life, perhaps the news might even sound his death knell. Whatever Cloot was going to tell him would precipitate urgent action, he felt sure, and an end to any vague hopes he had of not needing to shed blood. He felt the Colours pulse and then he heard the ugly tidings.

Eryn has been slaughtered by Goth. Her girls were beaten by the Ciprean guards who travel with him.

Eryn's dead? Tor needed more confirmation. It was as though he understood the series of words but not quite what they meant.

Cloot's hate for Goth had built during his flight home and finally crystallised into something impenetrable and determined. Goth must pay with his life for this cruel act. And he realised that Tor would avoid dealing death to any if he could; the only way to ensure Tor felt the full horror of Eryn's death was to tell it precisely as it was on the bright morning in Caradoon when a hint of summer had wafted on the morning air.

His voice was deliberately devoid of emotion, hard in fact, as he began his tale of terror. *He had stripped her naked and had her strung by her feet from a tree, whereupon he had slit open her belly and emptied its contents.*

None of the others were privy to this horrifying description of what had occurred in Caradoon and they could only watch the shock and grief claim Tor's lovely face. Alyssa heard his breathing become shallow and both Arabella and Cloot felt the power surge from their bonded one. Tor began to tremble. He stood slowly, very slowly and placed his falcon on a nearby branch and then he deliberately leaned against the tree, absorbing its strength and comfort as he retched long and violently.

Quist could see them now – faces blank, mouths grimly set. He recognised the uniform of the Ciprean Guard. Hela was right. And at the front rode a man in black. A man whose face was not blank. It was twisted into a snarl as he mercilessly whipped his horse, harder and harder in his furious desperation to reach the Great Forest. The pirate swallowed hard. It had suddenly occurred to him that the mere fact these riders were here at all meant they must have already visited Eryn.

He could not think on what that meant right now; it would make his hands shake and he needed a resolve of iron to serve him at this moment as he touched the burning kindling to the strange powder and tablet he had purchased years ago in the Caradoon apothecary. The dry, wizened fellow who had sold it to him called it Wizard's Flame. He had bought it as a novelty but had never got around to trying the deep red flakes which lay in a long line before him. His timing was perfect. He hoped the powder would work. It flared and then as the flames licked the pile in the middle where he had embedded the tablet, it exploded. The blinding flash and unexpected noise disoriented and terrified the horses as they approached at high speed. At least four bucked and threw their riders.

Good! Quist said to himself as he reached for his cutlasses and melted deeper into the dark to hack at the downed men. He killed three silently and swiftly before the man at the front, the one they called the Leper in Tallinor, restored some sense of order. The horses were spooked. Quist ran up from behind, leaping surprisingly high to sever one man's head from his neck and hacking off another's hand. The man began to scream and Quist felt a momentary rush of dark humour as he was reminded of Captain Blackhand and his penchant for removing his enemy's hands and hanging them from his mast, to blacken and wizen in the wind and salt air.

Quist rushed back once again into the cover of bushes but he knew the turmoil would not last long. Very quickly he would be discovered. This time Quist ran around to the side of the pack and, much as it distressed him to do so, he began disabling the horses. Now the terrified shrieks of injured animals began to mix with the groans of men.

The sharp eyes of Goth spotted him. He heard the man call out above the din and then point. So, this was it then. He made his final charge. Quist ran at them hard and managed to fell another two of the guards before he himself was brought down, the backs of his knees expertly slashed to cripple and force him to the ground, helpless. He counted seven of the thirteen men dispatched. Another two seriously injured who would probably be left to die and six of the horses no longer able to walk, another four missing. That left only three horses for five able men, he calculated. For one attacker, it was a good effort. Now he must die bravely, he thought, as he watched the Leper approach.

Goth began to clap. 'Very good, Quist,' he applauded. 'You've served her majesty proudly with your fire tricks and flashing blades.'

This was only the second time Quist had seen the former chief inquisitor of Tallinor. The first occasion had been when Goth, newly arrived in Caradoon, had asked questions in the brothel. All the girls had found him so creepy that Eryn had asked Quist to get rid of him. The pirate had shown him the door and Goth had left without further trouble. Quist had known who the man was but Quist was a Caradoon – so long as the man gave him no bother, he had no desire to open any discussion with the Tallinese who sought him. Reward or not, Quist was not a man to share Caradoon's secrets.

The last he had heard, this man was dependent on the stracca and had become useless. Yet here he stood, certainly half the width he had been, but strength still lurked in that body as cruelty still resided in the tormented face. His thoughts fled to Eryn as the Leper's boots came level with Quist's eye.

'Get him to his knees,' Goth ordered.

The pain was immense as they roughly jerked him into position in front of Goth. He could feel the blood pouring from the vicious cut which had severed tendons. He had no strength in his legs and wished Goth would just get on and finish it now.

'Where is the Queen, Quist?'

'Not here.'

'In the Forest?'

'No.'

'Where then?'

'Headed for Tal but you'll never catch her. They have fresh horses and yours I can see are already half dead, even without my contribution,' he lied.

'Tal, eh?' Goth's fist hit Quist so hard that, as strong as he was, he fell to the side heavily. 'You are lying, pirate. Would you like me to tell you how I know this?'

Quist said nothing. Goth must have motioned to his men because Quist found himself dazed but back on his knees staring at Goth's crotch this time. He had heard somewhere that a Kloek had removed the Leper's manhood and stuffed it into the chief inquisitor's mouth; left him for dead. It had to be a jest. No one survived that sort of punishment and, if they did, they would probably become a recluse. Goth's ego seemed intact, if not magnified.

'Look at me with your one eye, Quist, or I'll poke it out.'

Quist recalled losing his eye. There surely could not be a more exquisitely painful sensation than a thick splinter gouging deep into the eyeball. It had been a freak occurrence. Fighting had broken out during a raid, someone had swung blindly, madly, with a cutlass at him but hit a railing instead. The timber had splintered and a sharp piece had shot up into his eye, damaging it irreparably. The beam had saved his life, but at great cost – the physic at Cipres had removed his injured eye. The pain of his voyage back to Cipres had been indescribable and his crew had kept him permanently drunk and tied to his bunk, where he had writhed and screamed for the entire journey.

Janus Quist was not sure he could cope with another such injury. He would prefer to die. And to speed death along, but also to keep Goth lingering, he raised his head as asked and stared into the twitching, mauled face which was trying to smile.

'Ah, that's better. It would be awful to lose the one remaining eye, wouldn't it?'

Quist nodded simply to keep Goth happy and amused. Every minute he kept Goth interested in him meant he won his friends another minute of freedom – and safety, he hoped – as they sped towards sanctuary.

'I want to tell you how I know that you're lying about the Queen and her friends.'

'Go ahead,' the pirate said. 'I'm not going anywhere.'

Goth enjoyed his jest, laughing aloud. 'I like you, Quist. And because I like you so much, I'm going to give you the long version of the story rather than just bluntly telling you how much I enjoyed killing your wife.'

Quist felt no more pain. It disappeared along with all desire to live. So Eryn was not asleep in her feather bed, nor was she swimming with dolphins. She was hanging upside down from a tree outside the brothel; her body rotting, no longer of interest, not even to the creature scavengers. Eryn was dead. So was his heart. Now he just had to make it stop beating so he could go in search of her. He had done his best – he had bought them some time with men's lives and his own. It was up to the three of them now to make it to Gynt and somehow, somewhere, avenge Eryn's death. He could not care less about himself. His life had been full; its final reward the feel of his young wife's beautiful body against his and her affections . . . if not her love. But she had so much yet to live for and it was with this final thought as a catalyst that Quist found the anger and thus the strength to launch himself from his knees upwards towards the hated Leper.

One last blow just for Eryn.

Quist's skull connected hard with his tormentor's jaw and Goth was momentarily stunned. Rage coursed through him. How dare this scum, who lay with whores, married them no less, interrupt his speech. And he hadn't even had the pleasure yet of describing what it felt like to rummage around in Eryn Quist's body and scoop out its warm contents.

Goth got back to his feet, his teeth aching from the blow. He looked at the pathetic mound which was the pirate, who had clearly spent his last in that daring and rather nimble move.

Goth raised his sword and brought it crashing down on the man's neck. He kicked the pirate's head towards one of the Ciprean guards, sidestepping quickly the torrent of blood gushing from the headless corpse.

'We take that with us,' he said.

18

Game of Fists

Gidyon had in the end decided against taking the horses which the King had offered. He and Figgis were happier to move on foot, particularly now that Figgis was restored to good health. They had left the city of Tal far behind them as they headed north and then began to swing west towards Brittelbury.

Figgis was tireless. Each evening it was Gidyon who first began looking for the best place to sleep for the night rather than the dwarf who, in spite of his size, was strong and surprisingly fleet of foot. Gidyon had expected they would stay in inns but there were few in the northern reaches and Figgis had suggested they make do with a camp. With someone to share the outdoors, Gidyon found he enjoyed the adventure of sleeping beneath the stars far more than when he had journeyed alone towards Axon. And Figgis had many stories to pass the time. Gidyon learned much about the ways of the Rock Dwellers and came to admire them. He looked forward to enjoying his friend's promise to take him to his birthplace one day. But for the most part their conversation dwelled on the threat of Orlac and how they might, with the other Paladin and the Trinity, defeat him.

This particular day, as dusk stole across Tallinor, they arrived in a town which boasted two inns – both fairly crowded with men in from the fields – and a show which was being presented on the local green and had brought in plenty of visitors.

Gidyon was parched and weary. 'Come on, Figgis, let's treat ourselves to a bed tonight. We can share a room and I've got the coin my mother gave me – I've hardly used a drack of it.'

Figgis eyed him. 'You'd make a woeful Rock Dweller, boy.'

'I feel like an ale and a singsong and an enormous hearty meal – I could eat enough for two men in fact!'

They laughed together.

'All right, you win. Which one?' Figgis asked, regarding the inns.

'Well, let's see now. The Bull 'n' Stag or the Old Crown? Hmm . . . the first one, I think.'

'Lead the way,' Figgis said. 'But don't be surprised if they stare. My kind have not been seen around for a long time,' he cautioned.

They stepped into the lively inn and within moments much of its loud chatter and laughter had dimmed.

What did I tell you? Figgis said.

It doesn't stop my thirst or hunger. And I refuse to sleep on the ground tonight. Follow me, Gidyon said, shouldering his way through the crowded room.

The sight of the two strangers, odd companions though they were, did not bother the serving girls. They were more than happy to see such a tall and handsome traveller in these parts. Used to the roughneck villagers who came into town after an Eighthday working the fields, Gidyon was a treat for sore eyes. Neither of the girls was especially pretty but one had a bright, wide smile and a cheeky glint in her eye.

'Two of your largest ales . . . and what's on tonight?'

'Depends what you mean,' she said, grabbing a couple of enormous mugs from the shelf.

He grinned. It felt good to engage in something as simple as flirting and for a moment not having to worry about saving the world. 'Food,' he answered.

'Oh, in that case it's ploughman's pie or roast pigeon.'

'One of each,' he replied. 'Big servings,' and he winked.

'Take a seat, if you can find one.'

He turned and picked out Figgis who had already claimed a small space in a corner of the crowded room. 'We're over there,' he called to the girl and she nodded.

Gidyon joined Figgis. 'You see, you're forgotten already. A novelty only for a moment.'

'Give it time,' Figgis warned.

Their food arrived and they both ate heartily and drank copiously. The ale hit the spot for Gidyon and as he felt himself relax a gregarious mood began to overtake him. The serving girl frequently caught his eye and he began to entertain thoughts of what else the night might hold.

'Did you ask about lodgings?' Figgis said.

Before Gidyon could answer a roar went up in the alehouse followed by a burst of cheering. 'What's that all about?' he wondered aloud, standing for a better look. 'Another ale?'

'Why not?' Figgis said, also beginning to relax under the influence of the drink.

Gidyon made his way to the counter, once again pushing through the throng. The cheering was frequent now and the sound of men's voices became more boisterous. He ordered another couple of mugs and paid his coin to the other girl this time. He noticed the original serving lass pouting slightly at her sister getting to him first.

'What time do you girls work until?' he asked.

'Too late. And you keep throwing these down and you'll be drunk before we can enjoy your company.'

'Strumpet!' the innkeeper said, slapping the girl's rump with a towel. It was a friendly gesture and they both laughed. 'These are my daughters, young man, and they will be going to bed straight after their night's work.' He was an oily sort of character; there was intelligence – or was it cunning – in his eyes, in the way they sparkled. 'Their *own* beds,' he added just in case it needed clarification.

Gidyon grinned. 'Just passing the time of day innkeeper. No harm meant.'

'None taken,' the man said, pointing his daughter towards the tables which needed clearing.

She threw a backwards glance towards Gidyon but he knew not to trespass now.

'What's happening over there?' he asked the innkeeper.

'Oh, the Freak Show's in town. That's Londry the Strongman. He pays anyone who can beat him at Fists.'

'He doesn't look strong to me.'

'Cannot be beaten,' the man replied, a sly grin stealing across his face.

'How much?'

'Don't bother. He's never lost a single round and has

been coming here for years. Each season another young blood thinks he might beat him but he always goes home with his tail between his legs. I'd hate for you to lose your money,' the man said, but Gidyon did not think he really meant it.

Gidyon nodded. 'What's the Freak Show?'

'Travelling circus of oddbods. Your friend, the dwarf over there, had better watch out — they'll grab him for their show.'

'They'll have to catch him first,' Gidyon said, and grinned. 'Thanks for the warning.'

The innkeeper took his coin and Gidyon picked up the mugs of ale, returning to Figgis. He told him what he had learned. The little man shrugged.

'He's cheating,' he said.

Gidyon put his mug down. 'Who is?'

'The Strongman's cheating. He's empowered.'

'I imagine he would have to be, seeing how skinny he is. How do you know?'

'I can feel his magic. As soon as the cheering began I felt it but it's very weak. We've probably both had a little too much ale to notice it.'

'Can't have him winning all night, can we?' Gidyon said, draining his mug, his bubbly mood frothing over. 'Let's see if we can relieve him of some of his money.'

Figgis was still clear-headed enough to caution his friend. 'Come on, lad. We need a good night's rest and we still haven't sorted where we are sleeping.'

'Just one turn, Figgis,' Gidyon said, grabbing his arm and dragging him through the legs of people towards the now very loud mob of people gathered around one table.

Gidyon's height meant he could see with ease over the

shoulders of men enjoying the spectacle of Londry the
Strongman, his decidedly slim right arm linked with that
of his opponent – a young farmer, red-faced and perspiring
as he worked hard to prevent his arm being bent towards
the red ribbon which would pronounce him loser. He was
a big, burly lad, more than capable of beating most men
at a strong arm match but his strength could not pitch
itself against magic. Of course, he was not to know that
and so he laboured to beat the famous freak, Londry.
Londry pushed with his very simple powers and the burly
farmer capitulated to the sound of a massive roar of
approval from the onlookers, who thumped him on the
back and told him it was a close one. The farmer left,
disgusted with himself.

Leave it, Gidyon. We don't need this now. We're on a mission.

I hate cheats, Gidyon replied and moved forward.

He heard his companion sigh in his head but he ignored
it. 'Who takes the bets here?' he yelled over the din.

A loud applause went up as the crowd sensed another
contender. Londry eyed the new opponent, looking him
up and down. 'I take the bets,' he answered. 'It's a duke
a-piece. Winner take all.'

'I see you've been winning all night,' Gidyon said,
nodding towards the pile of coins at Londry's elbow.

'Ay, I have. I never lose,' Londry replied. 'Tell you what,
lad. You look like you've got the goods . . . but let's make
the bet more interesting,' he offered.

'Such as?'

'Let's triple the odds shall we?'

'Fine with me,' Gidyon said, pretending to sway a little
and give the appearance he was too hazy from the ale to
realise what he had just committed to.

'Show me your coin, lad,' the man said.

Gidyon dug in his pocket and pulled out a handful of his mother's money and slammed it on the table. He heard Figgis tsk-tsk in his head again.

It's just a little fun. He's been taking their money for years by cheating.

So you think you should teach him a lesson, eh?

Something like that.

Londry counted a small fortune in the pile before him.

'I can't cover that,' he said.

'I can!' It was the innkeeper who had sidled up and was greedily looking over the glinting money.

Ah, so the crooked innkeeper is in on the deal.

Does it matter? Figgis said.

They're cheats. Come on Figgis, where's your sense of justice?

Upstairs in bed, tucked beneath the sheets.

Gidyon chuckled over the Link before he addressed the crowd.

'I'll tell you what, good folk. I'm confident I can beat this fellow. Why don't we throw it open so you can lay bets too?'

He saw the innkeeper baulk. 'Ah now, that's not the deal,' he said.

'What are you afraid of, innkeeper? You told me yourself that Londry never loses. So, why not take the risk that he won't fail this time, either?'

The innkeeper licked his lips and glanced again towards the pile of coins which lay on the table. 'How did you come by so much money? Are you a thief, sir?'

'My parents saved it for me. It's everything I have — I'm prepared to risk it. Are you?' Gidyon hoped that would deflect any further delving on the substantial amount of money he really could not explain if pressed further. He could just imagine how this provincial crowd would greet the news that he was the son of the former queen of Tallinor.

Londry looked at his partner and nodded. Gidyon caught it and turned towards the innkeeper. Everyone around them waited expectantly for the answer. Greed got the better of the man.

'All right. We take bets. I cover them.'

A roar of approval and a frenzy of activity followed as men dug into their pockets and found their last coin to wager. Half the room liked the tall lad's swaggering confidence and placed their money on him. They knew it was a lost cause but they loved the idea that someone had pushed the greedy innkeeper to demonstrate that he was in on this annual event. He had always denied it, but tonight had shown him to be in partnership with Londry. The others in the room, not so confident and aware of Londry's unblemished reputation for winning at Fists, went with the Strongman, even though every one of them would love to see him beaten.

The two girls had written down the bets, the tally of which Gidyon now ensured the innkeeper sight and sign his name to.

'Everyone is witness that the innkeeper is covering these bets,' he announced.

They cheered as the innkeeper smiled nervously. He was confident of winning but he hated to see so much of his money even vaguely under threat.

'Take your seat,' Londry said to Gidyon. 'Don't get comfortable, you won't be in it long,' he said and laughed, showing two rows of teeth in various stages of decay.

Then Londry banged his elbow down on the table, showing his clenched fist. Gidyon followed suit and one of the girls tied the combatants' wrists with ribbons; one red to declare the Strongman the champion, the other blue, tied to his opponent. The red ribbon was stained from regular use. The blue ribbon had never yet declared a victor.

'I've put my last duke on you,' the girl whispered to Gidyon as she tied a firm knot at his wrist, making sure she caressed it surreptitiously before adding: 'Make sure you win.'

He rewarded her with a smile, which made her feel weak as she stared into the brightest blue eyes she had ever seen. Win or lose, she intended to reward him with something other than money tonight. She stepped away.

A hush fell on the gathered crowd.

The innkeeper quickly reminded everyone of the rules. 'One round only. Whichever fist touches the coloured ribbon of his opponent is declared the winner. I shall enjoy taking all your money.' He was booed by those who had bet on Gidyon and cheered by the rest of the mob.

'Ready?' he called, raising his arm.

Both opponents nodded and then gripped each other's hands; palm to palm, fingers wrapped tight. Gidyon could already feel the man gathering up his powers. Londry was sentient, it was true. But only just – he possessed enough magical ability, if used wisely, to be able to channel it through his arm and best just about anyone. His tiny frame was testimony to the fact that without the magic, he would rarely win in a test of strength.

Gidyon felt the Colours pulse gently. He also noted Londry tighten his grip as they watched the innkeeper's arm prepared to drop. Gidyon gave Londry a final 'devil-be-damned' grin before the innkeeper's arm dropped and the cheering erupted.

At first nothing much happened as their fingers gripped harder and they simply tested one another. Gidyon felt the weak sentient ability of Londry doing its best and he allowed it to flow over him. He knew the Strongman would not be able to detect his own powers; his father had warned him as much and so he decided to allow Londry to gain a sense of security as his rigidly held arm began to lean dangerously close to the red ribbon. The men in the inn were wild with cheers. Half the room was urging Gidyon on, begging him to find the strength to fight back. The other half was now chanting Londry's name, sensing yet another victory and more money in their pockets than they had arrived with. The innkeeper showed his pleasure, leading the chanting, loving the thought that he would be considerably richer tonight.

Finish it, Figgis suggested.

You spoil my fun, dwarf.

Remember Orlac. We have a job to do and need to be on the road early tomorrow.

It was Gidyon's turn to sigh across the Link. He looked towards one of the innkeeper's daughters – the one with the lovely smile – and winked. She looked confused, noting that Gidyon's fist was barely a whisker from touching the red ribbon. How could he be so cocky? She could hardly hear her own final encouragement to him over the monstrous din of the crowd. Men were now standing on chairs and tables; several of them, in fact, had even clambered onto the serving counter for a clear look at the boy's defeat.

Gidyon turned back to Londry, who was leering at him with his horrible teeth.

'What will you tell your ma and pa at losing their money?' the Strongman taunted.

Gidyon broke into the widest of grins. 'But I haven't lost yet, Londry,' he said and pushed ever so gently with the tiniest amount of the Colours. They responded, subtly surging against the weak power of Londry which had been pouring through Gidyon's arm. Londry's expression changed dramatically as he felt his arm weaken. What was happening? This was not right. He looked towards his grinning opponent as their locked fists gradually swayed away from the red. They held momentarily in the centre, fully upright where the contest had begun.

Londry cast a terrified glance towards the innkeeper and then felt the ghastly sensation of his own rigid arm moving inexorably towards the blue. The crowd became hysterical. The boy had found some deep hidden strength and was fighting back courageously. It was slow and graceful, the movement down to the blue ribbon. Londry wanted to believe his eyes tricked him. He tried to double his power but he had long ago used its full strength and this lad before him did not seem to be affected by it any longer.

And then something extraordinary happened. Londry had never felt such a sensation before. A sense of something cold sliced open in his head and he heard a voice. *Cheats cannot be allowed to prosper*, it said.

It was the voice of the lad. He was still grinning. Londry looked at his fist, knowing he was a beaten man, as it experienced its first ever touch to the blue. He could not hear his own thoughts as the inn seemed to explode. Men were cheering and thumping each other's backs;

others leapt from tables and jumped on one another. Londry, numb, felt his fingers being unlocked from the tight grip of his opponent who was being showered with kisses by one of the innkeeper's daughters.

'How did you do that?' he said, quietly.

Gidyon's superior hearing heard him. 'I cheated,' he said, and stood.

Londry watched all of his night's winnings disappear into Gidyon's hands and he looked towards the innkeeper, who wore a murderous expression as he was inundated by demands for payment from boisterous men, looking forward to clutching their winnings. Londry knew it would be a long time before the Strongman from the Freak Show would be welcome at this alehouse again and he had to wonder whether the innkeeper would even survive the huge payout he would be making tonight.

Gidyon pushed some coin into the hand of the girl that was still clinging to his neck. 'I have to go, but this is for you,' he said.

Let's get out of here, Gidyon, Figgis said, keen to get his companion away from the hysterical congratulations of all those who had placed their money on him. Figgis was relieved when Gidyon nodded.

Let's go, he said, piling money into his pockets and waving at his supporters.

It was a cool, clear night and they sucked in the fresh air.

Another night under the stars, then, Figgis said. *Let's head towards that small copse on the other side of town.*

I suppose it is, Gidyon said, referring to a night under the stars. *I don't feel like going back in there. The innkeeper looked ready to kill me.*

Figgis chuckled. *I reckon he got what he deserves.*

They've been running that trick for years and cheating honest men from their money. I presume they could only have devised it since the fall of the Inquisitor.

Yes, you'd be right there. Saxon told me that Goth punished people for many years. It's only recently that sentients have been able to proclaim their powers.

Are they always that weak?

I think so. Wild magic is never strong. It's just a trace of something passed down through generations.

And this is what King Lorys feared and had people persecuted for?

Figgis shook his head. *It's terrible what was done to them.*

Father said that he and my mother have the wild magic. But they are both so strong with it.

This is true. Torkyn Gynt is the One and your mother is special. None of us really understands. Their magic is perhaps an individual gift. Without either of them there is no Trinity.

It doesn't make sense to me, Figgis. There's more to it. If sentient people are weak in their powers, passed as wild magic through generations, then how do my parents possess such immense abilities – enough to consider taking on a god?

I'm not sure they are being given much choice.

Gidyon refused to accept it.

Well, what do you think it is then, if not the wild magic? Figgis asked.

Has it occurred to you that my parents may also be from the gods?

No it hasn't. It's an impossible notion.

Why?

Well, explain how?

I don't know. It's just a thought.

They were both so deep in their thoughts and private conversation across the Link that neither had paid much attention to the fact that they were now on the open road again, headed out of town and towards the motley set-up of carts and stalls which they presumed was the Freak Show. As they rounded one of the alleyways which would lead them towards the copse and shelter for the night, Figgis suddenly hissed.

We're being followed.

They swung around and saw half a dozen men approaching them.

Wait! Figgis cautioned, sensing the Colours flare in his companion. *Your powers are more than enough defence. Let's see what they want of us. If it's money, just give it to them.*

Pigs bollocks I will! But I'll hear them out.

It was Londry leading the pack.

'We want no trouble,' Londry said to them.

'Why are you following us? Surely you don't plan to steal my money?'

'We're not here to steal from you. I want you to meet someone.'

That's novel, Figgis murmured.

A ruddy-faced man stepped out of the shadows. He was as broad as he was tall, with a bulbous nose. 'I'm Vyk Tyne, proprietor of the Freak Show,' he said, holding out his hand. 'Shall we move out of the alley and into the open?'

No harm done. Might as well hear him out, Gidyon said.

They turned and followed the men back up the alley and into the main street.

Tyne turned towards Gidyon. 'Londry told me what happened back there in the alehouse.'

Gidyon shrugged.

'You are sentient and you travel with a dwarf,' the man said with some wonder. 'We haven't seen his kind in decades. I'm offering you a place in our show.'

Gidyon was taken aback. This was the last thing he had expected. He looked towards Figgis and they both burst out laughing.

'Why is it funny? You're both perfect!'

'Perhaps we are, but we are on a journey to Brittelbury and must make haste. I thank you for your interest,' Gidyon replied, with genuine politeness. 'Good luck, Londry.'

They both made to leave.

'Wait . . . please!' Tyne called. 'Brittelbury is one of our stops. We should reach there in a few nights. What harm then to travel with us? Help us earn some coin and earn some yourself.'

Gidyon turned. 'I'm not sure I need to earn coin, sir. Londry will testify we have enough to see us through.'

Londry nodded. 'I'm sorry, Vyk. I thought he may say yes.'

Tyne shrugged. 'Are you walking through the night?' he asked.

'Probably,' Figgis said.

'I thought you were mute,' Tyne said, incredulous.

'No, I can sing and dance too,' Figgis said, effecting a comical jig. He was relieved that the confrontation was not what he had imagined.

'Well, don't go yet. Please. Why not stay the night at our camp and we can talk some more? There's food for the morning and some manner of bed for the night. I'll be happy to extend some hospitality. Perhaps you can teach Londry here a few tricks,' Tyne offered graciously, nodding towards Gidyon.

He seemed genuine enough. They sensed no guile in this man.

'Come and share a drink with me before you rest. Your money's safe, I give my word. Who knows, I might persuade you to travel with us.' He smiled big-heartedly.

'All right,' Gidyon said. 'I could use a soft pallet.'

'Come,' Tyne said. They walked with the group. 'Let me introduce you to a couple of our performers: you know Londry, and this is our contortionist, Elby.' A slim man with a liquid walk smiled at Figgis who grunted a greeting. 'On the end over there is Selwyn, who you can see has no arms but balances on a tightrope. And in between them is Caerys . . . he's a snake swallower.'

Caerys held out a hand. 'I used to be with Cirq Zorros.'

Gidyon grinned. 'I'm not from these parts, I'm sorry.'

'Oh well, it's a very famous circus. It used to boast the Flying Foxes. But they broke up when Saxon left . . . and then Greta married Zorros . . .'

'Saxon,' Figgis said, 'the Kloek?'

'That's him,' Caerys replied, beaming that they might have a mutual friend. 'How do you know Saxon?'

'We go back a long way,' Figgis admitted.

They had arrived at the Green. 'This way,' Tyne said. The group broke up, headed towards their own caravans, but Caerys followed with Gidyon and Figgis as they ducked beneath awnings and stepped over rugs and various pockets of hastily made habitation. Tyne led them to the most ornate caravan and gestured for them to join him inside.

'I know you're both in need of rest but join me in a

nip of something stronger than ale. It will see you both off to a good night's sleep.'

Figgis eyed him suspiciously.

Tyne laughed. 'Nothing sinister, I assure you, dwarf. Just some excellent liquor I picked up on our last visit to the south.'

Caerys nudged Gidyon. 'You can trust us.'

They sat back in the relatively salubrious surroundings of Tyne's caravan and listened to his tales of how the Freak Show came into existence more than a decade ago. Gidyon was enjoying himself, letting down his guard, but Figgis kept a close watch on the door and on his bonded's state of mind. One more glass and he was sure the lad would pass out.

'Tell me about your circus, Caerys,' Gidyon slurred.

'They were wonderful days they were. We travelled up and down the Kingdom performing for the royals many times. You know, it's impossible to think it, but our Queen . . . well, King's Mother now, once lived with us.'

Gidyon nearly dropped his cup. 'Who are you talking about?'

'Queen Alyssa. She lived and travelled with us. She and her friend, old Sorrel.'

'I don't believe you.'

'It's true, I swear.'

Gidyon was just about to press the young man for more information when they heard an almighty roar.

'Apologies. That's our very big friend. He gets himself horribly drunk every night after a show.'

'Big friend?' Figgis enquired, putting down his cup and removing the one listing on Gidyon's lap.

'Yes, my word. He's enormous. The complete opposite

of you, my friend. The two of you would make a fine double act.'

'A giant you mean?' Figgis said, feeling a knot twist in his stomach.

'Giant? No, I don't think so. Giants were a tale from our imagination, weren't they? But he's a huge man. I've never seen the like of him. He draws enormous crowds.'

'What is his name?' Figgis demanded.

'He can't pronounce it until morning when he's sober again,' Caerys laughed.

Tyne offered to refill the cups but Figgis refused for himself and on behalf of Gidyon.

'He calls himself Themesius, which is such an old-fashioned name don't you think?' Tyne said, filling his own cup, not noticing the dwarf was on his feet and making for the door.

'I want to see him,' he said.

Gidyon yawned.

Up, lad. Now! We've found Themesius!

Tyne did not fully understand the urgency to meet with the 'Big Man' as he was known. They had always steered away from calling him the obvious title of Giant because it might scare the little ones. Themesius was scary to look at, with long, dark hair and an equally long dark beard. His huge arms were covered in a thick black fur of hair, as were his legs, and his voice was so deep you could almost hear it rumbling from any part of the camp. Yet, despite his terrifying appearance, he was a gentle soul who had wandered out of the Great Forest one day, disorientated.

It just so happened that the Freak Show had been travelling on a relatively unused track of the northwest, hugging one of the famed fingers of the Forest, and everyone had been edgy at being in such close proximity to the supposedly enchanted place. When a huge man had suddenly lurched from the trees he had startled the first caravan so badly that the horses had shrieked and reared, breaking the axle. They had had no choice but to make camp in the very place they had wanted to leave far behind. As it turned out, the stranger had lost his memory and had no notion of his home, any family or why he had been in the Forest. All he knew was that his name was Themesius.

He had intended no harm and his strength had helped them make repairs to the damaged wagon in order to be on their way — this time with the big man in tow. He preferred to lope alongside the train of wagons and very quickly became a popular member of the travelling troupe, winning notoriety wherever they went.

Tyne explained this quickly to his new friends as he led them towards the darkest part of the camp and Themesius.

'Do you know of this fellow?' he asked Figgis.

'I knew a Themesius. He was of giant stature,' he admitted.

'There surely cannot be two such people roaming Tallinor,' Tyne offered.

Gidyon stumbled along behind. His head was feeling very blurry and he decided he definitely had no stomach for hard liquor. The ale was bad enough but combined with Tyne's nip . . . all he could think of was to lie down and yet he knew if he did, he would feel the world begin to spin. It was an awful dilemma.

'Why does he drink so much?' he asked Caerys, who also accompanied them.

'We don't know. He's always stony sober of a morning but he drinks vast amounts of his earnings each evening. He's nice enough but I don't have much to do with him. He hates snakes, you see.'

'Ah, that's right . . . and you swallow them!' He felt sick just thinking about it, his belly already churning from the drink.

Caerys beamed. 'I used to make Alyssa really squirm when I did it close up to her.'

Gidyon belched unintentionally. 'You'll have to tell me more about our Queen some time.'

'Gladly,' Caerys said. 'We're here, watch your head,' he said, pointing to a low branch the others were ducking beneath.

They entered a tent. Sprawled in a corner against some cushions was the tallest, broadest man Gidyon had ever seen.

'Ho! Themesius. I've brought some guests to meet you. Friends in fact,' Tyne said, nudging the slumbering man.

'Is he asleep?' Gidyon asked.

'He calls out in his dreams . . . that's what you heard,' Caerys said.

The big man did not stir. He snored loudly.

Figgis had to stifle the smile which leapt to his face. He turned to Tyne. 'That offer you made about being part of the show. Do you mean it?'

Gidyon wasn't sure he had heard correctly. A look from Figgis told him to hold his tongue. He did. It was agonising to speak anyway.

Tyne's ruddy face lit up. 'Of course I mean it. Have you changed your mind?' he asked, wondering why the dwarf was doing the talking for the pair all of a sudden.

'Yes, but only as far as Brittelbury.'

'Deal!' the man said and spat on his palm and held his hand out.

Gidyon sat down hard and then felt he must find the courage to lie down or just pass out.

Tyne grinned. 'Don't think the lad has ever tasted such fiery spirit before.'

Figgis shook the man's hand. 'Perhaps I should have warned him about the famous yellow liquor of the south,' he said.

'Caerys,' Tyne called. 'Go and see if old Bensy has space in the caravan.'

'No need,' Figgis said. 'Gidyon is asleep and I'm in no mood to carry him anywhere. I'm happy to bed down here. Themesius and I have much to catch up on.'

'He'll get a surprise when he wakes up, then,' Caerys said, bright-eyed.

'Indeed,' the dwarf said.

'Sleep well, Figgis,' Vyk Tyne said.

The two men left and Gidyon slipped into the merciful oblivion of sleep before his stomach could heave up its contents. When nothing more but the gentle snores of the lad interrupted the night, Figgis opened the Link.

Wake up, you rogue.

The giant opened one eye to a slit. *You took long enough. I wasn't sure how much longer I could keep up this pretence! Drunk each night, indeed.*

Figgis laughed and then wept as he hugged his oldest and greatest friend.

19

Trapped

Lauryn watched the servant's graceful, economical movements as he prepared a small breakfast of fruit and cheeses which had been brought to their cabin. They were on a ship and for the past few days she had refused all food and drink, but this morning had relented and agreed to a few sips of water from the man who called himself Titus. The effects of fear and no nourishment had left her light-headed, to the point where she could not remember how long they had been on horseback or even which direction they had headed. She had no recollection of boarding a ship.

He knew she watched him. 'Sip that water slowly,' he said softly, not expecting a reply.

Lauryn had not spoken a word since she had woken from the magical stupor into which Orlac had put her. She had screamed once at the sight of Orlac and then drifted into a contained silence in which it seemed she did not hear a thing. Orlac had shown no regard for her weakening health, pushing them onwards towards the north where he intended to board a ship to the Exotic Isles. Adongo noticed that the horses travelled faster than a horse should and could sense the powerful enchantment cast over them. They reached Caradoon at impossible speed. It did not take Orlac long to negotiate a crossing with the amount of coin he was bandying about.

'Where is he?' she said in a flat voice.

Hearing her speak took him by surprise but he did not show it. 'Not far away.'

'And where are we going?'

'To Cipres.'

'People will follow,' she said, pushing at a wisp of hair.

'He knows this.'

'It's what he wants. Is that right?'

'Perhaps,' Adongo said carefully. He had to be very cautious about what he said. He knew full well that Orlac could and would eavesdrop on any conversation. He had been briefed by Orlac to win the girl's faith. So, they trusted him. But somehow he needed to convey that he was more than a friend to her. And yet he could not reveal himself – must be seen to be playing along with their plan. He could not risk contacting Tor again. The first attempt had been exquisitely dangerous and he had only just survived that scrutiny. Orlac would not permit more use of magics.

'He is not whom he pretends to be, Titus.'

'I am only a servant, mistress. I have no knowledge of these things,' he lied.

'He is empowered.'

'I understand it is so and I would caution you not to test it.' Adongo did not know what else to say. He hoped somewhere in his words a couched message would be heard by Lauryn. 'My master prefers that his magics are not listened upon by others, especially those who may be empowered themselves.' He glared at her, imploring her to understand but Lauryn looked away, already her mind wandering in a different direction.

She sighed. 'What will he do with me?'

Adongo shrugged, hating the fact that he could not tell her more or reassure her of his bond with her. 'We shall be there shortly.'

Orlac and his guest had heard the conversation between Lauryn and the Moruk. The red mist which was Dorgryl shimmered. *I do not trust him.*

He is a tool.

So you say. Do you trust him?

I have no reason not to. A servant is no threat to us.

Dorgryl grudgingly agreed but did not give up his argument without making a final thrust. *Then mark my words, nephew.* He sighed and changed the subject. *How long before we reach port?*

Orlac was in no mood to talk. He looked out at the sea which buffeted the ship's sides and wished they were on dry land. *A few hours.*

After they docked, Lauryn was left in her cabin. She had finally agreed to down a few morsels at the constant nagging of the servant, Titus. He had now gone on deck to take instructions from his master. She thought of the master as Sylc but now wondered at his real identity and the hidden magics he had wielded in her room many nights previous. Gyl was ever in her thoughts. How could she have thought it was a good idea to create such pain for him? She could still see his hurt expression at the attention she had paid Sylc. More to the point, how could she have been so infatuated with the Regent and encouraged his attentions?

In the sharp light of day, when her emotions were not

being churned by jealousy, she could see she had behaved
with great stupidity and now she threatened everything
her parents, brothers and the Paladin had worked so hard
to do, which was to reunite everyone. So far she had kept
her fear at having been stolen from the palace tightly
strapped down within herself, but it constantly threatened to take flight and burst from her. In withdrawing
herself from everything, including sound, she had survived
this far but she knew in her heart worse was to come.

To this moment, though, the man called Sylc had asked
nothing of her. He had hardly spoken more than a dozen
words to her, travelling in silence. She sensed he was
constantly using his powers but she could not trace them
as he expertly shielded himself from her probes. It seemed
odd they had travelled so far in such a short time. She
had always believed the far north was an Eighthday or
more away by horse and that the port in the far west was
another Eighthday on top of that. For some reason she
had it in her mind that they had only travelled for a few
days by horse . . . or was she imagining it? Lauryn could
not be sure.

The desire to cast out to Gidyon or her father was
tempting and yet she resisted, despite her fear. Something
nagged at her, suggesting that her casting might put them
in danger. And there was something about the way Titus
looked at her. It was as though he was saying one thing
but actually meaning another. The business about Sylc
being empowered – Titus had not shown surprise and he
had reacted with great caution. She had run over what he
had said to her several times and she could not help feeling
that what Titus actually meant was that yes, the man called
Sylc is sentient and does not like to have his magics noticed,

and the glare he had given her seemed to implore that she
– or was it he – should not display any magical ability.

Was she imagining this? Was Titus communicating a
hidden message and, if so, why? Who was he if not a paid
servant of Sylc and therefore dangerous? What was his
interest in her? She could not help but notice how he took
care of her, fussed around her. What was that about? Why
should he care if she lived or died? Perhaps his life was
on the line if she did sicken too much and die, hence his
keen interest in keeping her well nourished. She sat in
her stuffy cabin and pondered, her mind finally coming
around to Sylc and what he might really be. He was hugely
empowered. Sentients with the wild magic – as her father
had explained – had only weak powers. But when the
Regent had used the stuporing force against her he seemed
to but gently push his powers and yet as they touched
her she felt their incredible potency.

Likewise, when Sylc disappeared and reappeared, she
felt the enormous concentration of magic at his call
although he seemed hardly to tap what was available to
him. This then, she decided, biting her lip and feeling
more than just a vague fear grab at her throat, was no
ordinary sentient soul. His looks set him apart from most
men; taller than any man she knew and very strongly
built, he was like her own father, Torkyn Gynt. And his
eyes, those strangely violet and compelling eyes, they were
so unusual as to be commented upon by all who met him
– as was his appearance. How was it that one of the ladies
of the court described him at the time of his arrival?
Lauryn remembered the woman's whispered words. *He is
a god*, she had murmured with awe.

The lady of the court was referring to his stunning

looks, of course, but it seemed now to Lauryn that it had been a well-chosen turn of phrase. Lauryn felt the thought snap into place and her blood felt suddenly icy. This was no ordinary man, indeed. This was in fact no man at all. If she trusted her instincts – and she felt they served her well now – she was in the presence of a real god. An angry one, whose true name was Orlac.

Orlac! She felt sick.

So, he had come amongst them already and he had stolen her. Why? Lauryn began to pace to stop herself from trembling. He must have worked out that she was Torkyn Gynt's daughter. He would use her as a lure for his bigger prize, knowing full well that when her father found out he would leave the Heartwood and come after her. But how would her father know, unless someone who knew of her plight could contact him?

She thought of Gyl. Her disappearance would have been discovered by now and, presuming he did not assume she had left without word with a stranger in the dead of night, then Gyl would begin a search and he would follow every clue. There could not be many of those. Who else would know? Not her mother, she had already left before the theft had occurred and would by now, she hoped, be reunited with her father, bringing Saxon, Cloot, Arabella and probably Solyana together again. Sallementro? No, he could not use the Link – unless her mother had removed the disk which, now she thought about it, was not so unlikely given where she was and with whom. So that was a possibility. If Alyssa's archalyt had been removed by Tor and the Link was open to her Paladin, he could relay the news of Lauryn's snatching. It made sense.

Her mind revolved around the Paladin now and she

went somewhere with her thoughts that she had not permitted before. Gidyon had already been found by one of his Paladin, Figgis. Was it so improbable that she too could have been discovered by one bonded to her? She counted them off in her head. The only Paladin yet to show themselves were Cyrus, Themesius, Juno and Adongo. Two of these belonged to her but which two? Her father had spoken of Adongo, whom he had met when they were both being transported to Cipres as slaves. He had described him as a man of few words, always carefully chosen. He was a Moruk of the nomadic tribes from the Exotic Isles. Swarthy and long-limbed they were, according to her father, with hairless faces and long dark hair.

Was it such a leap?

As she turned this new thought over in her mind, the man she was thinking on entered.

'We must leave. Regent Sylc awaits you outside.' It was a deliberate warning to stop her saying anything further. 'Please follow me,' he said.

Lauryn touched his arm and when he turned at that touch, he saw her put her finger to her lips to hush any query as she dipped her finger into the cup of water nearby and then scribed *Adongo?* onto the wooden bench. When she had finished, he looked up from the bench at her, gravely. He nodded once slowly, almost imperceptibly, but it was enough. Her heart leapt and she mouthed *thank you* to him, her eyes beginning to water as she felt a sense of safety wrap itself about her. He was here to protect her. Her Paladin had found her. Adongo shook his head to prevent her spilling any tears and then pointed to the wet patch on the bench. She hurriedly wiped the letters away with her skirt.

'After you, my lady,' he said and this time it was he

who felt his spirits lift, as she gave him a gentle smile.

Adongo prayed that Lauryn would not try to open the Link; he was still not sure whether Orlac would be able to hear them. They had arrived on deck and Orlac ignored them. A carriage awaited and Lauryn was told to get inside. His master followed, but Adongo was required to sit outside with the driver. He felt afraid for Lauryn and decided to take a chance with the Link, recalling that Tor had once mentioned that he could not hear what Alyssa and Saxon said to each other. Perhaps the Link between Paladin and bonded were special, whereas on the occasion of his casting to Tor several nights back, it had been a very public use of his magic. Anyone with Orlac's power and sensitivities to magic would be able to tap into such a random cast.

He risked everything in the hope that the conversations between Paladin and bonded were private as he sliced open a cautious Link with Lauryn.

Try not to show your fright.

I am no longer scared, she answered surprisingly calmly, *now that I know you are here. Is it dangerous talking like this?*

I'm hoping he cannot listen to our Link. We'll soon know. It seems we're safe. He's not reacting at all.

What is he doing?

Staring.

At what?

Me!

I shall keep the Link open.

Don't leave.

Not until death, child. You are my reason for being now.

'What are you smiling at?' Orlac asked.

'Apologies, Regent Sylc. It is a private thought.'

He was taken by surprise when she answered him. She

had shared not a single word with him since her capture. He wondered what had brought about the change.

'My name is not Sylc,' he said softly, still staring at her, a little sad to see the dark smudges around her hollow eyes. She was thin, too. But the beauty still glowed back at him and he admired the new defiance in her voice. He would enjoy her.

'What would you have me call you?'

'By my true name.'

'Then I shall call you Orlac,' she said, hoping it shocked him.

It did. She also heard Adongo's sharp intake of breath. *Was that wise?* he asked.

I don't know but I'll be damned if I'll cringe before him.

Adongo did not have time to answer. Orlac spoke again.

'How do you know this?'

'Let's say we've been expecting you.'

'You and . . . ?'

'We have.'

The god smiled. There was real grit in this girl and if she was empowered, well . . . she had not even tried to use it against him. Clever and beautiful.

She makes a mockery of you! hissed Dorgryl, incensed by this girl's hold over his nephew.

Orlac ignored him. 'And what should I call you?' he said to Lauryn instead.

'You already know my name. I do not hide behind disguises,' she sneered.

'I like the name Lauryn, though I keep wondering what your father will think of me when he learns I am enjoying carnal knowledge of my niece.' Orlac did not look away as he said it. He had intended it as a blow.

Until that moment Lauryn had felt strong again but suddenly her fragile defence crumpled. He was staring at her in that way he had that seemed to drag her into a private cocoon.

'Oh, you didn't know?' he added, feigning innocence, once he noticed that the barb had struck home. 'Your father, Torkyn Gynt, is my brother. Isn't that cosy?'

'You lie!' she shouted, her voice sounding suddenly ragged.

'Do I?' he said. 'Think about it. You're a very clever woman. You worked out who I was . . . now work out how it all fits together and I think you'll agree that we are very much family.'

He took her hand and kissed it. 'We are here. Welcome to my palace,' he said and alighted from the carriage.

Orlac heard a deep chuckle from within himself.

A masterful move, Dorgryl admitted. *She will not recover swiftly from that*.

As Adongo stepped down from the carriage and bowed to his master, he kept his face deliberately devoid of all emotion, although inside he was anything but calm. Torkyn and Orlac were brothers! So, the King of the Host had sent his second son. He closed his eyes with silent grief at this news and what lay ahead.

Tor and Alyssa had spent a joyful night of rediscovery, giving themselves completely over to one another. They bathed in the pool where they had first made love and sat naked against each other's body, revelling in being able to share this special time.

'You've learned some new tricks,' Alyssa admitted, her eyebrow arched slightly.

'Are you complaining?' Tor countered, as he kissed her full and perfect breast.

'Not at all. I'm just wondering where you gained such experience.'

'Well, they say practice makes perfect and so I kept practising over and over and over again until I knew it was just right,' he said, a look of innocence on his face.

'Oaf!' She threw a stick at him. 'I hate you!' But she laughed anyway.

'But I love you,' he said, pulling her close again and kissing her softly.

'Have you loved anyone since me, Tor?'

'No.'

'What about that girl you were so distraught over . . . will you tell me about it?'

He became suddenly serious. 'Eryn – she was a very special friend. I still can't believe she's dead, and so horribly. Goth will pay with his life this time, I swear it.'

'We must make him pay for all the lives he's taken or ruined,' she said sadly. 'Tell me about Eryn.'

And so he did. Alyssa felt a stirring of jealousy, not that he and Eryn had been intimate, but that she had shared part of his life that Alyssa had not been permitted to enjoy.

She stroked his cheek. 'Don't be sad about her. Be angry. We'll avenge her death, I promise you. Don't let's spoil these few precious moments we have.'

'Are you sure you want to hear this?' he asked.

'I do. I hold no grudge, Tor. I just feel cheated that we were kept apart.'

'I know. And of course then there was Sylven . . .' he continued, a wicked undertone to his voice, goading her into asking more.

'The Queen!'

'No less.'

'Tor! Who haven't you bedded?'

'Well, let's see now . . . I'd always hoped I might sneak between the sheets with the Lady Augusta. I never got the chance though I got close once. She was—'

Alyssa punched him this time. Hard. 'Stop it! Vile man.'

'Well, you asked,' he said plaintively, trying to force down the smile bursting from him.

He hugged her, then stood, theatrically, moving his arms for effect. 'The truth is I have bedded plenty of women but I have loved none of them. I have only ever loved one girl, since she was nine and I not much older. Alyssandra Qyn of Mallee Marsh – be she Queen of Tallinor or simply Naked Wench of the Heartwood – is my true love; my heart's desire, the reason I breathe.' He grinned then. 'And you'll note I'm far too much of a gentleman to even mention the slight indiscretion of bedding a king or falling in love with him.'

She looked at him seriously now. 'I do thank you for that. It was never the same love as I experienced for you.'

He took her hand and lifted her to her feet, wrapping a cloak they had been lying on around her slim shoulders. 'I already know it.' He kissed her. 'There is nothing to forgive.'

They heard a sound and turned to find Solyana staring gravely at them.

Is it time? Tor asked, hoping Rubyn had been found.

Strangers approach . . . you are needed, she replied and loped away into the undergrowth. They heard her as she disappeared. *Meet at the clearing.*

They dressed and quickly made their way to the meeting spot where they found Arabella and Saxon waiting.

'Have you heard anything?' Tor asked.

Saxon held up a brace of rabbits. 'I was hunting just outside the Heartwood. Solyana summoned me.' He shrugged and threw the rabbits down. 'Plenty of rabbit stew tonight for all.'

Arabella nodded when Tor looked towards her. 'Solyana called me. Do you know who comes?'

'No,' Tor admitted.

'Is it Goth?' Alyssa said.

No one answered, for they heard the sound of people crashing through the trees and the snap and crunch of twigs and branches breaking underfoot. And then suddenly three figures emerged into the clearing, fright written over their faces.

'Locky!' Tor exclaimed.

He looked towards the lad's two companions. 'The Light save us! Is that you, Hela?'

Alyssa saw a handsome woman curtsy. She looked dishevelled but relieved to see them. She did not miss the glint in the woman's eye as she looked upon Torkyn Gynt again.

'It is me, Tor. And I bring with me, her majesty, Queen Sarel of Cipres.'

Tor looked aghast and turned his gaze fully on the statuesque young woman before him. The last time he had seen Sarel she had been sobbing over the body of her dead mother and seemed to be just a young girl with ribbons in her hair. Here stood a proud young woman.

There was a defiance in her stance which shone through

the obvious fear they were all emanating. He bowed. Saxon followed suit he noticed, though Alyssa he saw remained upright. He smiled inwardly; so the Queen of Tallinor does not bow to the Queen of Cipres. No time to think on it. He strode towards them.

'Your majesty.' He took her hand and kissed it.

She smiled. 'I'm glad we found you.'

He led her towards Alyssa. 'Sarel, this is her highness, the King's Mother; our former Queen of Tallinor, Alyssa.'

Sarel felt herself blush — she had been thinking how impudent of that golden-haired woman not to curtsy before royalty. Oh, she had a lot to learn about curbing her impetuous nature. She nodded graciously, bending very slightly to the older woman.

'Your highness.'

Alyssa followed suit Tor was relieved to see. 'Welcome, Sarel. But you arrive in such haste — are you being followed?'

Locky was at Tor's side in a few strides and Saxon joined them.

'Tell me quickly,' Tor said.

Locky rubbed his face. Curiously, he was suddenly very distressed now that he felt safe. Until this moment, he had found steely courage in getting the women into the Forest and to sanctuary. He felt as though he could pass all the fear of responsibility over to Tor now. The relief was huge and he found his knees were trembling; in fact he fought hard not to break down.

Saxon laid a huge hand on the boy's shoulder. 'Calm, lad. You're safe now. Tell us, but fast.'

Locky took a deep breath. 'Goth follows. He nearly had us just past the last village. Janus,' he gulped and then found his composure. 'Janus forced us to leave him behind. He hit the horses, made us gallop at breakneck speed towards the Forest. I . . . I don't know what's become of him. He stayed to fight them . . . delay them I suppose, alone. Eryn will never forgive me.' He looked devastated.

Tor stiffened at the mention of Eryn's name and was glad when Hela came up beside them and took his hand, preventing him from further explanation to Locky. Alyssa, who had encouraged Sarel to sit and catch her breath, did not fail to notice the intimate gesture but she forced herself to rise above the jealousy it provoked.

'Hela,' Tor said, and embraced her. 'What has happened here?'

They all gathered near Sarel, sitting down and allowing racing pulses to slow in the warmth and safety of the Heartwood as Hela related their story as quickly as she could, beginning with a dream visit from a woman called Lys.

Goth was furious. He was down to just a pair of men, having left the two horseless men behind to bury their dead and make their way back to the north. He could not care less what happened to them, in truth. His duty was to find the Queen and he simply could not wait to dispatch the troublesome maid. The head of Quist banged unhappily beside him in the sack, blood leaking through the loose weave of the hessian, but it gave Goth comfort that it was another of Gynt's supporters dead and done with.

They were upon the Forest now. Rather impossibly a donkey stood grazing ponderously at the fringe. It reminded him of the bastard creature that had created havoc at Caremboche all those years ago. He ignored it and spurred his horse on, kicking and whipping at it viciously to go straight towards the trees which it seemed disinclined to do.

He entered the cool of the dark Forest at high speed, ahead of the other riders, knowing the branches were more than high enough for a mounted man to pass beneath. And so it came as a powerful shock when he felt his cloak snag on a branch and lift him from the saddle. He wrenched at the cloak but more branches seemed to entangle and entwine him and suddenly his horse was gone from beneath him, galloping into the depths of the Forest, riderless and with no direction. He found himself swung about, which was odd for there was no wind, and the trees began to pinch his skin where they held him.

He screamed to the man racing behind but was stopped in his command by the sight of the donkey suddenly kicking with its back legs, high enough to connect with the rider who had no chance of staying in the saddle. He dropped like a stone to the Forest floor where the donkey, more than just reminiscent of the one at Caremboche, waited until the dazed guard staggered to his feet. Then with one more well-aimed and very powerful kick of his hind legs, laid the man out cold . . . dead, Goth presumed from the trickle of blood he could see emerging.

He yelled to the final rider who had slowed his horse. 'Get me down, you cur!'

The man cast a glance towards his fallen companion and then back to Goth. 'You can hang there and die for all I care, you scum. You are not one of us. You are a murderer and a coward to boot. Our men die and you care not. You torture women and kill without mercy.' He spat towards Goth. It was an empty gesture for Goth was way up in the trees. 'I go no further in this place. I've heard the legends of the famous Great Forest of Tallinor. I hope you rot in its branches,' he said. The man turned his horse and led it out into the sun.

Goth twisted and cursed but he was well and truly held. He had no idea how it could be so but he stopped struggling and set his mind to work out an escape. No brilliant idea had leapt to mind after several minutes. He was in trouble and alone.

Without warning and hardly daring to believe it was happening, he witnessed a large branch reaching towards him. He took a sharp breath and tasted fear – a rare sensation for Goth – as the branch wrapped sinews of itself around him. He could not cry out; he felt frozen and his throat too dry to make a sound. And then he was being whipped savagely from tree to tree. He lost all sense of which way was up or down. All Goth could focus on was the next fierce and unpredictable movement he would travel in. He felt like a child's rag doll as the strength seeped from his body and the trees had their fun with him. At one stage he felt his arm dislocate from its shoulder socket and the pain was immense but the trees cared not. They continued to sometimes throw, sometimes stretch him impossibly, but mostly whip him from branch to branch. Sometimes they grabbed him by the leg, other times the damaged arm and he screamed out in agony but no one heard.

Goth lost track of how long the punishment lasted. He was beyond registering the pain now. His body was so racked with it, everywhere hurt. The magic of it stunned him. At one point he thought he heard the trees whispering, laughing at him. He thought he must have passed out because he suddenly felt the huge thump as his broken body hit the ground with force. He lay there dazed and confused. Somehow he knew he could still move his legs and one arm, though all movement was painful. The other arm was useless. He wondered if the trees somehow knew not to break him completely.

Goth opened his eyes and stared into the pair of bright blue ones he hated more than any eyes in the Land . . . it was Torkyn Gynt.

'Welcome to the Heartwood, Goth. I'm delighted you could join us. There are others here who wish to offer their warm welcome too.'

Alyssa came into view. He felt a pang . . . was it a thrill, hate? He knew not. She said nothing, just stared at him with disdain.

He looked beyond her, squinting through his pain. The bastard Kloek stood looking pleased by her side, as well as a woman he did not recognise. Quist's brother-by-marriage, the lad, stood next to the despised Ciprean maid, Hela. They both had hate written on their faces.

'Greetings, Goth,' Hela sneered.

And then finally the Queen. The young woman he had been told to retrieve by a vengeful master. It was all over now.

'We beat you, Goth. You're pathetic,' was all she said before turning her back on him.

And in that moment of desperation as he realised he was indeed beaten he somehow found he could laugh.

'I've brought you something, Gynt,' he said in his effeminate voice, having noticed that the sack was still tied to his side. 'Open it.'

Tor would never know why he did as Goth suggested. He was still quite shocked that the former chief inquisitor had been delivered to him with such ease and in such a manner. The Forest must have dealt with any of his companions.

He tipped the sack's contents onto the ground. Janus Quist's bloodied head rolled to rest by his feet. He heard Locky retch and he presumed it was Sarel screaming behind him.

Goth laughed through his pain. Even now he impressed himself at the effect he managed to have on people. 'Like my gift?' he asked. 'I wish I could have brought you a trophy of the pirate's wife. But most of her is lying in a puddle providing a feast for the scavengers,' he said. 'Pretty body. Plucky thing, told me nothing; didn't even give me the satisfaction of a scream when I slit her belly open.'

He was able to say nothing more. Locky's boot connected so hard with his head, Goth was unconscious and motionless on the floor a moment later.

Alyssa's chest heaved up and down with the effort of staying calm as she and Saxon rushed to Locky's side. The lad buried his face in Alyssa and she soothed him as best she could. His sobs broke everyone's hearts.

'She was all I had,' he kept repeating.

Kythay reappeared, strolling towards the prone body of Goth. He shocked all gathered by urinating on the former chief inquisitor's head. It had the desired effect. The burning, acidic liquid brought the hated man back to consciousness, but only just. He groaned and the donkey strolled away into the undergrowth. It was a comic gesture but no one smiled.

'What now?' Goth said, his mind very blurred and his body in pain.

Torkyn Gynt's blue gaze of wrath burned into the mauled face of Almyd Goth and answered the question with two words. 'Your death.'

It was no surprise to Alyssa when Sallementro appeared a few hours later; another dishevelled and distressed rider. He refused all sustenance but asked for a few minutes to catch his breath. He had ridden, without stopping, until he reached the Great Forest.

He began to explain the situation back at the palace. Alyssa hushed him, explaining that they knew about the Regent Sylc.

'Sal, listen to me now,' she said to her babbling musician. 'Sylc is not whom he pretends to be. We believe he is Orlac.'

Sallementro's mouth opened and closed and then his eyes grew wider. 'Impossible! How can that be? He was amongst us!'

Tor nodded. 'Can you describe him?'

The musician gave a detailed summary of the man he knew as Regent Sylc and with each word Tor felt his already battered spirits spiralling downwards.

'It is him,' he said.

'How did he get her away without a fight?' Alyssa asked, seeing Tor's crestfallen expression.

Sallementro told them all that they had gleaned and managed to piece together. 'Gyl is wrathful. He has already left for the north with Herek and a full retinue of the Guard.'

Tor shook his head. 'He has no idea what he's dealing with. They are all doomed.'

'A boy is dead and if Sal's interpretation is right, then

the woman he may love has been stolen from his own palace. What do you expect him to do? Cringe and hope someone else rescues her?' Alyssa sounded angry.

'No, I'm sorry, Lyssa. Of course he's doing the only thing he can do.'

'That's right,' she said. 'If only to save face. I warned him about this, though. He is not completely ignorant.'

'Does he believe it?'

'He's sceptical but there've been too many strange occurrences for him to ignore the story I gave in colourful detail. If we could just intercept him somehow.'

'I'll go,' the musician volunteered.

'No, I will,' Locky said. 'I insist, Tor. I know the north better than most and I'll wager I'm a better, faster rider than the singer,' he said, his chin jutting towards the ever-present lute strung on the singer's back.

Sallementro did not have the strength to bristle at the insult. And Alyssa spoke to him. *He is young. He is not careful with his words . . . and he's just learned that his sister and her husband have been murdered.*

Tor asked Sallementro how long ago Gyl had left for the north.

The musician shrugged. 'We all left the same morning. He headed for Caradoon and I made for the Forest. I would estimate he is still two, possibly three days away.'

'Then I can make it back there in time,' Locky said. 'If I leave now.'

Tor walked away from the clearing. He needed to think. He hated the thought of Locky racing off alone to who knows what.

He is safest with the King's Guard. Cloot's reassuring voice entered his head.

I know . . . and it's everything he's ever dreamed of doing.

Let him go. Let him feel he is doing something towards avenging his sister's death.

Tor turned back to Locky. 'All right. Head off now.' He saw Sarel's face crumple. It could not be helped. 'I hope Gyl believes you.'

'Here,' Alyssa said, pulling something from her pocket. 'Give him this, Locky. Then he'll know you have come from me.' She handed the lad a small green disk.

'What is it?' he asked her.

'Something I will never need again. But the King will know you have come from his mother and that what you say is true. Tell him everything you know, including that we have Goth and will deal with him and that he should remember everything that I warned him about is coming true.'

She saw Sallementro cast a glance towards the bundle of black on the floor. 'Is that the famous Goth?' He had not noticed him until now.

'Not for long,' Tor said, his voice as hard as anyone had ever heard before.

'He's alive still?'

'Just,' Alyssa replied. 'His life must be ended, Sal. He is evil.'

'Oh, I agree. I was just thinking that it might be a waste to kill him here and now.'

Locky busied himself checking the saddle on a horse which between them Kythay and Solyana had managed to coax beneath the trees.

'What do you mean?' Tor said to the musician.

'Well, several years ago I was travelling through the furthest northern climes. Don't ask why, it's a hellish place.

I met a man who said he had once worked for Goth and knew some of the secrets. I think he may have been a man on the run because the inquisitors had been disbanded.'

He saw irritation cross Alyssa's face and knew to get on with his tale. 'Anyway, I was on the run too from my family and we ended up getting drunk together and he said he wanted to show me a place. I thought it wouldn't be far but we ended up travelling for two days into the mountains and there I witnessed the most incredible thing.'

Alyssa thought she might have to slap her Paladin if he drew this tale out much longer. *Sal, people could be dying whilst you tell this story, certainly many lives are in peril. Can you get to the point!*

He shrugged. 'Apologies, I tell stories with my music. Habits die hard. The man showed me the place where all the sentients are taken who didn't die from Goth's torture or bridling process. It just occurs that those survivors should have the satisfaction of seeing Goth's end.'

Apart from the noise of their surprise at his suggestion, both Tor and Alyssa took steps forward. He thought both were going to hit him.

'Sallementro, where is this place!' Alyssa said. 'Could you tell us how to find it?'

'Um . . .' He looked thoughtful. 'Yes, I think I could, though we would need someone who knew the mountains well.'

'You need Figgis!' Saxon said. 'If only we could make contact with him and Gidyon.'

I could fly to Brittelbury, Cloot suggested.

Tor noticed Locky was ready and keen to leave. 'Let's see Locky on his way and we'll make decisions.'

Locky left without further delay. He hugged Hela and

bowed low to Sarel before kissing her hand, promising they would see each other again. The Queen had gathered her composure, Hela was glad to see, and was showing that she had the mettle to make a strong monarch. Alyssa too had hugged him hard. Although they hardly knew one another she remembered the numb feeling of abandonment and loneliness, with everyone you love dead. Locky seemed to understand this, accepting her affection with a sad grin. Saxon wished he could go with the lad but his place was now at Alyssa's side and together with Sallementro they would put her life before theirs.

'Don't forget all I taught you on our first journey here,' he said, squeezing the boy in a bear hug. 'Remember me to Herek . . . perhaps you can make an impression on the man and make your dream come true.'

'I intend to,' Locky said. 'You watch me, I'll be Prime one day.'

Arabella and Sallementro hoped the Light would guide him safely and then only two remained to farewell.

Locky stroked Cloot and said something just for the falcon which he knew the bird could hear.

'He says likewise,' Tor replied on behalf of Cloot.

'Tor, we will avenge her, won't we?' Locky suddenly urged.

'I promise you, Locky, what you do now is part of that vengeance. Goth is merely a pawn in this much bigger game. Forget him. You get word safely to the King and Herek and you will have single-handedly made a major mark in helping to save Tallinor. I give you my word, Eryn will not have died in vain. She saved three lives by her incredible bravery and sacrifice . . . one of those lives is a Queen's. Quist too. His courage had no bounds when it mattered – he also gave his to save your life. Both of them will be remembered by the gods.'

Locky felt the grief gather and constrict his throat. But he also felt pride that he was part of this now and he would not fail them – as Eryn and Janus had not failed him.

'May the Light guide you, Locky.'

'And you,' he replied, hugging Tor. 'We'll meet again soon.'

He climbed onto the horse which seemed curiously refreshed and noticed his saddlebags were bulging with fresh stocks for his journey. He looked towards Tor.

'The Heartwood provides,' Tor said with a shrug and then Locky was turning his horse and moving away from them. He cast a single glance back for Sarel and waved once. Then he was gone.

He'll make it. Cloot said.

I believe he will, Tor agreed. *He's a brave lad.*

Everyone gathered around a meal which Arabella insisted they eat.

'No good decision can be made on an empty stomach,' she cautioned and despite their low spirits, they all tucked into the food which had miraculously been laid out beneath a tree near the pool.

As they ate, they talked softly. Tor reached over and took Alyssa's hand. It was then that he heard Solyana's soft voice in his head.

It is time.

He turned and saw the wolf. She wanted them to follow her. He squeezed Alyssa's hand and when she smiled gently at his touch he told her.

My love. I believe our son is due. He was amazed at how steady his voice sounded whilst his heart thumped against his chest.

Alyssa's eyes immediately misted. *Where?* Her voice was not so steady.

Come. Solyana wishes us to go with her. They stood and when the others looked towards them, he explained that the wolf had come for them. Saxon, Sallementro and Arabella nodded with understanding.

'We shall wait for you here,' Saxon said.

As soon as Solyana saw them approaching, she turned and led the way. Tor knew Cloot followed silently amongst the trees and he was glad. He dared not look at Alyssa. She held tightly to his arm and willed herself to stay calm. They walked, without talking, for what felt like a long time until they were in a part of the Heartwood neither had seen before. Tor commented on this to the wolf.

The Heartwood retains many mysteries, she replied. *Now we wait.*

Tor was holding his breath. The anticipation of this moment was too great and he expected it was the same for his wife whose fingers were digging into his arm as she clutched him close.

Cloot landed gently on his shoulder. They waited.

20

The Trinity and Paladin Complete

Orlac dismissed her two servants, telling them to take Lauryn to the baths and get her cleaned up.

'I shall see you soon,' he commanded before turning to Adongo and speaking quietly. 'Remember your role. I must have her trusting you. I don't want to see you leaving her side.'

'As you wish, my lord,' Adongo said, bowing low and thanking the Light for this stroke of luck.

'Where is Juno?' Orlac demanded, as his long legs took the beautiful flight of marble stairs two at a time.

A servant curtsied. 'She awaits the girl, my lord.'

'Send Juno straight up when she is done,' he ordered and disappeared onto a landing.

Adongo immediately fell in alongside Lauryn.

What now? she asked.

A bath. You'll enjoy it.

When does he mean to see me again?

He'll wait for a while. He'll need to keep Xantia happy.

Xantia?

As beautiful as she is dangerous. We need to keep her away from you.

And Juno?

You'll meet her now and we shall be complete. He smiled and it was a wonderful broad smile which lit up a face normally devoid of expression.

One of the servants who led them noticed his smile. 'What are you grinning about, Adongo? Was the trip with him that good?'

'No.' He did not elaborate and they wisely let it alone. Adongo was strange and they accepted his curious ways.

The girl pointed. 'Here we are, then. Good luck, Miss Lauryn. If you are a favourite of his, then perhaps you'll be safe. Just watch out for her.'

'Who?' Lauryn asked, guessing the answer.

'The bitch, Xantia. The whore who thinks she's now royal. I pray for the child of our Queen Sylven. She got away, brave thing. Didn't think she had it in her but perhaps one day she can return and save us.'

She was probably going to say more but Adongo hushed her. 'I shall take our guest from here. Thank you.'

The two women disappeared.

Come now, my lady, Adongo said kindly. *Let us complete the Paladin.*

I don't understand.

You will.

The Flames of the Firmament appeared, one by one winking into existence around them, increasing in speed until dozens turned to hundreds and flared into life, their chimes making their very own special music. They danced around the trio who waited.

They love you, Alyssa said.

They love the Heartwood and what belongs to it.

Do you belong to it?

I suppose I must.

Could you live here for ever?

Yes.

They know this. It is why they love you.

I keep wondering what they are . . . they talk to me sometimes.

Alyssa was going to say more but she felt Tor tremble. She could not see anything but held the Link open and remained silent.

Tor had felt the enormous surge of power before the air around them became brittle. He thought he could feel his hair standing on end.

He comes, whispered Solyana.

The shimmering intensified as did the thrum of a mighty magic being wielded. The song of the Flames had changed to a familiar welcome as their god, Darmud Coril, appeared.

And so we prepare to welcome back our son, the god said.

Tor, Alyssa and Cloot heard him and gave silent thanks. They watched the shimmering which now seemed to be focusing itself towards a great old oak – by far the largest they had ever seen in the wood. The shimmer began to change into a light which became stronger, splitting into thousands of colours and beginning to throb in time with the chanting of the Flames. Tor was reminded of the day he witnessed Cloot transform from man to falcon and felt sure the bird echoed his thoughts though he dare not whisper a word across the Link.

The light now blazed so sharply and so brilliantly white, they had to look away, closing their eyes tightly and in that moment of looking away, Rubyn was delivered

. . . returned to Tallinor. The deafening song of the chimes and the equally penetrating hum of the magic stopped instantly, creating an intense silence.

It was not Darmud's voice, nor was it Solyana who spoke. Nevertheless the voice Tor heard was so familiar. The voice of a man whom Tor thought he may never see again.

'Tor. Meet your son, Rubyn,' said Kyt Cyrus.

Tor looked towards the tree to witness the amazing sight of a young man emerging from the trunk of the oak. It seemed to unwrap layers of itself as branches lifted away and up to give him back to them. Rubyn raised his head to look upon his true parents for the first time. And they wept. He was the perfect combination of both. Where Gidyon was the duplicate of his father and Lauryn echoed her mother so strongly, Rubyn melded both. Tall, with honey-gold hair and soft grey eyes with flecks of green, he smiled tentatively and there was his father echoed strongly in that face.

Neither parent could speak, they were both so consumed by love and relief that their boy was safe.

'He has made a long journey to be with you,' Cyrus encouraged, understanding their churning emotions. 'We both have.'

Tor looked at his old friend. As their eyes locked much was said in a glance whilst still more remained to be said and explained.

But for now, the child was everything and Cyrus turned to his charge. 'Go to your parents, Rubyn.'

They all moved at once and Rubyn found himself caught up in a fierce embrace, his mother reaching him first; she put her arms around the child. At that moment the love she felt for Tor and for her three children, and her determination to protect them all, overwhelmed her.

Tor's long arms wrapped around his wife and his boy and his tears flowed freely that he was safe and that he was found. *Welcome back, precious boy*, Tor whispered across the Link.

Cyrus looked up into the trees and grinned towards Cloot, who flew to his shoulder.

They both had the same thought.

And so the Trinity is found.

Inside the villa dedicated as a private bath house, the day's light was softly diffused through various pastel-coloured panes of glass. A great haze of steam lifted from an exquisitely designed pool from which the scent of lavender and gardenia, mint, jasmine and orange blossom wafted. The deliciously mingling fragrances immediately soothed Lauryn and calmed her anxiety. Inhaling them, she looked about her and saw that the walls were adorned with gorgeous murals of the gods at play. The pictures had such arresting perspective that Lauryn could imagine strolling down one particular pathway through the perfectly painted archway covered with a pale pink climbing rose and into a sprawling orchard.

'It's so beautiful,' she said.

Adongo encouraged her to step further into the villa and then he locked the door behind them. Lauryn looked about the bath house with wonder and finally noticed a young woman, older than her but nevertheless still young and striking, standing in the middle of the pool. She was covered by a light shift for modesty but its dampness showed off a very neat and lovely figure.

'I would like you to meet Juno.' *She is your Paladin*. 'She will look after you and we will both see to your needs.'

Adongo saw Juno query his use of the Link and he nodded. They could see relief flit across her face.

Lauryn, I have waited many years to greet you, child. I will not leave you now, until death.

With those few words – as the final member linked with her bonded – the Paladin together felt a strange opening of their minds as the ten guardians and their five charges were finally linked.

Tor broke free from the embrace as he felt a shift within. *Did you feel it?*

It has happened, Cloot said. *Do you hear me, Cyrus?*

I hear you, bird, the former prime said dryly but reached to touch the falcon, showing his wonder at the moment.

Tor, we are complete. The last of the Paladin has linked with their bonded.

Alyssa had heard all of this. *Do you think it's Lauryn?*

Tor answered. *I'd guess it is. So this means Themesius and Juno are amongst us.*

'I'm a little hurt you haven't formally introduced us,' Cyrus said, approaching Alyssa.

Tor ran his hand through his hair. 'Light! I'm sorry. Alyssa, this is the famous Kyt Cyrus.'

And you well and truly surpass the beautiful woman he described, Cyrus said privately to Alyssa as he raised her to her feet. He bowed. 'I am privileged to meet you at last and honoured that your special boy was put in my care.'

'Cyrus, I want to hear every last detail of your tale but first, Rubyn, let us welcome you back to the Heartwood,' Tor said, extracting Alyssa from the handsome soldier's gaze.

Stealing my thunder, are you? Solyana said to Tor affectionately, and Rubyn looked up at her voice.

'Solyana!' He broke free from where they stood to lope towards the wolf and bury his face and hands in her fur. She permitted it and even nuzzled him herself, her huge tail thumping, for she was his bonded Paladin and in no small state of joy that he was returned to her.

Let us sit here and share Rubyn's past, she suggested. *Cyrus, you begin.*

Alyssa felt instantly drawn to the tall, handsome soldier. She had heard so much about him from Tor and she knew how distraught her husband had felt when he lost Cyrus to the Heartwood. Now they had the reason why he was taken. She listened to the story of her son unfold.

Cyrus explained how he was escorted that night by Solyana to a special place in the Heartwood where he was greeted by Darmud Coril, the Flames of the Firmament and all the creatures of the Forest.

'I was told I had a special role to play,' he said. 'But I didn't know what it was at the time. I just knew it was right. That this was where I belonged and what I had searched for since my family's death.'

'So you didn't know you were Paladin?' Tor sounded amazed.

'No. Not until the moment this large oak here, miraculously bent its branches down and handed me a newborn baby and Solyana told me that I would have to raise him, teach him everything I knew about his father and all that I learned of the Heartwood.' He looked at Alyssa. 'I was never permitted to see you when you lived here, more's the pity,' he said, appreciating her radiant smile. 'But Solyana told me all about you and of course Tor had bored us senseless with every minute detail for most of the journey to the Heartwood anyway.' He paused because his audience was laughing at Tor who shrugged and took Alyssa's hand.

'How could I not?' he asked.

'Indeed,' Cyrus replied looking towards Rubyn. 'He was such a fragile soul. I worried so much about you.'

'You still do,' Rubyn said.

That's a Paladin's job, child. I worry constantly about your reckless father! Cloot said into their minds. I could tell you some stories to make your hair curl.

'I think not,' Alyssa said, pretending to glare at the falcon.

I would like to hear those stories some time, Rubyn said, shielding and talking just to Cloot. He heard the bird's chuckle in his mind.

Cyrus continued: 'Anyway, between Solyana and myself, as well as the constant vigil by Darmud Coril and even the damn strange donkey who kept suddenly appearing, we kept Rubyn alive. And then, to my astonishment he began to thrive and grow. We knew he would be safe and that's when Darmud Coril told me it was time to leave the Heartwood.'

It broke my heart to let Rubyn go but I knew Cyrus would keep him safe. He needed the influence of his own kind around him too, Solyana said.

It was Rubyn who picked up the tale. 'And so the trees absorbed us, didn't they, Cyrus? . . . and took us to another world.'

The soldier nodded. 'That's right. We travelled not knowing where we were headed but we arrived at a place not so different from Tallinor and made it our home.'

'How did you live?' Alyssa asked incredulously.

Cyrus shrugged. 'Much the same as we do here. We

found a disused cottage nearby a forest. It suited the lad to be near the wood and I certainly prefer a quiet life and there we lived.'

'We had chickens and a goat, ducks and Cyrus even gave me my own pony. Then I grew too big for him and we bought a foal and raised her so I could ride to school each day,' Rubyn said.

'The local priory encouraged any gifted students they stumbled upon with an education. I think they hoped Rubyn would go into the priesthood. I didn't say anything which might sway that belief. I was happy he was learning his letters and numbers. I think he can even read!'

The last was said with deliberate irony. And Tor and Alyssa noticed the shove Rubyn gave to Cyrus and the obvious shared private joke at the soldier's comment. They were clearly very close . . . and why not, they both acknowledged privately on their Link. Cyrus was effectively the only parent Rubyn had known for all of his life. They, his parents, were the strangers. Tor urged Alyssa not to feel sad about this. It was natural for their son to feel this way about Cyrus.

They would have to earn his love. She agreed, of course, but all she wanted to do was hug him and never let him go. She wished she could gather up all three children and do the same.

Cyrus continued. 'Our lives were happy and blissfully uneventful. Until of course that day Rubyn collapsed and then not so long afterwards, a messenger appeared and told us we had to return to Tallinor.'

'Was her name Yargo?' Tor asked.

Rubyn answered. 'That's right. She was very lovely and said she had been travelling a long time to find me. She said you had summoned me.'

Tor nodded. 'I did. But I thought I was calling back the two children I knew of. She never told me about you, Rubyn.'

Cyrus and Rubyn looked puzzled. 'Who are these other children?' Cyrus asked.

Tor and Alyssa looked taken aback. 'Don't you know?'

Solyana's gentle voice explained. *They know nothing of them.*

'Tell us,' he said.

And so Tor told his friend and especially his son about the brother and sister who were born first. He also explained their individual tales of arrival into Tallinor and realised this was the first time their mother was hearing these stories too. He kept the burning of Duntaryn and the subsequent deaths as brief as possible.

'So Lauryn had already met Gyl?' Alyssa queried.

'Well, yes, that's right but I didn't know who this Under Prime was at the time. Neither did Saxon, who had been away during Gyl's appointment,' he replied. 'But neither of them have any memory of what happened before their arrival. It's interesting that you have.'

Cyrus shrugged slightly. 'Very little to recall, in truth. Our life really was very tranquil and remote.'

Rubyn had been thinking on all that Tor had revealed. 'So my reason for being is to be one of the three who make up the Trinity. Is this right?'

Tor nodded. 'Until Sorrel told us of your existence, Rubyn, we had no idea what the Trinity was. Yes, it's our belief that you three children are the Trinity.'

'So what do we have to do?'

'Wait for a visit from a Dreamspeaker.' Alyssa's sarcasm was unmistakable.

Rubyn looked at her, perplexed, whilst Tor gave her a sideways glance as quiet admonishment.

'We're not sure, Rubyn. But I think we will begin to learn more now that you are here.'

Perhaps we must reunite these children and then one hopes their role will be revealed, Cloot suggested.

Ever wise, Cloot, Solyana admitted. *We must bring all of our own back to the Heartwood.*

'First we deal with Goth,' Tor said.

He heard Cyrus growl. 'Goth!'

Alyssa and Tor both sighed. He answered the soldier. 'You don't know the half of it. And probably don't want to but there's a lot for you to catch up on.'

'Such as?'

Tor felt nervous. How to tell his old friend so much bad news. He knew the soldier demanded honesty and brevity. There was no point in hedging the truth.

'Goth is a long, long story in itself. I'll share that with you when we take you back to the others because you'll be pleased to know that he is presently unconscious and trussed like a pig for roasting . . . courtesy of the Heartwood's vines.'

'The Light strike me!' the soldier said. 'I can't wait to see this. And the rest?'

'Is all bad news,' Tor admitted. 'I'm sorry you hear it so bluntly from me but both the King and Queen you served are dead.'

They watched the former prime's complexion pale as his expression drooped into one of complete shock and disbelief. 'Lorys dead?'

Tor took Alyssa's hand. He knew she would not want to live through this again but he needed to tell this swiftly.

'Cyrus, I should tell you that you are in the presence of the former Queen of Tallinor. Alyssa was married to Lorys.'

It seemed impossible that Cyrus could be shocked further.

Tor hurried on. 'Lorys died after being struck by a lightning bolt not so long ago. But Nyria died first about a year ago because of her weak heart.' He tried to summarise their story. 'Alyssa, after watching me being stoned to death, remained at the palace and Lorys fell in love with her.' He realised this was not coming out well. 'Oh dear, this must all sound so confusing.'

Cyrus nodded very slowly, then gave a shake of his head. 'Wait, slow down. What do you mean you were stoned to death?'

Now everyone took a deep breath. This might take longer than a simple briefing.

Rubyn looked from his parents to his guardian, baffled by what he was listening to. Cloot rescued him.

Come, Rubyn. Solyana and I will take you on a stroll so you can reacquaint yourself with the Heartwood.

I would like that.

Cyrus has much to hear. Let them tell him and they will join us shortly, Solyana said gently. *Anyway, I want you all to myself for a while.*

Rubyn grinned and dug his hand deep into the silver-tipped fur of his wolf Paladin and together with the falcon on his shoulder walked deeper in the Heartwood, flames burning brightly and dancing around him.

21

Heading North

Figgis and Themesius talked into the early morning,
learning each other's colourful stories of how they came
to be where they were. When Gidyon finally stirred,
they suggested he take some water. They then risked
raising him to his feet but once upright he promptly
returned the recent drink. They dragged him outside
the tent in case there was more to come, which proved
a wise decision as Themesius was soon holding him over
the bushes, the two men feeling sorry for their young
charge.

'Your tale is impressive for a short man,' the giant said
over Gidyon's noise. Figgis was about to make some sharp
comment back when they felt the shift within themselves.
Even Gidyon, in his state, stood up.

'What's happened?' he croaked.

It has taken place, said Figgis.

We are returned. The Paladin is complete again. Themesius
uttered this reverently.

Gidyon looked at both of them. 'What does it mean?'

Figgis tapped him gently on the back. He knew how

wretched the lad must be feeling from the previous night's liquor. *It means, boy, that the last of us has linked with their bonded one. Now the real battle begins.*

The two Paladin looked thoughtfully at one another, speaking across their own private Link. *Let's allow him some peace whilst he can still enjoy it.*

Figgis nodded.

'So, with that thought in mind, how about breakfast?' Themesius offered and could not help but grin at the nauseous look on Gidyon's face.

His joviality was lost in the same instant as all three heard the voice of Torkyn Gynt across the Paladin Link.

Gidyon, son. Where are you?

Gidyon ignored his aching head. *Father! I am with Figgis and a giant of a man called Themesius, my second. We're in a town and headed for Brittelbury.*

He heard his father make a sound of approval at hearing that they were safe. *Lauryn?* he said next. They could all hear the worry in his question.

I'm here. Everyone heard her voice catch.

This is Juno. The seer spoke to save them hearing Lauryn weep. *She is safe for the moment. But we have to get her away from here.*

Juno, this is Lauryn's mother. What does he mean to do with her? Alyssa's alarm was evident and it was Lauryn who answered, keen to make sure she was not seen as cowardly, despite her fright. *It's a trap. He's using me to lure you to Cipres. Neither of you must come.*

Her father cut in. *Does he know who you are?*

That I'm your daughter, yes.

But does he know what you are? Tor persisted.

If you mean, does he know that I am one of three children

*and the Trinity . . . no, I don't think so. The Trinity has not
been mentioned.*

*Good girl. Be brave now. Tell him nothing. He won't harm
you. It's me he wants, child.*

Tor hated the lie he told his own daughter. He believed
Orlac would have no scruples over whom he harmed so
long as he could wreak his vengeance on the person who
represented the target of his hate. Alyssa knew it too. She
turned away from him.

Lauryn, she said. *We are coming for you.* She spoke over
her daughter's objections. *You keep her safe, Juno.*

Wait! Lauryn cried, desperate to tell them of the relationship between Tor and Orlac. But the seer closed the
Link and hushed her. 'Be still, child. We cannot risk these
conversations.'

Juno continued to pour warm water gently over her
bonded one to soothe her fright. She knew better than all
of them. She knew Orlac wanted this girl – had wanted her
from the very first moment she had described the woman
from the dream. The less Lauryn heard the better right now.
She would need a clear mind and strong heart. Any talk
over the Link at present would only undermine her resolve.

Gidyon had regained his wits sufficiently to realise that
Lauryn must be in trouble.

Where is Lauryn? he demanded of his father.

There was no point in not telling him the truth. *Orlac
has her.*

Figgis, Themesius and Gidyon felt the same spike of
shock the others had experienced earlier. *How?*

*It would take too long to explain. The fact is, she's trapped
in Cipres. I need time to think on this. I'm sorry, Themesius,*

that your welcome is so brief but it is nonetheless heartfelt and offered with the greatest of sincerity by Alyssa and myself.

The giant's great voice rumbled gently. *I am privileged to be Paladin to your son.*

What do you wish us to do? It was the familiar voice of Figgis.

Tor was firm. *Get the stone back quickly.*

We are on foot — four days perhaps from Brittelbury, Figgis estimated.

Has Gidyon still got that purse I gave him? Alyssa asked.

Hardly touched, he answered.

Buy horses, Saxon suggested. *Which town are you in?*

They looked at Themesius for an answer. *It's called Warbyn, in the northwest,* the giant said.

Saxon nodded. *I know it. There is a large stable complex in the town.*

But no horse big enough for me, Saxon, old friend. There was great affection in Themesius's voice.

A cart, then. Two horses. You should cut that journey by more than half. It cannot exceed a full day's journey from Warbyn, surely, if you get them up to a gallop for the most part?

Tell us when you have the stone, Tor said, *and hurry!*

Where will you both be? Gidyon asked, referring to his mother and father.

Dealing with someone who has long outstayed his welcome in this world.

The Link was cut.

Themesius scratched his beard, not understanding and realising his companions were just as puzzled by Tor's last response. Well, they had their task set and he felt it was best to put one foot in front of the other immediately and make a start.

'I guess we may have to pass on breakfast then, Gidyon.'

He watched the boy turn back towards the tree and could not help but enjoy the scathing look from Figgis.

Tor considered the row of people before him, all wearing expectant expressions. Their numbers had certainly swelled. His blue gaze came to rest on Rubyn, who, predictably, was seated between Cyrus and Solyana. It was right that he was but Tor felt a pang on behalf of Alyssa who, he could tell, just wanted to hold her boy tight and keep him safe.

I'm sorry I didn't tell them you are found, he said for Rubyn's hearing only.

When the time is right, his son replied, his expression unreadable.

Tor felt a different sort of pang this time. He realised that whereas Gidyon was self-sufficient and Lauryn was perhaps more dependent, the two of them were already close to him and both quite sociable in their approach to people. Rubyn was different. It was true that he had not shared any time together with this son, yet he already sensed the lad was very independent and self-possessed. Tor noticed how Rubyn sat neatly; his movements were precise and economical; and he seemed to waste no words nor show much emotion. Tor tried to pinpoint the quality he was sensing.

It was as though Cloot could read his thoughts. *Very contained isn't he?*

That was it. Contained. Rubyn had shared no one's life except Cyrus's and he stuck close to the former prime. *Will he be all right do you think?* Tor shared his fears with his friend.

Let's give him some space. He has not had the luxury of the private time in the Heartwood with you that Gidyon and Lauryn enjoyed. You three had that serene period to get to know one another. This poor child has been thrown to the dragons, so to speak.

I hate it when you're always so right, Cloot.

Yes, I know. It can be a burden for me too.

In happier times they would have shared a laugh over such a line. Cloot did so love to sing his own praises. But neither could today.

Goth, the falcon said. One word. It spoke droves.

Yes.

Did you think over what Sallementro said?

I did.

And?

You know your way around those mountains don't you?

I am a Brocken at heart. I haven't forgotten any of the passes. And with my falcon's view, it will not be difficult to find this place.

What do you think?

I think it's swifter and easier to stab him in the throat here and now but more appropriate to make the journey.

At that moment, Cyrus opened a Link to Tor and Cloot.

If I was a gambling man, I reckon I could win a lot of money if I wagered all I had on guessing what you two are discussing right now – Goth.

You'd be right, Cloot said.

May I throw in my thoughts, for what they're worth? the former prime asked.

We would welcome them, Tor said. *You're the soldier and strategist amongst us.*

Thank you. Cyrus smiled, enjoying the reminder of his glory days. *Sallementro's suggestion is laborious and possibly dangerous but I also believe it is the just thing to do. Goth does not deserve life. He was guilty of terrible sins even in my time and I daren't allow my imagination to even wonder what he's been up to in recent times. My recommendation is this. You and Alyssa should take Goth to this place the musician speaks of and deal with unfinished business once and for all. I will go after your daughter.*

But Orlac expects me, Tor cautioned.

Well, of course he does. His intention is to lure you by dangling the bait he knows you will bite. So don't. It is not cowardly of you not to go. It is wise. I will not fail. I will bring her back to her parents.

Tor considered it.

Cloot spoke first. *We must protect you at all costs, Tor. That's my daughter in danger!*

We know this, Cyrus said gently. *But we must not play into Orlac's hands. By keeping you away, it means he must come to you. The Trinity — I truly believe — must be in the Heartwood to prevail. And you are the One. It is you we all protect. As much as our dedication is to our bonded, it is Torkyn Gynt we must save.*

How do you know this?

I don't. Call it soldier's instinct.

I agree with Cyrus, the falcon said. *We should follow our original plan of making you the lure that brings Orlac to us.*

Tor knew they should all hear what was being discussed. *Saxon, Alyssa.*

They both answered and he told them what Cyrus had suggested.

What about Rubyn? Alyssa asked, frowning.

He answered for himself. *I would go with Cyrus. I can help.*

Alyssa baulked. *No! Orlac would then have you in his grip as well. I won't permit it.*

She looked desperately at Tor, imploring him to agree with her. He could not. Whichever way he looked at it,

Cyrus's reasoning was sound, and to force the lad away from his guardian and his Paladin now would be madness. Each of them needed their protectors.

Rubyn should stay close to Cyrus; we cannot separate him from both his Paladin.

He saw the despair cross her face and forced himself to ignore it. 'Here is my plan,' he declared and everyone gave him their full attention, including Goth who had finally regained consciousness but found himself immobilised against a tree by vines, of all things! The more he struggled, the more pain drove through his body and the tighter the vines seemed to cling.

He listened to Tor.

'Cyrus and Rubyn will travel to Cipres. I'm hopeful they will link up with the King and Herek's Company of men.' He turned to the Cipreans who had sat very quietly through all these hours. 'Hela, may I press upon you to accompany them? You know the city and, more importantly, you know your way around the palace. Your help will be invaluable.'

She nodded. 'Of course. But what of Sarel?'

'I'd like to return to Cipres,' the Queen said, fiercely.

'Not yet, Sarel,' Tor counselled. 'Let us make your throne safe first. We cannot risk you yet.'

'There is no risk,' she said, with grace, yet firmly. 'If the usurper follows the trail back to the Heartwood, he will forget about Cipres. It is nothing more than a dispensable tool for him. But it is my realm. Those are my people. I will return and claim my throne. He will be gone and I'm very sure you will see to it that he does not ever return to Cipres. It has been foretold in the dreams that you will protect my throne. I trust you, Torkyn Gynt, and I will no longer shirk my duty and cringe in another kingdom.'

It was the voice of a true Queen. Tor's eyes narrowed as he considered her emphatic speech. Meanwhile Alyssa noticed how Rubyn increasingly stole long glances at Sarel. She was relieved. The wheel of life and its loves and torments continued to turn no matter what was happening in the world, she thought. Here sat her son, surrounded by talk of battle, death and struggles, and yet he seemed concerned at this moment only with how his heart beat a little faster at the sight of a young woman. She looked at the Queen now, noting the determined set of her jaw and the imperious way in which she carried herself. And still so young. She shook her head and returned her attention to Tor.

'All right, Sarel. It is your choice and may the Light guide you safely back to your throne.' He saw triumph on the Queen's face. Sarel was right to stand up for what was her duty. Every bit her mother and more still, Sarel was destined to be a powerful ruler with a conscience and dedication to her people. He hoped she would forge strong ties with Tallinor now. Two young monarchs. If anyone could turn history around, it was them.

'Rubyn, we shall look to you then, to protect our Queen of Cipres on the journey ahead.' He said this deliberately, having also noticed the keen interest his son was showing in Sarel. Tor believed Rubyn must be given a mission or they risked his feeling even more isolated.

Rubyn betrayed little on his face at his father's instructions but chose careful words in reply. 'I shall consider it an honour,' he said and dipped his head towards the Queen.

She noticed him for the first time . . . or perhaps not, Alyssa thought with a sudden insight, as she caught the coy grin, promising something, which Sarel threw his way.

Light! She's a vixen in a child's body, she whispered to Tor privately.

She's young, I'll admit, but no child any more, my love. And she's trying to fill enormous shoes with no experience. I think she's wonderful. She'll be good for Rubyn, he answered and shot her a brief smile knowing how much of what he had just said would irritate Alyssa.

And what about Locky? Did you not notice his final glance back at her?

I cannot dwell on this now, my love. We have to ensure they all hold on to their lives and must allow them to sort out their hearts.

It was gently said, and Alyssa kept her peace as Tor turned to Arabella.

'Solyana and I will remain, as always – perhaps, Sallementro, you might care to stay with us and entertain us whilst we wait nervously for our precious ones to return?' Arabella suggested.

The musician looked to Alyssa. She shrugged, but not unkindly – it told him that this was his decision. He felt cornered. To remain might be seen as cowardly but to go seemed madness. What could he do? Sing them all to sleep in the evening?

It was Saxon who rescued him. 'Sal, stay. You are no fighter. And we surely need some of us to remain in the Heartwood in case preparations need to be made,' Saxon said, grinning and getting to his feet. 'I'm off to gather a few things. I presume we're headed somewhere too?'

Tor switched to the Link because he did not want to share any of this with Goth, whom he could see finally paying attention.

Sallementro is right. We should allow the persecuted to decide Goth's fate. Alyssa and myself, accompanied by Saxon and Cloot, will take Goth to this place in the mountains and he will be dealt with. We will return to the Heartwood as quickly as possible. I need everyone to be back here as soon as you can, he said. They all nodded. *Cyrus, we have to think about how to get you there swiftly,* Tor added.

That's easy, the soldier replied. *Rubyn has this curious habit of travelling amongst the trees. It's hard to explain, it's best to demonstrate.*

Oh? Tor said, remembering the incredible enchantment when the trees of the Heartwood had flung him between themselves on his journey towards Caradoon. *How far can you get?*

As far as the Forest extends. We can take its north-western finger which reaches almost to Caremboche. Then perhaps we can buy horses for the remainder of the journey to Caradoon, then on to Cipres by boat.

Sallementro announced that he had brought money. They should use that.

Alyssa voiced something which had been nagging at her since Tor had suggested the journey to Cipres to rescue Lauryn. *It's just occurred to me to mention the possibility that Cyrus will be recognised by Orlac. He is Paladin, after all, which means the god has already seen him, fought against him.*

Tor had not even considered this. Would this jeopardise their plans?

Cyrus rubbed at his short beard. *I don't think so. The Dreamspeaker, Lys, visited me only once in the time that Rubyn and I were away from Tallinor. During that visit she told me about my role as Paladin and how I had already fought and lost one battle against Orlac. I do recall that she said I am very different in appearance now and that I was even known by a different name. The reason I tell you this is that I believe I can go to Orlac as a stranger.*

You are different, Cloot admitted. *That's why I did not recognise you the first time we met at Hatten.*

Cyrus nodded. *Lys said I was known as Jerome Cyrus to Orlac. That was my great-great-great-grandfather's name, which, I'm presuming, was bastardised through generations*, he said thoughtfully. *She's clever, protecting me in this manner. Anyway, Orlac will not know me from the next man.*

They said their farewells, Alyssa clinging hard to Rubyn, he permitting it, sensing her despair at losing him again so soon. Tor said little, but a single glance at Cyrus provoked a private response.

I shall bring your daughter . . . and your son back to the Heartwood. Or I shall die trying. Cyrus said this to Tor alone and saw him nod in acknowledgement.

Now they had all gathered by the great oak, intrigued, to witness the unique way in which Rubyn could apparently travel.

'Are you sure we are all welcome to travel in the same way?' Hela asked, doubt written all over her face.

Rubyn grinned. 'The trees will protect all of us.'

'Does it hurt?' Sarel shared Hela's reluctance.

'No. But here, hold my hand. We shall travel together,' Rubyn offered.

Alyssa glared at Tor, purse-lipped.

I can see this shall be an interesting journey, Cyrus said to the two of them as he kissed Alyssa's hand.

Bring them back to me, Cyrus, she warned.

If only in order to kiss you again, madam, he replied and

pretended to wince at the sharp glance from Tor.

Rubyn held Sarel's hand and already she seemed very comfortable in his company. 'We'll go first. Cyrus, you know the drill.' He saw his Paladin nod. He glanced towards Solyana but whatever they said to each other was kept private. 'Take a deep breath, Sarel. It makes your tummy feel odd to begin with.'

He smiled self-consciously at the others and put his arms around her.

Tor watched with fascination as Rubyn leaned back against the vast trunk of the oak and whispered something in an exotic language he did not understand. Immediately, they could all feel the pull of the magic and were amazed to witness branches bend down from the oak and embrace the couple. As this happened, Rubyn and Sarel seemed to blur and in the next instant were gone, absorbed into the oak itself.

There was a collective 'Ah' before a hush. They all looked towards the former prime.

'Our turn, I think, Hela,' he said, offering his hand graciously, which she took.

'Light guide you, Cyrus,' Tor said before watching the same process occur.

And then they were gone.

'Incredible!' Saxon muttered.

Indeed, Cloot agreed.

They made their way back to where Goth was strapped even more tightly against the tree. He had seen none of the first group's disappearance.

'A drink, perhaps?' he croaked.

'Die of thirst for all we care,' Alyssa said. 'When do we leave?'

'Now,' Tor replied. 'Sallementro, you came with a cart, did you not?'

The musician nodded. 'I don't know where it is, though.'

I do, Solyana replied. *There's Sallementro's horse and two others which have kindly wandered into the Forest . . . probably belonging to Goth's men.*

'That's all we need,' Saxon said. 'Let's get our prisoner organised.'

'Keep him tied, wrists and ankles for the journey. I'll sit in the back with him,' Tor said.

'I don't want him anywhere near me,' Alyssa admitted, looking at the man who had previously struck dread into her. 'But I do want to see him die,' she said, surprising herself by the conviction in her voice.

More farewells and then the Forest opened paths and guided Saxon, who was driving, into a north-easterly direction towards the Rork'yel mountain range.

They had made steady progress, keeping to the Forest which would lead them right into the mountains. The Heartwood itself was now far behind and all of them, bar Goth, felt the loss keenly. Alyssa was grateful when Saxon finally called a halt to make camp for the night. Cloot returned when a small fire was burning and the smell of cooking drifted into the early evening air. He had already fed and set about cleaning himself as he listened to their soft talk. The falcon had ranged high constantly during the ride and had seen nothing ahead. They were lone travellers on a track rarely used. Few people had reason to head into the complex mountain wilderness and even fewer felt comfortable within the Great Forest. He noticed Goth had settled into a sulky silence, refusing food. So be it.

Cloot hoped he could live off his reserves just long enough to meet his fate at the hands of the sentient ones.

'Did it never occur to you to wonder where those people were sent?' Saxon asked, as Tor handed him a chunk of the roasted hare.

'Here's some bread,' Alyssa said, twisting off a piece from the loaf which they had found on the cart. All had learned not to question the mysterious ways of the Heartwood.

Tor tentatively chewed a piece of the hot meat. 'Ignorantly, I suppose, I thought they all died.'

'So did everyone, I think,' Alyssa agreed.

Saxon turned and not so much nudged as kicked Goth. His action made the former chief inquisitor wince from the pain. 'How about you, Goth?'

Goth grunted.

'Did you know they were taken somewhere?'

'Yes,' he replied but did not elaborate.

'At whose orders . . . surely not yours?' Tor blinked with disbelief at the idea of Goth giving a second's further thought to the lives of the people he had tortured.

Goth remained silent but groaned again when Saxon encouraged him to talk with the toe of his boot.

'King's orders,' he said through the pain.

Alyssa shook her head. 'Knowing Lorys as I do I don't believe he would ever have sanctioned the torture. I think we can safely presume it was an invention and privilege of Goth. As for the bridling of people I'd have to say yes, he condoned it, because he grew up believing sentient people were so dangerous. I know this is hard to understand but I feel if he was aware of the torture, then he taught himself to turn a blind eye. It's true it's at odds with how he behaved towards his people otherwise, but fear is a complex master.'

Cloot had listened with interest so far. He now chose to involve himself in the discussion. *I think Alyssa's right. Lorys lived with an ancient fear. He had been schooled to behave like this – it had probably been drummed into him as an infant that all sentients were evil – but the mere fact that he gave those orders to have people sent to what I presume is a haven in Rork'yel, is an indication of the difficulty he perhaps had in condoning their persecution.*

'Exactly! Thank you, Cloot,' Alyssa said, chewing absently on a piece of bread. 'And I've been thinking about something the King said. Tor, do you remember that curious message I told you he sent before he died, which made little sense to me at the time?'

Tor shrugged.

'I do,' Saxon said, wiping his mouth of the meat juices. 'Something about giving freedom to your people.'

'That's right,' she said as her mind roamed. 'It's bothered me ever since that I didn't comprehend what was obviously such a private and deliberate instruction. Of all the things he could have said he chose these words: *Forgive me, my love, for leaving you. Find your own people. Free them. Save Tallinor.* Herek told me that Lorys knew he was doomed somehow, which might explain him asking for forgiveness at leaving me but the rest left me baffled.'

Tor wiped his hands. He had no idea where this conversation was leading. He looked at Goth whose sharp eyes returned the hate as his face twitched in its incessant way.

Alyssa continued. 'I now believe that Lorys was telling me to find these sentient people. When he referred to my own people, he meant those who are empowered like us.'

Tor nodded. 'Well, it does make sense now that we know those who survived Goth's brutal attentions are alive and together in the mountains.'

Alyssa felt a small triumph. 'I wish Lorys had told me more.'

I think it was a confession of sorts, Cloot mused. They looked at him perched on his branch; his beak and talons now cleaned from the wood pigeon he had caught expertly on the wing. *You know, a man who foresees his death often feels compelled to rid himself of his secrets . . . his sins.*

Alyssa nodded. 'Your falcon is very wise,' she said to Tor, as she made a comfortable pillow for herself from a cloak.

They slept; Goth fitfully from pain. Only Alyssa dreamed. It was the first time she had heard the voice of Lys.

I presume you have been expecting me?

Not really. She felt relief but also anger that her time had finally come. It was a curious combination of emotions.

Why?

Why would I? For many years you have talked to all except me. I presume nothing regarding you.

Are you glad I have come?

Yes.

Will you tell me why?

In order that I can tell you how much I despise you and your manipulations of the people I love.

There was a silence. Alyssa refused to break it. She would make Lys pay – even in this small way – for her control over those she cared for. The silence lengthened and Alyssa believed the Dreamspeaker had disappeared. Still she chose not to make a sound. Just waited, listening.

I believe I do deserve that, Lys said finally.

And plenty more. People have died at your design.

Lys felt this was unfair but decided not to argue this. She knew Alyssa would have her say. *It was necessary. However, I would never choose it to be so.*

Lies! Go away, Lys. Spin your tales for Tor and those who follow you.

Your children are in grave danger.

Not because of me. But because of you and what you make them do.

Will you not help them?

I will help them the only way I can. You will help only your cause. If they live or if they should die, it matters not to you.

That is a strong accusation.

You have earned it. I hate you.

May I show you something?

It was a change of tone and topic Alyssa had not expected. *No. I wish you to leave me. Invade Saxon's dreams . . . or Cloot's. Better still, give Goth the nightmare he deserves.*

I want to show you why your children matter to me.

Well, I want nothing to do with you. Let me be. Let them alone. You will get no absolution here, Lys.

I don't seek absolution. I seek to show you who you are.

That caught her attention. *I know who I am.*

Do you?

Alyssa faltered, Lys could hear it in her shaky response. *I . . . yes.*

Come, child. This is more important than your hate.

Where?

Follow me. And Alyssa did. She permitted herself to be swept up and along with Lys – whom she could not see. They travelled in her mind and Alyssa found herself

watching the birth of a child. It was a boy. He was given
to the flaxen-haired beauty, his mother, but only briefly.
She wept bitterly when the baby was gently taken from
her by an immensely tall, dark, wavy-haired man with
brilliant blue eyes. He was instantly familiar and then
that thought was gone – she could no longer see him,
only his arms handing the child to a woman. The woman's
face was shrouded by a gauzy hooded cloak.

'Take him,' Alyssa heard the man say.

'Are we sure this is right?' the woman asked over the
bitter weeping of the mother.

'Go now,' he said and she did.

The vision became hazy.

Where is she taking him? Alyssa asked of Lys, helplessly
intrigued.

Watch.

The vision cleared and Alyssa was watching the shrouded
figure of the woman walking along a dusty road. She was
approaching a small hamlet. There was a familiar scene ahead
and she began to feel a chill creeping across her.

Flat Meadows, she whispered.

Lys said nothing.

Alyssa watched as the woman, carrying the infant,
entered Flat Meadows, walking towards the inn as she
turned off the main road to Tal. She did not want to
believe this scene.

I don't want to see this.

You must.

Alyssa held her breath as the woman walked up to that
well-known doorway and entered. Now she found herself
inside with the woman at a table, sipping on water, poking
at a meal. She could almost smell its delicious aroma

because she knew whose cooking this was. Sure enough, the cook appeared and she heard their conversation.

'Come on now, I won't have anyone pick at my food,' said the familiar voice. 'Here we are, then. Give me that babe and you eat my beef and leave none, mind. You're scrawny enough.'

On cue, the infant began to wail. The cook did not wait for it to be handed over. Instead she reached and took the child from the woman's arm and disappeared with it. When she returned some time later, the woman had finished her meal and the child was brought in from the back rooms. It was sleeping and content. Alyssa heard the cook explain that one of the lasses in the village had a new baby and more than enough milk for an extra mouth. She noticed that the infant was not yet handed back to the woman, who had removed the hood but her back was to Alyssa. And then in amazement she listened to this woman tell a tall tale about how she had come by the child. The cook, that dear plump lady, listened with increasing woe, her eyes getting wider as the story unravelled. She began to weep at the child's abandonment and the woman's story that the parents had died in a fire and no one from his village would take him.

Stop this! Alyssa screamed but Lys did not listen.

She tried to close her eyes but they would not obey. Instead she witnessed the cook lean forward and make an offer to the woman who accepted in an instant. Taking off her apron, one arm still cradling the precious boy, she led the woman out of the inn and now Alyssa wanted to look away but she could not. She did not want to see which dwelling the pair of women walked towards, talking in hushed tones. But there it was already . . . a familiar cottage at the end of the village sitting amongst pretty gardens. A happy enough home although it had never enjoyed the sound of a child's laughter. It was the home of the travelling scribe who had done well for himself; had worked hard to provide a solid roof over his head and that of his wife.

Alyssa felt dizzy. She tried to talk to Lys but knew it was useless. Lys intended her to see this vision through to its conclusion, whatever that was, and so she fought her nausea and looked on as Jhon Gynt put his arms around his plump wife, Ailsa, and smiled at the baby she carried in her arms. He welcomed the stranger who was already in a hurry to depart, claiming she was on her way to Tal and the infant had so slowed her up that she had lost income. They smiled and made small talk and then finally the stranger dug into her pocket and lifted out a small pouch, knotted at one end.

She handed it to Jhon Gynt, telling him it was to be given to the boy when he was 'of an age'. They enquired when that would be and she waved away their questions, rising to leave.

'You will know the right time,' she said. 'Take special care of this precious child. His name is Torkyn.'

And with that she turned, her face uncovered, and Alyssa saw the woman's face for the first time. She sucked in her breath with shock. She thought she may have begun to scream but she went unheard; she tried desperately to wake herself but she was still in her dream as she watched the first vision blur and disappear as another seemed to take shape.

Now Alyssa was staring at a village green. She caught her breath. It was Minstead. The spinsters were dancing and the men of the surrounding villages had gathered.

She could see her father. Her whole body began to shake with the tears she wanted to cry at the sight of him. He was young and proud. Not a handsome man but broad, with a bright smile and a wit which kept the other young lads laughing constantly. His sandy hair was neatly tied in a thong and his face clean-shaven. And whilst he laughed with his friends his eyes never left a woman who was too far away for Alyssa to recognise. She could see honey golden hair, loose, with two small plaits tied at the back with flowers. The woman finally tossed her bouquet and Lam Qyn courageously fought off all those who coveted that same bunch of daisies.

Alyssa cried out again in the next scene as she saw her father standing outside the cottage which had been her home for fifteen summers – she could even see the old apple tree where Kythay had once been tethered by her friend, Sorrel.

Then she was inside the cottage. She saw the midwife imploring a woman who was presumably her own mother to push her child out. The woman's thighs – all she could see – were sweaty and she made short, shallow breaths between contractions. The midwife was a tall, large woman blocking out her mother. Alyssa wished she could shove her out of the way but she could not. She could only wait and hope she would be permitted to see the mother she never had in life.

Alyssa thought she had begun to cry in her dream. She knew the ending of this tale. Her mother would die and she would live. She felt the old guilt grab her throat and twist as she wept, begging Lys to release her from this vision. Lys paid no heed.

You must watch this, child, she said. It sounded to Alyssa as though the Dreamspeaker's voice caught as she spoke. Was she moved too?

Her mother had begun to scream and push hard now, and then in a gush of blood a tiny, perfect child was brought into the world. She began to scream immediately and the midwife wasted no time in severing the thick blue rope which connected Alyssa to her mother. As her blade sliced through the tube, Alyssa thought she heard Lys cry out too. She looked back and saw that her mother had begun to bleed profusely. The midwife called out and Lam Qyn came running in. There was no time for joy at the birth of his daughter, who was bundled roughly into a linen and thrust into his hands as he was given the news that his wife was haemorrhaging.

'I doubt she'll live through this,' the midwife said matter-of-factly.

Were all midwives so callous, Alyssa wondered – so oblivious to the emotions of the people involved in the life and death struggle of birth? It seemed they were because not long after, a sheet was laid across her bleeding mother and the midwife told Lam Qyn she could do nothing more.

'Your wife is dying. Give me the child . . . let it suckle at her breast for as long as she can before her weak heart stops,' she said, wanting to snatch the child from her father who looked at the midwife with distaste and disbelief.

'You'd better say your farewell,' the midwife cautioned. 'She's not long for this world.'

How true, Lys thought, her cheeks wet with tears of pain and guilt as she watched her now-grown daughter live through the agony.

Alyssa heard a soft sigh and Lam Qyn call his wife's

name over and over again. He even shook her, grabbing the child just in time before she fell off her mother's breast. He clutched the child in one arm and encircled his dead wife with the other and sobbed in the same way she herself had heard him sob over the years. These were the tears of an inconsolable man. They had been married only ten moons.

And now his wife's spirit was gone. All that was left was her shell; cleansed and laid out by friends. She lay on her bed, flowers in her hair, dressed in a soft gown of palest cream.

People finally stepped out of the way and Alyssa could look upon her mother for the first time. She was beautiful with an ethereal quality – from her pale and flawless skin to the ghost of a smile on her dead lips.

She was the woman who had brought Torkyn Gynt to Flat Meadows.

The vision disappeared and there was silence again. Alyssa was breathing hard and her mind was racing . . . returning again and again to the same one place, to one woman, one single notion.

The woman who brought Tor to his parents was my mother?

The answer did not come immediately. *The dreams do not lie*, Lys finally said.

And this woman, then . . . she is you. There was no question in her voice. It was a statement, uttered in a flat voice of resignation.

Alyssa heard Lys sigh once again. It was heavy with regret. *Yes, child. We are mother and daughter.*

No. It can't be true. If my mother is dead, how can you be the Dreamspeaker who talks to all of us?

Because your mother was never an ordinary woman, Alyssa.

Lysandra was my grandmother's name. I took it when I passed through the worlds to enter Tallinor.

Lys waited. This would be the most difficult of all moments for her daughter.

What do you mean, through the worlds? Who are you?

You know I am Lys. Now you know that I am your mother and you must accept the truth. I am also the Custodian of the Worlds.

A god! Alyssa shrieked it so loudly in her dream, it took Lys by surprise. *My mother is a god?*

Your father never knew.

Alyssa took several deep breaths to find some calm in her voice. *Am I to understand that everything from marrying my father to dying in childbirth was a part of your plan?*

I am sorry but this is so.

It was too much to bear, too much to begin to understand. Alyssa began to scream.

Lys tried to calm her but it was of no use.

Leave me! Get out of my head!

She awoke, trembling and perspiring into the chill of the early morning. She stood and deliberately shook herself free from the touch of Lys. She stomped off into the lightening of dawn, not trusting herself to be amongst others. She needed to think . . . alone.

22

The Truth Discovered

Lauryn had been groomed and dressed in a plain but exquisitely fine shift. Her hair had been brushed until it gleamed and then expertly braided into a single plait. She was clean and tidy but anxious. What now?

Juno put her fingers to her lips. *I will see you soon. I must go to him now.*

Adongo?

We'll stay close. Try to remain calm. Consider these your rooms for now.

Juno left Lauryn nervously pacing. They were in unknown territory now and her own heart was beating faster as she contemplated what Orlac's desire could be for this girl. She moved quickly through hallways, making her way towards his suite. She was given immediate entry into the salon where she waited to be announced. The servant returned to bid her follow. The Fourth of the Paladin took a deep breath and stepped inside.

Orlac had bathed too, she saw. His golden hair was still very wet and he was towelling himself. He was not at all self-conscious about his nakedness and Juno marvelled at his incredibly perfect body. Again she was reminded of a sculpture but she could not imagine any artist had ever had such a beautiful model to work with. She had not realised she was staring and got a shock when she noticed him grinning at her. Even his bright, wide smile was completely disarming.

'Enjoy what you see, Juno?'

'Er . . . my lord, forgive me. I was far away in my thoughts and I did not mean to stare.'

'Don't apologise. I like you looking. It makes me believe all that iciness is contrived and that you really do desire me.'

Juno wished she could blush; that would help cover her true feelings towards him. Instead she steadied herself and ignored his delight in teasing her. 'You summoned me, my lord.'

He sighed. Juno would give him no sport today. 'Join me outside.' He nodded towards his bed chamber. 'She's sleeping.'

Outside on Sylven's favourite and huge balcony the servants had laid out a lavish spread. Tying a fresh towel about himself he sat down and began to graze on the food. Juno joined him at his request but as usual did not eat.

'How is the girl?' he asked.

'Frightened.'

'Is she comfortable?'

'As much as I can make her. May I ask where is she from?'

'Didn't she tell you?'

She shook her head.

She's lying, Dorgryl cautioned.

Be quiet! Orlac responded, not taking his eyes from Juno.

'My lord, she said nothing whilst I bathed or dressed her. She is young and it is perfectly understandable that she is terrified in this strange place.'

'I see. Has she said anything?'

'Yes. She asked me what you wanted of her?'

He laughed harshly. 'Can she not guess?'

Juno kept her peace and tried not to glare. She must do nothing to give herself away or put Lauryn into any further danger than she was in already.

He shrugged. 'Have you noticed anything about her, my all-seeing Juno?'

'I have, my lord,' she replied cautiously. 'It seems she is the woman from my vision.'

'Hah!' He clapped his hands with glee. 'I knew you'd pick it. She is everything you described and you were right, I desire her very much.'

'Is that your plan for her then, my lord? She will be your . . .' she searched for the right word and then found it, 'companion?'

He nodded. A sly expression seemed to shroud his handsome face.

'And Xantia?'

'Is also my companion,' he said, adding, 'when I choose.'

Juno left that alone. She despised Xantia and knew the arrival of Lauryn would mean trouble. 'May I ask her name, where she came from? It might help me to bring her out of herself for you.'

Orlac inhaled the fresh scents of citrus from the gardens below. Distant sounds of the city coming alive for another day could be heard. 'Is Titus with her?'

'Yes.'

'Good. Ask him. He knows who she is.'

Juno rose and bowed. She could push no further. He was closed to her now. 'Will that be all, my lord?'

'For now, yes. But I wish you to bring her to me tonight.'

The Fourth had not expected this and had to think quickly. 'Might that be too soon, sir?' She made it sound as though she was sharing a thought rather than asking a question or, more to the point, offering a rebuke.

He answered her query in the same casual way she had asked it. 'I think not. I think it is time we turned her from a girl into a woman.'

The god heard Dorgryl's rumbling laughter inside. *Nicely done*, he said.

Orlac felt his own heartbeat quicken at the thought of touching Lauryn. He ignored Juno's pursed lips. 'Don't defy me, Juno. I will expect her brought to my chambers tonight.'

'And Xantia?' She felt annoyed with herself for returning to the same question.

'Is of absolutely no concern to you, servant,' said the owner of the name, appearing on the balcony. 'Whom do we speak of, my love?' she cooed, wrapping her arms about his neck and kissing his cheek.

Orlac deliberately loosed himself from her. 'Of a young woman called Lauryn. She will be sleeping in my bed tonight, Xantia. Please move your things. I don't like that you seem to have set yourself up in my chambers in my absence anyway. You have your own rooms.'

Xantia's face darkened but not enough to betray herself. She turned brightly towards Juno. 'Is this one of your picks from the city?'

Orlac reached for a warmed, sweet roll. 'Pour me some of that, Xantia,' he said. He was purposely treating her in the same brusque yet polite manner in which he treated

all servants, but Xantia reacted as though he had just
called her by some pet name.

'Of course, my love,' and hurried to do as bid.

He continued. 'She is my choice. Juno had never met
her before.'

Xantia poured. 'From Cipres?'

'No,' he said abruptly. He did not even turn to the
Fourth. 'Thank you, Juno. Don't forget my instructions.'

Juno bowed again and left quickly, hurrying now –
just short of running – back to Lauryn's rooms. Upstairs
on the balcony Xantia was scowling behind Orlac. He
continued his grazing on the food.

'You met her on this trip?' She tried desperately to
make it sound casual.

'Yes.'

'So, she's Tallinese?'

'It would seem so.' He waved a hand towards her,
showing he was tired or worse, bored by her conversation.
'Xantia, when you leave in the next minute or two, could
you ask my aide to come by as soon as possible. I want
to see if there's any word from Goth.'

It was a dismissal. She had no choice but to depart.
Xantia tried to kiss him, but he brushed her affections
aside, finding the sweet cake more to his taste this
morning. She was enraged when she left. Her first call
was not into Arlyn's rooms as instructed. Instead she
hurriedly dressed, gave pinched orders to servants to move
her belongings from his lordship's chambers, and made
enquiries as to where she would find this woman who had
stolen her place in Orlac's bed. It did not take long for
the information to be delivered.

*   *   *

Adongo's warning was abrupt. *Beware of Xantia! She comes.*

Xantia swept past the nomad whom Orlac had insisted on taking with him to Tallinor. She hated him as much as Juno. Both watched her with guarded expressions and knowing ones too. 'Get out of my way, Titus,' she commanded.

It was amusing that Xantia treated the palace staff as though she was royalty and her orders must be obeyed. None of the Cipreans knew which was worse right now: the threat of the stranger's powers over them or the viciousness of the whore he had installed in the palace. Xantia wrenched open the door and froze as the small figure stood up from the chair on which she had been perched. In that instant she was dragged back years and all those old feelings of hatred returned to settle on her shoulders once again. Adongo sidled up silently from behind.

'Alyssa?' he heard Xantia whisper.

Lauryn heard it too and in that silent stretch of brief moments, she took in the blue disk of archalyt which glinted on the woman's forehead and marked her as coming from the Academie at Caremboche. She had learned this from her father when he was regaling them with tales of the happy years with her mother. As the woman stood there glowering, Lauryn's memory suddenly gave her what she needed. Her father had mentioned a vicious woman called Xantia who had hated her mother. So this was she. Lauryn was prepared now for danger. This was clearly no social visit.

'I am Lauryn,' she said, deliberately hardening her voice, pleased to hear that she could. 'And you?'

She stepped further into the room. 'Xantia. Orlac's woman.'

Lauryn breathed out. 'Then he won't be needing me,' she replied, moving towards the window to put as much space between herself and Xantia as possible.

'I wish that were the case,' the dark-haired woman said. 'It seems he is a little besotted by you.'

'I can't imagine why,' Lauryn said, stalling for time and wishing Adongo would rescue her as he stood quietly watching the exchange.

She is very dangerous. Do not make her angry, is all he said.

'Where have you come from?' Xantia asked, approaching, still staring intently. She looked like a predator, lining up her next meal.

Lauryn avoided that stare. 'Tallinor.'

'Extraordinary,' Xantia breathed close by. 'Face me!' she commanded and Lauryn was angry with herself for turning and doing just that.

Now they were barely inches apart, Xantia standing far taller and scrutinising her from on high. Lauryn was not expecting it. It was as fast as a snake might strike. Xantia's hand slapped across her face.

'That's for your mother, the bitch. You are Alyssa's daughter, I presume, because you surely can't be her twin?'

Lauryn was still trying to catch her breath. She had never been hit before. It was more than just shock; it was anger that claimed her now. So it was true. This was the same woman her father spoke of. The Colours swelled and as Xantia towered above her, a satisfied smirk on her face, Lauryn prepared to retaliate.

Don't! Adongo shouted in her head. He had felt the thrum of her magic gathering.

Lauryn stopped herself, breathing hard now.

She is protected by archalyt. I have a better idea for dealing with Xantia.

The Link closed and Adongo disappeared. She wondered what his plan might be.

'Answer me!' Xantia screamed.

Lauryn pulled herself back to her feet. Her hair had come loose and her face ached where she had been struck. 'I am the daughter of Alyssa and Torkyn Gynt.'

Xantia laughed. It was a manic laugh; one which told Lauryn that she stood before a woman whose emotions were suddenly out of control. With her lips pulled back and her eyes wide and wild, she looked deranged. She was.

'I knew it! So they married and had a child. How very nice for them. How are your parents, child?'

'I don't know,' she lied. 'I have not seen either in a while.' Lauryn played for time wondering when Adongo would return.

'Your mother and I have a score to settle,' Xantia all but spat.

'So I can see.' Lauryn was pleased she felt a level of control now. She would beat this woman.

'Let's say my mark on your face is a foretaste of what's to come.'

'Xantia.' It was said mildly enough but both women turned towards the voice, one with relief, the other with fright. 'Step away from her,' Orlac said.

Xantia wanted to say something placating. But it was too late. The sentient ones felt his minuscule push on his powers and Xantia was savagely flung back against the wall. She hit it hard and crumpled with a groan on the floor.

Lauryn instantly shielded herself. 'No need,' Orlac said,

moving towards her. 'I am not here to hurt you. Let me see your face.' He cupped her chin in one of his large, elegant hands and she could not help but feel a tingle of attraction once again for this man. He terrified her but his presence was so overwhelming he seemed to remove all resolve from her. She permitted him to hold her as he studied her cheek. 'I am truly sorry.' He meant it too and he stroked her face very gently. 'Titus!'

'My lord?' Adongo bowed.

'Fetch Juno. Have her see to Lauryn's face and hair.' He had not let go of her yet. She could feel the strength in his body which touched her now as he stood so close peering at her with those amazing violet eyes. He is my uncle, she told herself and tried to feel revulsion – but could not.

'At once,' Adongo said, not really wanting to leave her with Orlac.

'And have Xantia removed from here and deposited in her quarters. She no longer has access to mine.' Adongo smiled as he bowed. 'And at no time, under no circumstances, is she allowed to go anywhere near Lauryn's chambers. I hold you fully responsible.'

'You have my word, sire,' the Moruk said.

Orlac bent and kissed the spot on her cheek which hurt the most. The pain had settled to a dull throb now. Lauryn felt a Link slice open. She expected it would be Adongo but was chilled to hear Orlac's voice in her head.

You were wise not to use your powers against her.

She felt she stood there naked now. He knew she was empowered and he was not even perturbed. She no longer had barriers against him. He could link and enter her mind at will, brushing aside her shield as though it were not even there. Now he bent and kissed her hand, but this time spoke aloud. 'Until tonight.'

He left without another word nor did he glance back at the prone figure in the corner.

Alyssa was not just quiet, she was silent. Saxon had tried several times to link but she had shielded from him; asked him to give her time to think on something. He respected her privacy, knowing she would come to him when she was ready to talk about whatever was unsettling her. Tor, whose turn it was to drive the cart, did not notice her withdrawn state for several hours as he concentrated on steering the horses along the uneven track. He and Cloot maintained a constant Link, with their private chatter going back and forth – it kept Tor's mind occupied. Goth of course said nothing and everyone ignored him, quietly revelling in his groans each time the cart hit a bump and jarred his arm.

They were still in the Forest but it was beginning to thin. Before they hit open country, Saxon decided to water the horses at the stream which had run to their right for a good part of the trip, and give everyone a rest. He unharnessed the animals and led them away. Alyssa moved to a secluded area beneath a tree. Goth was slumped in the cart. Tor suddenly found himself alone and went looking for his wife.

'You're very quiet,' he commented, approaching her. 'Is something wrong?'

Alyssa pulled her knees close and rested her chin on them. She did not know where to start or even how to. Without choosing her words, she allowed them to tumble out.

'I dreamed last night.'

'Oh?' he said, sitting beside her. He wanted to hold her but sensed she did not want to be touched.

She wasted no words. 'Lys came.'

'I'm glad.'

'I'm not,' she said vehemently. Then added: *Look at me, Tor.*

He did not want to but forced his brilliantly blue gaze to meet her eyes. She looked into that lovely face and knew that whatever she said next would hurt him. But it had to be said.

'I met your father last night as well.'

He was not expecting this but he was expecting something, she noted. 'You . . . you met my father?' A quizzical grin appeared.

'Perhaps *met* is not the word. Let's say I saw him. And your mother. They are both incredibly beautiful people. Almost too beautiful, too perfect . . . like you.'

Tor was confused. He had no idea what this was about, nor could he interpret the subtle accusatory tone in her voice. He played it safe. 'I gather you are not talking about Jhon and Ailsa Gynt, then.' He attempted his usual brand of humour but it did not work for him this time.

'No,' she replied. 'I was not given their names but you really do look like your true father.'

Tor did not know what to say. He felt suddenly clumsy. 'Anything else?'

Her eyes narrowed. 'Plenty.' She cocked her head to one side. 'Why don't you tell me what you thought I was going to tell you about before I go on?'

He shrugged, saw her expression harden at his reluctance and knew he must not lie to her now. 'I thought,' he said, taking her hand – and was relieved she permitted it – 'that you were going to tell me about your mother.'

'I am. So you've known about her?'

Tor felt more nervous at the icy tone in her voice now. He looked towards Saxon, who was busy, his back turned. Cloot was privy to this conversation but sensibly remained still in the trees and silent.

It was best if he told her everything. 'When Orlac summoned me from the Heartwood and then cast me away, I found myself in the Bleak. I didn't know it at first – it was all very confusing and of course I was completely unexpected. It was my arrival which distracted Lys and allowed Dorgryl to escape.'

She nodded. He had already mentioned Dorgryl's escape during their time in the Heartwood whilst waiting for Rubyn. 'Go on.'

'I actually saw Lys – you see none of us had before that moment – and it was obvious to me that you and she were related somehow. Later, returned to the Heartwood, she admitted she is your mother. When she thought I might tell you, she forbade it.'

'And you always obey Lys, don't you?' she said, a pitying tone in her voice now.

'No,' he leapt at her defensively. 'That's not why. I agreed that she should be the one to tell you. Last night was obviously her chosen time.'

Alyssa smirked and took her hand away from him. 'Did she also tell you that it was she who brought you to Jhon and Ailsa?'

She could tell immediately that he had not known this and she felt a twinge of guilt at her bluntness. Nevertheless, she continued with her tale, particularly now that she had had time to think through everything she witnessed in her dream. Alyssa was sure she had pieced together an important part of the jigsaw.

'Or that she deliberately contrived to marry my father and then stage her own death at childbirth to leave me motherless and my father a broken man, never to recover?'

He shook his head, hanging it and running his fingers through his hair. He could not defend Lys against this accusation for it was all true.

'Tell me everything you saw,' he said sadly.

And she did, sparing him no detail. When it was told, Alyssa softened. She had rid herself of her anger now, glad that she had shared all of it. It was her turn to offer comfort and she reached to put her arm around him. She was relieved that he responded, turning his head into her shoulder and hugging her close.

Cloot blinked. They were stumbling onto the truth now. He opened the Link to Saxon so he could hear. The Kloek looked up from the horses towards where they sat as he heard Alyssa's voice.

'My mother is a god,' she said, her voice filled with the same disbelief she had felt in her dream. 'And do you know, Tor?'

He looked up and kissed at the tears on her cheek. 'What, my love?'

'I think your true parents are gods too.'

Tor sat back. 'What!' His worst fears were being confirmed. Tor had suspected as much but never once allowed his mind to accept the notion. To hear Alyssa utter the words was the confirmation he did not want.

She nodded. 'There's more. It's worse.'

'Don't,' he said and groaned.

'We must talk this through. We are meant to. That's why she came.'

'No.'

Yes, Cloot said into their minds.

She pulled Tor's shoulders around so he was forced to look at her. 'Listen to me. You once described the first vision Lys ever gave you in a dream.' He began to shake his head but she continued. 'You told me about the people in that dream. They were the King and Queen of the Host. Darganoth and Evagora you called them. They were the same people I saw last night. Evagora birthed you and Darganoth took you from her and immediately handed you to Lys, my mother. You know the rest.'

'No!' he yelled, leaping to his feet.

Let him go, Alyssa, Cloot said. *He knows what you say is true.*

Heavy of heart, she watched her love disappear into the trees, his Paladin flying after him. She too needed comfort and was glad to see that Saxon was coming towards her.

Cloot flew down to perch on Tor's knee and watched his bonded one stare in a sullen silence at the Forest floor.

How long have you known? Tor finally asked.

Always.

I thought we were friends.

None closer.

Why then?

I was forbidden by Darganoth himself. We were all told you must discover your identity yourself. I'm not sure why . . . I'm still unsure. But I have held true to my promise, as you held true to Lys in not telling Alyssa what you knew.

I'm not blaming you, Cloot.

I know this. But I need you to understand why I have not shared this. Would it have made much difference?

What, to know that the mad god who seeks to kill me and everyone I love and destroy the land that I call home, is my brother? Yes, it might have. Tor shook his head. *My brother.* He turned the word over in his mouth as though it was a foreign sound.

Can I just say this? Cloot asked. *When you finally lay eyes on him again, it would serve you well to remember that Orlac the man is a result of something terrible that happened to him as an innocent. As you feel now . . . cheated, devastated perhaps even vengeful – this is how the young Orlac felt when he discovered he was not mortal but a god. And yet all of his life he's been made to live the life of a mortal. It was not his choice. He was stolen – just a baby remember. There are times I can feel sorrow for him.*

Tor finally looked up at his Paladin. *Alyssa is right. You are a wise old falcon.*

The bird chuckled. *Aha, so you admit it at last!*

Tor wiped at his eyes, rubbed his face. *I don't know what to think any more.*

Survival for you and yours, Cloot said firmly. *He still wants to kill you and ruin Tallinor.*

Do you think he knows?

I can't guess at that. How would he know?

Dorgryl probably.

Perhaps. Here come Alyssa and Saxon.

Tor looked up. He could see by her red eyes that she too had been upset.

'Are you all right?' she said.

He nodded. 'Let's all sit.'

Saxon held up a sack. 'Let's eat as well.'

They shared a simple meal which included luscious blackberries Saxon had found. As they ate, they talked, sharing all the information they now possessed.

'How do you feel about Lys?' Tor asked Alyssa.

'Not sure,' she said, licking at her juice-stained fingers. 'It's a shock. I always wanted to know my mother. I should be deliriously happy but instead I feel tricked, angry, hurt.'

He nodded. 'I know. The strange thing is, I recall that as a child I always used to draw our family as being four. My parents, that is the Gynts, were amused that I insisted on putting a big brother into the picture.' Tor shook his head. 'I must have known, somehow.'

Saxon tossed him a knuckle of bread. 'Maybe you absorbed some of what was happening around you. Imagine how brave your mother had to be to give you up, having already lost one precious son to Tallinor. Who knows, that pain and knowledge may have seeped into your being somehow.' The Kloek shrugged. 'Perhaps I'm being stupid.'

Alyssa put her hand on his arm. 'No, Sax. You're not. My mother may be a god but Lam Qyn is very mortal I'm afraid, so I have his blood running in my veins too. Whereas Tor has only gods' blood . . . none of us can know what that really means and perhaps he did pick up on his mother's sorrow.'

It was time to lighten the mood, Cloot decided. They still had a lot to achieve and it would not do to have Tor in leaden spirits. *Of course you all realise we are in the presence of royalty. Before us sits a prince of the Host . . . an heir of the gods.*

Alyssa brightened. 'Your majesty,' she said, standing

to curtsy, which won a laugh from Saxon and even a grin from Tor.

Tor stood. 'Enough——' but before he could finish he saw Saxon plummet forwards, an arrow sticking from his back. Alyssa screamed and then Tor heard the same horrifying sound of an arrow leaving its bow and then the dull thump as it buried itself into her body, throwing her viciously forwards. She too hit the ground and lay still. He was so shocked, he just stared at his fallen friends before screaming to Cloot.

On my way! the falcon said, lifting powerfully from the branches.

Tor shielded for all of them. No further arrows could strike any of them, though he presumed the attackers had already fled. He dropped to his knees by Alyssa. She was unconscious, having hit her head on the tree as she fell. She was bleeding badly from that wound but he reassured himself with the knowledge that cuts to the head invariably looked worse than any other. He ignored the bleeding and felt for her pulse, which he found . . . strong and steady.

Checking Saxon, the Kloek groaned. 'Gods' bollocks, what hit me?'

'An arrow,' Tor replied. 'Be still.'

'Alyssa!' Saxon had just noticed she lay next to him.

'She's alive, Sax. Let me just see how bad this is and then I'll tend to her.'

Talk to me! he called to Cloot.

Three men. Two horses gone. And . . .

No wait, let me guess. Goth is gone too?

With great difficulty. But nevertheless he is with them.

Do you know who?

No idea.

Follow them but don't be seen. Goth will warn them of you.

He told Saxon the bad news and was not surprised when the Kloek growled, 'Get me up, Tor.'

'Wait!'

'He's not getting away again.'

'He won't. Cloot's following. We'll track him.'

'See to Alyssa,' he begged.

'I'm about to. You'll have to keep watch,' he cautioned.

The Kloek nodded, wincing as he sat up so he could see around him better.

Tor worked calmly. Now that he knew they were not immediately fatal wounds, he slipped into the role of physic, washing the area and surveying the damage. The arrow had buried itself in Alyssa's shoulder. She would not die but it was important to get the metal head out of her body before infection could set in. Whilst she was still unconscious, he summoned the Colours and the Flames, which were now ever-ready at his call. They materialised from the Great Forest. He focused, roamed with the Colours and let go, his spirit entering Alyssa and immediately travelling to the site of her wound. With his physical self kneeling over her, hands hovering above the arrow head and his spirit working from behind it, Tor let his Colours work their magics, easing the arrow head from her shoulder. He could sense she was surfacing from her darkness now and he must work quickly. With an immense effort he dragged himself backwards and out from Alyssa, returning to his body, where he took deep breaths, racked with a horrible trembling he remembered from the previous times he had tried something similar. There was no time for his recovery though. He needed to finish working on her wound. Weaving the Colours he worked from outside of her now, cleaning the gash the arrow had left, but mercifully it was a neat wound and he could see it would heal. She groaned but was still not fully awake.

The Flames instinctively knew what to do and as soon as he sat back on his haunches, exhausted from the spiriting, they set to work cauterising the wound. Alyssa opened her eyes and immediately began to vomit. Tor had somehow made his legs work and he had fetched water, tearing strips from his shirt to clean and bind her wound.

He spoke on a private Link. *You are safe. Hurt but safe. You need some healing time.*

What happened? She sounded drowsy and disorientated.

We're not sure. Bandits perhaps. You've been wounded by an arrow. And they've taken Goth.

She closed her eyes. *How many lives does that wretched man have?*

He's enjoying his last, Tor assured her. *I'm going after him.*

Alone?

Saxon was hit too. I must tend to him.

Her eyes flew open at this news. *I'll help you.* The truth was she was at this moment too weak to even lift her head from the Forest floor. She winced from the pain at her shoulder.

Be still, Alyssa. You may yet suffer the fevers from that wound and you need to just let it heal and save your strength.

The Flames had finished their task. They sang and Tor thanked them. It seemed only he understood their language.

Cloot's following them. He will not get away, I promise.

What do they want with Goth?

If they're common bandits, he probably promised them riches.

How bad is Saxon?

He'll live but he's going to be sore like you. We're lucky that they were such terrible shots.

Small mercies, she said and closed her eyes again. She drifted asleep.

Tor wished yet again he had some of the arraq liquid to ease their pain. It would heal them quickly too. But his satchel had been stolen and with it the precious vial he had used with such care.

Much later, a fire lit, both patients woke up to find themselves laid out in the back of the cart which the bandits had decided not to take.

Tor helped them both to sit up. 'Drink lots of this,' he said, handing them each a clay jar. 'All of it,' he cautioned.

Alyssa tasted various herbs mingling with nettles and grasses. It was the right brew to help them through the fevers should they visit. Her head throbbed too.

'What news?' Saxon croaked. He began to shiver and realised he would spend the rest of this night sweating it out as his body fought off infection.

'They've made camp north of here. Apparently, they've also broken cover of the Forest to try and throw off Cloot but he's too wily for them.'

'What are you planning, Tor?' Alyssa asked.

'To see you both through this night first,' he answered. 'Then I shall catch up with Cloot and our new friends.'

23

Lost and Found

Tyne would not hear of them leaving. He also did not want to give up his chance to earn money from Themesius.

'One more show,' he begged. 'We'll leave this morning and go straight to Brittelbury. We can hold the show there tomorrow night.'

It was tempting.

'But what about your other shows?' Gidyon asked.

'Of no matter. I'll make enough with this one if I promote it along the way. Now make haste. We travel in one hour.'

He left them no chance to change his mind.

Themesius scratched his head. 'Better this way don't you think, Figgis?'

'I do. Keeps us out of harm's way as well. The lad has a happy knack of getting into bother,' he said and they laughed at Gidyon's scowl.

Tyne was as good as his word and within the hour, the first of the caravans drew out of the town and headed west towards Brittelbury.

'What do you do in the show?' Gidyon wondered to Themesius.

'I just walk out . . . and everyone's jaws drop open.'

Figgis enjoyed this, chuckling to himself. 'A show-stopper, eh? Well, perhaps Gidyon and I can make a special contribution. What do you think?' he said.

'I have an idea already,' Gidyon said, not offering to reveal anything further.

On their journey, and particularly as they began to pass through outlying villages from Brittelbury, Tyne made regular stops, calling into inns and promoting the *Greatest Show in the Land* as he liked to call it. At each stop the performers were encouraged to remain hidden so none of the secrets were revealed.

'If people want to see our freaks, they'll have to pay.' It was his favourite saying.

As it turned out Brittelbury was a decent-sized town. No wonder Tyne felt he could risk missing his other planned stops as long as he could show off his star attraction here. People waved and welcomed them in and once again the 'freaks' hid themselves. Tyne posted hired guards around the perimeter of the Green where they would perform in order to prevent snoopers from getting an early look at the acts.

'Figgis, you'll have to remain here,' Gidyon suggested. 'You're too much like one of the attractions to go walking about the town and risk Tyne's despair.'

The Paladin nodded. 'You may be right. How will you find her?'

'I'm not sure. Start asking questions, I suppose.'

'What about tonight?'

'I'll be back in time, I promise.'

'Straight back,' Figgis cautioned with a stern face.

Gidyon ticked off his tasks. 'Get my stone, kiss the girl, back to the freak show.'

'Good lad,' Themesius said, his huge laugh bellowing. 'Are you going to tell us how we shall entertain the masses tonight?'

A smile broke across Gidyon's face. 'A balancing act like no one has ever seen before,' he said, tapping his nose knowingly. 'No need to practise, leave it all to me. Oh, and Themesius, ask Tyne if we can borrow the Fat Lady.'

'Whatever for?'

'You'll see,' he said and opened the tent flap, emerging into the sharp sunlight.

He squinted. Where should he head first? Gidyon decided to walk and see where he found himself. Brittelbury was larger than he expected and so he guessed it was unlikely Yseul would be found wandering about in the town unless she had work here. He headed towards the first inn, gingerly sipping on a watered ale for a while and getting a feel for the place. It was clearly a busy and thriving town; there was a rough quality to it which he presumed came from living in such an unforgiving region with the Rork'yel Mountains looming in the distance. Back out in the main street, people went about their business with little interest in strangers, who seemed an integral part of the transient nature of this town. People obviously used it as a last watering hole before heading west across mainly uninhabited countryside towards Ildagarth or perhaps further north still into Kyrakavia.

To make one's way west from here meant either moving directly through the northern finger of the Great Forest, or, as most people chose to do, taking the long way around it and skimming the lowest reaches of the mountain range, on a long and often cheerless journey.

Gidyon felt empty. He had not eaten since the previous sundown and whatever he had consumed had been returned at dawn. Now his belly roared its hunger and he went in search of food. He walked towards the market-place where he could see all sorts of wares on sale with people calling out their prices and attesting to the quality. It was a lively, colourful place and it seemed so normal . . . something very lacking in his life. His nose picked up the smell of meat roasting and he turned to see an eating house where rows of tables and chairs were set up outside under a makeshift awning of canvas. It was still quite early in the day and yet this place was doing a brisk business. He squeezed into a corner table, trying to tuck his very long legs away from the traffic of the serving women and waited. Soon enough a woman stopped and asked him what he would like.

'There's chickens coming out of the oven now,' she suggested.

He nodded. 'Perfect. Bread?'

'Of course. Can I bring you an ale?'

'Er . . . no thanks. Milk, please.'

She looked at him sideways. 'Milk?'

The smell of the ale at the inn convinced him he had consumed enough for a lifetime . . . or so he thought at that moment. 'Please,' he said, trying to ignore the smirk which had appeared on her face.

'Don't get much call for milk here. I'll see what I can do,' she said.

He leaned back, arms behind his head and looked about

him. The tables were now all taken, predominantly with men; once they had ordered their jugs of ale, he noticed they all got quickly involved in a rowdy game. It seemed to be a combination of dice and cards. He watched with such interest, he hardly noticed when his meal was set before him.

'We milked old Betsy out the back for you,' the woman serving said as she placed it on the table. If she was expecting a response from Gidyon, her barb failed to hit its target because he was intent on watching a particularly boisterous game in front of him.

'Oh . . . er thanks,' he said. He was devilishly handsome but no fun at all, she thought.

Gidyon caught her arm. 'Sorry, can you tell me what they're playing?'

'Light! Where do you hail from, stranger?'

He shrugged. 'A monastery.' He said the first thing that came into his head but had no idea how close to the truth it was.

'That figures,' she said, hand on hip. 'Explains the milk. They play Hari. This is a Hari House but I guess you didn't know that. Mark my words – don't get involved. For the inexperienced, you'll lose everything you own including the boots on your feet.'

'They aren't worth much,' he admitted, turning on his best smile.

She could not help but return it and he was saved from further conversation by someone calling her. 'I'm coming,' she yelled. 'If you find yourself alone later, come by.'

He sipped his milk, deliberately ensuring he had a ring of it around his lips. She left, a look of distaste at the edges of her mouth. That got rid of you, he thought, enjoying the taste of the warm chicken. He dipped the bread into the bird's roasting juices and concentrated hard on the game of Hari which was being replicated at various tables around him. It was a fast and furious game, and not only the participants bet on the outcome. The tables were attracting other betting folk. He had no idea of the rules but he began to understand the rhythm of the game and quickly worked out who was cheating. It was the man at the end of the table. He had a bright smile and played with the casual air of someone who really was not paying attention. He joked and chatted with those around him and always seemed to be lagging in playing his next card or rolling the die. By the time Gidyon had finished his meal, cleaned up the juices and drained his milk, he essentially understood that Hari was not so much a game of chance as one of bluff. If you could cheat, as the man at the end was doing, that increased the opportunity of winnings tenfold. He did it by having a partner in the audience, perhaps several even, who used some sort of signal to indicate which cards were moving where in the rapid game. Gidyon hated dishonesty but he was impressed at how well the man did it.

The player was as cunning as he was crooked. He did not down his cards every round with a winning hand. His wins were small and subtle. Gidyon noticed also that as the sun rose higher and the day got warmer, the players drank more, as did the audience. The consumption of liquor was great for business and also for the cheat who did not have to be so careful any more. For every jar of ale each of his companion players consumed, he sipped perhaps half a cup. Although the man pretended to be intoxicated, his eyes were sharp.

Just when Gidyon thought he had the cheat completely

worked out, the man lost everything he had won in a single round. Gidyon was shocked. All that effort wasted. They slapped him on the back and made jokes about his terrible calls and his shocking rolls of the die. It all became clear in the next moment as the now very merry players decided to have one last round for the highest possible stakes. All the other tables stopped to watch this particular round by the big spenders. The stake required to play was high . . . too rich for one player; they began to ask around for anyone who cared to take his place.

Gidyon stuck his hand in the air. 'Ho! I will,' he said, and gave them a crooked grin as though he was a bit slow.

A roar of approval followed. He was quickly welcomed to a place around the table.

'Your purse?' someone asked.

Gidyon dropped a pouch of heavy coins onto the table. Then he produced a second with a rather sheepish grin and then a loud belch for good measure. He yawned. The cheat smiled at him. This one was no threat.

'I'm meant to go to market today,' Gidyon admitted to the bearded fellow next to him, 'but I'm feeling lucky, perhaps I can impress father by coming home with a bulging purse.'

It was the cheat's turn to deal. So well-planned, Gidyon thought.

'Er, wait,' he said, holding up proceedings. 'I don't know the rules.'

It did not silence the now gathered mob but it might as well have. People looked at him aghast.

'I'm from a monastery.' He shrugged an apology.

'But you spoke about your family . . . your father and the heavy purse?' his neighbour queried.

'Oh I see. I meant the Abbott, we call him Father.'
Men cleared throats and grumbled around him.

'All right, lad,' the cheat said. 'No harm done and his money's already in so we can't let him go now.'

Gidyon smiled inwardly. He knew the cheat would not be able to bear the thought of losing out on the pile of coins clinking in the pouch.

'I'm a f-f-fast learner,' he said, enjoying his embellishment of the stutter.

People around him shook their heads and suddenly felt sorry for him. There was no way the lad was leaving this table with money in his pocket. Others just laughed and Gidyon joined them; he really did appear a simpleton.

It was the cheat who once again claimed order. In a quiet voice, he explained the basic rules.

Gidyon nodded. 'R-righto, I have it,' he said, before the man had taken a breath following his explanation.

'There are subtleties,' the cheat cautioned and looked as though he was about to explain some of those as well when Gidyon put his hand in the air.

'Don't worry, I'm feeling very l-lucky today. S-s-say no more.' He yawned again.

The cheat smiled. 'Is everyone ready now?'

Grunts of agreement were heard and furious betting from the onlookers commenced. The cheat dealt. Gidyon picked up his hand of seven cards knowing the task ahead was to achieve the highest scoring pack; the maximum of which was three suns and four dragons. That was hardly ever achieved of course and instead combinations of suns, moons, stars, dragons, gryphons, winged horses and various wild cards could make the winning hand. Gidyon wanted the three plus four combination of the sun and dragon. At present he had one sun, a moon, two stars, two dragons and a jewel. It was not a bad hand and he wondered if the cheat had contrived to give him a sense of early security. Everyone laughed at the way he peeped at his cards and then held them tightly to his chest.

Gidyon summoned his Colours and pushed as he opened up his cards to look at them in a more regular way. He immediately heard grumbling behind him and he also noticed the cheat rubbing at his eyes. Gidyon wondered how blurry the cards looked to the cheat and knew the poor chap behind would not be able to see a thing.

The round began. The cheat rolled the die blinking several times and got a three which meant three cards had to be exchanged from each hand to their left, whether the other players wanted to or not. And so it went. Gidyon had worked out that the cheat not only knew what was coming his way but what others were receiving and even how their hands were shaping up. Not at the moment, though. All of his carefully placed helpers were rubbing their eyes and finding it difficult to make out the cards they were spying on.

'Hold,' the cheat said. 'I have something in my eye.' He stood and rubbed hard, even dousing his shirttail with ale and cleaning his eyes.

Gidyon smiled. This was going to be fun, he thought, as he rolled the die and it landed on precisely the number he wanted. Another push and everyone around the table exchanged two cards in the way he wished.

It would not take long.

*   *   *

Later, whistling to himself and strolling through the market, Gidyon put all of his senses on alert. His purse was now three, maybe four times as heavy as it had been when he set off from the caravans and he knew he had made some enemies this day. He would need to be watchful. It was past noon and Gidyon had wasted many of his precious hours at the Hari House. Still, he would give undivided attention now to finding Yseul. He began to stroll amongst the rows of market stalls hoping to engage someone in conversation and start asking questions. Gidyon did not think the cheat and his friends would catch up with him as fast as they did but he was not surprised to see the familiar face with the keen eyes waiting for him at the end of one row. He turned and saw men he remembered from around the Hari table, blocking the other end. There was no easy escape route and so he summoned his Colours, keeping them ready for his call. He strolled casually up towards the cheat and nodded.

'We have a problem,' the cheat said.

'I guessed you may,' Gidyon replied.

The man jabbed him in the chest. 'You have money of ours.'

He smiled quizzically. 'I thought I'd won it.'

'Yes but we've changed our minds. We want it back.'

'Ah, well now I see you're right – we do have a problem.'

'I see your stammer's gone,' the man said as he suddenly realised he was no longer talking with a simpleton.

Gidyon grinned. 'It always works . . . regularly fools people.'

'And now I think of it, the closest monastery is a five day ride from here.'

'Correct again. What can I say?' Gidyon said, throwing up his hands in mock capitulation.

The man nodded in appreciation of the young man's arrogance. 'Shall we ask my friends what they'd like to do about this?'

'Why? We both know you cheated and we both know I cheated. Whoever you ask, I'll still come up with the same reply. The money's mine.'

'I'm intrigued,' the cheat said, chancing a look around Gidyon's body because he was not tall enough to see above his shoulder. He saw that his friends approached slowly. 'How did you dupe us all on your own?'

'An ancient skill. I can't show you, I'm afraid, or the guild of cheats will take me off its list of members.' He gave his most amused grin.

'Light! You're a cocky bastard,' the cheat said, suddenly losing his calm. 'I can't wait to pound your arrogant, handsome face to a pulp.'

'Charming,' said a voice Gidyon knew well.

'Yseul!'

'I knew it was you,' she said, throwing a look of disdain towards the cheat.

'Where were you? I've been looking for you?'

She snorted. 'Hardly. If you've got this man chasing you it means you've wasted the day playing Hari. What are you doing back here, Belcher? I thought the Mayor told you and your lads to stay away from Brittelbury?'

'We have,' he answered with indignance. 'It's been two summers since we were last here.'

'Well, that's not long enough,' she said calmly. 'Take them and go or I'll get the town guard onto you.'

He shot a look of hate towards Gidyon and glowered

at Yseul. 'I mean to get my money back, you whore.'

'Not only charming but polite as always, Belcher. Leave or I will call them. I've seen this man fight,' she said, pointing to Gidyon. 'He'll take six of you on and hold you off until I'm back with the guards.'

Belcher's eyes narrowed as he considered his next move. He chose to back off and with a gesture called off his henchmen behind them. Gidyon and Yseul watched them leave.

'I'm not sure you've seen the end of them,' she murmured. 'They turn up from time to time – I think they work the whole realm.'

'You're amazing.'

'And you're lucky I came along.'

He shrugged. 'I had it all under control.'

She laughed. 'Yes, I don't doubt you did, knowing what you're capable of.' Both of them suddenly felt shy. Yseul filled the uncomfortable moment. 'Er . . . look why don't you come over to where I have my stall and we can talk?'

'You have a stall?'

'Yes. My parents are the chandlers for the town. We're all involved . . . even Gwerys.'

'How is he?'

'Oh, he's fine.'

They walked together and Gidyon chanced taking her arm. She did not break step and he was pleased to have the physical contact, furious with himself for not kissing her hello and hating Belcher for spoiling their reunion. Now he would have to work towards a reason to kiss her again or Themesius would be disappointed.

'So he's over the trauma?'

Her smile faded. 'I'm not sure really. He seems happy

enough and it's wonderful for him to be home again with the family but he still has nightmares and shakes uncontrollably. I do my best to be there for him.' She shrugged.

It was instinctive. Gidyon moved his arm and gently draped it over her shoulder to pull her closer. 'He's a lucky boy to have you for his sister.'

'Oh, he's got four of us – all love him madly. I just have a special bond with him after all that we went through.' She pointed to a neat stall with a striped awning. 'Here we are.'

'How clever your family is,' Gidyon said, picking up candles and turning them around to marvel at the perfectly smooth and shiny wax.

'My father's family has done it for several generations. I think the knowledge just runs in our blood now.'

'And you sell them here?'

She laughed. 'No. We would only make a pittance if we did. Father takes them all around the Kingdom. Sells them to the monasteries and convents mainly. We make very special ones for the royal households and even more decorative candles for the crown ceremonies and events. We recently had to deliver a merry pile for the coronation. Did you hear about all the honoured guests . . . even the Cipreans sent a delegation.'

'So I heard,' Gidyon replied.

Yseul picked up a plain, creamy candle. 'These here are just for local use in households. My youngest sister normally runs this stall but everyone's sick in our family at the moment except me, my brother and my father who is away again.'

'Oh.' He did not know what else to say. They smiled and then their faces became more serious.

Yseul took a breath and put on a bright voice. 'So, you've come.'

'As promised,' he said and did a short bow.

'For the stone.' It was not a question.

Gidyon looked towards his feet and then back into her strangely light-coloured eyes. He nodded.

'Of course you did.' She attempted a brave smile. 'I don't have it here, Gidyon. Perhaps I could bring it to you?'

He shrugged. 'Yes.' Then, feeling stupid, he added, 'Are you busy this evening?'

'Busy? Um . . . no, the usual things.'

'That's right, your family, I forgot,' he said, wanting to rip his own tongue out for the clumsy way he was handling this.

'No, they'll be all right. What were you thinking of?' He noticed she seemed just as anxious as he was.

'Oh, it's just that, I'm here with some friends.'

'That's nice,' she said, nodding, not sure what he meant by this.

'We're in the *Greatest Show in the Land*.'

'You're in what? Oh . . . you mean the Freak Show . . . at the Green?'

He grinned. 'Apparently I'm so handsome, it's freakish.'

And he won the big laugh he wanted to hear from her. 'Is that so?'

'But tonight, my friends and I shall be performing a rather incredible balancing act. I thought you might like to come along, bring the stone . . . bring Gwerys.'

'You mean it?'

'Yes, I would love you to join us.'

'Is Figgis with you? I should like to see him again.'

'He is. And a new friend, Themesius. He's a giant. Gwerys's eyes will fall out of his head when he sees him.'

She burst out laughing again. 'You jest.'

He shook his head with a knowing look. 'Promise me you'll come.'

'All right. I'll bring Gwerys . . . and the stone.'

'Good. Tonight, then,' he said, putting down the candles he had been holding during their conversation.

Her pale eyes were shining and she looked so pretty and happy to see him, he could not help himself. Gidyon leaned down and kissed her. Yseul did not allow him to get away with a peck and flung her arms around him. When he pulled away from her embrace he felt breathless.

'I'm so glad you came,' she said.

'I can tell,' he said and with a final affectionate grin, he left.

On his way back to the caravans, a lightness to his step and a sense of joy in his heart, he opened a Link to his father. *I shall have the stone returned tonight.*

Good work, son. No trouble?

None. How about you?

Oh, you know, the usual trials . . . prisoner escaped, your mother and Saxon each shot with an arrow, Cloot's tracking the attackers . . . everyday problems.

Gidyon paused, trying to work out if his father was just larking. *This is a jest?*

His father sounded suddenly tired. *No, son. It's my way of remaining calm. I have just removed the arrow heads from your mother and Saxon. They're both sleeping now . . . and healing. I'm sitting here alone and wondering what in the Light will happen next.*

Are you all right?

Yes, yes, I'm fine. I'm worried enough about your sister and now this. The arrow was surely meant for me. They were such bad shots.

How bad are the wounds?

They'll both recover but they're going to ache for days which will slow us up. I'm hoping the fevers will pass through them swiftly if they have to face them at all.

And Goth?

As soon as they make it through this night, I'm going after him.

Alone?

Cloot and I.

Right, so we'll start backtracking towards you, then. You're going to need help.

Head east as fast as you can, son.

We'll leave tonight after the show.

Show?

A tale too long in the telling.

Fair enough. Get to your mother and Saxon. They're going to be fairly helpless for a day or two.

The Link snapped shut and Gidyon's high spirits came crashing back to the dusty road on which he walked.

Night fell and whilst Alyssa and Saxon shivered through the first touch of fever and Tor banked up the fire and watched them closely, Cloot stole ever closer to the group of men which included Goth. He was in obvious pain but the falcon had to admire the man's strength. He talked through it, telling these men how rich and landed he was. It was obvious they did not recognise him. But then why should they? No longer instantly recognisable to the untrained eye as former chief inquisitor, the men accepted his twitching, tortured face without familiarity.

Cloot listened carefully for any information he could pass back to Tor.

'Where are you men from?' Goth asked, edging closer to their fire.

The one who seemed to be the leader grimaced. 'Nowhere. Sailors originally,' he said.

'I'm surprised to see you in this Forest – and such a lonely part of it.'

'What's it to you?'

'Nothing more than curiosity. Most Tallinese are frightened of the Great Forest.'

'Not us. And not you, it seems.'

'True,' Goth said, lying. He had every reason to be afraid of the enchanted wood. He guessed they were men who had good reason to flee to deserted regions . . . even those considered dangerous. He changed the subject. 'Where are you headed?'

'Northwest. Caradoon.'

'Ah. I know the place well.'

They looked at him carefully now.

'It's not a place for gentlemen,' one replied.

'I didn't ever say I was one. I'm simply a rich man.' Goth laughed mysteriously.

The sailors could tell he was a man with secrets and dark ways. They joined him laughing.

The leader pointed. 'Then we are glad to have helped you – as you begged. But mind my words. If I don't see your promised coin soon, I shall slit your throat as easy as a lamb at slaughter.'

Goth nodded. 'I understand. You have my word. At

Caradoon, I shall reward each of you highly for taking me away from those people. Trust me.' He tried to grin but it never worked for him. 'And whom might I be sharing this journey with?'

'No names.'

'Oh, my good fellow, you need not fear me. I am impressed enough with you both to offer you work. There is no need to find a ship to take your service . . . which is what I presume you are planning to do in Caradoon. I will pay you handsomely to act as bodyguards.'

The men looked at each other, sizing up the offer.

'It's been a while since we were at sea, Nord.'

Nord glared at his companion.

'Ah, Nord,' Goth said. 'I am delighted to make your acquaintance and thank you for rescuing me from those people. Let me thank you properly by paying you a sizeable and regular fee for your protection services.'

'Starting when?' the huge former sailor said through slitted eyes.

'Right now. You don't think they will not give chase. I've already warned you about the bird.'

Nord snorted. 'I'm not scared of a bird . . . and your talk of magic don't scare me either.'

Goth nodded. 'Still, show caution. Do you accept?'

The sailor glanced at his men who nodded enthusiastically. 'Well, if I'm to share my name, I'll know yours too.'

'But you already do, my friend. I am Almyd Goth, former chief inquisitor of Tallinor and now outlaw in this Kingdom. However, I have since become the close and trusted adviser of the Ciprean monarch and I am here on secret business for my royal.'

Goth was the only one amongst them who was impressed by this speech.

'Money alone talks, Goth,' Nord replied.

'And it will talk heartily to you, my friend.' He held out his hand to shake on the deal with a questioning look on his face.

The man took his hand. 'The name's Nord Jesper.'

Cloot reported back all that he had learned, and wished he and Tor were together.

Why does that name ring a bell?

One of the sailors on The Wasp? Cloot prompted.

No. But it's so familiar. I shall have to think on it.

How are Alyssa and Saxon?

Sleeping, intermittently shivering and then come the sweats. It's for the best. At least I know their bodies are fighting back.

Any plan?

Tor laughed. *You always hate my plans!*

True, the falcon said sagely, *but I also always go along with them.*

I've spoken with Gidyon and he says he will have the stone shortly. He, Figgis and Themesius are leaving tonight, headed back east towards us. I'm hoping he can reach Alyssa and Saxon in the next two days.

So it's safe to leave them alone?

I'd prefer not to but they have each other and we all have the Link. I will not let Goth get away again. What about you?

Fine. Cold. Wishing for my Forest.

Have you eaten?

No!

Grumpy, then?

Very. They're all drifting off to sleep now. I don't think we'll hear much from them until just before dawn.

Good. Go hunt.

Tor felt the Link close and stared into the flames. The name of Nord Jesper continued to niggle at him but experience told him to let it alone and it would come back to him of its own accord. He checked his patients. Both were now sleeping soundly after their latest cup of his special brew, which he kept simmering gently over the fire. Good, the rest now would do all the healing.

He sat back and thought about Orlac. His brother. The moment Alyssa uttered her thoughts, he knew it was true. So he too was a prince of the gods and had been sacrificed to Tallinor in order to murder his brother . . . and now Dorgryl, who lived within Orlac. He shook his head; he had not shared this information with Alyssa. She was already suffering shock from the discovery of him being alive and the children's sudden arrival in her life, as well as despair at the death of Lorys. Yet still she moved forward doggedly, determined to see through her part in all of this. Learning of Lauryn's capture had been another blow, making her more fearful than Tor had ever seen her. To top that with the news that Orlac had been possessed by another god, one even madder and more vengeful, could break Alyssa's battered spirit. No, it was best that he withheld this information, whatever the consequences.

And what of the Trinity? Were they up to this new and terrifying challenge? How would they know what to do? Most importantly of all . . . what was their purpose? He turned these questions over and over in his tired mind, finally deciding that he should not look too far ahead. Deal with the immediate problem, he told himself. Follow the plan. Finish Goth. Then back to the Heartwood to finish Orlac.

His mind turned to Goth. How he hated the man. How many lives had been lost through him? And inevitably his thoughts fell sorrowfully upon Eryn and the permanent mental picture he carried of the lovely young woman hung upside down and left to die in such a barbaric way. Even Orlac had more capacity to kill humanely, he thought. In a way he was glad Quist had died too for he felt sure the man's life would have been ruined anyway without his great love. He hoped the pirate never learned of Eryn's death but it was unlikely Goth would not have taken the opportunity to torture Quist with the gory details before killing him.

Tor thought about Eryn's brief, sad life. She seemed to have lived it to the fullest and yet he had sensed a grief in her at their last two meetings. At a superficial level it was her ongoing disappointment that she and Tor might never be more than hidden lovers, great friends. But he decided it had been more than that. Eryn had not recovered from the death of Petyr. He knew she prided herself on having taken care of her brothers, ferociously protecting and raising them from tiny lads when she herself was hardly more than a slip of a girl. But it was Petyr who had broken her heart, he knew. Finding him dead as she had, unable to reach or help him, had scarred her permanently.

It made Tor angry. And then it hit him. Nord Jesper!

Nord Jesper! he cried, slashing open the Link and alarming Cloot who was feasting.

Yes, that's his name, the falcon said calmly.

Cloot, that's the name of the sailor who beat Eryn's brother, Petyr, leaving him half-dead. Petyr never recovered, ran away from Eryn and Locky and ended up in a stracca den in Caradoon.

She found him there, dead. She was just hours too late. Tor's voice broke on his last words.

All right, Tor. I hear you. You'll have your revenge, I promise. They still sleep. They're going nowhere.

I'll avenge Petyr for Eryn. It's what she wanted.

Get some rest, Cloot cautioned. *We'll talk in the morning when you can think clearly.*

More wise words from his friend. Tor said a brief farewell and closed the Link.

He curled up next to Alyssa, careful not to disturb her, and tried not to think about Lauryn and her fear of Orlac. Instead he imagined Goth and Nord Jesper at his mercy.

24

Surprises

Juno came reluctantly for Lauryn. Adongo followed her in.

'What does he want?' Lauryn said fearfully.

Juno glanced towards Adongo. Something may have passed between them – she did not hear – but Lauryn stared, frightened, regarding them both. She knew instinctively that they were trying to weigh up whether to tell her the truth.

'He wishes for you to spend the night with him.' Juno, at Adongo's bidding, chose honesty.

A series of shocks trembled through Lauryn's body, culminating in dizziness. Within two strides Adongo was holding her. She sat down heavily.

'You must be brave now, Miss Lauryn,' he said. *If you go to him willingly, he will not hurt you.*

Lauryn heard voices in her head and a buzzing in her ears. Her legs would surely not even support her weight now. She began to shake her head. 'I'm not ready for this. Surely you won't ask this of me?'

Juno winced at the pain in her bonded one's voice. *We*

must child. 'Don't fight this. He has chosen you above all others,' she said, hating herself.

Lauryn's whole body was trembling now as Adongo left the room and Juno first undressed and then reclothed her in a white gown in the simple, yet beautiful, Ciprean styling. Lauryn had withdrawn mentally, overwhelmed with panic at the thought that she was about to lose her self to Orlac – the very enemy they had been born to destroy. Her father's brother would rape her. She remained within herself, tears silently coursing down her face as Juno gently hummed a soft tune, hoping to soothe the girl. She brushed and dressed her hair with fresh white, fragrant flowers.

I must speak with my father, Lauryn announced, returning to the scene around her.

Please, child, I beg of you. Do not risk casting. The cursed one may be listening. You may jeopardise all our lives. I care not for mine but you must survive this trial and soon we will destroy him.

I can't, Juno.

Juno stood behind Lauryn, both of them staring into the mirror. She pretended a bright voice for any eavesdroppers. 'You are very beautiful, Miss Lauryn.'

Don't make me do this.

We have no choice. We must get through it so we can live another day to fight the final battle. 'Would you prefer the antler or tortoiseshell clasp?'

Lauryn refused to answer. *I will fight him. He will hurt me and I will blame you and Adongo, my Paladin, who are supposed to give their lives for me.*

It was an unfair stab but Juno accepted it for she knew she must. The child was terrified and rightly so. She chose the tortoiseshell.

Adongo entered. 'It is time, Miss Lauryn.'

I hate you both! she said, masking intense feelings behind a face devoid of all expression now.

We love you, they said together. *And we will avenge this*.

Lauryn looked between them; knew well they were hurting but did not care. She could not cry any more but she was not able to stop her body trembling. It was no longer fear, it was anger. Inside, something snapped into place in her mind and she found a calm, the foundation of which was pure, white rage like lava overflowing into her body. Lauryn stood.

'Let's get this done with.'

She walked steadily between them, refusing the Link they attempted several times to open. Lauryn had shielded herself so completely, not even they could reach her. She would not contact her father, nor would she allow him to witness this terrible event. As they climbed the marble staircase in silence, Lauryn began to reinforce her mental, magical walls about herself. He could do what he would with her body but he would not touch her mind. She would not permit him access to a Link. She was strong enough to withstand his mind probes and she would deny him what he would know was her true self. It was only via the Link that he could truly possess her. She would refuse him. *I can be anyone*, she reassured herself. *I could be Xantia for all it would matter. Or a corpse*. She finally decided on the latter as it best described how she would behave.

When they arrived and were permitted into the salon, her Paladin tried once again to offer some encouragement but she rebuffed them with a cold stare. And when she was asked to enter by Orlac's servant, she stopped when they moved to go with her. Lauryn held her hand up, her face hard and unyielding. It was clear she wished to enter his chambers alone. She permitted the servant to open the door and as she glided in with the air of detachment she had finally achieved, she gave one last sad thought to Gyl.

It should be him, she wished, not allowing herself to cry over it.

Night's dark mantle had closed around evening. Orlac had dismissed all servants. The last of them showed her out onto the balcony and then left. Lauryn's superior hearing noted the door close. She was alone with her torturer. He stood at the furthest end of the balcony with his back to her. He was strikingly dressed in a loose white shirt over white breeches. His long black boots accentuated his height and the long lean lines of his body. She did not move and in that moment of watching him, anticipating him, she realised she was terrified.

Finally he turned. His long, golden hair had been combed back and tied into a single club. His skin looked bronzed and polished.

'Thank you for coming.'

'Did I have a choice?' She tried to sound strong in her words but her fear betrayed her and they came out sounding nervous.

He did not answer but flashed her an almost shy smile. He approached but did not touch her. Instead, she was surprised to see him bow before her. 'Not really, but it doesn't spoil my pleasure at seeing you. Lauryn, you are more beautiful than I've even imagined in my thoughts.'

Gone were the arrogant tones of Sylc, his innuendo, his peacock mannerisms. This man spoke quietly. His garb, though hanging superbly off his body, was plainly styled and lacking in the colour favoured by the Regent. And where Sylc used elevated language, bordering on poetic, Orlac had a simple, straightforward way of talking. It confused her momentarily. She wanted to hurt him with a caustic reply but none came. Again her anxiety betrayed her. One aspect of him which had not changed were those violet eyes; they were drawing her closer, willing her to accept him.

He gestured towards the table. 'Will you join me? The chef here is from a long line of famous chefs, apparently. I gather your father knew him.' He smiled. 'Actually he saved his life. It seems our mutual relative enjoys hero status with my cook.' This was not said unkindly. If she had read it right, it was said to make her smile, relax even.

Desperately wanting to be churlish, Lauryn snapped her eyes away from his inviting violet gaze. 'Given his loyalty to my father, are you not afraid he may poison you then?'

'I have taken precautions,' he said gently. 'Although I fear Ryk is too passionate about his cooking to risk spoiling it with anything which could make it bitter.' He sighed very softly, taking her arm without putting any pressure on it. 'Well, that's what I like to think, anyway.'

There it was again — that self-deprecating manner. Lauryn wanted to refuse his food, ignore him, make him force himself upon her, but against her wishes she found herself permitting him to guide her to a chair.

'I've taken the liberty of finding out your favourite foods.' He shrugged a little self-consciously. 'We haven't had time to learn much, of course, but Ryk has done his best. I hope it satisfies you.'

She gave him a quizzical look. She tried to pinpoint a new quality in him – it was not nerves because Orlac was graceful and assured as always but Lauryn picked up how intent his need was to make her feel comfortable. He was trying to impress her as any new lover might. It was so perplexing. And his courtesies, his beautiful voice – not dissimilar to her own father's, she grudgingly admitted – and, she had to accept it, his thrilling looks, only served to make her confusion more complex.

'It all looks very appetising, thank you,' she said, in mild disbelief at her own good grace.

He asked if he could pour her some wine. 'You will like this,' he said, only pouring a little into her glass. 'But taste it and tell me. If you don't, we shall order something different.'

She did. It effected an extraordinary explosion of taste in her mouth and she could not believe she was smiling. 'It's very fine.'

He beamed, pleased at the compliment, and filled her glass but modestly. Clearly, he had no intention of deliberately trying to get her intoxicated.

'Oh, and I have this for you,' he said, suddenly leaping back to his feet. At the end of the table was a velvet roll. He handed it to her and then looked away. 'It's just something I'd like you to have.'

Now he was embarrassed. Light! She could not work him out. Lauryn really did not want to unroll it but he watched her as if he was holding his breath.

'Would you like me to look at it now?'

He shrugged, the awkward grin back on his face. He reached for his wine and took a gulp. Lauryn unrolled the velvet. Inside lay a necklace of dazzling sea-green gems.

Each one looked as if it had a flame burning inside it — the candlelight reflecting fantastically from the surface of each jewel. She was taken aback. Orlac glanced at her sideways. Impossibly, it seemed to her that he was unsure of what to do next.

Why do you woo her, nephew? She is your slave. We promised you that you would have your every desire with her. These courtesies make me feel ill. Throw her on her back; have your pleasure and be done. Then do it again tomorrow night until she feels used and depraved. How else will you get her to call to her father?

And you make me feel ill, Dorgryl. Withdraw.

I warn you—

Withdraw! he shouted within, knowing the pain of his despair had crossed his face and his guest had seen it.

Dorgryl's mist backed down and away, curling within itself. Sulking.

Lauryn did not know what was expected of her and she had been watching his face for some sign. She noticed he seemed to be disturbed and this frightened her more. He seemed to be so many different people. She forced herself to look away from him and back to the velvet roll. Well, she was to be his whore and she presumed it was right that she graced her body with whatever he wanted her to wear.

Lauryn had already decided to think of herself as Orlac's whore. Only by so doing could she not confuse this relationship with the way she felt about Gyl. She wanted to be Gyl's lover. She wanted no other man to touch her in love. And because Orlac intended to have her, then she would be his object.

'Do you wish me to put it on?'

He seemed composed once again and made a depre-
cating shrug. 'Only if it pleases you. I chose it to match
your beautiful eyes.'

Lauryn swallowed hard. He was not making it easy to
hate him. Instead he looked like a lost boy.

'May I?' he said, pointing to the jewels.

She nodded. What else could she do? Spitting in his
face or throwing them over the balcony would only enrage
him, and both Juno and Adongo had counselled her
strenuously against bringing such rage on. They had told
her how petrifying he could be when his ire was aroused.
She had had no indication of this but she would not
provoke it.

Lauryn felt his presence behind her as he hooked the
gems around her neck, but not once did he attempt to
caress her; not once did his fingers, so close, even briefly
touch her skin. The jewels sat perfectly against her collar
bone, heavy and cold. Orlac walked around to admire her.

'They are lovely and you do them justice. It is your
beauty which sets them off and makes them look as perfect
as they do around your neck.'

She bowed her head in acknowledgement of the compliment, at a loss as to what to say to him.

'I have one more gift for you tonight,' he said. 'You may
like it better than the necklace.' He grinned and left the
table. 'I will be only a few moments, please help yourself.'

He disappeared into his chambers. Lauryn shook her
head to clear her thoughts. So far only his smile and that
gaze had touched her. She had thought he would leap
onto her body as soon as she entered his rooms. If anything,
he was being as charming and attentive as any man could
be to a woman.

He reappeared. 'I thought he may prevent you from being too lonely here.' In his arms was a tiny, fluffy creature.

When it lifted its head, she saw it was a puppy, barely weaned she felt sure. Her mouth opened in surprise and her heart melted at the sight of its large, dark, trusting eyes. It yawned from Orlac's arms and then yapped once; he handed it to Lauryn who was instantly in love with her golden dog.

'I didn't presume to name him but he will grow into a fine beast and you will need to give him a proud name to match his stature.'

He sat down and again she noticed that tentativeness.

'He's too beautiful.'

'Not as beautiful as you. But like the jewels, he is a good match.'

'Thank you,' she said, this time unable not to show her pleasure at this unexpected gift.

'He will always protect you, Lauryn. No bad will come to you once he is grown.'

For some strange reason, these words sounded prophetic and they affected her deeply. The jewels, the sensitivity of his attitude and now this most appropriate and thoughtful gesture of giving her company. She wept. He sat silently, watching until she had found her calm again. The dog had drifted into a puppy's blissful sleep in her lap.

She sniffed. 'I shall call him Pelyss.'

'Ah,' he said and smiled. 'After the god – protector against all demons?'

She nodded, not really knowing how she knew this to be right.

'An excellent choice,' he admitted, reaching for his wine. 'Now eat, Lauryn. You need feeding.'

And so in these strange and unexpected circumstances she found herself dining and conversing with Orlac. It seemed preposterous. All her loved ones were preparing for torrid battle whilst she sat there with a puppy on her lap, exquisite gems about her neck, quaffing superb wine and feasting as her enemy told her about Cipres and all that he had learned about that fabulous city and capital of the Exotic Isles. Lauryn was ashamed to admit he was brilliant company; far more engaging and witty than Sylc, making her laugh out loud several times. And she could tell he revelled in his ability to do so. The night stretched on and the candles burned low. Still Orlac had made no move that could alarm or disgust her.

'Would you care for a stroll in the gardens? They are especially fragrant at night.' He picked up two refreshed glasses of wine to take with them.

It meant leaving his chambers which was a reassuring thought. 'I would,' she replied, looking towards her sleeping pup.

'Pelyss will be safe here,' he said.

So, he intended bringing her back to his rooms, she realised sadly. She was not going to be released from her fate. She nodded and even dared take his proffered arm as he led her towards the stone stairs which would take them into the gardens below. They strolled through the rose gardens and then the orchard in silence. It was not uncomfortable but Lauryn could not relax as she knew he had intended she might, but to reassure him of her quiet pleasure, she allowed him to guide her with his arm and she even leaned against him and laughed gently when he helped her across a small pond with stepping stones.

He led her towards a bench in an enclosed formal herb garden with a wall of heavy-scented honeysuckle which added a special lustre to the various fragrances which permeated the mild night.

'I like it here most of all.' These were his first words since leaving the balcony. 'I hope you don't mind if we sit a while?' He handed her one of the glasses.

'Not at all,' Lauryn said, taking a sip, knowing every moment here was one less spent beneath his body. 'It's very beautiful. Your Ryk must enjoy all these wonderful herbs for his dishes.'

He nodded and pulled a face. 'Beware that Pelyss does not take his daily ablutions in here.'

She laughed. 'I'll be watchful.'

After another long silence which Lauryn was now finding hard to fathom he sighed and said: 'Tell me about my brother.'

This was her biggest surprise so far that night. Lauryn took a deep breath and considered what she should say. She would have to be careful for he could be deliberately leading her into a trap; goading her into spilling information he could use against them. She began by describing Tor to his elder brother in as much detail as she could recall, from his impossibly blue eyes to his manner of speaking.

He did not interrupt her.

'Talking to you now, you remind me of him,' she said, not wishing to say any more about her father, lest it be dangerous. It was the only phrase she had uttered in the past few minutes which she had not carefully considered.

He was thoughtfully twirling his glass of wine, the

buttery yellow liquid glinting in the bright moonlight.

'We shall meet soon and try to destroy one another,' he said, no emotion in his voice. He was simply stating a fact.

Again she said what came to mind, knowing it was fraught with danger. 'Why must it be so?'

'It is.' He shrugged, his eyes firmly looking down.

Lauryn leapt towards this sensitive moment. 'You are blood. Does that count for anything?'

His voice was smooth. 'You have not suffered as I have.'

'But my father is not the reason for your suffering.'

He lifted the glass to his lips and drained it. 'He is all I have to level my despair at.'

'And by killing him, killing me . . . will that restore you?'

He finally turned a large and sorrowful violet gaze towards her. 'I will not kill you, Lauryn.'

She held his intensity with her own look directly into his eyes so that he knew she meant what she was about to say. 'Well, I shall do everything in my power to kill you and to stop you hurting my family.'

'I know,' he said, in something close to a sad whisper. And then he leaned forward to kiss her so very softly. In those fleeting moments of his kiss she sensed his fierce affection for her. There was something else, too, and she prolonged his withdrawal from her mouth trying to figure what it was. She probed and in that moment of his weakness she glimpsed an internal battle. She did not know what it was or why but she could somehow tell that Orlac desperately wanted to be the person he was with her but something inside him wanted him to be the opposite. She felt him push back at something sinister, deciding it must be his darker side wanting to wreak the revenge he had lusted after for so many centuries.

He pulled away. 'It is late,' he said. 'I imagine Juno and Titus will be heartsick by now. I see they are already as smitten with you as—' He did not finish what he was going to say. Instead, he stood. 'I must let you get back to your rooms.'

Lauryn was too terrified to say the wrong thing, which might make him change his mind. Could she really be this lucky to escape the nightmare?

He helped her to her feet and then bowed courteously to touch her hand, this time with his lips. 'Thank you for allowing me to kiss you.' A fleeting smile touched his mouth and then it was gone. 'I shall send Pelyss immediately. Your chambers are that way,' he said, pointing towards a lit wing.

And then he was gone, long legs striding back upstairs. Lauryn sat down on the bench again, her feelings churning, knowing her knees trembled too much to walk anywhere. She had escaped. And Orlac had allowed her to. He was an enigma to her. Worse . . . she no longer felt contempt or disgust . . . not even fear. All she felt for him was pity.

Finally returning to her chambers, she was greeted sombrely by Juno and Adongo, both with fearful expressions full of anticipation of what she might have endured these past hours.

We did not want to disturb your thoughts, child, Juno whispered gently into her mind explaining the lack of their Link. *Are you in pain?*

Lauryn shook her head, too numb from her jumbled feelings to speak with them.

Come, we have drawn a deep and scented bath for you.

Still unable to find the right pattern of thought, she remained silent. They took it as despair and helped her towards the warm water which might wash Orlac from her body.

For the next three nights Orlac and Lauryn dined together and strolled the gardens. On each of those occasions, Orlac was charming and attentive and Lauryn said to a confused pair of Paladin that she would be lying if she did not admit she was enjoying these evenings. She went so far as to comment that she looked forward to the time she spent with him. Neither Adongo nor Juno could understand Orlac's actions. Both had expected the worst, that he would force himself upon Lauryn, leaving her a broken woman. It was beyond their comprehension that he would woo Lauryn and, worse, that she was reacting towards him with an unwitting friendship. Juno sensed Lauryn had begun to pity the god. If only she knew what they had been through to be here now, Lauryn would not pity him, she would despise him. But Juno understood the clever machinations of the god's mind. This must be a ruse.

Adongo agreed. He went so far as to suggest that it was only a matter of time before the calm before the storm broke.

He was right.

Locky rode like the wind, stopping only to feed and water his horse. He slept for snatched periods in bushes and lived off the supplies he found stashed in his saddlebags. Mostly, though, he fed off his determination to succeed in this task and rid himself of the guilt that he had survived whilst Eryn and Quist had died. And so he drove himself and his horse grimly towards Caradoon with the single aim of getting there in time to meet with King Gyl.

Luck rode with him. Locky wiped the dust from his eyes and slowed his mount as they entered Caradoon proper. He could see the small town had swelled dramatically in population and the oriflamme of King Gyl flew brightly along the streets which seemed to be owned by the royal guard. A smirk crossed his face as he wondered whether the Caradoons had gone into hiding. They would not be enjoying such attention from Tallinese rulemakers, nor would they relish the scrutiny of the King himself, known as a fair player who ruthlessly pursued lawbreakers in his role as Under Prime.

Locky took a deep breath. He had done it. He had kept his promise to Tor and he had made it to Caradoon on time. He got off his horse and led a thankful mount through the town towards the brothel he once called home. Assuming the inn was still operating, he did not want to meet any of the girls, so he skulked around to the back where he found fresh hay and sweet oats for his courageous horse. He watered the mare and took a few minutes to rub her down, remembering Saxon's warnings to always take care of his horse first. As he did so, he wondered about the brothel, realising it was now his. With Eryn and Quist dead, there was no one else. Well, he could pursue that later. Now he must find the King. Without even wetting his face, he sneaked back into the town looking for a way to win a meeting with the sovereign.

He asked directions from several soldiers, most of whom just stopped short of giving him a cuff to his head. King indeed! However, the last man he spoke to looked like an old campaigner and through squinted eyes he regarded the youngster who stood before him.

'Looks like you've done some riding, lad.' His voice was gruff.

'I've ridden from the midlands, hardly pausing.'

'You're in a hurry, then,' he said, scratching at his beard, 'to see the King I mean?'

'I have to speak with him. I have news he must hear.'

The old fellow could see the lad was as exhausted as he was dusty and hungry. 'Over there,' he said pointing towards a dwelling in the distance which Locky knew had been vacant for years, 'is where the Prime has set himself up. You talk to him and it's as good as having the ear of the King.'

Locky's face lit. The Prime! Those two words had more effect on him than the notion of meeting the King. 'Will he agree to meet with me?'

'Ah, now that I can't answer. I can only point you in the right direction, boy. 'S'up to you to do the rest.'

Locky thanked the older man who moved on, wishing him luck over his shoulder. Locky turned to watch the house from where the Prime was operating. There were men coming and going constantly. Obviously messages were moving frantically back and forth through the chain of command which stopped in that house where the senior commander now gave his orders. Locky swallowed. He must impress this man. With that thought gripped firmly in his mind he walked towards the house and was promptly stopped by two guards.

'Ho, lad. You're not allowed in here,' one said.

'I was told I might speak with Prime Herek.'

'Oh? By whom? His mother perhaps? . . . because I think that's the only person who can still wield that sort of power in his life.'

They both laughed at the jest. Locky was unmoved.

He took a deep, steadying breath. 'A soldier said I could get an audience with the King if I spoke with the Prime first.'

Now the guards were hugely amused. 'Oh, it's the King now? Well, lad . . . why didn't you say so! Of course the King will see you. He's got nothing better to do than take drinks and sweet pastries with a stripling like you.'

The other guard poked him. 'Go on, lad, be off with you. This is serious business we're about here.'

'I know. That's why I'm here trying to speak with my sovereign about matters relating to this serious business you speak of.' He kept his voice steady and stern.

The joking had stopped.

'I won't tell you again,' one of the guards said. 'Leave now or we'll tan your backside for you.'

'You may care to try that but then the King won't get his message from his mother, which I alone bring.'

They snorted. 'King's Mother eh?' one said.

He nodded.

The other one boxed his ear and Locky fell to the ground. 'The King's Mother is at a convent outside of the city recuperating from her loss, you hairy-arsed vagabond. She wouldn't be talking to the likes of you,' said the man who had hit him.

Locky's left ear sang a song all of its own. He shook his head to stop the strange sound.

'Hey, you guards, leave the boy alone.' It was the old soldier. He helped Locky back to his feet. 'I thought they might do something like this.' He looked back at the guards. 'Give him a chance and do as he bids. You know we've been told we need all the information we can get and the King won't thank you if you turn valuable knowledge away.'

The guards looked sceptical. 'We have our orders,' one said.

'What would it hurt? Just ask the question.'

The other guard shrugged and trudged towards the house.

'Tell them I can prove it,' Locky called after him. He turned to the soldier. 'Thanks.'

'You can buy me an ale later,' the man replied.

The guard returned not long afterwards and shoved Locky towards the house. 'You've got one minute to explain yourself.'

Locky turned back to the old campaigner. 'Wish me luck.'

'Already have,' the fellow said and watched Locky make his way to the door.

Inside was a queue of men receiving orders. Locky could not see the Prime but he could hear voices raised – he wondered which of those was Herek's.

'Wait here,' a soldier said, pointing him back to the wall just inside the door.

He did as told, trying to neaten himself but his efforts were in vain. The soldier had returned and was beckoning at him. 'One minute is all you have.'

'So I've been told,' Locky murmured and followed.

They pushed through the men crowding the desk until Locky found himself face-to-face with the man he had dreamed of meeting. Herek was thin and of medium height but it was clear who commanded respect in this room. And when he spoke, his voice was quiet. He regarded the dust-encrusted lad in front of him. 'How long have you ridden, boy?'

Locky knew his time was short and he had to make a good fist of this meeting. It would not do to cringe or be overawed by the moment. 'Three days, sir.'

'From?'

'The Great Forest, Prime Herek.'

'Alone?'

'I rode alone, yes, sir. I was not alone in the Forest, sir. I was with Torkyn Gy—'

Herek cut him off, gave some signal and men began to disperse. He looked at Locky and raised a finger very slightly. It told Locky to be still whilst certain ears were present. A few moments later, with the room they were in now fairly empty, the Prime addressed him again.

'We speak freely now. Have a seat.'

Locky was grateful for it and even more surprised when Herek himself poured a mug of water and handed it to him. 'Here, drink this down and then we'll talk. Have you eaten?'

Locky shook his head awkwardly as he gulped the sweet water to slake a raging thirst he had not even been aware he had. Herek nodded and someone immediately disappeared to find food.

'Better?' the Prime asked as Locky finished his drink.

'Much. Thank you, sir.'

'Good, tell me what you came here to say.'

Locky ordered his thoughts. This was the head of the entire army he was now speaking to – the Prime. It did not get any higher bar the King himself. The man would react well to a brief, accurate report.

'You said we can speak freely?'

The Prime nodded.

'The new sovereign of Cipres, Queen Sarel, is being hidden in the Great Forest—'

Immediately a cry of voices interrupted him.

'Whoa, lad,' Herek said. 'The Queen of Cipres?'

He nodded. 'Let me tell you it all, sir, and then perhaps I can answer any questions.'

Herek was impressed by the youngster's composure. 'All right, let's start with who you are first.'

Locky began, telling an increasingly anxious Prime everything he knew of what had happened since the two Cipreans had arrived on Tallinese soil.

'. . . and we decided someone had to get word to the King. I was chosen.'

Silence reigned in the room.

The Prime finally rubbed his face with both hands.

'Torkyn Gynt was stoned to death some years ago. I was there at the execution. I witnessed him take his last breath, just before the stones split his head open as one might ripe fruit.' He stared at Locky. 'It is preposterous.'

Locky wanted to shrug. He had known none of this. 'He is alive, sir. I have spoken with him on countless occasions these past years. We sailed to Cipres together where he saved my life . . . twice in fact, I believe.'

Men smirked at this but not Herek, whose eyes had narrowed considerably as he regarded this earnest boy.

'Describe Gynt to me.'

Locky did and it was accurate.

'Where did you meet?'

'On a ship, sir. *The Wasp*, bound for Cipres as I mentioned.'

'So you have met the Queen? I was not aware her name was Sarel,' Herek said, picking holes in the incredible tale he had just heard.

'Sir? Um . . . Queen Sylven was murdered. Tor believes it was by the hand of Goth—' He stopped talking as he watched the Prime bristle at the mention of that name.

'Goth? Almyd Goth, former chief inquisitor of Tallinor?' It was asked in a whisper. 'Be careful, boy. I want the truth.'

'Yes, Prime Herek. I speak only the truth. That is the same Goth I speak of. It is he who murdered the Queen and her daughter is on the run from the usurper, Orlac.'

'So Goth is in Cipres, eh?' Herek said, beginning to pace the room.

'Er . . . no, sir,' Locky said.

'But you just said he killed Queen Sylven.'

Locky felt his heartbeat increase in tempo as he fought back the bile of Goth's grisly work back on Tallinese soil. 'He is returned to Tallinor, sir. Not long ago in Caradoon he executed my sister, Eryn Quist. He also murdered Captain Quist, her husband, who rode with me and the Cipreans.'

Herek could hardly believe all that he was hearing. The lad's story was becoming more and more complex.

'You have seen this, know it to be true?' he asked, confused yet intrigued beyond his doubts.

'The Light saved me from seeing my sister killed in the brutal manner he chose, sir. He gutted her,' Locky said, his hands balling into fists. 'I saw the head of Janus Quist in the Forest. Goth kept it as a memento for all of us.'

'Where is he now, boy?' Herek had grabbed Locky by his shirt.

Locky did not struggle or try and fight him off. 'He is held captive in the Heartwood, sir. Torkyn Gynt has him.'

He saw a light blaze into life in those fathomless eyes of the Prime, who slowly uncurled his grip on the lad's shirt. 'And you say Alyssa . . . er, the King's Mother, is in the Great Forest with Saxon and Sallementro?' There was a tone of utter disbelief in the Prime's voice. When the hell did a musician get involved in all this adventure? 'I was told she had gone to a convent to recuperate from the loss of her husband.'

'I'm sorry, sir, that your information is wrong. I left the King's Mother a few days ago.' He shrugged. 'She hugged me farewell,' he added and Herek could not help but smile inwardly at this brave lad.

'Eat something, Locky. Your tale makes my hair curl.' He pointed to the plate of food which Locky had not dared touch whilst he was giving his report. He ate with gusto now. 'And you say you can prove it?'

Locky nodded. His mouth was too full to answer.

'Wait here,' Herek ordered. He whispered something to his men and then he disappeared.

Locky ate and the men around him maintained a detached silence. He began to wonder whether anyone believed him. Herek was gone a while.

The back door finally burst open and Locky saw him reappear with another man. This one was not especially tall but he was strongly built and had a clear air of authority about him. He was dressed as a soldier – simple clothes, a sword at his side and a blade in his boot. Locky was instantly impressed by the man's presence.

'Is this him?' the stranger asked.

Herek nodded. 'Locky, you may care to bow. This is your sovereign, King Gyl.'

Locky did not know whether to bow first or spit out what was in his mouth. And so he did both, unloading his mouth into his hand as he bent quickly to acknowledge his sovereign.

'Your majesty,' he said, hoping he was following correct protocol.

'As you were,' the King said.

When Locky stood upright, the King was holding out his hand in welcome. Locky felt horrified for his own right hand was full of food. He immediately threw it onto the plate nearby and then wiped his hand on his trousers, rubbing vigorously. Then he shook hands in the Tallinese manner. The King did not seem to notice his anxiety nor his grubby hands.

Instead Gyl grinned to put the lad at ease. 'The Prime has just told me an extraordinary tale which you've brought to us today.' Locky nodded. 'And the reason I believe you is that I have met with Torkyn Gynt and I am aware that my mother is not at the convent. Apparently you have some proof that you have recently left her?'

'I do, your majesty . . . if you'll pardon me,' Locky said, digging into his pockets – several of them, in fact, until he found the right one. 'She asked me to give this to you so that you would know all that I've told is true.'

He held out his hand and the King did the same. When he looked into his palm, he saw that Locky had dropped a pale green disk, a sliver of a gem, into it.

Gyl took a breath. 'It would seem, gentlemen,' he said, addressing the others in the room, 'that this lad speaks true.' Now he eyed Locky. 'You have your audience, Locky. Tell me everything you know.'

And Locky told his tale again . . . this time impressing on the King that Lauryn was not held captive by Regent Sylc. Sylc was a manifestation of Orlac, the stranger Alyssa had warned him about.

'They're frightened you may walk into a trap, your majesty.'

The King nodded thoughtfully. 'This does change things. Did they offer any advice?'

'No, your highness. Alyssa said you would do what you had to do to retrieve Lauryn.'

The King turned back to Locky. 'You have been courageous, son. We must reward you for your efforts.'

Locky shook his head. 'No, sir. I want nothing. I did it for my dead sister and her husband.'

The King nodded. 'Is there anything we can do for you, Locky?'

'Yes, your highness.' This was his moment.

'Well?'

'Your majesty . . . um . . . all of my life I have dreamed of one thing only.'

'Yes?' the king said, with a slightly bemused expression as he cast a glance towards Herek.

'May I address the Prime, sir?'

'Go ahead.'

Locky turned to Herek and bowed. 'Prime Herek, I offer you my service. I wish to join the King's Guard and protect my sovereign's life with my own. It is my extreme desire to be a soldier. Saxon the Kloek said you might bestow the opportunity upon me if I impressed you enough. He said he would speak on my behalf.'

The King winked at Herek now.

The Prime addressed him. 'How old are you, Locklyn Gylbyt?'

'Sixteen, sir,' he lied.

Herek could see the lad was gilding the truth. 'I see, well that makes you of an age to join the Company although I suspect you have some growing yet to do?'

Locky flicked a nervous glance up from the ground towards the Prime. 'Yes, sir. I gather I'm small for my age but I can read, write and fight with heart, sir.'

Herek reached forward and laid an arm on Locky. 'We don't need your brawn, lad. The Company recognises a bright mind when it sees one. You have proved yourself to be brave and resourceful and men like you are rare. Welcome to our army, Locky. Go with my man, now, and he will kit you with what you need.'

'We need good men like you, Locky,' Gyl said. 'Especially those who know Cipres. You're coming with us.'

Locky dropped to his knees to thank his sovereign but Gyl stopped him.

'Come on, son. You need some rest whilst we find a fast ship.'

'Have you not got a ship?' Locky asked.

The King grimaced. 'No, we don't tend to drag them behind us on wagons. We had hoped to secure some vessels here, although your story makes me think I must re-work our plan.'

'Your majesty, er . . . I have a ship you can use. She cuts the waves faster than any ship in Caradoon.'

Gyl and Herek turned to the lad.

'*Explain yourself*,' Gyl requested.

'Janus Quist's ship, *The Raven*. She's mine now, your majesty. And I extend her to you for swift, safe passage to the Exotic Isles.'

'Light, lad, but you're a constant stream of surprises.'

Locky grinned. 'I even have a reliable crew, your highness.'

'Herek, let's get this boy sorted and then get down to the docks immediately. If he's as good as his word, we sail tonight.'

25

Surrender

The four companions emerged from the Great Forest on
the outskirts of Ildagarth with Hela and Sarel impressed
by and just a little breathless from Rubyn's enchanted
mode of travel. Rubyn whispered his thanks to the trees
but if the Forest replied, they could not tell.

He deferred to Cyrus. 'What's our next move?'

The soldier's eyes narrowed as he scanned the land
ahead. 'It's nearing dusk. I'd recommend we head into the
city and take some rooms for the night. We'll make better
decisions on a full stomach and after a good sleep.'

Hela smiled her approval at Cyrus, admiring not for
the first time, his fine looks and stature. In just the short
time they had known one another, she found she was helplessly drawn to him. True, he had looks any woman would
admire, but his appearance was not what truly attracted
her. There was something else. Something about his closed
manner as well as his direct gaze and the strength which
she detected bubbling just beneath his calm exterior.

'I'm presuming none of you have visited Ildagarth?' he
asked.

They shook their heads.

'Then you are going to enjoy this city. It is the most beautiful in all of Tallinor with a rich history and culture.'

They entered the wondrous city as night fell and Cyrus suggested they wait by an especially ornate fountain which seemed to be a popular meeting spot. There were sufficient people milling around that the strangers would not be noticeable. In any event, Cyrus noted, Ildagarth received hundreds of curious visitors each year. A few more new faces would not register as odd.

'Let me make some enquiries,' he said, nodding at Rubyn. 'Keep a sharp eye out, boy. Sarel is our precious charge.'

Rubyn made no move in acknowledgement but something obviously passed between the two men and Sarel presumed they spoke across the Link. It fascinated her as much as it irritated that they had this private skill.

They watched Cyrus stride away, Hela noticing something new and attractive about him in the arrogant gait and the way he carried himself, so tall and straight-backed, head high.

'You two seem very close,' Sarel said quietly to Rubyn as they waited.

'He is the dearest friend I have. More than friend, in fact,' Rubyn replied, not elaborating as he reached into the cool water of the fountain to rinse his face.

Sarel knew precisely what he meant by his careful choice of words. She followed suit, dashing refreshing water on her hands and face. 'I never knew my father.'

Rubyn said nothing.

'But you knew the intense love of a mother, child,' Hela offered. It was the most gentle of rebukes.

The Queen smiled shyly, realising the clumsiness of what she had said and how perhaps it might affect Rubyn. She glanced towards Hela who made no more of it. 'I hope that now you are returned to Tallinor, Rubyn, you will enjoy many years making up for all that was lost but is now found. You have two parents in your life again.'

Again she looked towards Hela who smiled her approval, not wanting to acknowledge the hollowness of such words when she considered what Rubyn, Cyrus and their friends were up against.

If Rubyn knew it, he shared nothing. He only nodded briefly. 'Cyrus comes.'

'Good and bad news,' the former prime said in his usual direct manner. 'We can get rooms at a decent establishment called The Rose and Thorns but I've heard that the Cipreans were recently through here enquiring not so gently about two women who go by your description.'

'I see,' Hela said, hoping he had a suggestion. 'Is it still risky then?'

'I would prefer not to take any risk with you ladies. I have an idea but it may not be to your liking.'

'Sir. Anything which offers us protection from danger is welcome,' Sarel said.

He inclined his head towards the Queen. 'Of course, your majesty.' This was said in a whisper to prevent any passers-by from hearing. In a more level tone he outlined his idea.

'You can disguise your appearance a little if you each cover your hair with a scarf. I'm suggesting that Hela and I arrive and book in as man and wife. I can be a soldier on leave bringing my lady on a special trip north to see this wondrous city. We can carry such a story off without trouble. It will be harder for the two of you,' he said turning to Rubyn and Sarel. 'Can you pretend to be brother and sister? You are travelling through Ildagarth on your way to meeting family at any one of the northern towns . . . let's say, Saddleworth.' He noticed Hela's astonishment at his suggestion out of the corner of his eye but deliberately ignored her.

'And where are we from?' Rubyn asked.

Cyrus considered this. 'Mexford,' he said. 'You've taken the slightly longer journey because you preferred not to travel through the capital and instead wish to see Ildagarth.'

They both nodded. 'Who are we?' Sarel asked, frowning.

He could see Hela would have her protest and did not answer the Queen immediately.

'Light! Are you mad all . . . of you?' Hela hissed. Then spoke in a harsh whisper. 'Do you think I'm going to let the Queen of Cipres sleep with a stranger?'

'But I see you are not protesting at sleeping with one, Hela. Please fret not either for my modesty or my chastity. Rubyn will respect both.'

There was that haughty Queen's tone. Hela's jaw gaped open at what was just short of a dismissal. Rebukes flew to her lips but none escaped. She reminded herself this was no longer a child to be admonished for her cheek. This was a Queen about to reclaim her throne.

Cyrus could see he needed to calm troubled waters and made a point of looking around. 'Ah, there's an excellent restaurant called The Tapestry here which is a favourite of mine. We can nut out a proper background for ourselves over our meal. Everyone hungry?' He glanced at them all but eyed the elder woman. He needed to help her claim back some status. 'Hela, what do you think?'

'Again, a most suitable plan,' she said softly.

He offered her his arm and Hela took it. 'For the purposes of The Tapestry, we are family travelling together. I'll do the talking,' he said.

Later, with their bellies full and stories rehearsed, they had also hatched a new plan – much to Hela's added despair – to stay in separate establishments overnight after Sarel had mentioned that they might be notable by their lack of luggage.

'A single couple arriving at an inn without bags may be swallowed. Two apparently separate couples travelling without luggage and checking into the same inn on the same evening could draw attention,' she had suggested. Cyrus had nodded sagely, looking uncomfortably towards the Queen's companion.

'She's right,' he responded, hating to add to Hela's woes.

They were all surprised when the maid agreed. 'I know she is. We must do whatever we can to protect her life.'

Cyrus glanced towards her, glad that she had wrestled with her objections and found them wanting. She had followed sound advice; done what was right despite her heart, and indeed head, begging differently. She enjoyed his soft, fleeting smile of pride in her decision and felt a tremor of helpless excitement now that she would be sharing a room and a night alone with this man.

Not long after seeing Rubyn and Sarel wave to confirm the successful booking of a room with two beds at The Rose and Thorns, Cyrus was smiling at the innkeeper's wife at The Lily Pond . . . another highly reputable establishment.

'Just you and your good lady for tonight, sir?'

'That's right.' He smiled graciously for the woman's benefit.

'I imagine you'll be wanting the double bed then, sir, rather than the two single pallets.'

Cyrus's smile hesitated. The single beds would be far better.

'Of course,' Hela intervened. 'I had forgotten how cold the nights can be in the north.' She winked at the lady behind the counter.

'Oh my, my, sir. You'd better have our best room then, the one with the fire and armchairs.' She tapped her nose suggestively.

Cyrus had to fight back the urge to glare at her as an old pride flared up until he reminded himself that he was no longer anyone of status in this Kingdom. No longer Prime; no longer the revered head of security and protector of the King. Instead he was pretending to be an officer on leave, bringing his wife on a short holiday to the north. He forced the smile to return to his face.

'Thank you.'

'I'll have our lad send your bags up, then.'

'No bags,' he replied, perhaps a little too quickly.

'Oh?' the woman said, confused. 'I thought you were taking a holiday in these parts, sir?'

'We are,' Hela said, intertwining her arm through that of Cyrus. She had noticed his face darkening. For someone who was going to do all the talking, he really was not very good at deception. 'Do you know, madam, our luggage was lost on our way from the east?' She lied smoothly and convincingly.

'No.' The woman's eyes widened with disbelief.

'Yes indeed. I am mortified, for how am I to travel without my clothes and toiletries?'

'Stolen?'

Hela shrugged. 'It matters not how they've disappeared, that we don't have them is what troubles me.'

'Well, quite,' replied the woman, warming to her guests' plight.

Hela giggled coquettishly. 'I shall need no clothing for tonight, madam, of course,' she said, glancing towards Cyrus who looked aghast, 'but tomorrow I'm afraid I shall have to do some damage to my husband's fortune and replace all my goods from your beautiful city.'

Cyrus squeezed Hela's arm. 'The coachman said they may still turn up on the next journey north, my love.' He smiled through slightly gritted teeth.

'This is true,' she agreed.

'Is there anything I can send up for you good people then?' the lady asked.

Hela smiled back. 'I hear Ildagarth is famous for its drink known as zabub?'

'Indeed, my lady.'

'That would be lovely.'

'Have a carafe of Morriet sent up too,' Cyrus said, wresting back control of the conversation.

'Right away,' the woman replied. She handed them a large key. 'It's at the end of the landing on the top floor. The climb is worth it for the view over the city,' she said, adding, 'but don't tire yourself, sir. Your wife has plans for you.' She returned the wink to Hela and left, giggling to herself.

Cyrus sensibly chose to keep his irritations to himself and Hela wondered if she had overstepped the mark for as soon as they were out of sight up the stairs, he untangled himself from her arm.

'I hope I did not offend?' she asked and received only a grunt for her enquiry.

They climbed the next two flights of stairs in stony silence but the ascent was worth the effort when they finally entered their spacious room and unlocked the shuttered windows. They were rewarded with a magnificent view across the city of ruins lit by the moon and smiled upon by thousands of twinkling stars in the clear night skies of the north. The balcony was framed by beautifully carved pillars – it reminded Hela momentarily of Cipres.

'Forgive me for any indiscretion. I merely wanted to keep our disguise authentic. This was all your idea, after all, and you seemed to be having difficulty convincing the curious innkeeper's wife.'

'I understand,' he said, holding a lighted taper to the fire's kindling which caught immediately. 'It is cool outside,' he added distractedly.

She turned around to face him. They both looked at one another and then towards the double bed as if in concert but Cyrus immediately looked away and busied himself with poking at the flames. Hela took a deep breath and was pleased to hear a soft knock at the door.

'Come in,' she called.

A serving girl entered, balancing a tray. 'Your zabub, madam,' she said, looking towards a small table. 'And your wine, sir. May I set it here?'

'Of course,' Hela replied. 'Thank you.'

The girl left almost as soon as she arrived and Hela found herself back with the difficult silence of Cyrus.

He finally cleared his throat. 'I can rest on these chairs pulled together.'

She did not know what to say. How best to put him at his ease again with her. 'Can I pour you some wine?'

'Thank you.'

She cringed inwardly at their stilted words and responses. For his part, Cyrus watched her move towards the table and made himself pull his gaze from Hela's lovely shape. He knew he had made her feel awkward and felt compelled to say something conversational. 'You should enjoy your first taste of the famous zabub.'

'I intend to,' she replied, handing him his glass of wine.

There were two armchairs and they settled back into them, facing one another. She watched Cyrus sip his wine and was quietly amused by the contented look which stole across his face at its taste. His expression relaxed as he closed his eyes to savour the Morriet.

'I can see it's been a while since you've enjoyed such fine wine.'

'Indeed,' he murmured, taking another mouthful but not opening his eyes.

She sipped her own drink. It was surprisingly potent but its taste was nonetheless rich and exotic. 'Mmmm,' she said, helplessly. 'Incredible.'

'Told you,' he said, his voice much softer.

'Are you tired?'

'No, just enjoying a simple pleasure and my own thoughts.'

'Would you prefer me not to talk?'

He said nothing, which just served to confuse her further and so Hela kept her peace, sipping her zabub which was truly delicious. The silence lengthened and although she realised they should light a candle or two, she dared not disturb his peace and in fact began to wonder whether he had fallen into a doze.

She hated the silence; could no longer help herself. 'Are you married, Cyrus?' Hela stunned even herself with the sudden asking of such a personal question.

'Once,' he replied, his eyes remaining closed.

'Oh?' She found herself studying the lines of his face in the glow of the firelight. He must have been a handsome young man she decided, but life's events were now etched on his lovely face and their lines disappeared into the moustache and beard he kept trimmed very close. Life had definitely made his handsome face far more interesting. She realised he had offered no further information.

She pressed on doggedly. 'What happened?'

'She died.'

She had not expected this and Hela now felt terrible for asking. 'I sense you carry that sadness still,' she said gently.

'You are correct.'

'No other women?'

'Plenty.'

'Ah,' she answered reflexively to his direct response. Her thoughts were roaming and she found herself erratically wondering what it might be like to be his lover. His body looked hard and fit and she also noticed his hands were meticulously cared for; in fact everything about him was neat and ordered, smart and precise.

He surprised her by saying more when she thought the conversation was over. 'None who could touch my heart.'

'I have never known a love as deep as that.'

'Love of this nature should be treated with caution. It can mean pain more than joy, as in my case.'

'Would you prefer not to have known her, then?'

His eyes opened now and she felt impaled by the hard grey gaze of Kyt Cyrus; a look which used to strike fear into his men. 'No.' The single word seemed to chill the room.

'Forgive me,' she said. 'I meant nothing by it.' She felt her cheeks burn. She had done nothing but apologise to him since entering this inn. Light! This man was unnerving. His eyes were closed again and his glass empty. She took the chance of tiptoeing to the table, fetching the carafe and refilling his glass. She also took the opportunity to light a single candle which cast new shadows around the room.

'Thank you,' he said quietly.

'And family?' She hoped this was safer territory to tread. They had a whole long night to get through and conversation was clearly all they would share.

'A son.'

'Is he grown?' She sounded surprised. How could he have left his own child to raise someone else's?

'He died with his mother . . . soon after his birth.'

Now Hela wanted to bite her own tongue out. She gulped down the zabub, scalding her mouth. When she looked back at him, he was staring at her.

'I have made you uncomfortable.'

'Yes, you have.'

He looked suddenly amused. 'It is a special gift I have.' She found herself grinning despite her discomfort.

'I'll recover,' Hela finally said, liking that this enigmatic man could amuse her at the height of such awkwardness.

He sipped. 'Perhaps we should start again. Why don't

you tell me about your life while I finish this carafe of Morriet?'

And she did. She described her early life in a sleepy hamlet of Cipres before she ran away from home with a man who turned out to be no good. The promise of marriage disappeared as soon as their money did and Hela explained that she was fortunate to have been taken pity on by one of the courtiers at the palace. He wanted her body enough to find her a position on the Queen's personal serving team. She told Cyrus about life on Sylven's staff, describing how over the years she had climbed the ranks of the servants to become a personal maid to the Queen and finally her aide and companion.

'We were close and I know she would have liked you, Kyt Cyrus,' she said.

'Why is this so?'

'Because you are something of a mystery.' She noticed how he smiled at that. 'I think most women would find that compelling, but as much as Sylven would have loved to unravel your secrets, I believe she would have been mostly engaged by your complexity. It is a quality many women can find threatening, to be honest.'

'But not Sylven.'

'No. She would have thrived on it.'

'Do you find me threatening, Hela?'

She was cross she hesitated. 'No. I find you to be remote.'

'Is that so?' he said, opening his eyes and turning towards her. She felt her heart skip. Slumped in his chair, his long legs stretched towards the fire and his shirt slightly undone, this man looked very desirable indeed and the conversation was headed towards dangerous territory. Behind him was the double bed towards which her eyes flicked uncharacteristically nervously now, betraying her thoughts, her desires.

She took a deep breath. 'But I think it's contrived, sir. I don't believe for one moment that you are not a warm and affectionate man.' She shrugged. Might as well say it all. 'I just think you deliberately hide behind a wall of remoteness, and layers of mystery. It's safe. Your wife and son died. Your heart broke. You believe you can never mend that heart and give it to another and so you make love to many but love none. It ensures you can remain at a distance from women.'

She held his gaze and noticed his eyes had strangely darkened.

'You seem to know a lot about me.'

'I know only what my own senses and instincts tell me, sir.'

He stood. 'Time for our rest, I think. You take the bed. I'll go out for a walk until you are settled.'

Hela felt disappointed with herself. She had not handled him at all well and men were her specialty. She liked this one; not that she expected anything to come of it but she genuinely felt she had somehow failed him this evening. Their mission was dangerous and small pleasures such as quiet conversation, perhaps just getting close to someone, would be brief, if even at all possible. Tonight was a chance for her to forget their perilous life and simply get to know more about an intriguing person and yet all of her charms with men had abandoned her.

'Damn him!' she muttered. He had made her feel like a cheap whore. And yet he did not even want her. When it boiled down to it, what was truly frustrating her was that Kyt Cyrus had showed no sexual interest in her whatsoever. She watched him leave without another word and felt hollow. She knew men desired her. If Hela had to describe herself the word 'worldly' would spring to mind together with 'provocative' and 'erotic'. It disturbed her greatly that these qualities appealed not to Kyt Cyrus.

She stripped, washed her undergarments and blouse and hung them discreetly on the balcony to dry for the morning. She untied her hair, lamenting the lack of a brush and fingered through it to loosen it. Slipping beneath the fresh sheets, she thanked her luck that Cyrus had good enough taste and purse to ensure such a decent inn for them – a small consolation after a desolate evening – and then fell into a fitful doze awaiting his return.

Cyrus had to get out of the room. He inhaled the crisp night air and walked, no particular direction in mind. He linked with Rubyn who said they were fine but not especially sleepy. Cyrus felt the companionship with Sarel was good for Rubyn.

Be careful, lad. Remember you are in the presence of a Queen.

See you in the morning, Rubyn replied and cut the Link.

The old soldier was rarely troubled by his charge's contained manner. Rubyn had been like this since he was old enough to talk; nothing had changed. If anything he rather admired Rubyn's manner; it sometimes reminded him of himself. However, he would be the first to admit that the boy needed to grow and experience the world. They had led such a quiet existence all of these years that he realised both of them desperately needed to mix with people again, women especially. Which is why he found himself strolling the beautiful streets of Ildagarth – he had been intimidated by a woman and that was a new experience for Kyt Cyrus, the self-assured, arrogant and brilliant former commander of the Tallinese army. Men and women had worshipped him in his glory days but he had called no man friend – except perhaps Torkyn Gynt – and had only ever loved one woman. She had departed his life without warning, leaving him bereft, he now realised, of the ability to love another.

He had permitted Gynt to get under his skin but they shared more than friendship. They shared the Heartwood and its secrets and now they shared Rubyn. Although Cyrus never allowed himself to admit it, Rubyn was as good as a son. He had cradled him as a newborn in his arms and since that day, Rubyn had rarely been out of his sight or his care. They were as close as a father and son could be and yet Rubyn belonged to another man who had recently come to claim him and put him in danger. That alone was alarming.

And the conversation with Hela had served to unsettle him far more than he had first thought. He had initially decided to leave her because he thought their conversation was headed in a direction he might regret. It was obvious the woman was lonely, desperately in need of some male companionship, and all it would have taken was a smile or a look from him and they would be rolling between the sheets right now. He hated his having deliberately set out to undermine her, make her feel uncomfortable, but he realised she was more than just one of the vast array of women he had bedded in his time. Hela possessed a razor-sharp mind and she had countered his comments and come back quick as lightning with her own, which took his breath away.

Why? Because she was right. Hela had nailed his uncertainties and insecurities as effectively as Corlin had once nailed him between two trees. For all his posturing as a brave son of Tallinor, Cyrus knew he was a coward. A coward when it came to affairs of the heart, that is. The pain experienced at the loss of his wife — a woman so gentle, so serene and so perfectly matched to him — had been too much for him to bear and so he had ignored his agonising memory of her. Locked it away. Never allowing it to surface. He had almost forgotten the curves and lines of her face.

He knew he had never really resurfaced into the light of day from the moment of her death, for ever walking within a private haze of darkness — her legacy.

He enjoyed women but kept them purely as objects of lust. Once he was satisfied, he was courteous and always gallant but he rarely saw the same woman twice and despite knowing it might hurt her feelings he never looked back nor made any apology for his ways.

But Hela had touched him somehow. Learning her story he had to admire the tough exterior she too had built around herself for different reasons. She was so different from the courtly, elegant young women who had all but thrown themselves at him when he was Prime. From such a young age Hela had needed to fend for herself and she was courageous and loyal — qualities he personally admired so much he had to look away from her when she was retelling the story of their escape from Cipres and later from Goth. It was Hela who had kept Sarel strong and Hela who would hopefully restore the Queen to her rightful throne. The Cipreans owed much to this small, resourceful and very desirable woman.

That he desired her was not in question. Her dark features and petite, curvy build spoke to him of satisfactions between the sheets he had perhaps not experienced. It would be so easy, but Hela seemed to look into him; saw him for what he was and that was unsettling. To share a deeper touch such as a kiss and all that it might lead to frightened him and Cyrus was not a man to be easily frightened. And so he walked without purpose for more than two hours until the moon was fully risen, the people on the streets thinning and he found himself standing on the landing outside their room once again.

He hoped she was sleeping. Hoped they had nothing more to say to one another and could start afresh in the morning knowing the circumstances they found themselves in this night would probably not be repeated. He opened the door with caution and stepped soundlessly inside. Cyrus held his breath but he let it out quietly as he could see Hela asleep; her dark hair loose and tousled on the pillow. He could hear her rhythmic breathing and relaxed. All was well. No demons to confront this night.

The fire burned gently now and would die to embers very soon. In its soft glow he studied her face. It was not arrestingly beautiful like Alyssa's, nor did it have the high, superb cheekbones of his wife which had given her a serene, chiselled look.

Instead her face seemed to be a collection of nice enough features which formed a pretty arrangement. And yet the darkness of the features was extraordinary. Long lashes lying against her cheek; the hair soft, shiny and long; the sleeping eyes feline and dark – so dark as to be almost black.

He sighed softly and then, watching her face for any

sign of waking, dragged together the two armchairs –
wincing at any noise – not very comfortable but it would
do. He pulled his shirt over his head and stretched tall,
turning away from Hela now to gaze from where he stood
by the fireplace out of the long windows.

Hela had always been clever at deception. Pretending
to be asleep was one of the easiest of all ruses and she
knew she had capably tricked Cyrus or he would not be
so relaxed in front of her. She opened her eyes to slits and
stared at him stretching. She had been right. His body
was hard and muscled, still very lean for an older man
and no sign of the paunch of age and prosperity around
his belly. For one of the few times in her life, she was
confused over a man. What to do? She wanted to somehow
put things right between them but she did not know how
and Hela did not want them to go to sleep on the
awkwardness which lay between them. To do that would
mean waking within the same unresolved atmosphere and,
with all that was ahead for them, she could not bear the
thought of it.

So Hela turned to her cunning. She used her best
attribute and hoped it might win the day. Stirring,
pretending not to notice him she sat up in bed and
stretched herself, allowing Cyrus a perfect view of her full
breasts as she pulled her hands up over her head and then
allowed her hair to fall lazily down her back. She could
hear his sharp intake of breath and knew he was trapped
and semi-naked himself now by the fire. She continued
the pretence of not realising he was there, faking that she
was sleepy and still in a dreamy state as she moved her
legs from the bed to the floor.

She pushed the sheet away, feeling very vulnerable in

her full nakedness but determined to see where this might lead. Hela yawned and sat there a moment or two, swaying slightly as though still needing to find full consciousness and then she stood.

This was it. He would either give in to her or cut her to the quick by making some sharp comment which would have her rushing back to her sheets and covering up. She was ready for it.

He said nothing. The silence was deafening but she ignored it.

Hela took the chance, opened her eyes, still not turning towards the fire, and walked to the small jug of water near the window. She knew now she was giving him full view of her delectable back in all of its curvy, naked loveliness and she let him enjoy it for as long as she considered one might possibly linger over a few sips of water.

And then she turned, seemingly fully awake now and made to shriek at seeing him standing there and looking directly at her.

'Hush, Hela,' he said softly. 'It is Cyrus.'

'What are you doing standing there in the dark?' she said, trying to cover herself with her hands and hair but deliberately failing.

'Forgive me. I thought you were asleep.'

'Were you watching me?'

'Yes.'

'Why?'

'Because you want me to.'

She was glad it was too dark for him to see her blush at the truth of his comment. 'That's a stupid answer, Cyrus. Why were you compelled to stare at me in my sleep?'

'Actually I did all the staring whilst you were awake and showing yourself off to your best advantage.'

Did she see a trace of a smile there? Perhaps not. Too hard to tell as he had moved into a shadow.

He repeated himself. 'My apologies, Hela. I will leave again.'

'No!' she said, loud enough to startle him as he turned to walk to the door. 'Don't leave,' she added very softly now.

He sighed, not looking at her. 'Hela, I can't.'

'Not can't. More like won't,' she said, her voice a little harsh.

He cleared his throat and leaned one long, muscled arm against the mantle but made no further move to leave. Suddenly in the dying glow of the embers he really did look the fully sad man that he was. Proud, strong, impressive but nonetheless vulnerable.

Hela moved swiftly to stand next to him. 'Look at me,' she said. It sounded like a command. 'Please,' she added.

And he did.

'Is it so wrong that you could desire me?' she asked with feeling.

His eyes never strayed from hers. His voice when he finally spoke was soft. She had not heard that gentleness in it before. It melted her. 'Not wrong at all. What is wrong is that I would use you and you deserve better.'

'It is my choice. I'll take the risk.'

'No.' He shook his head slowly.

'Then *you* take the risk!' she said a little angrily now. 'Risk it, Cyrus. Chance that you might actually like me. Your wife is dead – long dead by the sound of things. Step back into the light and allow yourself the opportunity to love someone. I'm not naive enough to believe it may be me but risk that it might be. What is so wrong with loving each other for a night?'

She saw his grey eyes soften and mist a little. This was hurting him. And he was so controlled. So strong. Most men would have at least reached for her naked body by now, helpless against such temptation – but not him.

'Touch me, Cyrus. I want you to. And I will risk that in the morning you will not want to touch me again. But tonight enjoy me as I will enjoy you. We are two lonely people with no one to love except a child each, neither of whom are ours. We are kindred spirits you and I. And we are walking directly into danger, perhaps death. Who knows? I do it gladly for that same young woman I love. You do it for a young woman you had never met before now. You risk so much for a stranger . . . why not risk your emotions for someone you know and who holds you to no obligation?'

He hesitated and in that moment's uncertainty she reached for his hand and when he did not resist her, she laid his elegant fingers against her cheek and at his touch let out the breath she had been holding. When she took her own hand away from his, she felt her heart surge when his other hand moved from the mantle to cup the other side of her face.

He held her there for a moment as he looked deeply into her eyes and then he leaned down; Cyrus faltered just for a second and then, as though letting go of all his internal protests, he touched his mouth to hers and for a blissful period forgot everything – from his long-held heartache to his fears about what they faced.

The former prime could no longer distinguish his surrounds – everything was Hela; all he could feel were her hands on his body, the smell of her lingering spicy fragrance, the touch of her tongue, the taste of her smooth skin. He cast away doubt and released years of passion, allowing his hands to roam over the small, lithe body and his mouth to search hers – sometimes gently, sometimes more forcefully.

Wrapping her legs about himself, Cyrus effortlessly lifted and carried her to the bed where he laid her down, but she refused to let go of his neck, refused to allow him escape from her kiss and so he lowered himself gently and finally surrendered to the intimate pleasures of her body.

26

Promises

Gidyon scanned the audience. The auditorium had filled quickly with happy, chattering folk keen to see one of their favourite travelling ensembles. The acts changed regularly enough on its slow journey around the Kingdom but there were favourites, such as Caerys the Snake and Sword Swallower, who made his name with the famous Cirq Zorros.

Gidyon had briefed Figgis and Themesius on their 'turn', as the giant liked to call it.

'Are you sure?' Figgis had asked.

'No one will be able to account for it,' Gidyon had replied. 'And it's quick and simple. Let's not forget what my father urged. We must leave as soon as we can.'

The giant had nodded then. 'I have spoken with Tyne. It only involved a small lie. He understands.'

'Good,' Gidyon had replied. 'What about the Fat Lady? Is she happy with my plans?'

Themesius had smiled at this. 'She's intrigued . . . and er . . . more than happy to be handled by a young man.' His deep voice had rumbled with amusement. 'Said it would be the first time in a long while.'

'I'm going to check for Yseul.'

Gidyon stared out across a sea of people who had taken the advice from Tyne's hastily posted message that for one night only, the Greatest Show on Earth would play in Brittelbury.

Gwerys, his eyes shining with anticipation, spotted him first and waved, nudging his sister. She turned and a look reserved for new lovers softened across her face. Gidyon's heart felt as though it had flipped. He remembered their kiss from earlier that day and wished he could taste it again. Was this love? He did not know. All he wanted to do was to hold her close and never let her go. She raised her hand and waved shyly. He swallowed hard. How would he find the courage to leave her?

Several acts preceded theirs, all enjoying loud and boisterous applause from an eager audience, happy to lap up all of Master Tyne's curiosities and strange people with even stranger talents. None, Gidyon could tell, had wielded any magic and so when the tall young man walked out on stage looking anything but odd, an expectant hush gripped the crowd.

He chanced a glance towards Yseul and Gwerys; both looked radiant for different reasons – he could not help but flash a smile for them alone. Gidyon had given Tyne only a brief description of the act they would perform tonight. The Master of the Show could not believe his ears but the young man's confidence forced him to permit what sounded like utter folly.

Tyne told the audience this was their most dangerous act. He truly believed it too. 'Could everyone move back as far as possible and give Master Gidyon the room he requires,' he said in a reverential tone. His sombre expression encouraged them to take him seriously and the crowd shuffled backwards as one. This was all showmanship – Gidyon needed no more room than he already had but he did not tell Tyne this.

Tyne introduced Figgis, who walked out proudly into the arena to applause. Dwarves were not common but neither were they particularly spectacular, so the applause reflected a polite appreciation of a race long forgotten. He took a bow. Next it was the Fat Lady's turn. The audience had already met the Queen of Pork and although familiar with her incredible bulk they greeted her once again with resounding appreciation for her enormity. She smiled and waved warmly. Now it was the giant's turn. No one in Brittelbury had caught a peep of Themesius prior to this moment. The huge, strong man strode out into the main arena to shrieks of disbelief at his size and roars of approval for a genuine 'freak'.

Meet a real showstopper, he said, for Gidyon's and Figgis's benefit, grinning widely.

Figgis, keen to get the whole thing over and done with, turned to Gidyon. *And so you just want me to leap towards you now? Is that right?*

Gidyon nodded. *At my signal.*

The audience hushed again until several hundred people finally managed to achieve silence. A slow smile spread across Gidyon's face.

'To me, dwarf!' he called loudly, reaching out his hands.

Figgis sighed inwardly but ran as commanded and as their outstretched arms touched, the dwarf flipped into the air and landed, feet first, on Gidyon's hand which was raised high into the air.

Impressed?

Only slightly, like them, he replied, nodding towards the audience.

The crowd cheered warmly to reward the grace of the dwarf and strength of the man holding him in one hand, but they expected a lot more was yet to happen. It was supposed to be dangerous after all.

Gidyon ignored Figgis's contempt. 'To me, Fat Lady!' he yelled, his voice carrying into the night.

Everyone laughed as what was surely the Kingdom's largest woman did her best to move quickly. Arms outstretched, she managed to get up a surprising gallop. No one in the audience for a second believed she could do anything much more than bowl the handsome young man and his balancing dwarf over into the dust. They held their laughter as her hands made contact and then silence again as she too flipped effortlessly into the air, balancing on his other hand.

Her own shocked expression told the watchers that this was something beyond comprehension. It had to be trickery for no man was that strong. No woman as large as that could flip into the air with so little effort or balance with such ease. Murmurings of disbelief combined with wonder could be heard.

All heads now turned towards the giant and then back again to the trio. Gidyon moved to balance Figgis on his head.

Is anyone going to believe this? the dwarf asked, a little bored.

Does it matter?

I suppose not, Figgis replied. *Don't tell me the Fat Lady now stands on my head!*

I'm afraid so, Gidyon said and with a small flick threw

the Fat Lady high into the air. She screamed hysterically. Her terror was picked up by the already tense mob as they watched her spin with grace and land on the tip of her toes on the head of Figgis. The dwarf sighed theatrically across the Link.

Now ask her to do what I told her earlier, Gidyon asked Figgis.

'Fat Lady!'

'Yes?' Everything was wobbling.

'Do what he instructed earlier.'

'I'm not sure I have the courage,' she hissed.

'Just do it,' Figgis offered gently. 'You will not fall.'

Delicately she lifted one foot away from the dwarf's head and struck a dancer's pose.

The crowd went wild.

Gidyon began to laugh. He could keep this up all night. It required so little of his power.

Next Themesius stepped forward. It could not happen. This man already stood head and shoulders above the exceedingly tall younger man. Surely these three people could not balance on top of each other with the anchor man at the bottom just grinning.

'Themesius . . . to me!' Gidyon suddenly called.

Many could not watch, including Gwerys, but as the giant began to lope towards the other three, Yseul burst into laughter and whispered to him: 'Trust Gidyon.'

Not only did the giant flip, he managed several somersaults before landing in the arms of the Fat Lady.

The crowd broke into shouts of laughter. They pinched themselves, fully convinced they would never see such a bizarre sight again. Now Gidyon began to circle with his load, even daring to do a little jig which won more rapturous applause. Waiting in the wings, Tyne rubbed his hands gleefully. It was a pity the three men would leave tonight, although the giant – his prize – had assured him they would return shortly. Tyne could only think of the riches to be earned from this act alone. He began to imagine how he might structure the show around this piece, making it the climax – if only he had known earlier how spectacular it would be.

Gidyon circled the arena once more with his friends suspended magically above him and then one by one they jumped down to be caught by him. People were still shaking their heads. If any suspected magic, it was not talked about. No one wielded that sort of enchantment these days, if ever.

Back at the main caravan, Gidyon and his friends were congratulating themselves on a fine performance. The Fat Lady accepted their warm thanks but she was still in some shock and was in urgent need of a tot of something to steady her nerves.

Once she had departed, Figgis looked seriously towards his friend. 'What about the stone?'

'Yseul has brought it. Would either of you mind if I escorted her home? She's with her small brother.'

They both shook their heads.

'Tyne will be here any moment, I imagine, so you might as well make your escape now,' Themesius suggested. 'Where does she live, anyway? We can meet you there with the cart and horses.'

Gidyon gave the same directions he had learned from Yseul earlier.

'Hurry, lad,' Figgis cautioned. 'Keep your farewell swift.'

'See you both soon,' Gidyon said making to leave.

'Gidyon!' Figgis watched him turn back. 'Make no promises to the girl. Dangerous times are ahead.'

Gidyon nodded and disappeared into the dark. He found Yseul and Gwerys waiting for him at the back of all the travelling caravans where he had suggested they find one another. The show was continuing so the crowd was still to disperse.

'Gidyon!' Gwerys yelled and ran towards him.

Gidyon grabbed the youngster and swung him high. 'You were marvellous,' the boy said breathlessly.

'Was I?' he replied, eyes only for Yseul who stood back a little self-consciously yet enjoying her brother's pleasure.

'I see you continue to be a man of many strange talents,' she said. She leaned close and kissed him lightly on the cheek, pressing the stone into his hand at the same time.

Gidyon was flooded with relief at having the stone back in his possession. He felt it gently hum in his palm before he pocketed it.

He bent to hug Gwerys. 'It's good to see you again,' he said before swinging the little boy onto his shoulders. 'Hold on tight.'

'Could you balance me like you did the giant?'

'With the greatest of ease.'

'Oh, do it!' the boy begged.

'Don't you dare,' Yseul cautioned.

'I'd better not,' Gidyon said to his excited friend. 'Your sister will be furious.'

'Oh, she gets cross with me all the time. I try to ignore her.'

'And all your other sisters as well?' Gidyon asked, taking Yseul's hand.

The boy sighed. 'Yes, they're all very tiresome,' he said.

This made Yseul laugh as much as it did Gidyon.

'Women just don't understand the needs of boys, do they?' Gidyon said.

'Exactly,' Gwerys answered, matter-of-factly. 'Which is why it's nice to have Papa home.'

'Your father's back?' Gidyon said with surprise.

Yseul nodded. 'This afternoon he returned. It's lovely to have him back, if only to help with the patients,' she said ruefully.

They walked slowly into the town.

'How are they all faring?'

'Much better, thank you for asking. One of my sisters is recovered, I believe. My mother feels well enough to cook again so that's a very good sign. The other two . . . well, they should be up and around before long.'

'That's good, then,' he said, suddenly feeling uncomfortable but not sure why. 'May I walk you both home?'

'Oh yes!' Gwerys answered. 'You can meet everyone.'

'No, little fellow. Not this time. I'll see you home safely and perhaps visit when everyone is in good health again.'

Gwerys said no more, pleased to watch his small world from this great height as they walked slowly back towards his home in the darkness.

'You're leaving again,' she finally said flatly.

'I have to.'

She nodded and he felt her hand tighten against his.

'I travel with Figgis and Themesius now,' he said for no particular reason. The discomfort had deepened to awkwardness and this seemed the best he could come up with as they left the main part of the town behind them.

'I see,' she said, then added: 'Do they protect you?'

He paused. 'That's a good way to describe it.'

'Where do you travel to?'

'Tonight we go east. People are waiting for us.' He was pleased she did not seem more inquisitive about their direction or the people about whom he spoke.

'Is it safe?'

'I'll be safe, I promise,' he replied, avoiding her question.

'There it is, Gidyon,' Gwerys said pointing. 'That's where we live.'

Gidyon saw a large, neat cottage; a glow of light in the window and a chimney smoking. A small garden surrounded it and he caught a waft of lavender scent.

'It's such a pretty fragrance . . . my mother's favourite,' Yseul said, noticing his pleasure.

'Your home is lovely. It looks like a welcoming and cheerful place to live,' he said, setting the boy down on the ground again.

'It is,' she acknowledged. 'You go on in, Gwerys. I just want a quiet word with Gidyon.'

'Are you going to kiss him goodbye then?' he asked, grinning.

'Oh, I hope so,' Gidyon answered, before she could. 'Give me a hug then, scamp, until the next time.' The lad obliged. 'Now take care of your sisters. When your papa's away, you're the man about the house.'

Gwerys nodded seriously. 'Come back soon. Thank you for the show.' And then he was gone, skipping away to the back of the cottage.

They looked at one another in the darkness, the glow of candles burning in a few of the houses offering scant light. His sight was so good though, he could see her eyes shining with tears she seemed determined would not fall.

'I was thinking,' she said. 'With my father returned and everyone recovering that perhaps I could—'

'Don't,' he said, putting his fingers gently to her mouth. 'Please, Yseul. You cannot come with me.'

'Why?'

The question hurt his heart. Why indeed? He wanted to be with her more than anything at this moment but he remembered his father's sad voice in his head and imagined his mother lying wounded in the middle of a deserted track.

'Because I follow a dangerous path just now.'

'Can't you tell me?'

He shook his head. 'No.'

'Is it connected with that stone?' She was sharp.

'In a manner, it is,' he answered, hoping that was enough for her.

She nodded slowly, biting her lip. Then she summoned a bright voice he knew was a disguise for her true feelings. 'Well, it was a treat to see you again. Gwerys will talk about this for days.'

'And you?' he asked, wishing he had not.

'Me?' she said, looking up now into his eyes. 'I shall regret your coming because it makes saying goodbye so hard . . . much harder than before.'

'I'll come back, Yseul.'

'You said that last time,' she said sadly.

'And I kept my promise.'

'Yes, but you had something to return to me for . . . your precious stone. You have no reason to come here again. You have left nothing behind.'

He cast aside his doubts and took his chance, pulling

her towards him. 'Yes I have. I have left something far more precious behind this time.'

She did not resist his touch. 'And what is that?'

Gidyon leaned down and whispered in her ear. 'My heart. I'm giving it to you for safe keeping. I need you to take the greatest of care with it because it's fragile.'

Her tears did fall now. They were not plentiful nor were they loud. Soft, silent drops down her cheeks which he kissed away.

'I shall come back and claim my heart and its owner,' he said gently.

She composed herself. 'You have to mean this. I won't be able to believe it when you're gone if I don't believe it right now.' There was an edge of desperation in her voice.

'I mean it. I love you, Yseul. I will return to you as soon as I can.'

Time was short. He knew Themesius and Figgis were not that far behind, possibly moments only did they have left. He pulled her towards the back of her cottage where it was dark in the street and kissed her, long and deeply. She responded, standing on tiptoe and wrapping her arms around his neck and losing herself in his kiss until they heard someone clear their throat softly. Gidyon, of course, had heard them long before they arrived but Yseul, it seemed, was surprised and she pulled herself away quickly, embarrassed.

'I'll be there in a second,' he said, quietly.

'We'll carry on,' Figgis said, just as softly. *Catch up quickly, boy*, he added, a note of caution in his voice. *Remember what I said about promises.*

The cart rolled forwards and out of sight. 'I must go,'

Gidyon said, kissing her face tenderly and wiping away the last of her tears. 'Make your candles; be happy with your family and think of me kindly. When next I return, it will be to ask your father a question.'

She made a sound of surprise. 'Do you speak true?'

'I make no jest. It is a promise.'

'Then go now about your strange business and hurry back to me.' She pushed him and he began to walk away. Then he returned for one more kiss.

'I love you too,' she whispered. 'Be safe. I'll watch over your heart.'

He gave her one final hug and then reluctantly left her arms, loping away quickly into the darkness to catch up with his friends.

Make no promises to the girl. He tried to ignore them but heard the carefully chosen words of Figgis again. Had he listened to the sound advice? No. He had ignored it and made a wild pledge of love and marriage to a beautiful girl who trusted him to keep that promise. Would he? Could he?

Gidyon shook his head free of his doubt. Yes, he would keep his word. And with that firm promise to himself he broke into a run in order to catch up with his Paladin and whatever his destiny held.

Cyrus awoke with a start and sat up. He was disoriented but only momentarily. Old habits die hard and the soldier gathered his wits in an instant and was out of the bed and on his feet in even less time. He was naked. He turned around to see Hela dressed.

'Is that your normal waking technique?' she asked innocently.

Cyrus cleared his throat. 'Actually no. I save that particular routine only for the ladies.'

She smiled at his jest. 'Last night was lovely, Cyrus – really lovely. But I have no need to discuss it.' She meant it as reassurance that he owed her nothing.

'I'm glad to hear it,' a wicked look of amusement stealing across his face. 'Because recalling now all those intriguing things we did to one another, I think it would make savoury conversation over breakfast with Sarel and Rubyn, don't you?'

'Speaking of which,' she said, 'we'd better hurry and meet them. Two young, hot-blooded people in a room overnight. Anything can happen.'

Cyrus was almost dressed. 'Indeed. It can even happen to two old, hot-blooded people!'

They shared an intimate smile.

'Let's make a promise that last night carries no implications for either of us,' she suggested. It hurt her to say these words but she knew releasing him from obligation was the only way she might win this man.

'Agreed,' he said, without looking at her.

Cyrus linked and learned that Rubyn and Sarel had already left The Rose and Thorns and were now happily munching on hot cakes and bacon at one of Ildagarth's eating houses.

You'd better hurry, Cyrus. We have no money to pay for this. Why are you so late anyway?

Mind your business, boy.

Ah, I understand. Perhaps I too should have slept in.

Perhaps not, with the company you were keeping.

Cyrus was pleased to sense Rubyn's amusement before the Link closed. It was a rare thing.

They swiftly made their way downstairs, nodding their farewells and heading in the direction Rubyn had told them to follow. Both were relieved to hear, over a hearty breakfast, that Sarel and Rubyn had sat up most of the night talking. The youngsters shared their thoughts.

'I agree totally with Rubyn,' Sarel said, determined to convince Cyrus. 'If we allow the Tallinese King and his men to arrive in Cipres uninvited, in number and clearly in no mood for discourse, our people will take umbrage. They will fight. Our people are peaceful but, like yours, if provoked or their land is threatened, they will do battle to protect it.'

'Yes, and in the meantime,' Rubyn said munching on Hela's bacon, 'Orlac, warned by such activity, could spirit Lauryn away if he was of a mind.'

Cyrus scratched softly at his beard in thought. They were both right.

'What do you think?' he asked Hela, giving himself more time to consider the option.

Hela noticed beard scratching was one of his habits. She rather liked it. She had discovered too that he was no clumsy bedmate; in fact he was skilled in his lovemaking and it had taken all of her creative wiles to finally surprise him. She loved feeling his body tremble in anticipation and that afterwards he had sought her mouth and kissed her more deeply than she could ever recall a man kissing her. Then Cyrus had held her close for several hours. She thought he had fallen asleep but he was just lying still, enjoying the closeness and the length of their bodies touching.

Hela blinked and realised all eyes around the table were on her.

Cyrus grinned. 'Did I just speak in Elutian?'

Sarel started to enjoy the joke but Hela admonished her with a glance.

'I'm sorry,' Hela replied. 'I missed the question.'

She saw the enjoyment of her discomfort in his eyes. It was as though he knew what she had been thinking. She tried to reassure herself that he could not, of course, but this did not lessen the blush which rushed to her cheeks.

'I wondered what you thought of this new plan?' he said.

'Well Sarel is right, of course. The Tallinese are surely wrathful that the Cipreans came galloping through their Kingdom. Why should it be any different the other way round?' She shrugged. 'Though I believe the Tallinese have an understandable grudge on their side.'

'All right, then,' Cyrus said, draining his mug of herb tea. 'We leave immediately for Kyrakavia and hope we can intercept the King.'

Alyssa's eyes fluttered open. She felt drained of strength but found a smile for the concerned face of Tor hovering above hers.

'Is it morning?'

He nodded. 'Just dawn.'

'I'm not sure I can move,' she whispered. 'Saxon?'

Tor reassured her. 'He woke a little earlier. He's weak but I helped him to bathe.' Tor smiled. 'Said he wanted to wash away the fevers.'

She closed her eyes momentarily again and felt Tor reach for her hand.

'Gidyon is coming, my love. He will be here soon

with Figgis and Themesius. They will take care of you.'

Alyssa was awake again. 'And you?' she asked, already knowing the answer.

'I have to go after him.' He saw her baulk and put his finger to his lips to hush her. 'I have to. There's a tea brewed. Drink it, both of you. Your strength will begin to return through this day. By tonight you'll even be hungry. There's plenty of food in the cart.'

Saxon arrived by their side. 'Morning, sweet one.'

She smiled for him. 'It had to be us that got in the way, didn't it?'

He was amused by her dry tone and knew this meant she was going to be fine. Saxon kneeled and helped her to sit up.

'Punch him for me,' she said to Tor.

He looked momentarily puzzled. 'Goth?'

'No. Whichever sod let fly with the arrow!'

Tor grinned . . . it was wolfish. 'Oh, I'll be doing much more than that to him, my love.'

'I want to be there with you. I want to share it,' Saxon admitted angrily.

'Your place is here with my wife,' Tor said and looked chagrined when they both turned to stare at him with surprise. He shrugged. 'I can't think of you any other way . . . I'm sorry.'

'Don't be,' she said. 'Go hunt your prey. Come back to me safely.'

Tor kissed her. *I promise*, he whispered into her mind and then stood, as did Saxon. They touched fists in the Tallinese manner.

'Happy hunting,' the Kloek said wistfully.

As he swung into the saddle, Tor reminded them both:

'Remember to drink the brew until it's finished. We'll talk soon.'

Saxon nodded. 'Be wary – I don't know how to save *you* from an arrow's touch.'

Tor nudged his horse forwards; he looked once behind at Alyssa and then opened his Link with Cloot.

Where? he asked his falcon.

Follow the track. They haven't even stirred as yet.

How long?

I'll see you well before you get close. Just ride quickly now and listen for me.

The Link closed and Tor pushed his horse into a gallop.

Cloot's voice entered his head. *Slow down now. Tether your horse beneath the shade of the trees you see coming up.*

I see the open country soon closed up again.

Yes. The Great Finger points into Rork'yel. They'd have to head east now to escape the Forest or the mountains. It seems they don't want to lose the cover.

Where are you? Tor asked, having slowed his exhausted horse to a slow walk. It had been a wild ride.

Here, Cloot said, swooping from behind Tor and landing neatly on his shoulder.

Light! I've asked you not to do that.

I'm getting so good at it, though.

Tor stroked his bird and immediately softened. *I don't like us being apart.*

I know. I feel the same. But this is too important.

They led the horse to shade. Saxon had sent a water bladder and thin leather bucket which it now gratefully drank from. A bag of oats had also been packed.

He thinks of everything, Cloot commented.

When it comes to horses, Tor said dryly.

How are our patients?

Grumpy, he answered. *Especially my wife. Gidyon's travelling east as fast as he can now with Figgis and Themesius.*

Yes. Thank you for letting me share that conversation. I'm glad he's got the stone back.

Mmm, but I'm wondering what he might have promised in order to get it.

The girl?

Tor nodded, stroking the horse as she drank.

Cloot paused before asking: *Why does this trouble you?*

He's so young.

Does it matter?

Tor said nothing.

Cloot continued. *In fact I seem to recall you telling me that you fell in love with Alyssa when you were just a spotty youth and she wasn't yet a decade of summers.*

But that's—

Different? I don't see how. Gidyon is so like you. Why wouldn't he take after you in affairs of the heart? Relax, Tor. Your children know so much grief. If this Yseul brings him joy . . . why not? It could be as real as the love you feel for Alyssa.

I cannot say goodbye to her again, Tor suddenly blurted.

I know.

I'm frightened for her.

She's stronger than you give her credit for.

How much more punishment must she take?

Don't underestimate her, Tor. She could hate you for that. Alyssa has a purpose in all of this. I don't suspect for a moment it was only to birth your children. The blood of the gods runs strong in her veins. She will prevail.

Shall we?

All of us shall, somehow.

And none of us will die, Tor replied sombrely, not believing it.

I didn't say that.

Let's not talk about this.

We can't run away from destiny.

I hate that word.

It is what has shaped you . . . what drives you — me, all of us.

He's my brother, Cloot.

And you are his. Promise me you will wait — make no decision yet — and let's see what that relationship means. For now, we deal with what we can. And that means Goth.

27
Valley of the Sentients

Goth had been awake for hours. He knew they would be followed — the falcon he presumed would keep them in sight. He was now convinced that the bird somehow communicated with Gynt. Every time he considered this concept it left a bitter taste in his mouth. Magic! How he hated it.

He recalled how the trees had claimed him. He could feel their hate; knew they wanted to tear him apart. And yet they had only broken him slightly and had deliberately preserved his life. He presumed they did this for Gynt . . . for retribution. Did Torkyn Gynt and the mysterious Great Forest work as one? They must, but why? And what was Gynt's purpose? No matter how he considered that question he could never give himself an answer which satisfied him. He had learned to accept that where Gynt was concerned there were never satisfactory answers.

But Goth chuckled quietly to himself as he lifted the small vial he had discovered the previous night in the satchel stolen from Gynt. Arraq! No more pain. He took another sip and felt its familiar healing burn to the tips of his toes whilst the pain was just numbed away. He would be able to ride now, and swiftly. The arraq would protect him.

A new thought occurred to him. Until the arraq had begun to work he had not been able to think clearly. Now, after a deep sleep, his head felt clear again and all his guile was back. Why not escape? . . . not only from Gynt but from the man called Nord Jesper who was still sleeping nearby. No one in this party had stirred. They had all drunk heavily, having found some skins of liquor in the cart. He figured they might well sleep off their stupor for a while yet. It would give him sufficient time to steal away with one of the horses.

He decided that with the way his luck was running, anything now was worth a try. Goth got to his feet silently, slipping the arraq vial into a pocket, knowing he would need it later despite feeling strong at this moment and headed to where the animals were tied up. He realised the mare he had ridden was still saddled. She would be tired and cranky for that reason but it saved him the time – and the nuisance . . . and noise – of having to saddle a horse.

The mare nickered with reproach when he began to untie the reins. Goth was perspiring in the cool morning from the effort of remaining silent. He even stroked her muzzle – an action foreign to him – to keep the beast quiet. He noticed her ears suddenly prick up and forwards although he himself had heard no sound. He turned anyway.

'Hello, Goth,' Gynt said, the falcon on his shoulder. 'Were you going somewhere?'

Goth wanted to scream his frustration. So close. If only he had thought to leave before first light.

Tor smirked. 'I would have tracked you down, anyway,' he said, as though he could read the man's thoughts. 'Shall we wake your friends?'

Goth noticed the mare still carried the bow. He was an excellent shot. As Tor turned to look at the slumbering figures, he reached for the bow, sliding a single arrow from the nearby quiver.

You'll be quite amused at what Goth's up to behind your back, Cloot cautioned, as Tor walked towards the group of men.

Tor shielded casually for both himself and Cloot. Nothing from Goth could hurt them now.

He kicked the men, one by one. They came to slowly; everything a blur. Finally Tor turned back to Goth who barked a harsh laugh.

'Shall I shoot the bird first, or you?'

Cloot tsk-tsked in Tor's head. *Trying, isn't he?*

The men beside them were fully awake now, confused, and slowly standing up.

'What's going on here?' Jesper growled.

Goth let fly the arrow which pierced the chest of one of Jesper's companions. The man dropped like a stone. Not bad, Goth thought to himself, although the heart would be a cleaner target next time. In a blink, Goth had nocked another arrow. His former travelling companions were suddenly wary.

'We can rush you, Goth. You can only get one of us in the time it will take us to throw you to the ground,' Jesper warned.

'Yes, but which one?' Goth asked gleefully, another arrow flying with horrible speed to its target. Jesper's second companion joined his friend on the ground in death.

'That was just stupid,' Jesper said. 'This gormless sod and I will now finish you. You'd better choose quickly which of us you like least.'

'Well, that's not an easy decision but I must admit, I don't owe him money,' Goth said, nodding towards Tor, still enjoying himself.

Tor turned to the sailor. 'And I despise both of you and will certainly not join you in anything, Nord Jesper.'

The sailor looked stunned. 'How do you know me?'

Tor's voice was hard. 'I only know *of* you but that's enough to welcome your death, either by his hand or mine. I care not.' He lied. He would prefer it to be by Goth's bow.

Jesper looked between his two would-be killers. 'What have I done to either of you?'

Tor felt his anger rise in concert with the man's whimpering tone. 'Apart from felling two of my companions you mean? . . . one of them my wife.'

Goth stepped closer. His wife? He could only mean Alyssa. 'Is she dead?' he asked.

'She lives,' Tor replied, not even looking Goth's way. 'Apart from them, you killed a friend of mine. His name was Petyr Gylbyt.'

Nord Jesper scratched his head nervously. 'I don't recall.'

'No, I don't suppose you do because that's how much his life was worth to you.' He turned to the former chief inquisitor. 'Kill him, Goth. I see your strength has curiously returned.'

Goth smiled. 'Yes, I do appreciate the healing properties of your arraq. Well, well . . . whoever thought we'd be on the same side, Gynt.'

'Only this once,' Tor said and again the wolfish grin crossed his face as though he knew something the others did not.

Jesper had begun to beg for his life and Tor turned away, walked a few steps and sat down. 'I shall wait here for you,' he said to the man brandishing the bow.

'Your arrogance amazes me you know, Gynt,' Goth said, shaking his head. 'Yes, wait for me and the arrow I have reserved especially for you. Then I'll go back to where Alyssa is and finish off what my travelling companions failed to do.'

The Colours flashed. Tor could kill him here and now but he remembered the wise counsel of Cyrus. Justice must be done. He was not the person to administer it.

Go Cloot. To the trees. The falcon obeyed. Goth did not notice the bird lift silently from Gynt's shoulder.

In his fright at imminent death Jesper had emptied his full morning bladder.

'Oh dear,' Goth said with fake sympathy. 'That is a shame. What an untidy way to go to your gods.'

Tor looked at the grass. He heard Jesper make one more plea and then the terrifying sound of an arrow as it left the bow and thudded home. A wet, gurgling sound was quickly replaced by silence. Goth had done the dirty work for him; Nord Jesper was dead. Eryn's promise to avenge Petyr's death had been kept.

He lifted his bright blue eyes to rest on Goth who had taken several more steps towards him. In the bow was nocked one final arrow. Tor noticed the quiver was empty.

'I suppose I had better make this one count,' Goth said, knowing his enemy had seen this arrow was his last.

Tor nodded sombrely, his gaze not leaving Goth's twitching face.

'Is there anything you want to say?' Goth asked, slightly perturbed by his victim's calm countenance.

'Hurry up, perhaps?'

'Oh, you're in a rush to die, then?'

'No. I must make haste for your judgement.'

Now Goth was hugely amused. He laughed heartily. 'I might almost miss you, Gynt. I just wish I could get you and your hideous bird with one arrow.'

'You can hurt neither of us,' Tor said softly.

'Shut up, Gynt. And now you die. Lift your chin and I'll make sure it goes straight through your throat.'

Tor obliged.

'Farewell,' Goth said and loosed the arrow which whizzed through the air with a sickening sound.

Tor made a small motion with his hand and the arrow followed that path, sliding past him to land harmlessly in the ground behind.

The tic on Goth's face intensified wildly.

Tor regained his feet. He spoke in a measured tone. 'There are several ways we can handle this now—'

Goth had started running. Once again, Tor was amazed at the man's speed and agility. The arraq had certainly worked its wonders.

Cloot flew down again to his shoulder. *How far will you let him go?*

Until he reaches the top of that hill he's making for. I think we should wear him out first.

He heard the falcon laugh in his head as they watched Goth's pumping legs carry him nimbly but less swiftly up the steep incline.

Goth was reacting on pure instinct now. He knew Gynt would catch up with him. Still he must try. He made a desperate lunge towards the top of the hill, knowing that if he could just get over the other side, then he might have the chance to put some space between his pursuer and himself. Perhaps Gynt's magic only worked over a short distance?

His hopes were short-lived. As he crested the hill, he felt his body lurch to a stop. It was not his choice to halt even though he felt tired. His legs simply would not move. Next he was thrown to the ground, which winded him. Goth lay there gasping for breath and wondering what horrible death was in store. Now he was being dragged backwards down the hill, his arms and head banging hard against the ground. Nothing gripped him; it was the most eerie sensation – of being pulled against one's will by something all-powerful.

Tor sat through the rest of that day in a stony silence. Goth tried to engage him, first cajoling and then insulting him, but nothing induced him to pass a word with his enemy who was battered and bleeding from his humiliating journey down the hill. Tor maintained a gentle flow of his Colours which pinned Goth against a tree.

Goth detested the feel of the enchantment wielded against him. He despised all magics and realised Gynt had been using such powers in his presence all the time they had known each other. He snarled as he recalled the miraculous recovery of Queen Nyria; one minute about to step through the gate towards the Light, the next sitting up against her pillows, colour returning to her face. This had been achieved with Gynt's ministrations, he now realised. Then there was that amazing disappearance from Caremboche by Gynt and Alyssa, when he had certainly had them cornered and cringing. He recalled how a rainbow of blinding colours had appeared and the pair of lovers vanished.

He tried to shake his head clear of these useless thoughts but they nibbled away, reminding him again and again of Gynt's arrogant use of magic in his presence. How about the execution? Goth barked a laugh but Gynt did not so much as stir at the sound. He remembered how he had witnessed the corpse hanging from the timbers. How could life ever be breathed back into a broken, dead body? . . . And yet here he was. Despicable magic was the only way. Other events roared through his mind now . . . the coincidence of being on *The Wasp*; Blackhand's death; the ship's sinking; Gynt's escape from the pirates; and his turning up in the arms of the Ciprean Queen. Goth had to marvel at it all — even the saving of that wretched Locky Gylbyt from the Maiden's Kiss must have been Gynt at work.

Goth watched the despised falcon arrive. He noticed the way it cocked its head to one side as though listening to Gynt. He was sure of it now . . . they communicated through magic. He hated them both more than ever.

The hours passed slowly and his constant companion was pain. It would not kill him but it drained his energy and his resolve to survive this and destroy Gynt once and for all. The sun began to lower and day slipped into dusk and still the pressure of Gynt's silent magics kept him pinned and motionless against the tree which also spoke its hate to him, over and over.

Finally the sun's glow deepened in the west and

darkness arrived quickly. Not long after Gynt stood. He seemed to have heard something but Goth could only pick up the scampering of tiny creatures and insects. Gynt strode off deeper into the Forest and before long Goth could hear several voices.

Five other people emerged with Gynt into a brightly moonlit clearing by the track. There was Alyssa who refused to even look at him — he could see she favoured one side and he took some delight that the injury was obviously paining her. And yet how beautiful she seemed . . . pale and ethereal. The bastard Kloek, as always at her side, was looking none the worse for his arrow wound, he noticed. And there was the initial shock of seeing a dwarf and what surely had to be a giant within a couple of strides of each other. Goth was astonished; these races died out centuries ago, surely? Still, not even the sight of these two people could spare him the genuine cold shock of clapping eyes on someone who resembled his enemy so closely that Goth could swear even in this light that they were identical. However, when the young man stepped forward to glare at him, he could see this was the Gynt he remembered from many years ago. So, Goth thought, a son. How perfect.

They all ignored him, talking quietly amongst themselves for a while after an initial flurry of hugs at seeing each other again.

As the others rested and watered their horses, Tor and Alyssa stole some time alone. Gidyon, who was digging out dried fruits and cheese so everyone could snatch a hasty meal, saw his parents move away from the main party. He wished he could share what they talked about but respected their privacy.

Tor put his arm gently around his wife. 'I'm so relieved to have you back with me. How are you feeling?'

'Oh, now don't you start, Tor. Your son has been worrying away at me for hours on the same subject. I'm fine, as you can see.'

'My eyes never lie, Alyssa. You look extremely pale, you favour one side; your expression tells a different story from what you would have us believe.'

She softened her gaze. It was not fair to take out her bitterness on him. She knew she should tell him. But not yet. Not until she understood it better herself. 'Fret not, my love. Your herbals worked, but not on my anger, I'm afraid. That will only be sated when justice is meted to Goth.' Alyssa hated feeling like this. Goth brought out all the bad in her. All her scorn, resentment and rage over so many years, always brimmed up where he was concerned. She tried to pretend that the new fear was just that . . . a fear – and not something tangible – because there was no proof. It was a dream, that was all. She hurriedly changed the subject. 'Saxon says you carry a special liquid fire which will heal anything.'

Tor smiled. 'Arraq. It is incredible. You will take some before we set out.'

'What now?' she asked, her head nodding towards Goth but still her eyes not touching him.

'We waste no further time. I know everyone is weary but we push on. I just feel that we must get everyone back into the Heartwood as fast as we possibly can.'

She nodded. 'I agree. But we need to give the horses a proper rest. I've suggested to Gidyon we eat something, however paltry, even if just to kill some time for the beasts.'

Tor took her arm. 'Come then,' and led her to where her son had laid out food.

Later, when everyone was re-saddling the horses and Goth had been placed back in the cart, it was Gidyon's turn to take his mother aside.

'Did you tell my father what ails you?'

She gave him a firm look of admonishment. He had seen her give Gyl this similar look. It meant she would brook no further discussion on a subject. He refused to be cowed by it.

'Tell me.'

She sighed. 'It is nothing, son.'

'Please.'

Alyssa looked at Gidyon's earnest expression and was transported back to that day at Minstead Green. He truly was a copy of his father. Something about that happy memory of dancing with the other spinsters and laughing as Tor caught her posy cut through her resolve not to share the reason for her troubled mood with anyone.

'I am dreaming too much.'

He moved his head to one side. 'Lys?'

Her brow creased. 'No. Xantia.'

'The woman from the Academie?'

Alyssa nodded. 'She keeps baiting me . . . laughing at me.'

'About what?'

'Lauryn.'

Gidyon took her hand. 'Mother, for the time being we know that Lauryn is about as safe as she can be.'

They heard Tor call them. Gidyon looked over and motioned that they were coming.

'In the arms of a mad god. Safe?' The fear which crossed

his face stopped her saying more. 'It's a dream, Gidyon. I told you it was nothing.'

'Tell me what frightens you in it.'

She took a long breath and looked back towards the loaded cart. 'Coming,' she called, before answering his question. 'That I believe I will be forced to face her again and fight her to save my daughter.'

'Tell the others.' He saw her baulk. 'At least tell him. Let Father help you,' he all but begged, now feeling her fright although not really understanding it.

'Not yet. I will await Lys, first.' She put her finger to her mouth to show him she would not say any more on this. 'Come. Your father wants us to make haste. We must travel.'

Gidyon and his Paladin had made the journey east from Brittelbury in surprisingly fast time, thanks mostly to the trees which guided them. Most Tallinese had to travel around the Great Forest because of their fear of it but the trio were able to cut straight through and were welcomed by its tall, leafy sentries which opened up new paths, ensuring their swift arrival at where Alyssa and Saxon waited.

Alyssa was overjoyed to see them, if not a little overwhelmed by Themesius who towered above her.

Saxon too was still clearly hurting but he refused any fuss being made of his wound – in fact he seemed embarrassed by it. His emotional reunion with Themesius also created some sorely needed amusement as the huge man tried to hug the Kloek gently so as not to make his wound bleed again.

The tender reunion between Paladin was being repeated

now, as Themesius wept at the sight of the magnificent falcon – his great friend and fellow warrior . . . was this really brave Cloot? And when Cloot travelled on his tall shoulders no one believed the grin of pleasure would ever leave the giant's face.

Reunited, the group let the Forest guide them on their way, rapidly shortening their journey to hours rather than days, until they could sense the mysterious Rork'yel Mountains closing in around them. The trees began to thin as daylight broke over the vast northern finger of the Great Forest.

Home, Cloot sighed softly across the Link. Everyone but Goth heard.

They settled at the fringe of the Forest. The horses could be taken no further and were safest there.

Rest everyone, Cloot said. *Let me scout and get our bearings.*

The falcon's wings beat powerfully and Cloot very swiftly disappeared over the first tall ridge. Themesius immediately began to tend to the horses having noticed how weary Saxon appeared. When the Kloek moved to help, he waved him away, suggesting he tend to Alyssa who looked exhausted. Tor had noticed it too but had not said anything. He would keep his worries to himself for now. They left Figgis in charge of their captive.

Don't let him speak to Alyssa, Tor cautioned. *He will do his best to unsettle her. She is ailing enough without his mischief-making.*

Figgis nodded. *I'll see to it he speaks to no one.*

Tor and Gidyon set off in search of the water they could hear not far away and firewood, in case.

Alyssa watched her two precious men disappear into

the Forest. She knew all too well what would be discussed during their private time together.

Are you worried for her?

Is it that obvious? Tor asked.

Only because I am too.

Has she said anything to you?

Perhaps you should urge her to speak with you about all that troubles her.

Tor stopped walking. He knew they were out of earshot of the others. 'What do you know, son?'

'She won't tell me much.'

Two pairs of remarkably blue eyes regarded one another. Tor realised his wife and son had entered into a confidence. He was mindful of not breaching their trust in each other. 'Is there anything you believe I can do to help her?'

Gidyon shrugged, started to walk again and was relieved his father followed suit.

'I think the arrow has injured her more than we realise.'

'No. I have seen to that wound. It is clean. Painful, certainly, but healing. That is not what troubles your mother.'

Gidyon stayed quiet.

Tor tried another approach. 'Ah, there's our stream. Let's fill these skins first.'

As they bent to their toil, he added, 'I keep wondering if Lys is visiting her dreams and troubling her.'

'Oh no, it's not Lys, it's Xa—' Gidyon stopped, angry with himself.

Having got closer to the truth Tor covered the mistake expertly, talking over his son as though he hadn't heard him. 'It's just that when Lys visited her for the first and only time, she upset your mother so badly, Alyssa became remote and untouchable . . . just like now.' He dropped a full bladder on the ground and cupped his face to his hands. 'Ah, that water's chill and delicious.' He smiled at his son. 'Thirsty?'

Gidyon took a drink as well, glad to have glided over his error with such ease.

'Is she a secretive person?' he asked his father.

'Light, no. Alyssa is very open, very direct. I don't understand her reluctance to share her worries. Perhaps she has spoken to Saxon?'

Gidyon shrugged again. 'Perhaps.'

They stood and collected kindling and some larger branches in their sack, Tor talking softly all the while to his son, searching gently for the right way to ask the hard question he needed answering in full.

He watched Gidyon's expression change from troubled to one of relief, as though he had made a decision. 'Father . . .'

Just when he thought Gidyon might yield he felt the cold slice of the Link open and recognised Cloot's distinctive cast.

I've found it!

They spoke no more of Alyssa; instead gathered their load and hurried back to the others.

Goth's time had come.

It was as though they were stepping into a new world. Led by Cloot, they went on foot. Goth walked slowly in pain; his arms tied and tethered to Themesius in front, his every move scrutinised from behind by Gidyon, who had taken an intense dislike to this vile man with the twitching face and permanent sneer. Figgis led with Saxon. Tor brought up the rear with Alyssa, who pretended she needed no help and yet gladly accepted his hand to clamber over most of the ridges. They had to trust the falcon for none of his suggested twists, turns and periods of what felt like walking back on themselves seemed to make any sense. He insisted they follow his instructions precisely.

A few know these mountain passes. But only a Brocken can find the one we move towards. Trust me.

They had been trekking for several hours now, glad that the sun was not yet high in the sky and of having set out at dawn. If Cloot had not flown down to Tor specifically to direct their gaze to an exact spot, they would certainly have missed the narrowest of passes. It had a cunningly concealed entrance and the track ahead was overhung by branches from either side which formed a cool and dark canopy for several hundred steps.

Goth could not fathom what was to be done with him. It was as though they all knew something which he was not privy to. Could they all speak without sound, using some sort of magic? He dismissed the thought as soon as it bubbled up and yet he had already convinced himself of the same between the falcon and Gynt. Why he was being led here baffled him. If Gynt wanted him dead, then why not kill him now . . . or even yesterday, when he had Goth at his mercy . . . or indeed long before that when he was first captured by the trees? It was as though Gynt did not want to dirty his hands.

Goth smiled to himself. Perhaps he could survive this after all. And yet Gynt doggedly pushed him towards something. What was he doing here?

His question was partly answered as one by one they emerged into a sun-drenched valley surrounded by soaring rockface on all sides, including the slim precipice upon which they all now stood. Below them they could see people moving about. There were not just a few either – a population as thick as that of any big village seemed to be roaming down there.

Cloot arrived on Tor's shoulder. No one said anything. Even the Link which was open between them all remained eerily quiet.

It was Goth who broke the awed silence. 'Why am I here, Gynt?'

'For justice,' Tor replied, his voice cold. 'Look more closely. I suspect I have better eyesight than you, Goth, but as we get nearer pay attention to some of the children whose faces you took great delight in disfiguring with your branding iron.'

They all turned to look at Goth, who felt as though his blood had turned to ice. 'The sentient ones?' he whispered.

For the first time since clapping eyes on him again, Alyssa addressed the man she hated most in the world. 'They alone are qualified to judge you.'

'But they're dead!' he screamed. 'I was told they all died for their sins and from my punishment.' His voice lifted higher, drawing attention from below as it echoed around the walls of rock.

Alyssa poured all her years of hate into her scorn. 'You were given false information, Goth. At King Lorys's behest, the ones who could survive were treated and then brought here to live in secrecy and peace, away from your cruel horde.'

The tic on the side of his face was jumping again to the point where Alyssa became blurry. His fury was such that he could not respond in his usual articulate manner and it came as a relief when he felt Themesius roughly tug him and shove him forwards.

'Walk!' the giant said.

It took them an hour, following Cloot's instructions, to wind their way down to the valley floor via precarious tracks and unexpected openings, which included a short trip via a cave. And all of this time the sentient ones below were gathering, a hush falling over them as they watched the strangers descend. None of them had seen people from the outside world since their arrival. They believed the Tallinese inquisitors were finally back to kill them.

Tor could feel their magics pooling, culminating in the more aggressive amongst them organising some sort of retaliation. He understood why but nevertheless he allowed the Colours to rise up. The others sensed it too and stopped walking.

Are we in danger? Alyssa asked first.

I imagine they would consider us enemies. Inquisitors even, he answered.

Saxon halted everyone. *Shall I go out first? Talk to them?*

Tor smiled. *No, we should not fear them.* Then he grinned. *As a precaution I shall shield for all of us. They cannot hurt us.*

Not even combined? Figgis asked.

Tor shook his head.

Goth watched these strange and silent proceedings. He noticed their eyes moved constantly as though communicating. Some nodded or smiled. He saw Gynt shake his head. They were talking! Their evil magic allowed them to talk to one another without speaking. It offended him so deeply that he could feel his anger returning. The shock of knowing that many of those whom he had thought dispatched to their gods were alive and living in this valley had passed. Now fury replaced it. He had been lied to by the cowardly king he had served. A king who had loved his pathetic subjects more than that which his crown had stood for. His predecessors had done their best to rid the land of sentients and Goth thought Lorys had been following suit. Clearly not. His blood boiled.

Themesius pushed him again. He trudged on with his bleak, angry thoughts. They finally emerged from the cave into sharp sunlight. The sentients had obviously expected them to appear from the direction in which they had first spotted them. But Cloot's clever design had brought them through an opening which allowed them to get used to the brightness and gather their wits.

'We come in peace,' Tor cried and they all turned swiftly, looking around to see where the voice had come from.

They were spotted and many cried out in awe at the sight of Themesius, standing so much taller and broader than Tor or Gidyon. An older, strong-looking man pushed to the front. One whole side of his face had been melted and fused by the branding iron. He regarded them silently with his one eye, taking in the fact that they carried no weapons – nothing, in fact. They were a motley collection – hardly soldiers or the strutting peacocks of the inquisition.

'I am Lyam. Name yourselves,' he commanded.

Tor stepped forward and offered his hand in the
Tallinese manner. The man called Lyam refused it but Tor
smoothly continued.

'I am Torkyn Gynt, former physic to their majesties,
King Lorys and Queen Nyria, but I am more famously
known as the treacherous sentient who seduced an
Untouchable from Caremboche.'

'Sentient?'

Tor nodded. 'This is Alyssa Qyn of Mallee Marsh.'

The man stopped him. 'Are you of Lam Qyn's family?'

Alyssa bowed graciously. 'I am, sir. I am his daughter.'
She smiled.

'Well, I'll be . . .'

'Have a care, Lyam. Alyssa Qyn now goes by the title
of Her Majesty, the King's Mother.'

People had shuffled closer. Some reacted with surprise
at this comment.

'Don't be ridiculous, man. Lorys is fifty summers if he's
a day. This girl can be no more than—'

'Not Lorys,' Tor interjected, softly. 'King Lorys is dead.
His son . . . Alyssa's son,' he glanced towards her and she
appreciated the graciousness of his words, 'Gyl, is the
newly crowned King of Tallinor.'

Loud murmurings broke out amongst the crowd. Fear
had been replaced by confusion.

Lyam found himself bowing. He was not sure whether
he could believe this tale but the woman had a certain
bearing.

Tor continued. 'This is Saxon. He is a brave Kloek
whose heart is with Tallinor. He serves King Gyl and is
a Protector of the King's Mother.'

Saxon stepped forward and offered his hand in the

Tallinese way. This time Lyam reacted favourably and took it, responding in a like manner.

'We come in peace,' Saxon repeated.

'My son, Gidyon,' Tor said, walking a step back to touch his son on the shoulder.

The man nodded. 'Yes, I can see that.'

Gidyon nodded back at him. 'We mean no harm, sir,' he reassured the listeners.

'That is my falcon up there. His name is Cloot. And over here is Figgis.'

Lyam frowned, perplexed by the small man. 'Dwarf?'

Tor nodded. 'He is a Rock Dweller. A fine race. And to his right is Themesius.'

'The giant,' Lyam concluded, no little awe in his voice.

'Yes,' Tor said. 'He is friend to you and your people, as all of us here are.'

Lyam pointed. 'All except that one scowling, who is tied to your giant, I see.'

'Ah yes, indeed,' Tor responded smoothly. 'Which brings us to why we are here. May we talk in private with the elders of the community?'

The man stared at him for a moment or two. 'Yes. Follow me.'

Tor realised that the people close enough to see the features of Goth were not comprehending the prisoner's identity. He was not meant to be there. He was out of his accustomed context and it was true that he no longer looked like the proud, strutting Chief Inquisitor of Tallinor. He was a thin, snarling wretch with a terrible affliction of the face. Perhaps closer inspection might reveal him soon enough, Tor decided, and he began to follow Lyam.

Themesius asked whether they had a post or rail anywhere nearby.

'Over there,' Lyam pointed. 'We keep our few donkeys tethered when required. For the most part, they graze wild in the small pastures beyond here. We have no reason to leave, you see.'

Themesius nodded. 'Thank you.'

'Why?' Lyam could not help but ask the question. 'Surely you won't tie your man there?'

Themesius strode to where the post was, Goth struggling to keep up with the huge man's strides. Now everyone, intrigued, turned to watch this vignette play itself out. They saw the giant firmly tie the bound man to the hitching rail and leave him there. The man, who possessed the most dreadful of faces, began to shriek and curse his captors.

'Don't mind him,' Themesius said. 'All will be revealed.'

28

Atonement

They were seated on rugs on the floor of a vast cave. It had a similar feel to the Great Hall in the palace at Tal, Alyssa commented. Lyam smiled. He was still trying to work out the relationship between the man called Torkyn Gynt and the former queen of Tallinor. They seemed so close – their eyes spoke droves to one another. It was all very confusing and indeed shocking to think so much had happened in their home and yet time had passed so slowly and uneventfully here.

'I have never seen the Great Hall of Tal, your highness, but this is certainly where our community gathers. I imagine matters of State are not much different.'

The two dozen or so people who had assembled laughed politely, hoping they did not offend this woman who claimed royalty.

Alyssa nodded a bow and smiled softly. 'True, indeed. And to let you in on a small secret, King Lorys never did like holding court in the Great Hall. He always said his best meetings were over a glass of wine in his chambers and his best decisions were made on the back of a horse.'

Now they laughed heartily, all strains of politeness gone. Tor privately marvelled at her ease amongst people, especially strangers. How quickly she had won them over and put their fears and concerns aside.

His thoughts were disturbed by a woman who bent down before him with a tray. 'Will you share some food?' she asked kindly. 'You must all be tired after your journey.'

'Marya!' Tor cried, attracting instant attention from all.

The woman looked stunned. 'Do we know each other?'

Tor shook his head with a combination of dismay and pleasure. 'Not exactly. You are from Twyfford Cross originally?'

She nodded, confused. 'That's right.'

'And you have several sisters.'

Her eyes became misty. 'Yes. I have not seen them in many years, of course. But tell me how you can know this.'

He had everyone's attention and regretted his outburst now. 'I was at your bridling, Marya,' he said softly.

She looked as though he had slapped her. He watched her fingers tremble and reached to take the tray as she sat down heavily in front of him.

'I have tried not to think on it for a long time. This is my life now. And yet your mentioning it brings it all back so vividly.' She began to weep.

Tor turned to Alyssa for help. Without another word said, Alyssa moved from where she sat and was at the woman's side. Everyone felt suddenly very uncomfortable at hearing Marya's soft sobs and Tor began to make gentle apologies. No one seemed to feel resentment, though the sadness in the cave was palpable as everyone began to recall their own fate at the hands of Goth and his cruel men.

Lyam shrugged at Tor's apology. 'It happens. A memory . . . some small reminder. We are scarred in so many different ways beyond the physical. My face – it is nothing to what else I lost. I was forced away from a young wife and three little ones. I have made myself forget them. I have not mentioned them in years until this moment,' he said, great sadness in his voice. 'I lost so much over so little. My powers are so weak as to be laughable but not to that cursed wretch, Goth. He found me and punished me.'

Tor shifted uncomfortably. He still needed to make amends. 'Marya. It was I who made you unconscious. I could not bear him to hurt you or your family a moment longer. I cast aside your magic because it was not strong enough to hurt them but I knew it would bring terrible hurt to your family.'

She looked up from Alyssa's arms. 'You?' She strained to remember him, searching his face. 'The scribe?' she suddenly said.

He nodded. 'I wanted you to live. I hoped you would. The village folk, after . . . .' He cleared his throat. 'After they had put you in the cart, the village folk all came up and touched you – each one – to assure you that they would take care of your mother and sisters.'

She nodded. 'Thank you for telling me this. They should all be safe then.'

So little had he brought her, he thought. 'Marya, we can go back. You can go back, now. You have nothing to fear any more.'

'How can you say this!' Lyam asked, clearly shocked. 'We live in constant fear of the inquisitors.'

Alyssa stepped into the conversation, pouring her calm about her and soothing with her voice.

'Lyam, Marya . . . all of you, listen to me now.'

She stood in the centre of the circle in which they sat. 'Torkyn Gynt speaks the truth. King Lorys disbanded the inquisitors.' She paused, knowing this would provoke a strong reaction and she was right. People were leaping to their feet and calling out questions. 'Hear me out, good people, please. We have very good reason for being here, which Tor will explain, but I want you to know that by royal decree no inquisitor roams the Kingdom of Tallinor. Sentients are free to live their lives without punishment for their talents.'

She watched their expressions change from dismay to surprise. 'Yes, talents. Lorys married a sentient and came to learn that we are not to be feared. That we are not rampaging sorcerers bent on taking over the world or destroying its people. For most of us our skills have been a burden but Lorys came to understand that these same skills could be put to good use for Tallinor. I give you my solemn word as your former queen and now as the King's Mother, that he has officially pardoned all sentients and I have his authority to grant you your freedom.'

There was uproar in the cave. Shock, despair, elation all mixed into one loud rage of voices. She let it peter out until all eyes looked at her expectantly.

'There are no guards outside this valley. We can lead you to freedom from here – if that's what you wish. Perhaps some people in your community have been born here and grow happily here. They may not choose to leave but for those of you with families or a desire to return home, well . . . we will help you to find your way back.'

Tor could see that Alyssa was close to breaking down

now. She was fulfilling Lorys's final wish for her — that she find her people and free them.

Lyam was shaking his head in disbelief. 'No guards? For how long?'

Alyssa shrugged. 'I don't know. But the inquisitors have been stamped out for several years . . . since their chief, Almyd Goth,' her voice had hardened now just saying his name, 'was captured and put on trial for his sins.' She did not detail those sins.

This brought a fresh wave of cries and alarm.

She implored them to hear her out and when she had quiet again, she continued. 'Goth was found guilty and sentenced to death by burning, but he escaped with a cunning companion and has been on the run from the Crown ever since.'

'Had you never thought to escape?' Saxon asked, in some wonderment that people could accept imprisonment so readily.

'What was the point in fighting back? We are just peasants most of us — ordinary people. And anyway, they would persecute our loved ones if we did. We remained humble to save our families' lives, not ours,' Marya answered.

Lyam interjected now. 'We were brought here and left alone. We assumed there were guards somewhere. But to tell you the truth, finding our way out seemed impossible. Several of our people tried and we presumed either got lost or died at the hands of guards. We could not risk any more of us. And our lives here haven't been so bad. They've left us to ourselves and we've built some semblance of normality here which is more than tolerable. It is a good life. Safe from persecution. We were not to know the persecutors were no longer out there to hunt us down otherwise perhaps more of us would have tried to leave.' He shrugged and others murmured their agreement.

Alyssa held her hand up for quiet. 'The King's final private message, which I'm told he sent on the night he died, was for me to find my own people. I did not understand his communication at first but now I know he meant all of you . . . the sentient ones. He wanted me to ensure your freedom.' She stumbled slightly on her next words but composed herself quickly. 'Lorys sought your forgiveness. He regretted deeply that his reign was tainted with your persecution.'

A strained silence filled the cave at these last words. Forgiveness. Could it ever be given, Tor wondered?

It was Lyam's turn to clear his throat. He glanced around at the eyes which watched him closely. He hoped he spoke for all of them when he turned and addressed the former queen. 'Your majesty. I'm not sure we can ever recover from the pain and loss, the humiliation and despair which we have suffered. But none of us, I'm sure, have lost our ability . . . no, our desire to look for the good in people. Lorys is dead you tell us and his son sits on the throne now. Hopefully he is a good man . . . a more tolerant man than his father; perhaps even more broad-minded and prepared to accept that as sentients we are just as loyal to our Crown as the non-empowered.' He saw Alyssa nod, desperate for them all to accept her words as true. 'We gain nothing by matching hate with hate. As a people we can only grow and go forwards by tolerance and acceptance of all walks of life.' He cast a final quick glance around the cave to ensure he was reading the mood correctly and that he was expressing the sentiments of all the people gathered.

'We accept your gracious apology. We may not necessarily bestow our forgiveness but, your majesty, we do gladly take our freedom and acknowledge your claim that we have our own place in Tallinese society.'

People began to clap. The applause resounded throughout the cavernous space and Tor stood to put his arms around Alyssa and Marya, both of whom were hugging each other. Saxon, Themesius and Figgis joined in the cheering. Gidyon stood a little apart, perhaps still in awe of his mother's commanding presence.

Tor cast to him. *She may be ailing and fragile but she's amazing, don't you think?*

Gidyon grinned back. *Light! I feel proud to call myself her son.*

When the celebrations finally died down, Lyam asked the question that was on everyone's lips and Tor had hoped they would ask.

'So what became of the hated Goth? Is he still roaming our Land?'

It was Tor's turn to take the floor. 'That is a tale in itself,' he said, suggesting they all be seated again. 'It's why we have come here today.'

'You have news on his whereabouts?' someone asked.

'I have more than news,' he replied, gravely. 'I have brought him to you.'

He expected an eruption of voices but was surprised to be greeted by a frigid silence.

'Here?' Lyam asked. 'In the valley?'

Tor nodded. He was about to say more when Lyam suddenly stood.

'The man at the post!' he cried. 'That's Goth! You jest, surely?'

'He does not,' Alyssa said, calmly. 'That is the man who destroyed your lives. We have tracked him down and brought him to you for justice.'

The silence became even heavier now. Their tormentor was at their mercy. How many times had they concocted a fantasy of how they would deal with him should they ever be this lucky?

'Almyd Goth awaits your justice, Lyam. Yours and your people's. He has been sentenced to death several times over and the victims of his lust for killing are no longer restricted to those who possess minuscule amounts of magical power. He now enjoys killing innocents and most recently killed a friend of mine – a young woman – in a manner so barbaric I will spare you the listening.

'Since hearing that news, I have allowed him to live only this long in order that the sentients he showed nothing but heartless cruelty towards will decide his manner of execution.'

Alyssa could sense their terror and reluctance to take much joy in this news. 'We realise this must be a shock for everyone here. Perhaps you would like some time to think on this matter, in private?'

Lyam nodded, as did most of the gathered.

Marya stepped forward. 'I would gladly kill him myself if someone would hand me a blade and give me the permission. I would have no qualms.'

Alyssa took her hand. 'I feel the same. He has done me many inhumane injustices which I prefer not to speak of now. All I will say is that Goth cannot live. His King demanded his death. He must die.'

'And what of our King . . . was he not tainted with our blood as well? Was he not as guilty as Goth?'

Alyssa felt as though a blade had been plunged into her own heart to hear the accusation that she herself had felt over and again at the palace before she had got to know Lorys and all the goodness in him.

She paused, not only to gather herself but to make sure she chose the right words. She took a deep, steadying breath.

'Lorys died alone . . . during a terrible storm, the likes of which I have not seen in years. He was trying to get home to me.' She tried to smile at them but failed. 'He had been attacked that day by a flock of ravens.' Many in the crowd made a warding gesture. 'Lorys knew he was a marked man. Shrouded by death, I believe he knew it stalked him for his own sin of permitting this terrible sentence to be visited upon people of his realm. His death was tragic but swift. A hand of lightning struck through his body towards the land, pointing one of its fingers directly at him as though in accusation. I saw his corpse – wept many hours over it. The lightning bolt hit his heart, blackening and shrivelling his skin on its journey towards the earth. He paid for his sins.'

'The gods,' someone murmured.

She nodded. 'Yes, indeed. The gods punished my husband for his sins of which I can truly say, he had only two. One was to love me when I did not belong to him. The other was ignorance as far as sentients were concerned; to look aside from Goth's evil doing. The gods punished him in their way and now you must punish Goth in yours. We will leave you to your deliberations.'

And with that, Alyssa, former queen of Tallinor, bent

graciously to her audience and then stepped regally from the cave with Tor and their retinue following closely behind.

They had eaten quietly in a separate cave much smaller than the one they had all gathered in. It was Marya's home which she shared with two other women, both part of the group who were making decisions on Goth's fate. It impressed all of them that the three women had managed to make a cave comfortable – hand-woven rugs and hand-crafted furniture gave it a cosy feel whilst a woven length of fabric, pulled back during the day, provided privacy and shelter from the night's cold. Marya had brought them food and left.

The others had finished their meal and had decided to explore the valley with Cloot as a guide. Tor appreciated the time this gave him with Alyssa.

'You were marvellous,' he said.

She looked embarrassed. 'Was I?'

'Every bit a queen.' He took her hand and kissed it.

'I'm not sure I can honestly say I've ever felt like one. I've always believed I was some sort of pretender.' She shook her head. 'I still do.'

'No, Alyssa. If Lorys was alive now I think Tallinor would be seeing its finest ever times. Nyria . . .' he thought carefully first before saying, 'well, she deferred to Lorys. They came from similar backgrounds and, as much as she had a conscience and loved her people, she was still a priv-ileged soul who could never really appreciate how devas-tating the inquisitors were to those same people. She hated Goth for sure, but for other reasons. But you brought to Lorys's reign his true conscience. You are sentient. You

are from that same group who had suffered at the hands
of Goth and the power he wrought. No.'

He shook his head. 'Far from pretender, my love. You
were Tallinor's best queen, albeit short-lived. You would
have made important changes . . . and you still can,
through your son.'

She leaned over and kissed him very briefly and then
she sighed. 'I don't think I shall see him again.'

She tried to smile but her eyes carried such a depth of
grief that Tor felt a flash of alarm.

'What could you mean by that?' he asked.

She moved to sit within the circle of his arms. 'I don't
understand it either. It's a vague but very real feeling –
I sense that my time is done.'

Now Tor moved. Swiftly. He was kneeling in front of
her and took her by the shoulders. 'You must not think
like this. Of all of us, you will survive this. You will go
on.' He had never felt such intense fear as he did now.

Now she did smile, fully and in love with the man
who held her. 'I love you, Tor. I always have, but you are
a terrible liar. You've never been capable of guile.'

His voice had dropped to a whisper. 'This is not guile.
I believe it.'

'Then this is good for all of us. But I do not feel the
same way. I sense something dark and evil approaching.
But it is directed at me alone.'

Tor pulled her close. He was shocked. 'No! Alyssa you're
fearful because of Goth and all that we have yet to do. It
is unnerving and I understand how easy it is to frighten
yourself.'

She pushed away from him. She said nothing for a
moment but stared into his remarkably blue eyes. She had

not focused on them so intently for years. Alyssa realised she had forgotten how devastatingly bright they were. Truly the eyes of a god. And the line of his jaw: strong and suddenly no trace of that boyishness about him any more. He was a powerful-looking man. She touched his lower cheek and felt the stubble of a beard. She loved Tor shaved – it showed off his striking looks – but still she rather liked the rough feel of short, tough hair against her fingers.

Tor felt his mind swimming. Alyssa looked as though she was fixing his face in her mind for the last time.

Alyssa! Stop it!

Why? she asked dreamily. *I don't want to forget your face this time. I did for a while when I thought you were dead. Not this time though. I want to take it with me where I am going.*

Please, he cried. *Please stop this now. I don't understand what you mean. Where are you going?*

I have to face her, Tor.

Who?

Xantia.

Tor was stunned. He thought that was the name Gidyon had been about to say earlier but he had dismissed it, not wanting to probe his son for more information. But it was true. Xantia was the person Alyssa feared.

But why? How can she hurt you?

Alyssa came out of her dreamlike state. Her look was now hard, unyielding. 'Not me. My daughter. And I will not permit it.'

'How do you know she hurts Lauryn? How can you know that she is even near her?' he asked, fully confused.

'Because she baits me. She invades my dreams and

laughs at me. She is calling me, Tor. And I must go. She has my daughter at her mercy.'

Tor tried to rationalise with her. 'These are nightmares only.'

'Stop! You believe your dreams and your visions from Lys. I know what I am seeing in mine. It is real. I feel it in the pit of my stomach. All my instincts tell me she is not so much in danger from Orlac as from the company he keeps.'

Tor did not believe it but he knew Alyssa was set on a course – a destructive one – and he could not allow her to face it alone, particularly in the bleak mood that enveloped her now. 'Then I will help you.'

At this she turned once again to look at him and her whole expression had softened; melted back to the gentle one he knew and loved so very much. 'You cannot, my beloved. This is my final part in this whole scheme. It is my destiny. I must face it as you must face your destiny.'

He shook his head, refusing to accept her words.

'Poor Tor. You've never really understood that neither of us have been in control of our lives since Merkhud came into them. Rue the day at Twyfford Cross when you intervened and saved Marya's life. If not for that, he would never have discovered us and we would be married and living quietly in the southern shires.' She smiled very sadly now. 'But what's done is done and now we must play out our roles to their end. Lys has her designs for both of us. My mother is cunning indeed. Can you not see? She has never permitted us to be together. And she never will.' Alyssa stood. 'Now kiss me once more, my beloved husband, and then we must finish what we came here to do.'

Tor, too rattled to do anything but obey her wishes, stood and held her close. His feeling of helplessness was so great that he took comfort in the only thing he could – her lips and her touch. He lost himself, pouring every ounce of his love into his embrace, willing her to believe him that he would somehow save them both.

Lyam came for them and when they stepped outside, they saw that all the sentient community had gathered. Their faces were grim; none looked at ease with whatever decision had been reached. Tor understood. These were not cruel people – some of them perhaps, after all these years, were unable to feel the same hate for the pathetic man chained to the post, still cursing and snarling.

Gidyon and the others had gathered near Goth. Cloot was perched above the prisoner. It was a deliberate show of power over a man who had struck such fear into so many.

Lyam addressed them. 'We have made our decision,' he said sombrely.

Tor nodded. He spoke loudly so all could hear. 'This man is guilty of so many heinous acts. It is a mercy to the land to destroy him and I promise you I take no man's life lightly . . . not even his.'

He could feel Alyssa rigid by his side. Her gaze was focused on Goth, who squirmed beneath it, ranting his hate for all sentients.

'Tell us your decision,' Tor said finally.

Lyam cleared his throat. 'He must burn as Tallinor pronounced he should.'

'And may he never find the Light,' Alyssa whispered for Tor's hearing.

Lyam continued. 'It must happen quickly. At sunset.'

'Will you make the necessary preparations?' Tor asked, his voice devoid of all emotion now. He knew this was right.

'They have already begun. At sunset, follow Marya.'

Tor thanked the man and then took Alyssa's hand and walked to where Goth stood. The former chief inquisitor's fury was palpable. The sentients began to disperse, uncomfortable with the situation forced upon them.

Tor spoke now for the benefit of his own small group. 'Be quiet, Goth!' he commanded and miraculously the man stopped his noise. He eyed Tor balefully, his face a constantly moving canvas of hate. He ignored the others, focused on his enemy and laughed at him. 'I do not fear you,' he said.

'It matters not. I want you to understand that you have been brought here to face your justice, long overdue. You are dead many times over for your deeds, Goth. This is simply the closing chapter in your vile, sad life. Tonight you will die as ordered by the royal decree of his majesty, King Lorys of Tallinor.'

'And are you my judge and executioner, Gynt?'

'You were judged a long time ago. I am here only to bear witness to your death.'

'Leave me!' Goth spat. 'I wish no longer to see you or any of your evil spawn.'

Gidyon could not help himself. 'We do Tallinor a great justice in ending his life.'

Themesius nodded. 'I've known him only days and he makes my skin crawl.'

'I've known him too long,' Saxon said quietly and then he looked at Alyssa. 'Tonight he will be delivered.'

*   *   *

As the sun began to lower behind the mountains, Marya came for them once again. 'It is time,' she said and everyone stood, their nerves on edge after a day of high tension.

She pointed. 'When a Brocken dies, he faces west.' They heard Cloot click his agreement across the Link. 'We feel it's appropriate that as Goth will die in the Rork'yel Mountains, he should follow the Brocken way.'

It is too good for him, Cloot replied for their benefit alone.

'Follow me,' she said. 'Who will bring him?'

'I will,' Themesius answered. He strode towards Goth who had been strangely quiet for the afternoon.

Now the prisoner began to struggle at the sight of the approaching giant. He could see his hated enemies watching and he had been aware for some time now of a stream of people slowly and laboriously snaking their way up through the rocks on a track.

Marya looked towards that column of people now. 'We go to the top of this mountain to pray. It is fitting he goes to the gods from this peak.'

Everyone followed Themesius, who had slung Goth like a sack of flour over his shoulder. It was done effortlessly and he walked without breaking stride, as if there was no burden.

It took them some time to reach the summit. Tor once again helped a curiously weakened Alyssa on the trek upwards. She seemed to be sinking in time with the sun to a place even Gidyon could not reach. Tor was worried for both his wife and son now. He tried to comfort Gidyon by explaining that his mother was melancholy, but even to his ears the words sounded contrived and hollow. He probed towards her and found she had shielded. Tor knew he could break down her shield, but to what end? Her wrath probably. She had somehow broken free of him and withdrawn. All he could do was keep her safe until she came back from where she was hiding and stopped being afraid.

It was a silent and bleak group that at twilight finally crested the mountain top. It was eerily quiet up there and without a breeze. The sky, appropriately aflame in the dying orange of the sun's glow, would soon deepen to pink as dusk descended. No children were present, but as many of the community as could stomach this event had gathered and stood now to watch Goth being brought up over the rise by the giant. Themesius unloaded his cargo, which was bound and still snarling.

Lyam had decided on no further formalities. There had been enough talking. It was clear he wanted this deed done.

'Tie him,' he commanded of two men.

'Wait!' It was Marya. Her eyes were wide and burning with a fervour that those gathered could only imagine was revenge itself. 'He must be naked, as we were. Stripped and humbled.'

Lyam nodded. 'Do it.'

It was done, despite much kicking and shrieking by Goth. Many were appalled at the sight of his naked body. None of these people had heard of his mauling at the end of a Kloek blade. He was bound swiftly to a tall boulder which had stood in that spot for centuries. Each of the sentients filed past and threw rushes at Goth's feet. It had been determined that each of the sentients who had felt his branding iron would play their own part in his execution. He – no longer sane it seemed – cursed every one of them, as spittle from his lips flew and his manic eyes rolled back in his head.

He looked like a demon and many of the women turned away once their rushes had been thrown down.

Tor noticed none of the rushes were damp, as they would be in the favoured method to prolong a burning for the victim. No, these people wanted their tormentor dead and gone; his ashes scattered to the winds amongst the forbidding Rork'yel Mountains.

The rushes were laid. The sun had set. Dusk had arrived . . . that strangely magical time between day and night when a soul could flee easily to its gods.

Lyam turned towards Tor and Alyssa. 'Does any of your group want to say anything before Marya touches with the flame?'

'I do,' Alyssa suddenly said.

'Don't,' Tor cautioned.

'I must,' she said.

She glanced towards Saxon who nodded. *Have your say, beautiful girl. He took the most precious thing from you. Now throw it back in his face*, he said on a private Link.

Tor wished she would not. This situation felt strangely dangerous. All the hairs on his arms had lifted. He felt an old fear grip him. Cloot arrived at his shoulder. Impeccable timing as always. The falcon's talons, large and strong, centred him.

All right? Cloot asked.

I will be when this is done, he answered, his jaw clamping his teeth hard.

She must do what her instincts instruct, Tor . . . as we must, Cloot gently counselled.

Alyssa walked around to face Goth, who mustered an evil grin for her.

'Alyssa, I'd ask you to suck my cock for old time's sake, but as you can see, I am without.' And he went into a fit of manic giggling.

She shivered. 'You were created by fire, Goth,' she said, frowning. 'It is fitting that the flames dismantle the creature you have become and burn away your sins. Go to your gods – whichever of them will have you. You can hurt me no more.'

She nodded towards Marya, who lit a bushel of dry wheat from a nearby torch which had been carried, burning, to the peak. Everyone held their breath. Tor felt the world spin slightly. It felt to him as though an important milestone in his destiny was being reached.

Marya looked into the victim's twitching face but Goth only had eyes for Alyssa. She touched the flame to the rushes. They caught fire instantly.

Goth began to laugh. He began to speak gibberish. His ravings and rantings had fallen into utter madness and his face contorted with the insanity which was finally taking him over.

Saxon watched him wrestle against the bindings and wondered if they would hold against his strength. He mentioned it to Figgis who nodded sombrely. 'We should have seen to that part ourselves, I fear.'

Themesius heard and bent down to whisper, 'Let's hope the fire consumes him quickly.'

Gidyon had heard this exchange too and stepped towards his mother. Tor did likewise. Both of them hated her making herself so available to Goth's eyes which were refusing to leave her. She seemed mesmerised as the flames began to engulf the pile of rushes.

Tor spoke gently. 'Step back, my darling, please.'

She resisted his touch. 'No, I will watch him to his end.'

Gidyon and Tor stole a worried glance at each other. *Then we stand beside her*, Tor said to his son privately. *This is not good for her*.

And so they stood and watched their enemy writhe against the heat of the flames which were yet to touch his already once-burnt skin.

A soft breeze blew through and some sparks lifted and landed against his face. Goth was shocked back to reality. They could see those sparks had blackened his cheeks. His eyebrows shrivelled and his legs seemed to be ablaze. It was horrible but still Alyssa fixed her eyes on the man she hated.

He focused on her again. 'Alyssa!' he yelled above the roar of the flames now. 'I'll always be the first man to have had the pleasure. Never forget that. It will haunt you for ever, my pretty thing. You were mine; I marked you!'

That was it. She could take no more. No more pain from this man; no more taunts or cruel words. He had stained her life with bitterness and fear and now she would rid the Land of him once and for all. Tor felt the rising wave of power but did not react quickly enough. Alyssa gathered her strength and screamed as she hurled her magic towards him. Flames exploded bright and white about Goth. Gidyon was reminded with horror of his own terror at Duntaryn, which had created a similar white flame that had burned its victims to ashes.

Goth burned quickly now. His skin melted like butter and he screamed his agony into the blackness which had stolen across the sky. In the intense brightness of the flames, Alyssa felt dizzy; she sensed herself being sucked uncontrollably into a void. And in that black space, she saw Xantia.

See what we do to your daughter, coward. Won't you try to save her?

She saw beyond Xantia to where a huge, golden-haired man, naked and erect, was lowering himself over and into her prone child. Lauryn was sobbing and begging for mercy.

No mercy, the god yelled as he penetrated her.

She screamed her pain and despair but the god did not stop.

Call him! he ordered, as he rode her body viciously. *Call him to me and I will stop.*

No! Lauryn gasped, her eyes wide with agony and fear.

He arched his back and pushed harder. *I can keep this up for hours*, his ugly voice called to her.

I will not summon him, you devil. Orlac! Save me!

Forget Orlac. You are for my pleasures now. Look at me, girl. I am Dorgryl, your ruler . . . the new ruler of this Land.

Xantia's wicked laugh could be heard above her master's rasping voice as he lost himself in vile pleasure.

Tor watched in horror as Alyssa's body went rigid – her eyes were staring and wide, pupils dilated and oblivious to anything in front of her. Tor grabbed her to prevent her falling, and in that moment, the burning figure of Goth began to strain against its bindings.

Hold, damn you, Saxon cast, begging the rope which held Goth not to yield.

But Goth was strong. Even as his flesh fried in the ferocity of Alyssa's flames he found impossible strength to rip himself free and lurched, screaming his hate, to the edge of the clifftop and plunged to the valley floor below. Themesius, Figgis and Saxon rushed to the edge to watch the fiery figure drop to its death.

It was only then Saxon noticed Tor and Gidyon bent over the prone figure of Alyssa. Tor was begging his wife to listen to him; shaking her by the shoulders, screaming her name over and over. They could feel him casting powerfully, probing all around her, trying to chase her to wherever she had gone.

Gidyon was too shocked to speak. He crouched by his parents and it was Themesius who finally came and lifted the young man to his feet.

'Gidyon!' he commanded. 'What occurred?'

The voice of his Paladin snapped him out of his stupor. 'She went rigid and fainted. I know not what has occurred. Help him, help my father find her!'

Figgis put his hand on the shoulder of Tor who kept up a stream of encouraging words, begging his wife to return.

Torkyn Gynt! Figgis spoke only to him. *We need you.*

Tor looked into the dwarf's face. *She's gone.*

Does she breathe?

Tor did not seem to understand.

'Themesius . . . does Alyssa breathe?' Figgis asked.

The giant bent to the tiny chest and the others shooshed everyone about them.

He looked up finally. 'Her heart beats but is faint.'

Both Tor and Gidyon found their wits. 'Quick, Themesius, we must carry her to the Forest. We must leave now,' Tor said, standing and running his hands wildly through his hair. 'Is it over?' he asked the Kloek, referring to Goth.

'He threw himself over the ledge . . . his favourite trick,' Saxon replied.

Cloot! Tor called.

On my way, the falcon replied flying high and then stooping to drop in a deep dive towards the valley floor. He would check to ensure the smouldering body was dead.

Lyam ran up. 'What has happened to the Queen?'

Tor's distraught expression told him there was no good news. 'We don't know. Goth inflicted terrible cruelty on her and her family,' he answered, sliding around the truth. 'She has fainted it seems, but I think we must leave here now.'

Themesius picked her up as though she weighed no more than a feather. Her body was now limp; her eyes closed to them.

'You're leaving now, at night?' Lyam asked, astonished.

'Yes.'

Saxon began walking with Themesius. Figgis followed with Gidyon who barely felt the guiding hand of his Paladin.

'I'm sorry to leave you in this manner,' Tor said and meant it.

Cloot arrived back. *Goth is no more.*

Are you sure? Tor said, his voice raspy in the falcon's head.

He is dead.

'Goth is finished,' Tor said to those who had begun to gather about him. He looked at Marya. 'We must leave. Our work is done here.'

'You're leaving us now?' Her voice was full of disbelief. 'But you promised to lead us from here . . . those of us who want to return.'

Tor's voice softened. He was eager to join his friends, get Alyssa to safety, but knew he must give these people an answer . . . some hope. 'I meant my promise. We will return. We will come back for you and bring you back safely into Tallinor proper.'

'When?' Lyam asked. 'I'm not sure I will be one of them, but there are many who have expressed a desire to return to their homes.'

'Soon, I promise you. I must get Alyssa to help outside this valley. We cannot take you with us through the night. Let me do what I must and one amongst us will return for you. You have my word.'

'Keep that word, Torkyn Gynt. You owe it to these people,' Lyam counselled. 'We will await your coming and make our preparations.'

'Thank you,' Tor said, relief flooding his body. 'I must go now.'

'I can't say we thank you for leaving the Crown's business to us but we do thank you for tracking Goth down and releasing us from his hold.'

Tor nodded and offered the Tallinese handshake. 'Until we meet again.'

Cloot flew on ahead and Tor jogged until he caught the others up. 'Any change?' he asked breathlessly.

'None,' Saxon said. 'The Heartwood is our only hope.'

The going was difficult because it was so dark but Cloot's instructions once again guided them flawlessly through the strange twists and turns which would bring them back out at the fringe of the Great Forest. Along the way, Gidyon tore strips from his own clothing and tied them to branches or placed them beneath stones.

'Why?' Figgis asked at last.

'One of us has to come back for them,' was all he said.

No one wanted to think on the implications of why it would not be all of them.

They reached the Forest several hours later but had made good time – despite stopping frequently to check Alyssa's pulse, which remained faint and her breathing appeared very shallow. Once back amongst the trees, Tor took her in his arms.

'Make your way back to the Heartwood with the horses as quickly as you can. Danger approaches.'

'And you, Father?' Gidyon asked.

'I can take her back to the Heartwood in my own way. Make haste!'

They watched him hold her close to his chest and then they all felt a mighty power gathering. Tiny flames burst around the pair, chiming, and then a vast rainbow light gushed around them, blinding and deafening them with the roar of its power. When they could look again Tor and Alyssa had disappeared.

29

A Forest Falls Silent

Tor no longer needed to draw on Darmud Coril's power to travel through the Forest. He now understood the magical complexities of transportation into the Heartwood and, fuelled by fear for Alyssa's life, wielded his power with terrifying speed and skill to bring them both to the very centre of the Heartwood, where their children had been conceived.

'Darmud Coril!' he cried, his voice hoarse with fright.

'I am here, Torkyn Gynt.'

'Save her. Use my life if you must but save her!'

'Give her to me,' the god commanded and the branches of the trees which served him reached low. Barely able to part with her, Tor placed his wife gently amongst them.

She was lifted high into the trees and away from his sight. Tor fell to his knees, begging the Heartwood to use all of its magics to rescue his precious Alyssa, over and over again offering his own life in exchange.

Solyana appeared, padding silently to where he knelt. She nuzzled him and he put his arms around her.

'She's gone,' he wept into her thick, silver-tipped fur.

'I've tried everything to reach her but I can't even sense her there.'

We love her too, son of the Heartwood. Be brave. Solyana could think of nothing else to say — no words of comfort came because she too felt hollow. *Tell me what happened while we wait.*

The wolf knew it would help him to regain some balance if he talked and she was right. He related everything — all the events which had happened on their journey north.

So Goth is finally dead, she said.

Yes, but somehow he took Alyssa with him.

I don't think so. From what you say, Alyssa went to wherever it is of her own accord. She looked up. *Hush! Darmud Coril comes.*

Tor leapt to his feet but when he saw the limp body of his wife being lowered from the trees, he knew in his heart they had been too late.

Alyssa was placed tenderly on the ground but Tor could not look at her. His eyes were riveted on the lines of sadness etched across Darmud Coril's own gentle face.

'We have lost her, my son.'

Tor swallowed. He could make no sound come. His throat had failed. He wished it would close completely, shutting off his breath and allowing him to die beside her.

The god continued. 'Only her body is here. Her spirit has gone. She has covered her trace expertly and I cannot find her. I am unable to call her back.'

'But perhaps . . .' Tor wanted desperately to clutch at something, anything which might give him hope.

Darmud Coril shook his head and Tor stopped

speaking. The trees rustled and creaked their distress and the Flames of the Firmament appeared to chime softly about the precious couple.

'She already cools, my child. It is too late. Alyssa is dead to us.'

Tor knew it to be true.

He said no more and lay down on the ground next to her; burying his face into her honey-golden hair he poured out his sorrow.

Solyana sat nearby, grief-stricken herself and worried about Tor. She must watch him closely. He and the Trinity were their only hope. Slowly the Heartwood fell silent. Nothing moved; not even the lake rippled. Despair reigned for countless hours as Alyssa's body began to stiffen beside Tor and then cool to a deathly chill.

It was how the others found them the following day; curled into death's embrace.

She wished now she had said something before she left which might bring him comfort, but seeing Lauryn, hearing her despair and Xantia's hideous cackle, had pushed her beyond her tolerance. She had cast a warning to Xantia, she thought, and then lifted free of her body. What an odd sense of freedom she had felt. She had looked down on her husband and son, feeling their fright, wanting to tell them she had made a decision.

Alyssa had lingered far longer than she had intended, travelling with Tor to the Heartwood and feeling his grief so intensely that she wanted to reach out and touch his soft, wavy hair and reassure him it was for the best. She watched him receive back her body from Darmud Coril and saw his agony as he accepted the truth and slumped beside her. Her spirit was trembling now with shame at bringing this upon him – causing him so much sorrow when there was still so much to be done.

Yet she had had no choice, she told herself. Her and Tor's needs were not above their children's. The monster, Orlac, was raping Lauryn and Alyssa knew all about rape. She had had Saxon to rescue her yet Lauryn had no one. Her Paladin were nowhere to be seen! What could they do anyway against such power? She recalled the broad, powerful back of Orlac and the way his lips had been pulled back in a frenzy of ecstasy combined with hate. Beneath him screamed her child who refused to call her parents to the trap.

Alyssa tried to shake herself free of the vision; she needed a clear mind for what she had to do. The only puzzle, she thought, was why Lauryn had called for Orlac to save her when it was Orlac who rode her as if she were a whore. It baffled her but time was short now. She was no more for this Land . . . she knew that now; she must follow her true enemy, Xantia. Perhaps she could use Xantia to divert the attention of Orlac and win her child some respite from his attentions, if not safety.

Alyssa looked down one final time upon the man she loved. She could neither touch nor link with him.

Farewell, darling Tor, she called to her husband, who could not hear her. *Be no longer sad, beloved. The gods have chosen that we were never meant to be together.*

She thought of Gidyon; someone she loved so much already – a sensitive, affectionate young man who would not recover from this blow easily. Her spiritual heart broke for him.

And Rubyn. Unknown to her but the bond between

mother and son still had strength. His face was etched in her mind. She hoped his father would live through this to tell him more about her endless love and regret for not being near him as he grew.

Finally, she spared a thought for Gyl. Her beloved son . . . her King.

Then she was travelling . . . racing after Xantia, whom she intended to destroy.

30

To Cipres

Lauryn withdrew as far within herself as she could and cowered there. Pain had passed; now it was just the detestable feel of him against her, over her, that she must endure. And Xantia, laughing manically at her suffering.

She thought of Tor and felt strengthened that she had not capitulated to the monster's demands, although several times when the fear of him threatened to overwhelm her it had been tempting – to link with her father; link with them all and let happen whatever was to be. But in the next second she had thought – through the pain, through the humiliation and the despair – of all those counting on her to protect their identity, their location.

The horror had begun three nights earlier. Somehow she had found the will to survive. Today, though, the fourth day, when he returned to take her again, she felt that resolve ebb. How many more times would he visit? How much longer could she resist his demands? They were always the same: she was to call her father for help. But then, just a few moments ago, when her resilience was at its lowest and even the notion of his hurting Gidyon seemed almost fair to her in her terror, she had heard the voice.

I will save you from him. Be strong, Lauryn. Just a little longer.

And then the voice had disappeared. It sounded weak but it was there and it was making a promise. She could hear the determination and the fury within it before it disappeared again.

It was the voice of Orlac.

It was then that Lauryn realised the man who was hurting her was not the same one who had wooed her so carefully. This Orlac was different, both in voice and posture. Somehow, Orlac's body had been overpowered and possessed by an impostor.

Her senses heightened by terror, Lauryn found her mind was open to Orlac's. Perhaps he had been reaching for her since the terror began. Now he promised to rescue her. Curiously, it was relief she felt. Relief that this horrible thing was not, in fact, the Orlac who had spent so many evenings talking about everything and anything with her. They had shared so much in that time and in all those nights he had done no more than kiss her hand. It was as though he had been too shy to touch her. But the monster within him was not.

Lauryn could not be sure her presumption was correct, but she suspected her instincts served her well. And she recalled now that Juno and even Adongo had tried to warn her. Had they seen the impostor perhaps?

She would survive. She would let him do his horrible acts over and over but she would not be cowed by his threats or demands. As long as she did not call her father, he would have to keep her alive. She was as good as dead, Lauryn decided, if she so much as uttered Tor's name. And so she hid his trace. Buried all pathways to him. He was the One. He must be protected by her. Orlac would save her and with that thought – as the beast who hurt her made his demands again – she sensed something new.

It was Xantia now. Xantia casting out! Could she follow that Link? Lauryn did not know if it was possible but she had to try. From her withdrawn self she focused . . . felt her Colours; kept them small and private and through her new and special self she sensed and was shocked to see her mother's tormented face through a ring of flames – could even listen in on her mother's thoughts. She believed she might scream for she sensed her brother's and father's presence and she pulled back instantly, running away from them, desperately hoping the thing which inhabited Orlac would not find her out.

Lauryn's luck held. Dorgryl was lost to the pleasures of the flesh and in his ecstasy did not sense her casting out through Xantia. Lauryn withdrew herself again as he became still. He shoved her hard backwards. She heard Xantia's horrible laugh but showed nothing. She scrambled aside, pulling up her knees to her chest; no longer caring to hide her shame in front of these two creatures.

She pretended to swoon. Xantia slapped her hard to see if Lauryn was faking but Lauryn felt it coming – she steeled herself and went limp, allowing the sting of the slap to tingle across her face whilst her expression betrayed nothing but a slackness indicative of sleep.

They spoke in her apparently unconscious presence and she listened, not so much as twitching a muscle.

'Thank you for giving me my freedom from the archalyt, Dorgryl,' Xantia cooed.

Lauryn noted the name, cheered inwardly. It was not Orlac. Dorgryl! She hated its ugly sound in her head.

'Don't mention it,' he said, seeming to turn on his charm. It did not work — the deep voice was still laced with scorn. 'Use your freedom wisely, Xantia. Do anything stupid with it, like following your own mindless and petty hates, and I will take your life as easy as blinking.'

The words were uttered softly but there was no disguising the threat in his voice. Lauryn could sense Xantia shudder. The Witch was scared of him but she was helplessly attracted to his power.

'Stay with me, Dorgryl. Don't let Orlac come back. I will serve you with a loyalty like no other,' Xantia begged.

'He is as much at my mercy as she is,' he said, looking over at Lauryn.

She held her breath.

'Do you think she will call her father?'

'She cannot take much more of this and I have plenty to give.' He laughed harshly. 'She will call him. A day or two more, no longer.'

'Why can't you just go and finish him yourself? I think we can all guess where he hides.'

'Because I want him to come to me!' Dorgryl shouted. There was no warning in his manner or his speech that his anger would ignite with such terrifying speed or burn quite so brightly. 'I want him begging for the life of his daughter. I know him. He loves others more than the power he owns; more than what he is or who he could be. He worships the woman you hate and the children she birthed. They are his weakness. He will come.'

They left Lauryn finally but not before Xantia had thrown a jug of chilled water over her and promised they would return later. Just before she pulled away, Xantia whispered to her.

'I gave your mother a little insight into what you get up to in Cipres, you wicked child.'

Lauryn noticed, for the first time, that Xantia no longer wore the disk of blue archalyt on her forehead, though it had probably been removed for days. It did not scare her to realise that this woman was reconnected to her powers. She rolled back to face the Witch and somehow found the courage to give the leering face a look of scorn.

'That was stupid. Now she can trace you, she'll destroy you.'

'Light be praised!' Cyrus said. 'He's still here.'

They were standing at the docks of Caradoon having travelled at speed from Ildagarth. The soldier was impressed with how quickly they had covered such ground. Although the great northern city and this relative backwater were close in terms of the size of the Kingdom of Tallinor, he recalled such a journey would normally take two, possibly three, days. They had made it in the course of a day.

Did you have anything to do with how fleet of foot our horses were?

Rubyn only barely smiled. It was answer enough.

'How can you know?' Sarel asked.

Cyrus looked away from Rubyn's smug expression to the Queen. 'Because only when the sovereign is aboard can a ship fly that pennant . . . or so it was in my day,' he replied.

'Do we just stride up then and present ourselves?' It was Hela. 'Because we look very conspicuous right now and it's a matter of moments, I'm sure, before soldiers ask us to move on.'

She saw Cyrus's normally serious expression change to one of amusement. He scratched gently at his closely-shaved beard.

'I think I've just spotted our way into an audience,' he said softly. 'Follow me.'

They did as told, trailing his long stride a few steps behind. Hela felt a tingle of pride on his behalf. He's magnificent, she could not help but privately admit, as she watched the confident – and indeed arrogant – walk of Kyt Cyrus.

The ship was clearly being readied to sail and if Cyrus's still sharp eyesight served him well, frantic activity was underway which seemed to be under the command of a civilian. Perhaps he was the captain – this was no royal vessel and certainly no warship. The only ships which left from this port were pirate craft . . . usually slavers.

A look of distaste crossed his face. He had always hoped to do something about Caradoon and yet it had been his idea to leave it alone. He had finally decided that to monitor it closely – have spies even – would be a more subtle way to control it. Lorys had not been keen but he had appreciated the good sense of his Prime who argued it would be best to keep potential troublemakers in sight. Heavy handling would only send them all scurrying to new regions, the Prime had assured, adding that as long as the problem did not spill south – could be kept contained within Caradoon – then it was as good as controlled. Lorys had finally agreed, and so as much as it galled him to leave the town of scoundrels alone, Cyrus had bided his time, infiltrating the pirating community with two or three men who lived amongst the Caradoons for many years, reporting back cautiously but frequently once they knew they had been accepted.

He looked again at the man in charge. He seemed

awfully young to command his own ship. Cyrus checked the name – *The Raven* – and his thoughts moved swiftly, racing back amongst his memories to bring to mind the name of the owner of this ship.

'Janus Quist,' he murmured. The others looked at him and he explained. 'But that's not Quist. He was distinctive to say the least.'

Rubyn's much keener eyesight focused on Locklyn Gylbyt, barking orders. 'He's about the same age as I am, perhaps younger.'

Sarel squinted into the distance. 'It's Locky!' she suddenly squealed.

Hela admonished her for the loud voice although none of the busy soldiers seemed to take any notice.

It was Hela's turn to narrow her gaze towards the young man. 'I think Sarel's right. His brother – well, brother by marriage – is Quist. The captain was exceptionally generous towards us. He helped us to escape from Cipres when we fled.'

'Good news. He might be useful,' Cyrus said. 'But he's too far away right now to do us any good,' he said, nodding towards the three soldiers approaching them.

'Ho, you people,' the youngest one said. 'What do you want down here? This wharf is a protected area until that ship sets sail.'

Cyrus smiled disarmingly. 'And you are?'

'A soldier of his majesty's Shield and not answerable to you, sir,' he replied. 'We must ask you to leave.'

'Is the King on board?' Cyrus continued, ignoring the young man and turning towards the eldest one in the trio. Cyrus did not recognise him but he hoped the man was old enough to have a long memory.

'What's it to you, may we ask?' the older man said.

The first soldier bristled at being ignored as he was obviously of superior rank and Cyrus could not help but smile as the older man gently raised his hand. It was not the act of a subordinate but it was not confrontational and his younger superior wisely held his tongue.

'The King will be interested to meet me.'

'Your name?' the same man now asked.

'Cyrus.'

A uncommon name but certainly not rare. The man nodded.

Cyrus could see the younger fellow was about to explode into a tirade of orders, presumably along the lines of asking them to leave, so he cut across him before a sound came out.

'It's Kyt Cyrus,' he said firmly, his piercing look narrowing and hardening as he impaled the eldest soldier with a look once legendary amongst the King's Guard.

The older man's attention was equally riveted now. He frowned. 'Very familiar although forgotten by most. I never knew him, of course, so I am not the one who can verify the face that goes with such a memorable name.'

'But he can,' Cyrus said, nodding towards a very senior ranking soldier coming down the gangplank of *The Raven*.

They looked over. 'Now look here,' the young guard said. 'If you think I am bringing him into this conversation, you are sadly mistaken. He is not disturbed happily by trite requests from strangers.'

'I am no stranger to him, boy, and there is nothing trite about my coming here.' Cyrus's voice had an edge. 'Fetch him.'

The soldier could take the insult of being ignored but

being referred to as some sort of snivelling lad was an indignity he would not abide.

'You and your friends can either leave of your own accord or I shall have you forcibly escorted from this wharf. Make a decision.'

Hela had to smile to herself. Cyrus was so calm. He seemed to pour more scorn with his eyes than any words could. She saw that he simply looked beyond the officer giving orders and addressed the elder subordinate.

'Fetch Herek.' It was no polite request.

The older man nodded and stepped away.

'You will do no such thing,' the officer commanded. 'I am in charge here,' he said, realising it was already too late. His superiority had been calmly and brilliantly undermined as the older soldier shrugged and continued to approach Prime Herek.

'Guards!' the younger man yelled to some men loading goods onto a cart.

'Oh be still!' Cyrus cut in, his voice hard and commanding.

Sarel and Hela had to stop themselves laughing at the poor speechless soldier. Rubyn looked away, knowing how humiliating this would be for a young man in front of women and himself.

The guards ran up but the officer could already see it was useless. Herek was looking over – he was squinting towards their group and then beckoned.

'Thank you,' Cyrus said to the officer. His words were polite. The tone was not.

The others silently followed Cyrus as he walked towards where the Prime of Tallinor stood and watched them approach. He had his captains nearby. They also stopped their activity as the group arrived. The Prime of Tallinor stared. It was as though all the frenzied activity of the wharf was muted as he stood there in obvious shock; his ruddy complexion paling to waxy.

'Herek,' Cyrus spoke very softly and they could hear the catch in his voice too. 'It's good to see you, man.'

The Prime's mouth opened and closed. He shook his head.

Cyrus saluted before clasping his friend's hand and then briefly hugging him. Herek, the shorter of the two, returned the Tallinese handshake, clearly moved. Everyone around them had stopped their tasks now and watched in surprise their normally dour Prime displaying such an outpouring of emotion. Both men began to laugh and baffled smiles began to appear all about them.

They finally stood back from each other. 'What? Where? Why?' Herek said and grinned. It was the old trio of questions Cyrus used to impress upon his captains over and again. *Facts!* he would argue. *Give me the facts. Then we'll talk about the solution.*

Cyrus acknowledged the old line. 'Indeed, Herek. You are owed much explanation but our time is very short. We come on urgent business for the King.'

'He is on urgent business too,' Herek said with a sigh. 'I am imagining that your urgent business and his urgent business are one and the same.'

Cyrus nodded more sombrely now. 'You would be right. Herek, this,' he said reaching for Sarel and gently pulling her forwards, 'is none other than Her Majesty, Queen Sarel of Cipres.'

Loud murmuring broke out and soldiers took off their caps. Herek looked astonished, his eyes flicking between

Sarel and Cyrus. His former prime nodded and Herek went down on one knee. 'Your majesty.'

She stole a quick glance towards Hela whose eyes told her to go ahead. She was Queen. She must now act like one. Sarel bent to take Herek's hand. 'Please,' she said, encouraging him to stand. 'You and your men,' she smiled, looking about him, 'are most gracious. We come with news for King Gyl. I beg an audience, sir.'

'And you will have one,' Herek assured her.

Sarel turned and introduced Hela. 'This brave woman helped me to escape the usurper's clutch. We owe much to her for keeping the royal line of Cipres intact.'

Herek bowed to Hela. She liked him already.

'And this,' Cyrus said, putting his hand on Rubyn's shoulder, 'is the son of Torkyn Gynt.' He carefully did not mention Alyssa as all these men, he knew, were loyal to Lorys and now to his son. They had served Queen Alyssa briefly too and all would know her as wife to their former king and now King's Mother. It would not do to inflame emotions at this delicate stage.

Herek's response was subtle. He took Rubyn's hand in the Tallinese way. 'I think I could have guessed at your parentage. You are most welcome here, Rubyn Gynt.'

'Sarel!' They all turned at the sudden outburst as a young man nimbly ran down the gangplank.

The Queen smiled demurely.

'Locky,' Hela said.

'Light! How come you're here?' Locky asked the women, his eyes shining.

Sarel nodded. 'It is good to see you again, Master Gylbyt.'

'Thank you, your majesty,' he replied, remembering himself. 'Er, they call me Captain Gylbyt now,' he said, casting a glance at her male companions, his eyes resting on the tall young man with fair hair who stood beside her. He nodded towards him. 'You remind me of someone,' Locky muttered, not actually saying that the man reminded him of two people very strongly.

'I am Rubyn Gynt, son of Torkyn Gynt and—'

'And I am Kyt Cyrus,' he cut across Rubyn. *Best not to talk of your mother in this company, son,* he cautioned.

Locky nodded and then smiled at Hela. 'Hello again,' he said, real warmth in his voice.

'Brave Locky,' she replied. 'You made it. We all knew you would.'

He grinned.

'If you are captain of this ship now, may I ask where Quist is?' Cyrus asked.

'Dead.' Locky answered flatly. 'At the hands of Goth.'

Now both Prime and former prime bristled and glanced at each other.

'It is in hand, Locky,' Cyrus reassured him. 'We have much to tell you all.'

'Come, then,' Herek said. 'The King must hear it first.'

Alyssa shielded her spirit as she felt herself coming closer to Xantia. She had gathered in the trace, pulling herself nearer as she hurtled blindly, relying on her senses. She wondered if Xantia would be waiting; ready to strike at her? Alyssa slowed herself. The sense that she was now upon her target was very strong. She must be wary. And suddenly she could see her, standing in a room – a beautiful room – her eyes riveted on the two people with whom she shared it.

The god, Orlac, was laughing at her child again. She could see Lauryn backed against a window. He was taunting her and her heart broke to see Lauryn pull her very thin satin wrap closer around her petite frame. He would strike again soon – how many times already, she wondered? But Alyssa had plans for him too.

Xantia! she called into the woman's mind. *I am here, you black-hearted witch. Come face your destroyer.*

The Raven had sailed three days and was now barely hours from docking in Cipres. Locky could not understand it. The voyage, in good weather, took about six days, and yet here they were on the third night virtually at their destination. The ship was fast, for sure, but not this fast – he had sailed these waters enough times to know this crossing was impossible in the time they had achieved.

He gave an order which was passed on to the lookout and then his attention came to rest on Rubyn. It then shifted to Sarel whose eyes, he had already noticed, rarely left the newcomer. Rubyn seemed oblivious to her gaze and somehow Locky knew not only did the son of Torkyn Gynt wield a power which had brought them here so soon but he also wielded a different sort of power over a queen. Locky swallowed hard and then took a gulp of the fresh breeze. He had lost her then – not that she was ever his – but somehow he had hoped their paths would cross again. That final glance in the Heartwood had spoken much. He knew he had not imagined it. Sarel had communicated more than just camaraderie brought on by their terrible circumstances. But in his absence, whilst he had galloped away to entreat a king, another man had stepped into focus.

And why not? he asked himself as he swung back to face the sea, banging his fist on the rail. He is everything she would want in a man and empowered to boot. Why

would she ever look at a common sailor, a man whose
only ambition was to be a soldier?

It was as if Herek could read his melancholy thoughts.

'Well done, Captain Locky.'

He worshipped the Prime. 'Thank you, sir, though I
fear the swift sailing has been out of my hands.'

Herek leaned over the rail, matching Locky's stance.
'You've done your bit, lad. You've impressed everyone
including the King, since your arrival. Whatever other
forces are prevailing we'll take if they help us in our
mission.'

'Yes, sir.'

'I understand it not either, boy. We are navigating
through strange times and even stranger events. If the
likes of Torkyn Gynt are on our side, we are fortunate.
He is a good man.'

'That he is, Prime Herek. No question.'

'And so his son comes from good stock . . . mother
and father.'

Locky nodded.

'We must help one another. No room for pettiness.'

'My heart is not petty, sir.'

'Ah, so I have been following the wrong thought
pathway, son. My apologies. I cannot advise your heart
. . . only your head. She is a queen, Locky.'

'As was his mother, sir. They are well suited.'

Herek sighed and squeezed Locky's shoulder. It was
probably best to leave the lad alone to lick his wounds.
Soon he would receive the news that he was to be trained
and appointed as captain to Herek, if he still wanted to
join the King's Guard, although the Prime could not
understand why he would give up life on the sea. He was

obviously an excellent sailor and already a captain. With a good crew, perhaps ridding *The Raven* of her pirate mantle, Locklyn Gylbyt could be a rising star as a merchant and sea trader, buying and selling legitimate goods. He would talk to the young man when this was over – perhaps on the voyage back to Tallinor.

Herek looked over to where his King and their guests stood on deck. Gyl and Cyrus – similar characters, though Gyl had some years to put under his belt to achieve Cyrus's level of poise and experience. Herek felt quite the odd man out, obliged to hand over the reins of command to his former chief. Cyrus had sensed this of course and had moved to quash that inclination very quickly. Cyrus had not returned to claim back his position; he had come back with a far loftier mantle falling on his broad shoulders.

Herek and Gyl had listened in some awe as Cyrus, over these past three days, had related the most incredible tale. Gyl accepted it immediately, which surprised Herek at first – but on reflection he realised that Gyl had learned to accept a great deal of strange and challenging notions since Torkyn Gynt had come back from the dead. And if Gynt could, why not Cyrus? They had learned as much as Cyrus could tell them of his recent past. Gyl had drained a cup of wine at one point and then stood and paced the chamber distractedly. Herek recalled the conversation.

'And so you were captured by the Heartwood and—'

'Not captured, sire. Invited to remain.'

Gyl had looked at Cyrus and been met by an equally firm gaze. There was no guile in Cyrus. Herek had long ago related tales to the young Gyl of the legendary Prime. The King had grown up on stories of Kyt Cyrus and felt no little sense of wonder to be in his presence now.

Gyl had nodded, although it was obvious he found this story hard to swallow.

Herek remembered how Cyrus had continued the story; telling them about raising the weakened newborn with the aid of a silver wolf and the god of the Forest. When the boy was strong enough, they were transported.

Cyrus had given the same details as those he had given not so many days ago to Tor and Alyssa, citing how at Orlac's arrival in Cipres, Rubyn had fainted and then they had been called back by a mysterious messenger, called Yargo.

The King's eyebrows had lifted at this. The story was getting stranger in its telling. He continued to pace. 'Go on,' he had encouraged.

And Cyrus had, bringing them up to date with the meeting with Rubyn's parents in the Heartwood.

'As far-fetched as this all sounds, it correlates with Locky's tale of my mother's adventures in the Heartwood,' he had said, ruefully, digging out a pale green disk from his pocket. 'She sent me this. It is hers alone. I know she is there.'

'But she is no longer there, sire.'

At this King Gyl had stopped his pacing. 'Where is she?' he had demanded.

'I left her and Gynt making plans to take the butcher, Goth, into the mountains.'

'Why?'

'Apparently there is a valley where all the surviving sentients Goth tortured were taken.'

'Did you know of this?' Gyl had asked Herek.

And Herek had shaken his head, as baffled as his King at the news.

'It was at Lorys's instructions,' Cyrus then confirmed. 'He wanted them taken somewhere safe and remote where they could live without fear of further repercussions from the inquisitors. I imagine he assembled a small and reliable team of soldiers, Herek. He would not have told me either . . . don't feel bad.'

'No I don't. I feel proud that he made such a decision. It never sat comfortably with me that we perpetrated such terrible things in the name of our realm.'

Cyrus had only nodded. He too understood the feeling of helplessness and recalled many conversations he had held with King Lorys to stop the madness and cruelty.

'So what are you telling me, Cyrus?' Gyl had asked. 'My mother is taking Goth for judgement by the people over whom he made judgement for years?'

'Yes, that's exactly what I'm telling you, sire.'

'She'll be the death of me, that woman,' the King had muttered and yet no one in that chamber missed the tinge of pride in his tone.

'They asked me to get to Cipres and get their daughter back. I thought it best to meet with you first, sire; prevent any . . . well, any unnecessary show of strength being visited on our neighbours. Hela can get us into the palace and Rubyn has the . . .' he had searched again for the right word, 'the skills to get us back out with Lauryn.'

Gyl had seen the sense of his reasoning and immediately called for word to be sent, ship to ship, for all his men to turn back. The two ships following had slowed, confused, and finally turned, uneasy about leaving their King to sail into the unknown. But everyone on board the principal ship knew it would take a covert arrival to allow them to somehow snatch Lauryn back. Arriving aggressively with weapons and soldiers would prevent any surprise element or indeed the opportunity to reach her.

And now they found themselves on the deck, not long from mooring at the famous Ciprean docks. Thankfully it was night and all was still.

Herek approached and heard the King say, 'Do you have a plan?'

Cyrus shook his head. 'No, sire. But trust me.'

Herek had laughed then. 'You haven't changed a bit.'

And then Cyrus had turned serious. 'We take as few people as possible ashore.'

The others had nodded.

'Providing you don't say "and the King stays here because he is to be protected" . . . in which case I shall pull rank and throw you off this ship, former prime or not,' said Gyl.

Cyrus grinned. 'Hela to get us in. Rubyn is critical. Sarel.' He saw both men baulk at the Queen's name. 'My bet is that the impostor will flee . . . he will head to Tallinor. She is safe from him for now.'

'How can you know this?' Gyl asked.

'I have explained I am Paladin now. I know what Orlac wants. And once we remove Lauryn, his desire will not be to remain in Cipres. He holds her purely to attract her father. Without the bait, he must hunt him another way.'

'What does he want?' Herek questioned.

'Torkyn Gynt.' They had both looked amazed at this and Cyrus nodded. 'Gynt and his family. They all threaten him.'

'I don't understand,' the King admitted.

'And the history as to why this is, is too long in the telling for now,' Cyrus offered sagely. 'Another time and I will tell you a fascinating story.'

He continued.

'Sarel must come so that we secure her throne and get her crowned Queen. Hela will see to all of this once she can gather the Ciprean Council of Elders, if they are alive,' he said ruefully. 'Herek, you'll need to handpick half a dozen men. We are dealing with a mightily empowered soul here. No weapons will help us. What we need is stealth and cunning and some of the same sentient power to wield of our own. Locky must have *The Raven* ready to sail.'

They nodded again.

'Are you sure I cannot persuade you to remain, your majesty?' he asked Gyl. 'Your life is worth everything right now to the Tallinese people.'

'Yes, and the woman who would give me its heir is in that palace. No, Cyrus. I will be at your side to claim back my betrothed.'

This shocked everyone. So far the women and Rubyn had been silent, although listening carefully. When everyone's exclamations had died down, they saw that Gyl looked embarrassed.

'Forgive me. No one knows of this yet; I pray you don't speak of it outside of these ears.'

'And does your intended bride know yet?' It was Rubyn, posing his question with a deadpan face.

Gyl bristled but held his famous temper in check. 'I understand she is your sister, Rubyn—'

'Sire, I do not even know her. Feel no embarrassment on my behalf.'

'I don't, be sure of it. I just thought it polite to tell you that I am very much in love with Lauryn and I think I am right in saying she feels the same way about me. We just did not have a chance to make such a thing public before her capture.'

This is not helping, Cyrus cautioned.

He's just awfully cocksure of himself isn't he?

I hope so, damn it! He's the King of Tallinor and just a year or so older than you, lad. You have no idea what this young man is up against or has faced in recent weeks.

'My apologies, your majesty. Lauryn is fortunate indeed.'

Gyl sensibly left it alone.

Later as they were mooring — everyone dressed in civilian clothes and Locky making his profuse apologies to the port's master for arriving at such an hour — Cyrus took his chance to speak with the King privately.

'Your majesty, I want to say I'm sorry for the lad's curious manner.'

Gyl eyed Cyrus. He had liked him on first sight, recognising someone of similar ilk to himself and his father. Cyrus had continued to make an impression on the young King throughout the short voyage and he was much relieved for the older soldier's wise head and counsel.

'He is a strange sort.'

'Rubyn has not led a normal life. He is very . . . disconnected from people. I think he needs to learn a great deal about social etiquette, particularly in the presence of his sovereign.'

Gyl smiled and Cyrus relaxed. He already recognised some of Lorys's traits in the youngster — from his swaggering walk to his easy manner — he would make a good King with the right people around him.

'No offence taken. I can't say this to anyone around me, of course, but I'm learning this royal business as I go. Everyone, except Herek I have to say, seems to think that with the crown came instant wisdom and experience at being a king. I know nothing about this, Cyrus. I am a soldier, like you. I can fight and ride, I can drink and swear with the best of them. And I can lead men. I'm hoping it's the latter which will get me through. It was thrust upon me – I didn't ask for it, didn't even wish for it, though I would be lying if I said I hadn't entertained the notion that it would be perfect to have Lorys as a father. He and I were such good friends.' Gyl sounded sad.

Cyrus nodded. 'He had his failings but he was the best king our realm has ever seen. I don't know you Gyl, but if you open your heart to the sentients and remember where you've come from, I think you'll make an even better king than your father. Choose your counsel wisely . . . and keep Herek close. There is no more loyal subject than he.' Flouting protocol, the soldier tapped the King on his shoulder in a fatherly gesture. Then he turned to join the others.

'Cyrus!' Gyl called him back. 'Could I persuade you to be part of my counsel? I need men like you. Men who know battle as much as protocol and who especially know Tallinor inside and out. Will you join me?'

Cyrus smiled gently and kindly. 'Perhaps we should have this conversation when you have your bride back safely in your arms and I'm not buried on Ciprean soil.'

'We're all coming back to this ship, Cyrus. Alive!' the King said, fiercely.

'I pray you are right, sire.'

31

A Mother's Ire

Xantia flinched. Alyssa!

Be very sure you want to meet me here, Xantia. There's no turning back. It was Alyssa's turn to taunt.

Xantia growled, as one possessed.

Dorgryl was shocked at Alyssa's sudden interruption and he turned away from Lauryn, who had also heard her mother's mocking words. She did not waste a moment in adding her own derision for the woman she hated.

'Scared? I knew you would be, you cringing cowardly wretch.'

'Xantia! Be still,' Dorgryl commanded, not sure whether to grab his accomplice or strike the woman who jeered at her.

Lauryn pushed her luck. 'Hide behind him, Xantia. My mother is too strong for you.'

That was all it took. Inflamed with fury, Dorgryl made the wrong decision. He cast his powers, letting out a roar, and Lauryn was hurled across the room. She crumpled in the same manner as Xantia once had at the end of Orlac's anger. She lay still and unconscious and was no longer of any use to Dorgryl or his planned entertainment for the next hour or more. In that moment his attention was diverted to glance at Lauryn, Xantia screamed her own fury and, unsure whether she could do it but determined to meet the destined confrontation between herself and her long-time enemy, she lifted free of herself and sent her spirit travelling at speed to do away, once and for all, with Alyssa.

Dorgryl spun around at the sound of Xantia's body collapsing to the floor and this time his fury bubbled over. He smashed the exquisitely plastered wall with his fist, breaking bones in Orlac's beautiful hand.

One other mind had heard Alyssa's taunts – hidden as he was in the deepest recesses of himself – and smiled. His silence these past three days had not only surprised Dorgryl but quietly troubled him. Nothing he said or did seemed to awaken the anger of Orlac and to Dorgryl this was a bad sign.

Had the young god given up? Or was he plotting something?

Orlac had indeed been plotting; waiting for a moment to strike. He desperately hoped Lauryn had heard his private communication – he knew Dorgryl had not, which meant he had a chance. And now this. Lauryn's mother was indeed a courageous woman and although he could not imagine how she had achieved such a thing, he thanked his few blessings that somehow she had managed to pull off what was surely a masterstroke.

Orlac was not aware that Alyssa had the blood of a god running in her veins; it would have shocked him – as it would have Dorgryl – if he had known of her mother's identity. Still, in his ignorance Orlac silently thanked her because he now had a slim chance of giving freedom to her daughter. That he loved Lauryn there was no doubt, although he refused to allow his mind to listen to his heart. He had tried to convince himself that she was merely the bait for the father and when that had failed – when he found himself unable to tear his eyes from her or dismiss the lilt of her voice and her laugh from his mind – he had told himself that she was merely a diversion, nothing more. By keeping her close, the father was kept occupied too – defensive and scared for his child. Torkyn Gynt would never be able to mount any serious threat to Orlac as long as Lauryn was in his possession, or so he reminded himself when the mere thought of seeing her threatened to undermine his driving need to destroy her father.

What he had not counted on was Dorgryl's sudden change in tolerance. He thought he might have sensed the older god's power gathering to strike but he had not. Dorgryl had shielded himself superbly and when he had taken Orlac's body from him, it was done with such speed and might, his nephew had been caught unawares. Worse, he realised it was because his mind had been lost in his thoughts about Lauryn.

Lauryn had paid shockingly for his mistake. Orlac had been forced to bear witness to her despair, humiliation and pain. Dorgryl had relished every moment but Orlac had made a promise he would make his uncle pay.

At some point during those three traumatic days, Orlac's perception of his own destiny re-shaped itself as he acknowledged that ridding himself of Dorgryl – and not of Torkyn Gynt – was his first priority. Gynt suddenly seemed to matter less, as did the razing of Tallinor and its people. Dorgryl had to be beaten.

Whatever it takes, he repeated time and again to himself as his body, without his permission, inflicted its terrible humiliations on the woman he just wanted to love. In her strength in not capitulating Orlac found renewed faith – a power to be still . . . to be silent . . . to outwit what he now believed was the darkest, most agile mind in the Host and thus in all the worlds.

He must destroy Dorgryl but he had no idea how. His only immediate thought was to free Lauryn from the god's clutch and Alyssa had given him a tiny sliver of light which he saw as hope that he could succeed.

Inwardly, as he felt Dorgryl rage about him, he cheered his brother's wife, begging any god who heard his private plea to help her succeed.

One did . . . and obliged.

Here! Xantia shrieked.

Alyssa did not react immediately. Everyone she loved and had ever loved seemed to crystallise before her and she found herself mentally farewelling each one . . . for she knew this was her end. It was her destiny, she realised, to rid the Land of Xantia.

She had not realised she had any substance; had thought she was just some sort of spiritual presence but now that she actually looked she saw a softly shimmering gleam. She was an apparition of herself. Alyssa turned and there stood Xantia, shimmering darkly and true to the form that Alyssa remembered; older, perhaps more voluptuous and even more beautiful in a sinister sort of way.

Hello, Xantia, she said sweetly. *I'm surprised you came. Do you think I fear you?*

Not at all. I thought you were a slave to him . . . to Orlac.

Ha! Orlac?

I've seen you with him.

Your eyes deceive you. It was Xantia's turn to sound cloying. *You see only Orlac's shell. You hear and witness the spirit of the greatest of all gods . . . his name is Dorgryl.*

Dorgryl! Alyssa shuddered. She had read of the god in Nanak's Writings: Darganoth's brother, Dorgryl had unsuccessfully attempted to usurp the throne of the Host from its rightful King. He had been cast into the Bleak as eternal punishment. But now, it seemed, he had somehow escaped.

She realised, as Xantia's face broke into a snarl which passed as her smile these days, that this was why her daughter had been calling to Orlac, imploring him to help her.

I shall have to kill you, Xantia said.

Is that so? Perhaps you're too late.

When I'm done with you, Alyssa, and I return—

Ah! So you don't know. I did try to warn you.

Warn me?

Are you aware of where you are? I am no longer attached to Tallinor. I've made my choice and so have you.

Xantia faltered. It was the first trip of her confidence.

Alyssa shook her head as condescendingly as she could. *Let me enlighten you. We are in a place known as the Bleak. Have you not heard of it?*

Xantia, in spite of herself, obediently shook her head.

Oh, then you will find this intriguing, Alyssa said.

I have no time for this! Xantia spat.

But you do . . . you have all the time in the world.

Xantia laughed but it was tinged with nervousness. *Where are we?* she yelled.

I've told you. The Bleak. From where there is no return . . . for either of us. Alyssa took great relish in saying the final words.

You lie!

No need for lies now. Try to go back and you'll see you cannot. This is a place of eternal death, Xantia.

Her enemy shimmered.

Alyssa continued. *I have already said my goodbyes. I'm not sure you had a chance but then it matters not to me.*

You were never as strong in the darker Power Arts as I, Alyssa. You will be the one to suffer. Xantia began to circle.

Alyssa remained still despite Xantia's threatening movements. She laughed. *You don't seem to understand. None of that matters now. Nothing between us matters any more. I have already destroyed you by luring you here.*

And what about your husband? Xantia sneered.

He will prevail.

It was Xantia's turn to laugh.

Not against Dorgryl, I promise you.

Alyssa bluffed. *Oh no? Even now Dorgryl is weakened, without you. He made the wrong choice – his anger dulls his mind and he makes foolish decisions. Mark my words . . . it will be his undoing.*

Xantia growled.

Whatever you do to me has no effect on what occurs in the Land. We are no longer of our world, Xantia. He should have stopped you coming. Instead he chose to hurt my daughter some more. He will pay the ultimate price. Enjoy the Bleak, Xantia. It's perfect for you.

Xantia's patience snapped and she cast out towards where she knew her body was . . . and felt nothing. Anger and hate spilled over as she hurled her magics towards her enemy. She expected to see Alyssa scream out in agony as the first powerful blow struck home. What Xantia did not know, could not know, was that her former friend did not possess a weak, wild magic like her own. She had no inkling that the spiritual person before her was part god, with powers she had not even begun to tap into. It was perhaps the greatest shock of Xantia's young life to see the shimmering Alyssa suddenly flash to golden.

Is that it? Alyssa asked, her voice hard.

Xantia's shimmering presence threw herself towards the woman who taunted her, biting, scratching, tearing Alyssa again and again, having no effect on the golden woman, blazing with power.

What are you? Xantia whispered through her sobs.

She is a god, said a new and terrifying voice, but Xantia, in her excitement at the arrival of an ally, did not hear the warning. She ran towards the red, shimmering mist. *Dorgryl! I knew you would come for me.*

Alyssa's spiritual heart sank.

Dorgryl ignored the cringing woman. Instead he addressed Alyssa directly. *Very impressive. I had no idea a god's blood ran in your veins.*

The red mist moved threateningly towards her and Alyssa knew her fight was lost.

She had failed her own destiny.

Shadows moved stealthily from the Ciprean docks. Against his better judgement, but trusting the instincts of the former prime, Gyl agreed for only a handful of them to make their way to the palace.

The King, a soldier at heart, saw safety in numbers and might. They were six, two of whom were women and one a lad who could no more lift a sword than fly. Although he quickly reassessed that opinion – he had no idea of what Rubyn was capable of in terms of his sentient ability. Nevertheless, how could three fighting men hold off a city if it chose to rise against them? He permitted himself no further fearful thoughts. At the end of this journey was Lauryn and his mind followed only that single track, not for a second allowing himself to consider whether she was still alive.

Herek meanwhile was permitting his mind to wander down all of its terrifying paths, the worst of which being that he and his Prime – he could think of the brilliant Kyt Cyrus as nothing less – were now defending two monarchs, both of whom were putting themselves into the most dangerous of situations. That he would give his life for his King was not in question but his life was not enough to save Gyl if things went badly here. He followed in a grim silence, stuck in gloomy thoughts of how to save his monarch.

For several hours Rubyn had been casting towards Lauryn. He did not know her trace but he used the familiar trace of Cyrus and hoped one of her Paladin, if not she herself, would hear and respond. So far there was only a bleak silence. He understood that Lauryn perhaps might have shielded but he had no reason to believe Juno nor Adongo would.

With Cyrus's encouragement he kept trying, finally suggesting that he believed Orlac might have somehow cut off the Link to Lauryn's Paladin.

Their plan was simple, if audacious. Hela and Cyrus would go first, testing the way was clear and assuring safe entry into one of the palace's secret passageways. The others would follow, then Gyl, Rubyn and Cyrus, once inside the palace, would find Lauryn. They made it no more complicated than that. That was their one task – to get her and bring her out safely and back to the waiting ship. If necessary, they would cast off without the others. All were in agreement with this.

Meanwhile, Herek, Cyrus and Hela would get Sarel to the elders of the city. When Herek had asked how they could prove her birthright, Sarel produced a ring.

'This is my mother's . . . and her mother's before her. It belonged to all of my grandmothers down the ages. It is the great seal of Cipres.'

Even Hela had been surprised. 'I told you to bring nothing,' she had admonished.

'I am the rightful Queen of Cipres, Hela. This ring only left my mother at her death. I have hated keeping it secreted away. And from this night on,' she said, slipping it onto her finger, 'it will only leave my hand in death too.' Then she had lifted her face in defiance, daring any of them to argue it with her.

Gyl had wrapped his own large hand around hers. Those present sensed the strong symbolism of this gesture. 'You will wear it for many decades, Sarel, I promise. And if you ever need Tallinor's help to defend your crown, I pledge it now.'

All were moved by his powerful words. Cyrus had quietly shaken his head. Lorys would never have thought to create a union between these two realms and yet his son had achieved it in a simple, proud statement. Great things might yet come of this strange wheel which was turning.

For his part, Gyl had been impressed with Sarel from

their first meeting. She was so terribly young and yet her grooming for sovereignty was not only impeccable, but her composure and inherent royalty were so strong that he envied her all those years of knowing her destiny. If only he had known his destiny; if only he had known his father from birth, he would already be a far better King to Tallinor. He could not dwell on that now but he took heart from the faces around him who appreciated the wisdom of his pledge.

They found themselves now on the fringe of the city. It was far quieter than Hela believed it should be.

'How long will you give us?' she asked, deliberately not looking at Cyrus – but in these strange and threatening days since she had woken up beside him, she felt that delicious warmth when he answered.

Even in this situation – so fraught with danger – she found herself admiring his voice, his steady gaze, the way in which he shifted his tall body onto one foot. Suddenly everything about this man seemed to outshine any other. She fully accepted it was her failing – her lovestruck heart seeing him as so perfect – but she could do nothing about it. His mere presence seemed to control her which was irritating because she was a strong, independent woman. She wondered vaguely if she was having the same effect on him. She doubted it. He had not referred to their night of passion once since that morning in Ildagarth, nor had he shown her any particular affection, although she felt she was searching for every nuance. Every smile felt like a thousand fragranced flowers dropping on her. If she was affecting him in any way, he certainly did not show it. And what annoyed her most of all was that it was this remote manner of his which most attracted her. His damaged soul he kept so private and yet she had tapped into it that night and truly believed she had offered some healing.

She turned towards his voice, trying to concentrate on the matter at hand.

Cyrus sensed extreme nervousness in this small group. All but Rubyn seemed to feel they were walking towards certain death.

'Herek, remember the Shield song?' he asked.

Herek frowned. 'Yes, sir, of course.'

Cyrus grinned. 'Then sing it and when it's finished – all ten tedious verses, mind, and with the chorus between each – come after us.'

Herek smiled and Gyl joined him – he knew the song well too.

'Oh, and Herek,' Cyrus added, a note of irony touching his words. 'I shall order you back to the ship if you don't stop calling me sir.'

The Prime nodded. 'Habits die hard,' he admitted. 'It's good to have you back.'

The two men clasped hands in the Tallinese soldiers' salute.

'Go now,' Herek said softly to the only man he had ever truly admired. 'Make our way safe.'

Cyrus and Hela stole off into the night leaving Rubyn and Sarel with bemused expressions as the King and his Prime, comically, very softly, broke into song.

Orlac felt the oppressive presence of Dorgryl lift away from him without warning. He was momentarily disorientated but then he was rising, pushing himself upwards and outwards into his own body, claiming it back.

She did it! he thought. Alyssa – may the gods bless her

— had lured Dorgryl from his cosy spot. It was all he needed. Orlac turned back, searching for Lauryn with the blurry vision he was desperately trying to readjust. There she was, slumped pitifully in the corner, her robe disarrayed, showing her nakedness which seemed somehow shameful to him. He took no pleasure in seeing the gentle curves and soft skin.

He realised he was holding his breath as he softly pulled the satin robe around her neatly and retied the sash.

'Come, beloved,' he whispered. 'You do not belong here amongst us.'

Orlac lifted Lauryn to cradle her in his arms. This was the most intimate moment he had experienced with her and he could not help but appreciate the irony that she should be unconscious as he laid his first soft kiss against her lips. She stirred and he pulled away, lingering a moment or two to gaze at her face.

Under normal circumstances to carry Lauryn would be effortless for Orlac but, still feeling awkward in his body, he swayed as if drunk as he hurried out of her chambers down the corridors. He broke into a run, realising Dorgryl could return at any moment, taking the marble steps three at a time. Where he was taking her he had no idea. He just had to get her out of the palace and beg someone to take the limp body from him and hide her away.

Cyrus and Hela did their best to walk casually but their hearts were pounding; Hela's from fear and Cyrus's from the thrill of action. Suddenly he felt like the Prime again and without thinking he took Hela's hand, whispering, 'I think we must hurry.'

She nodded, relieved to feel the reassurance of his grip

and they increased their pace. 'It's just around here,' she whispered back.

As they swung around a corner, they could see a group of the Ciprean guard walking towards them. They had not been spotted yet and although neither could think of a single reason to be worried, both felt instantly wary and guilty. Cyrus pulled Hela into a recess in the outer wall of the palace and immediately embraced her.

'What are you doing?' she asked, confused.

'What does it look like?' he murmured, pushing his lips against hers.

A few moments later, the men passed by and several whistled. Hela pulled back and whispered so low even Cyrus had to strain to hear her.

'Let me talk. Your accent is strongly Tallinese.'

He nodded.

Hela and the men spoke. She immediately adopted a coquettish pose, glancing towards Cyrus several times and then laughing with the men. He could not hear but he guessed it was at his expense. The men moved on and she returned.

'What was that all about?' he asked.

'Information.'

'And what have we learned?'

'That there is no guard for another hour on the western side. It is perfect. We can enter the main grounds from there. I know a way.'

'What did you tell them?'

She shook her head. 'Nothing.'

'Hela. You forget that I am a soldier. Guards are always posted around any palace. There's no such thing as no guard for another hour.'

She looked at him but remained silent.

'What did you tell them?'

'That we are lovers and that I need somewhere nearby for us to lie undisturbed for a few minutes.'

'And why would they do this for two lovers . . . strangers to them?'

'Because I have promised something in return.'

He looked suddenly appalled as understanding dawned.

'Cyrus, we have no time for this!' she groaned beneath her breath. 'We are trying to save lives!'

He blinked. She was right. Whatever it took, the destiny of the young woman they were trying to take away from Cipres and that of the young woman they were returning to Cipres, were far greater than any individual sacrifice.

Cyrus nodded sharply. 'What now?' he said, looking around.

'I'll show you how to get in. Then we go back for the others. Herek and I will take Sarel. You three somehow get the girl.'

The red mist had no form but Alyssa could feel its cold touch and hear the deep voice like a chill within her.

She is nothing, it said. *But you should be heartily afraid of me.*

Get away, demon, she spat, the hard words firing her anger, helping her to remain brave.

It laughed; genuine amusement. *Welcome, Alyssa. Do you like where they put me for eternity?*

She backed away from the mist which continued to drift towards her.

I am already dead, Dorgryl. Why do you waste your time with me?

I'm not sure.

Destroy her! Xantia screamed from behind.

Why? it asked. *Because you could not?*

Give her to me, then. Let me try, Xantia offered, her bravado increasing with his presence.

Shut up! it said. *You bore me. You are no match for her.*

Dorgryl! I was always stronger than her.

He laughed again. It was riddled with scorn. *Xantia, you have pitiful wild magic. Nothing more than circus tricks. Your companion here is so much more. Look at her. She is beautiful isn't she? Shining and shimmering in her golden god's light.*

God?

Alyssa lifted her chin with defiance. She enjoyed watching the confusion on Xantia's face.

You speak lies, Xantia spat.

But I do not! Dogryl countered angrily. And then he laughed again, lacing it with irony. *She is a clever woman isn't she?* he said, as if to himself.

Of whom do you speak? Alyssa replied, knowing the longer she could keep the red mist occupied, the greater chance her daughter had of escape — if she could gather her wits.

The red mist shimmered brightly. *I think you know.*

Alyssa shook her head.

Now that you are here before me I realise your likeness to her is striking. I never knew. She kept a grand secret.

Move away from her, Dorgryl! commanded a new voice.

Ah, I wondered when you might join us.

You were stupid to come back here. Now you are trapped.

Xantia felt her confusion and anger spill out. *Who is this?* she shrieked.

Can't you tell? Dorgryl said calmly. *This is Lys, the*

Custodian. Can you not see the resemblance? She is your friend's mother. How about a deal, Lys?

No negotiation, Lys replied, moving behind her daughter. Alyssa had not so much as glanced her way yet but Lys could tell she was shimmering with relief.

Oh, but I think you will this time. I can guess what your plan is. And I will not permit her to go.

You know nothing, Lys said cautiously.

Choose, he said, enjoying himself. *You can keep me here as your prisoner and thus imprison your daughter because I will never permit her to leave; or you can let me go back and you can do what you will.*

Alyssa turned ferociously. *Don't you dare,* she said, clapping eyes for the first time on her mother. She had no idea what they were talking about but it smacked of a bargain. Dorgryl was negotiating for his life back in Orlac, back to torment Lauryn, back to destroy Tor. It would make her own death pointless; make her a failure.

Lys knew it was she who was trapped. She turned sad grey-green eyes towards her daughter. *I cannot abandon you again. You must come with me.*

Aha! Dorgryl said, shimmering brightly. *You see, Alyssa. She gave you away once. She will not let it happen again.*

No! screamed Alyssa.

I can't, Lys said, her golden-honey hair shimmering in her golden light.

My children! Alyssa wept and sank to her knees. *Save them, mother. Save Tor. I beg you.*

Dorgryl giggled. *Touching, very touching. Farewell, Xantia. I must flee before she changes her mind. I can do nothing for you. But I did warn you not to follow your petty hates. Live long,* he said.

Alyssa shouted her despair and her wails were accompanied by the cries of Xantia.

Xantia, spoke Lys, her voice commanding now. *You are dead. Accept this. The Bleak is where you will dwell for ever. Your powers are not strong enough to escape its clutches. It is a fitting end for you and your bitterness.*

No, Xantia cried, still not understanding.

Come, child, Lys said to Alyssa. *This is no place for you.*

Alyssa looked up at her mother, shocked by the remarkable likeness the woman bore to herself. *How could you?*

Easily, came the reply. *I can save you.*

And the others? Alyssa dared ask.

I cannot interfere, child. We must believe they will prevail.

Alyssa shook her head. *But you could have saved them.*

I made my choice, her mother replied. *I should never have given you up. But I was given a chance to claim you back to your rightful position. I had no idea, Alyssa, that you would be brave enough to send yourself to this place. You have enormous courage, child, to give up all that you love including your own life.*

Mother, it's because I love them that I can. Why can't you love me enough to help them?

Suddenly Alyssa felt a powerful shield close about her.

Xantia, Lys said, regretfully. *It is no good. You cannot hurt her any more. Your magics are useless here. Your magics always were. We leave you now to ponder your sad life.*

I would rather be dead, Xantia snarled.

I'm sure you would but this was your choice.

Where are you going?

To a place you will never see, can never reach.

Alyssa turned to the woman who had caused her so much harm. It was over then. Her destiny was to be separated from Tor and she had failed in giving her life to save his and those of her children.

Farewell, Xantia, she called quietly and then she felt herself travelling.

32

Sanctuary

Rubyn squeezed Sarel's hand. 'I will see you again.'

They were following Gyl and Herek as they made their way towards the Ciprean palace. There was no time to think, let alone for her to stop and acknowledge his words so seriously spoken. But she did now. She pushed caution aside. Her situation was perilous enough not to worry further.

Sarel pulled him to a stop, leant forward and kissed Rubyn. 'And I will see you.'

He nodded, his face grave and his expression focused entirely on her as though he was unaware of the Prime moving back towards them, frustrated by this stoppage.

'You will make a great queen,' he whispered, bowing to kiss her hand.

'Your majesty, please,' urged a breathless Herek. 'There is no time for this.'

'There must always be time for love,' she said, turning to gaze at the perplexed soldier. 'Come!' she added, grabbing Rubyn's hand again and breaking into a run.

Gyl had already reached Cyrus and Hela. There was

relief written over everyone's face that they had made it
this far.

Cyrus addressed his King. 'All right now. We split up
here. Your highness, if you would accompany Rubyn and me,
we will leave Herek and Hela to get Queen Sarel to safety.'

Gyl nodded, turning to Herek. 'You know what to do.'

Herek saluted in the Tallinese way. 'I do, sire and . . .
may I add that you are not to wait for my return at the
ship. Once you have Lauryn, leave.' He stared at Cyrus.
'That's an order.'

Cyrus saluted as well. 'Go!' His gaze moved swiftly
towards Hela. He said nothing; no expression showing on
his face.

Hela felt hollow. This no longer felt like a farewell. It
felt like a final goodbye. Suddenly the full sense of their
flight from danger came home to roost and the chirpi-
ness and courage she had always been able to dig deep
and find deserted her. And there was no time to linger.
She let her sad eyes do the talking. His never left hers as
Herek shook his hand and the King offered words of luck.
Her throat was too dry and choked to say anything and
she found herself being jostled away from him.

And then finally he whispered something towards her.
She just caught it. 'May the Light guide you safely.'

'And may it guide you back to me,' she whispered but
knew he had not heard for he had already turned and was
moving into the shadows towards a small, unguarded
entrance on the western side of the Ciprean palace.

Orlac was running, Lauryn limp in his arms and oblivious to his bid for her freedom. He careened around a
corner into one of the lesser used wings of the palace and

startled a servant hurrying in the opposite direction. Recognising him she froze. All the palace staff – except Juno and Titus he realised – were terrified of him. He wondered briefly how Lauryn's companions fared since Dorgryl had had them locked up and under guard in one of the dungeons.

When Dorgryl had stolen and then attacked Lauryn that first night, Orlac – even from his withdrawn place – had noticed that both had cast out anxiously. Dorgryl had noted it too. *So, we have two sentients amongst us*, Orlac recalled him saying scornfully. *You make an interesting pair. I shall find out more later.* And then he had stunned them with a bolt of his own magic, wisely choosing to keep them alive until he had time to find out exactly who they were. He had ordered the guards to keep them drugged until he returned. But Dorgryl had not returned, preferring his entertainment with Lauryn.

Orlac brought himself back to the present and the terrified maid. 'Is there a way out down here?' he hurled at her, hoping to frighten her into speaking.

She shrank back, looking around for an exit. 'Sire?'

'Answer me, damn you! Can I get into the gardens from here? Quick, woman, this is urgent.'

She found her wits. 'Yes, sire. But don't go that way. There are three strangers . . . armed, sire. I – I just happened to be taking a short cut into the palace and saw them. I must raise the alarm.'

'Who are they?' he demanded, reaching for her arm then thinking better of it when she looked as though she would start screaming.

'Tallinese, sire. One wears the crimson!' She took off like a frightened bird, fluttering down the corridor.

Orlac's mind raced. Tallinese? Luck was with him tonight. He ran straight towards them.

Herek and Hela flanked Sarel as they moved stealthily into the city itself. In any other circumstances the soldier might have found himself intimidated by the magnificence of this city, so beautiful in every way. Yet curiously, in his tension, he found himself admiring even the exquisite manner of the way its artisans had fashioned everything, from doorknockers to drains. Tal was an imposing city but it had none of this elegance or grace.

Hela was speaking and he dragged his mind from some admirable ironwork.

'. . . his house is not far.'

'Sorry, Hela. Whose?'

She had not noticed his vagueness and repeated herself without pausing. 'Councillor Heyn. He is the most senior of the Elders. He will recognise me, if not his Queen.'

'How do you know he will help?' Sarel asked.

'Because he owes me a few favours,' Hela quipped and winked at Herek, who decided he would not press for any further information.

Cyrus put his finger to his lips. He pointed towards a small, fairly inconsequential doorway through which he had seen the maid scurrying. The soldier knew they had been spotted but they were far too committed to this cause now to turn away. She would surely raise an alarm. So be it. He motioned for Gyl to draw his blade. They both did so together, silently.

Rubyn grimaced knowing how inconsequential a blade was against what lay behind those doors but he realised that to these men, a weapon felt safe. He shielded for all of them. His thoughts drifted once, briefly, to Sarel, the incredible sensation of her mouth so fleetingly against his lips. He would taste those lips again, he promised himself.

Cyrus nodded. They stepped out of the shadows towards the doorway and faltered with alarm as an incredibly tall, golden-haired man suddenly appeared in it.

'Where are you?' the man demanded. 'Show yourself.'

In his arms was a woman, barely covered by a satin robe.

Without thinking Gyl rushed forward. 'Lauryn!'

The tall man turned at the sound of the man's voice. He recognised one as the King which impressed him. Most sovereigns would not risk their life in such a foolhardy manner. Blades were drawn and pointed at him. But his attention was snared by the calm countenance of the slim, fair-haired young man. The powers swirling about him were immense and Orlac could sense he had built a strong shield about them. It was an impressive show – this was no ordinary sentient.

He cast towards the young man. *She lives but not for long. Take her. Get her to safety. Dorgryl comes. He will kill you all.*

The other two were unbalanced by his lack of movement or even eye contact towards them.

'Give her to me, Sylc,' Gyl demanded.

'Welcome, your majesty,' Orlac said, his voice betraying no emotion.

This politeness only served to unbalance his enemies further. He handed Lauryn gently into Gyl's arms. The King had to drop his sword to take her and Cyrus, baffled as to what was going on, bent cautiously to pick it up.

It was a shock to see Orlac again, so alive, so much larger than life. He felt his gut twist at the sight of him, wondering whether the god would recognise him. Of course he would not, but it did nothing to comfort his sudden fear of the mighty power which stood before him.

Rubyn spoke, unable to tear his gaze from the golden man. 'He says we are all in danger from someone called Dorgryl, especially Lauryn.'

'You must run,' Orlac added to the warning. 'He will try and recapture her and in the process will kill all you. Every second you waste here threatens your life.' He gazed at Lauryn. 'And hers.' He looked straight at Gyl. 'Get her to safety.'

'Why do you help us?' Cyrus asked. The question was loaded.

The god shook his head and answered the most obvious. 'She deserves her life. She is braver than all of us. Tell her father to await me. I come soon. Now go! Dorgryl will already be searching.'

Gyl and Cyrus began running but Rubyn lingered.

He nodded at the golden man. 'You are more noble than we anticipated.'

Orlac smiled ruefully. 'Don't pass your judgement so soon.'

'I am Rubyn. One of the Three.'

'The Three?'

'We will destroy you.'

'You can try.'

'We will meet again in the Heartwood.'

'Appropriate. Are you her brother?'

'I am Torkyn Gynt's son, yes.'

'Her puppy is somewhere about these gardens. If you see it, you must take him. His name's Pelyss. She would miss him sorely.'

Rubyn looked at the golden man with curiosity.

Orlac suddenly felt the touch of Dorgryl on his mind. He flinched. He knew Dorgryl felt it.

Orlac nodded. 'It is a privilege to meet you, nephew, but I suggest you leave right now.'

Rubyn stared at him for just a moment longer. He bowed once to his uncle. When he looked back he saw Orlac's eyes had turned red.

The King had thrown Lauryn over his shoulder. It was not one of the most respectful ways to carry one of the three people on whom the Land's survival counted, but he accepted it was the only way he could move quickly and efficiently and still keep his weapon arm free.

They were approaching the docks when suddenly Cyrus stopped.

Gyl turned. 'What! What's wrong?'

Cyrus looked stricken. 'Oh Light! Oh no.'

Rubyn caught up with the two men. 'What's happened?'

Cyrus looked towards the palace and then back towards the docks. 'How could I have overlooked them? I have to go back.'

'Don't talk madness, man. Why? Who are you talking about?'

Cyrus smiled sadly at the King. 'Take her. Get the ship moving. Take my boy with you,' he said, looking at Rubyn with love. 'Do not wait.'

'Cyrus! Where do you go?' demanded Rubyn.

The soldier turned back to them, regarding their shocked faces. He took Rubyn into his arms and hugged the young man fiercely. Then he looked at the King. 'I'm sorry, your majesty. I have left behind friends. In my anxiety I had forgotten they were here. Adongo and Juno . . . they are Alyssa's Paladin. We cannot leave them behind.'

Gyl was out of his depth here but he could tell it had something to do with his mother's magical friends, having heard the name Paladin before. 'Cyrus. You cannot be serious. They must be injured or perhaps dead if they are not with her. You must come now.'

Cyrus was already moving away from them. 'I would know if they were not alive. Get *The Raven* sailing. Rubyn . . . somehow get yourself and Lauryn to the Heartwood. Don't wait for Herek either.'

He turned and ran back up the hill towards a place where angry gods lurked.

Dorgryl fled from the Bleak, gloating over how he had rid himself of Xantia and cleverly entrapped Lys. He had known she would not fail to choose Alyssa over him – she had to let him go to save her daughter. And Lys's powers so well matched his own there would be no point in her trying to fight him to hold him in the Bleak and risk hurting Alyssa. No, he had given her the best option even though she did not like it.

Throughout his time in the Bleak, Lys had been there for every tedious moment. It was the only way she could maintain another god's imprisonment. The only break in that power had come at the precise second Torkyn Gynt had accidentally blundered into the Bleak. Dorgryl laughed. Lys had faltered at the unexpected arrival and Dorgryl had taken his chance. And now she had faltered again. To save her daughter she had to leave the Bleak but in doing so relinquished her hold over him.

Oh how he loved it! Arrogant, stupendously confident Lys . . . thwarted not once but twice.

And where had Orlac got to, he wondered. He congratulated himself on not giving up his hold on the god's trace. If he had done, Orlac might have been able to escape his sensing.

Suspended between the Bleak and arrival back in Orlac's body he linked. *You cannot escape me yet, nephew.*

He reached out for his host and made contact. Orlac flinched.

Ah, there you are, he whispered and travelled urgently, arriving just in time to see a young man running away. *Who was that?*

No one special, Orlac said. With Dorgryl's presence inside him, he felt ugly and abused again.

I was extremely impressed by your trick.

Which one was that?

The one where you go very quiet and pretend not to hear me. The one where you wait – oh so patiently – for a moment when my guard is down.

Oh, that one.

It will never work again.

Then I shall have to devise a new trick.

I presume she is hidden then?

You are right.

I think I had finished with her anyway, Dorgryl said, casually. *Nice body, your Lauryn has, but she never joined in.*

Orlac deliberately kept his emotions under control. He took a deep breath. *Dorgryl. I am finished with Cipres. I am finished with you. I now travel to finish Torkyn Gynt and fulfil my promise to Tallinor . . . whether you care for it or not.*

Dorgryl did not so much as hesitate, speaking smoothly with a tone suggesting he was surprised Orlac had ever doubted him. *Oh but I do, nephew. It was always our plan wasn't it? And I do believe I owe you an apology. My behaviour has been abominable in taking over your body so completely. I don't know what came over me.*

Orlac knew he had one of two ways to go. He steadied himself, remembering Lauryn's sweet smile and that he had won her freedom – which not so long ago had suddenly seemed all that counted – and he forced his voice to neutral; forbade his body to show in any way its fury. He lied just as smoothly as his uncle. *You were right. I had lost my way for a while and you were correct to remind me that we show no mercy.*

Oh? Dorgryl was not that easily fooled. He probed deeper, searching for any sign of guile and came up wanting.

Orlac continued, ignoring the probe as if he had not felt its touch. *I cannot permit you to do this again. But I am somehow grateful that you did what you did. It has reawoken me.*

Dorgryl laughed. It was edged in such cruelty, Orlac felt his control teeter. He could so easily take a knife to himself and end it all now. Dorgryl would then have to wander within the body of whomever happened to be passing by for he surely could not survive long outside of Orlac's. But it was the vision of Lauryn which forbade him such action. The thought of possibly seeing her again made him choose life over death and this despair over peace. He knew they could never have anything between them except hate; he recalled how she had told him she would do everything she could to destroy him. And he had promised her there would be a confrontation between himself and his brother.

Dorgryl's amusement ended. *I do not believe a word of it but if it means we are not going to fight over my possession of your body, then I'm happy to go along with this.*

You do not trust me?

No. Do you trust me?

You have not shown yourself to be trustworthy. But we have an agreement do we not? Once we have defeated Gynt and those who would protect him, I will help you defeat my father. Then we part company.

That's an excellent plan. Dorgryl's voice was tinged with sarcasm.

Once again, Orlac forced himself to remain focused and calm. *Do you have a strategy?*

It will shape itself. Do not fear on that account.

I mean how will you summon my father?

No need. He will be present. Trust me.

And although Orlac did not trust him, he smiled.

It was Gidyon who made it first into the clearing.

Gently, son, spoke the soft, smooth voice of Solyana.

The great wolf sat beside his parents. They were curled like lovers on the damp floor of the Forest. Not far away, Arabella and Sallementro sat stunned. The others came into view. Saxon's eyes searched Sallementro despairingly – who would not meet his gaze – but then the Kloek did not need to be told anything. He had already felt the special brightness die within; guessed its import. It was the brightness which had been his connection to Alyssa since the moment he had seen her on that fateful day when the Cirq Zorros had introduced the famous Flying Foxes at the town of Fragglesham. He knew before this moment that Alyssa had gone to the Light; had known it the very second of her collapse amongst the forbidding Rork'yel Mountains. But he had not wanted to accept what he knew and so he had continued the charade of making it back here to see whether the Heartwood could save her.

Now he had to face the truth. Alyssa was dead. He was her Paladin and he had failed to protect her – had failed to give his own life for hers as was the creed.

Gidyon had halted in his tracks at the wolf's words, unable to tear his eyes from the prone figures. A glance at Arabella and Sallementro told its own tragic story. Death was here. Saxon staggered past him and Gidyon's two sturdy Paladin soon flanked him. Themesius pressed a hefty hand against one shoulder and he felt their Link open. No words were spoken but strength flowed through it. To his right, Figgis held his arm and joined the Link.

Be brave now, boy, the dwarf whispered.

Gidyon could not be brave; could not do much more than feel numb as he watched Saxon collapse to his knees next to Alyssa. He hated feeling it but relief coursed through his body when he saw his father stir and then rise to look about him. His face was dirty and tear-stained; his hair dishevelled; his expression as dead as the body which lay next to him.

'She's gone. I couldn't save her,' he mumbled and a heavy silence gripped them all as the words of truth were forced upon them and finally sank in.

The silence was broken by Cloot's arrival. Something passed between Tor and his falcon because Gidyon saw fresh tears overcome his father as the bird settled on his shoulder.

Saxon stroked Alyssa's hair and her cold cheek. It was the last time he would gaze on that beautiful face.

No more troubles for you now, my girl. I am undone by my failure. Forgive me for losing you, child. Be safe in the Light.

But Alyssa could no longer hear him.

Tor roused himself and Cloot moved soundlessly to the treetops above. Whatever the falcon had said had steadied Tor. He looked about him with new composure and felt the leaden grief of the others.

'Darmud Coril could not reach her. It was her decision.' He stepped towards his son and took him into his arms. 'Your mother made a choice. I don't understand it but she would never have left us without reason.' He hugged his boy tight and then addressed the others. 'Alyssa gave her life for something which threatened us. We must not let her sacrifice be in vain. We must prepare for the coming of Orlac.'

Solyana's calm voice spoke. *We must give her back to the trees.*

'No!' Gidyon shouted, spinning around, tears stinging his eyes.

Themesius and Figgis were once again at Gidyon's side as Tor bent down to pick up his beloved wife's corpse.

It's where she belongs, child, the wolf said.

Saxon bent and kissed the trailing hand. 'Will Darmud Coril take her?'

Tor nodded. 'Sallementro?'

The musician, stricken into silence, walked towards them and bent to kiss his bonded one. The others followed until there was only Tor and Gidyon left to say their farewell.

I will not say goodbye to her, Tor whispered into his mind.

Somehow I will see her again. Perhaps not until we both meet in the Light.

Gidyon kissed his mother's cheek, unable to check his emotion. *Perhaps sooner, Father. I don't believe she would let you go again so easily.*

I don't think she did, child. I think she let go with the greatest of difficulty.

They heard Darmud Coril's voice summoning them.

'My children,' he said, with great sadness in his lovely face. 'Give me our beloved Alyssa. I must return her body.'

'Where to?' Gidyon asked.

'To its rightful place,' the god answered.

Orlac saw the man approach but shielded the sight and any knowledge of it from Dorgryl, who was, as usual, airing his thoughts. Orlac rubbed his eyes as though a piece of grit was bothering him, and pretended to pay attention to Dorgryl's comment.

I don't believe our friends in the tower are telling us everything, the elder god mused.

Oh? replied Orlac, turning his back on Cyrus. Why would the man be so stupid as to come back? And for what?

There's more to them than meets the eye, as I always suspected. Speaking of which, what's wrong with yours? I can't see a thing.

Dorgryl's words suddenly threw open a door in Orlac's mind. Of course! Titus and Juno had been protecting Lauryn. Who were they? He turned his back on Cyrus who was hiding in the shadows. Orlac sensed the man cast out. So, the soldier too was not what he seemed. Dorgryl continued to talk but Orlac ignored him; he needed time to think. He sat down on a nearby bench, deliberately turning his shoulder from Cyrus but keeping his senses open to him. Now Dorgryl sounded cross.

Orlac flashed inside. *What?*

I asked, repeated the elder god, *what we are doing here? Smelling the lavender?*

No! Leave me alone. I wish to think.

Dorgryl had more to say but Orlac stopped him.

Withdraw! he commanded. He felt stronger for having said it. He remembered the ugly feeling of Dorgryl's possession of his entire body. He would never allow that to happen again.

His uncle became sulky. *Tell me when you're ready to talk. We have plans to make.*

Orlac inhaled the night air and allowed his thoughts to roam. If Titus and Juno had been protecting Lauryn from the start, it meant they had known from the beginning who he was. He thought about Juno and the clever way in which she had always handled him – never discourteous or even vaguely disobedient and yet never quite under his control. Those watchful eyes, that careful, cautious manner of hers. He took himself back to their first meeting and realised how skilfully she had dissuaded him from bedding her which had been his full intention. Why? She was not afraid of him as the others in the palace all were. No, Juno was not afraid, she was respectful – and he knew that respect was not born of fear. It came from something far more subtle. He racked his clever, agile mind until the answer came to him. Until what had been staring him in the face for so long finally settled into place.

Juno was of the Paladin.

He had no proof of this – he just knew he was right. The Juno he had known had been mightily empowered yet aged, and this young woman was many ages her junior, but he accepted they were one and the same. And Titus . . . he did not even have to think long on this. He was the Moruk, Adongo. Of course. It made sense.

And this man, creeping around the Ciprean gardens, had surely returned to rescue the Paladin. Why else would he risk so much? Although Orlac had spent aeons battling the Paladin he had to admire them. Their courage was vast.

Another idea hit him. Perhaps this soldier was Paladin too. He was sentient, so why not? Orlac considered it for a moment and then could not stop the smile spreading on his face.

Cyruson . . . the old rogue. The wiliest of the ten. He had always liked him. Light! He had silently admired all of them and the way they pitched themselves against such power. And here they were again defying him.

What are you smiling about? Dorgryl asked.

'I was just thinking,' Orlac said loud enough for Cyrus to hear, 'that I don't wish to go to the dungeons tonight.'

But I want to question them. Why do you speak aloud?

'Because it pleases me to do as I wish. Not as you wish. If I choose to speak aloud I shall and if I don't want to go to the guardhouse and speak to the maid or the Moruk, I will not.'

And if I do? Dorgryl asked, confused by the sudden change which had come over his host.

I care not what you want. You will do exactly as I wish now, uncle. I am tired. I wish to sleep.

I shall keep you awake.

I think not. I shall let you know in the morning my plans for Tallinor.

Why wait so long?

Because it is the early hours of the morning. Later, rested, I shall think clearly. It's your own fault for exhausting my resources so.

Why do I feel you are up to something?

No secrets, uncle. We want the same thing, you said. Let me rest this body of ours and tomorrow we sail for Tallinor.

In the shadows, Cyrus could not believe what he was hearing. Was it a trap? Or was Orlac deliberately conveying to him where to find those he had returned for? It puzzled him. Orlac was too dangerous to second guess so he dipped deep into his own instincts to gauge their advice.

Distracted in thought but noting that Orlac had drifted away into the gardens and was, he hoped, bound for his own chambers, Cyrus did not hear the man come up behind him. When a hand landed on his shoulder only his years of training prevented him from shouting out.

He turned, raising his sword, so alarmed that it took him a moment to realise it was Herek who had startled him.

'Sorry,' the Prime said softly.

Cyrus forced his breathing to return to normal. 'What are you doing here, man?'

It was exactly how Cyrus had spoken to him in the old days. Herek, normally so dry and serious, grinned. 'Couldn't leave you.'

'Those were my orders.'

'I overrode them. I believe I am the senior officer. Anyway, why are we here?'

'Paladin. Juno and Adongo. They have been protecting Lauryn, their bonded. We need to rescue them.'

'From?'

'The guardhouse apparently.'

'How do we know this?' Herek whispered, cautiously looking around.

'Orlac told me.'

Herek was silent for a moment as he considered this. 'Why would your sworn enemy give you helpful information?'

Cyrus shook his head. 'Search me. I was trying to weigh up whether to trust it or not when you startled me.'

'And?'

'Undecided. Is Hela safe?'

Herek gave his old superior a sly glance. Fortunately for Cyrus it was too dark for his friend to see how angry he was with himself for asking after Hela and not Sarel.

Herek answered, 'Queen Sarel is hidden for now. Your Hela is with her.'

'She's not my Hela.'

Herek shrugged. 'The women are safe and protected by the senior member of the council of elders. Lauryn, I'm glad to say, is safe at the docks too.'

Cyrus swung his attention from a puppy which had entered the gardens to glare at the soldier crouching next to him. 'You mean on *The Raven* which is now sailing for Kyrakavia?'

Herek sighed. 'No one will go without you.'

'Damn you, Herek. I gave orders!' Cyrus hissed.

'And I told you. I overrode them. Now let's get these people out and then we all go.'

Cyrus fumed in his silence.

'Are you going to consult your instincts again?' Herek asked, daring the legendary anger of Kyt Cyrus to boil over.

It did not, thankfully. Cyrus suddenly stood and Herek

followed suit. 'He knew I was here. He's too clever. He gave me the information as deliberately as he gave Lauryn back to us.'

'Do you understand any of it?'

Cyrus shook his head. 'No. But my memories have returned since all of the Paladin linked. And I do recall that there was a certain nobility about the madman we battled for centuries. When one of us succumbed to his powers, he would stop the flow. There was something rather principled and dignified about the strange way in which he would give us time to mourn our loss. He was ruthless and his strength enormous and yet he showed odd mercies.'

'And you think this might be that nobility coming out . . . telling you where your friends are?' Herek asked in amazement.

Cyrus shrugged. 'I don't know. I have no explanation for it. He gave us back Lauryn. Why would he do that? He could have killed me earlier in less time than it takes to blink – Light! – he could have killed all of us including the King. But he didn't. It's baffling. He's never been predictable, that's for sure. But in this he has me in confusion.'

'Can you talk to your two friends, as you do the boy?'

'I would but I fear he might be listening.'

'But he's already paved the way.'

'No. I mean the other one he spoke of. Dorgryl.'

'Then let us make our way to the guardhouse. Time is marching on.'

'Indeed,' Cyrus said. 'I can't imagine the guards will yield their prisoners happily. Are you ready to go down fighting next to me, Herek?'

'I always have been, sir,' Herek said, drawing his blade.

* * *

Rubyn insisted. 'I have to go to him.'

Gyl rubbed his eyes. 'I forbid it.'

Rubyn did not flinch; his expression did not change. He just locked stares with the King. Then he spoke quietly. 'You and I are similar. Neither of us have known our real fathers but we've known a love which comes close.'

The King was taken aback – not just by the sudden switch in topic but by the fact that Rubyn seemed to know such intimate details.

'And?' he replied, defensively.

'That's all,' Rubyn said. 'I must go. Lauryn has woken. I think you should be at her side.'

'How do you know? I checked on her just moments ago.'

'I am her brother, sire. We are . . . connected.' He turned and Gyl watched the young man leave the ship and walk purposefully into the night. What a totally baffling character he was.

Gyl moved towards the stairs which led to the chambers below but then shouted new orders to Locky.

'Ready when you are, sire . . . and when Prime Herek returns to my ship. I'm not going without him,' *The Raven*'s captain replied.

The King told himself heads would roll over all this insubordination. But the truth was his sense of danger was overcome by the knowledge that in the old captain's stateroom lay a young woman he loved very much – and suddenly not much else mattered at this precise moment other than knowing she was safe.

He took the stairs two at a time.

* * *

They had almost made it; almost pulled it off without a drop of blood being spilled or so much as a single man being bludgeoned senseless. Cyrus could believe that Orlac might have even withdrawn part of the watch that night because it just seemed too easy to enter the guardhouse and find their way down to the holding cells.

'Where is everyone?' Herek whispered nervously.

'Just count our blessings but watch my back.'

The two soldiers stepped cautiously, back to back, along the short, darkened corridor. A single flame burned pitifully at one end but it left the other end – where they were headed – in darkness.

They arrived at the last cell and peered into the shadows, blinking. In its recesses they could just make out bodies curled on the floor.

'Adongo?'

'Who goes there?' It was a woman. Cyrus did not recognise the voice. She sounded startled.

'Juno?'

There was a rustling as the figures stood. 'Who is this?' A man this time. Cautious. 'There is no Adongo here. I am Titus.'

Cyrus could not help but smile. It was such a familiar voice. 'My old friend. You cannot fool me. This is Kyt Cyrus. You knew me as Cyruson of the Paladin.'

Hands reached through the bars of the cell and suddenly Cyrus was gripped in a strong hold; a swarthy face came into view. 'We owe you thanks.' The words were simple enough but the eyes of the owner who spoke them conveyed a far stronger emotion. Cyrus returned the grip. He nodded, the thrill of the reunion with Adongo catching at his throat. 'The Light has guided us together again.'

'Into danger again together too,' said a petite, pretty woman appearing at Adongo's side.

Cyrus showed his appreciation. 'Well, that's not the Juno I remember,' he admitted.

They laughed.

Herek hushed them. 'Cyrus, we must hurry.'

'This is Herek. He is the Prime of Tallinor. I am privileged to call him friend.'

Despite his fear for their situation, Herek felt pride at such words. He nodded politely at the prisoners. 'Time is short. Keys?'

'Over there,' Juno pointed. 'Prison security is slack in Cipres. We are its first of prisoners since some pair faced the Kiss of the Silver Maiden.'

Cyrus frowned. 'Don't ask,' Adongo cautioned.

Herek fetched the keys and attempted to open the door as quietly as possible.

'Where are your guards?' the Prime asked.

Adongo shrugged and Juno answered. 'They were called away a short while ago. We have no idea where to or why.'

'Our luck,' Cyrus said, pulling back the door and then hugging Juno. 'I definitely like the new Juno.' He grinned and pulled Adongo close.

The Moruk's smile faded. 'Where is he?'

Cyrus knew whom he meant. 'Occupied.'

Juno could not bear to ask the question but knew she must. 'Tell us of Lauryn.'

'Safe,' Cyrus said. 'We have her on a ship which is being delayed because we had to come back for you two.'

Their relief at good news after three days of suffering the torment of not knowing Lauryn's fate was evident on their faces.

'You should have left us,' Juno admonished.

'Well, Herek wanted to, of course,' Cyrus said nodding towards the stunned Prime. 'But I could not contemplate such a thing.'

He winked and Herek scowled. 'I think we must get out of here now.'

As he said it, three guards arrived at the other end of the corridor.

'Swords, I think,' was all Cyrus had time to say before the men were upon them.

Rubyn entered the Ciprean palace by the same western gate as he had earlier that night. This time, however, it was manned and he took the precaution of making himself invisible for the short time required to silently pass the man on watch. The soldier was not paying much attention anyway as he relieved himself at the side of the road. Still, Rubyn was not taking any chances and the push of magic was small. Invisibility was his favourite trick and he had often driven Cyrus to distraction by teasing him with his skill from a very young age.

Tell me you felt that, Dorgryl grumbled, confused by their inactivity.

I felt it, his nephew replied calmly.

Well?

It is the son. Gynt's third-born, Rubyn.

You seem to know him.

We met . . . whilst you were otherwise engaged.

And?

Nothing. He told me who he was when I gave him back his sister. He shrugged. *I mentioned her dog, I think.*

Dorgryl growled. He was angry again. *You are weak like your father!*

Only you can know that, uncle. I have not met him since I was an infant, remember?

The elder god continued as though Orlac had not spoken. *Weak like your father and weak like your brother. Be careful, Dorgryl.*

His uncle wisely held his tongue.

They felt the push of magic again. This time it was Rubyn casting. They listened.

Where are you?

They heard Cyrus reply amidst the clang of metal. *Tell me, damn you, that you are not here.*

I am here.

Cyrus grunted and hit out hard with his sword. *Then help us! Herek is down.*

Cyrus fought back hard. They were trapped in the dungeons, their backs to the wall and as each Ciprean guard fell to the blade of Cyrus, another took his place. Herek was bleeding badly from a gash to his groin; a cowardly blow from a downed guard who slashed upwards with a dagger and connected.

'Adongo!' Cyrus cried, not able to see what had happened.

'He lives. Not long for this world though unless we can get help.'

Cyrus began to fight like a man possessed. He bared his teeth and drove his attackers back. The former prime's talent with the sword had been unmatched in his time at the head of the Company and every nuance, every subtlety of his skill came to the fore in this corridor of terror. Even as his lifeblood spilled about him Herek smiled. It seemed to Juno who clutched him, begging him to hold on, that his smile came from far away as he admired once again Kyt Cyrus brandishing his sword. To Herek he looked like a dancer with every cut in the air precisely made, wearing his opponent down until a deathblow could be landed. How could he lie here in a pool of his own blood as this man fought valiantly? No, they must die together. Side by side. He would not desert Cyrus until the Light took him away.

With one almighty push, using strength he did not know he possessed, Herek gave a loud Tallinese battle cry and shoved himself to his feet, making a timely slash and almost hacking off one guard's head with his passion to stand once more alongside his former prime. Alas, it was the last dash Prime Herek would make in this life. He tasted death at the end of a viciously jagged Ciprean sword, falling heavily at the feet of Cyrus as the Light finally claimed one of its bravest.

Cyrus could feel himself tiring as another man queued to take the present fighter's position as soon as he fell. He knew they were dead without Rubyn's help. It seemed to him that Adongo and Juno – like him – had not been bestowed with any special powers. He was a warrior. His job now was to fight to the death and protect those behind him. But when Herek had suddenly screamed, 'Honour the Crimson', he felt a surge of blood fire his fury. It turned to despair as a Ciprean stabbed forward and took Herek square in the belly. And as he faltered, staring at his friend fallen at his feet, he felt the lift of the blade that was destined to cut through his left shoulder close to his waist.

He anticipated it. Did he welcome it? He could not

be sure. But he braced himself and spared one last thought for the young man he loved as much as the true son who had died too young.

The blow came but it was not one which drew blood. Instead he felt as though all the air was suddenly sucked from his lungs and a burning occurred around him. The impact of the sensation forced his eyes shut and he grimaced through this strange pain. If Cyrus had turned around he would have seen a similar expression on the faces of Adongo and Juno whilst in front he would have noticed only one of complete shock on the faces of his attackers.

At his feet, Herek's face was slack. He felt nothing.

Why? Dorgryl boomed in his mind, blood-red mist spilling up where Orlac did not want to feel it.

Orlac forced it back, used his strength. He knew how to wield it better against the old god now and felt the give. I will beat you, he said smiling to himself. To his uncle he merely shrugged.

The elder god was unnerved by the power. Orlac did not quite have his measure yet but Dorgryl had told himself, since he first clothed himself with his nephew's flesh, that he would have to rely on his wiles. The young man was incredibly strong with the power and even now he had barely tapped its well.

Answer me! he roared; his anger all he had left to use against Orlac.

His nephew sighed and spoke quietly. *I will do this my way, not yours.*

You will go to the Heartwood?

Yes. It is fitting.

*   *   *

Cyrus felt his body crunch down hard. He rolled onto his back, groaning, still not daring to open his eyes. He knew he still had his sword in his hand and was ready to strike just as soon as he could drag in a lungful of breath.

He thought he could feel boards beneath him now and the freshness of a sea breeze stirring his hair. All of his senses had returned and he could smell fish, hear the creak of a ship about him. His eyes opened in shock and he sat up, breathing hard.

'What the—'

'Cyrus,' said the familiar voice of Rubyn. 'Be easy.'

The former prime stared wildly around picking out the faces of the ship's young captain, Locky, and various soldiers and crew he recalled.

'*The Raven*?' he said, disbelief crowding his voice as he looked for Rubyn.

Hands picked him up gently. It was the King who looked as shocked as he felt.

'I don't understand this,' Gyl said.

Nearby Adongo and Juno looked similarly drugged and blurry-eyed as they too gathered their wits.

Rubyn appeared in front of him. 'We are on *The Raven*, yes. We must go, now.' He emphasised his final word and Locky – still too shocked from seeing Herek's corpse to speak – nodded, giving orders immediately through well-practised signals his stepfather had taught him. He was grateful for the experienced, albeit smaller, crew which reacted instantly to his signal. The ship had been ready for hours and it felt as if only moments passed before they pushed away from the quay as quietly as they had arrived. The gods smiled on them that night and the breeze Cyrus had felt gathered strength and guided them swiftly into open waters. *The Raven*, true to her reputation, slipped through the waves as keenly as a knife, rushing her precious cargo towards the coastline of Tallinor.

Cyrus shook his head to clear it and looked to the King.

'Herek is dead,' Gyl said, his voice choked.

'I know. Is he here?'

The King nodded, stepping back to reveal the prone body of his loyal Prime.

'Ah, Herek,' Cyrus said sadly, moving towards his old friend. He kneeled beside him and touched his face. 'Brave Herek.' He took the soldier's hand and held it against his own heart, murmuring special words whispered only by warriors over the bodies of their fallen brothers.

Cyrus passed his hand over the man's eyes, closing them, and felt the presence of Rubyn kneeling beside him.

'Thank you,' he said, turning to his bonded one. 'Thank you for bringing him with us.'

With strong winds aiding its escape, *The Raven* made her
fastest ever crossing towards the coastline of Tallinor. She
would moor at Caradoon in a matter of hours. A gloom
had settled heavily upon everyone since their departure
and conversation was sparse. The death of Herek had left
Cyrus and the King deeply disturbed and they found
themselves drawn to one another, often talking quietly
late into the night on deck, mostly about Lorys. It was
through the former prime's eyes that Gyl viewed the early
reign of his father and appreciated what a great friend as
much as a loyal warrior to the Crown Kyt Cyrus had been.

Hurting just as deeply was the captain. Seeing his
beloved Prime Herek dead had affected Locky profoundly
and there were moments when he felt the return voyage
was being achieved by memory rather than his expertise.
He thanked his closest crew more than once for their support
as they closed ranks about their very young captain and
steered the ship through familiar waters to its home port.

Lauryn seemed recovered but strangely closed on her
trauma. She continued to shield against Adongo and Juno

and although she did not avoid them or speak ill to them, both felt the chill of being shut out. However, both her Paladin held centuries of wisdom, and despite their concerns understood that what Lauryn had lived through was more than most could bear. They knew she and Rubyn were talking using a private Link and deemed this to be a good thing.

Rubyn's masterstroke had been to arrive out of thin air, not only with four people but holding a wriggling golden puppy which Lauryn had immediately claimed as her own. A gift, she had explained. Rubyn's kind gesture was the ice-breaker in the new relationship between brother and sister. Although a little shy around each other at first, even Cyrus had to marvel at how often Rubyn would laugh out loud at something Lauryn had communicated. It was especially noticeable because his laugh was rare, but dazzling when it came.

Lauryn was on deck now, pulling a shawl about her to ward off the stiff breeze. She allowed Gyl to wrap his arms about her.

'You believe in our powers now, don't you?' she whispered.

'I have witnessed strange magics with my own eyes. How can I not believe in you?' he whispered back into her soft hair.

'You have to trust us.'

'Us?'

'My father, our mother, my brothers . . .' her voice trailed off.

'Lauryn . . .'

She shook herself. 'I'm all right. I get waves of fear when I think about my family under threat.'

He hugged her harder as he watched the docks of Caradoon draw closer. 'I will never let any harm come to you again. I pledge my life to protecting my Queen.'

She turned, trying to smile but failing. 'You cannot protect me, my King. Not from him.'

'Then I will die trying.'

'Then you will die,' she said, softly. 'He is coming and he is driven by evil. I have heard and seen the evil within. We may all die.'

Gyl could not summon any words of comfort. Her resignation was too complete. 'Then we shall take our last breath together, my love, for I do not want to live without you.'

Her gaze met his strongly now. 'No. I will not let him hurt you. Tallinor needs you.' And reading the fervour in her eyes, Gyl believed her.

Cyrus noticed the King and Lauryn sharing what was probably a final private word. *The Raven* would moor soon and the final leg of his centuries-old journey would begin. Beneath his fear at what was coming, his despair over Herek and his anguish over how to protect Rubyn from the mad god, he felt his leaden spirits lift slightly with the knowledge they would be back amongst the trees soon.

He let us go, didn't he? Cyrus said, sidling up close to Rubyn who was gazing back out to sea whilst everyone else looked towards Caradoon.

Rubyn nodded.

Why do you think he allowed us to escape?

I think he helped us to escape.

But why help us to make safe passage to our zone of strength? He surely knows about the Heartwood.

The youngster shrugged. *I can't guess why . . . perhaps he wants to conquer us in the very place where we feel at our strongest. So his victory will be all the more sweet.*

Do you believe that?

No.

Rubyn, please. Tell me what you're thinking.

The young man sighed. *I think he wants us to destroy him. That's why he is allowing us to get to the Heartwood, where we are strong . . . where we do feel safer.*

They had not shielded their Link securely. Lauryn arrived on Rubyn's other side.

I agree. She shrugged. *Sorry for eavesdropping.* Neither of them seemed to mind so she continued. *Orlac suffers. I have seen it.* She faltered and the men kept their silence, staring out to sea as she composed herself. *When Dorgryl did his worst . . . and we were joined . . . I could feel Orlac's hate and despair. We can use that against him but we need to speak with Father.*

Cyrus nodded. *Last time we linked they were just entering the Rork'yel Mountains with Goth.*

When was that? she asked.

The night before last.

His work is done then.

Should we link to him?

She shook her head. *I'd like to surprise him, if no one minds, although I feel he will probably contact us soon,* she replied.

All were unaware that as they shared this private conversation, Alyssa was being lifted gently from her husband's arms for the last time.

Her children would never see her again.

*   *   *

'Will you not come with us?' the King said softly to the young man who had brought them safely back to Tallinor.

Locky bowed deeply. 'Sire. I must return home and set my affairs in order. There are others to take care of. I must see to their welfare,' he said, thinking of all the young women at the tavern. He straightened and looked into his King's face. He even attempted a smile. 'Besides, I don't possess the magic. I am of no further use to you.'

'I might make my own judgement on that,' Gyl replied dryly. 'Herek told me that you wished to join the Shield.' He saw the light blaze again in Locky's formerly dulled eyes.

'Yes, sire,' he said, blushing furiously now although his pluck did not desert him. 'I have always had ambitions.'

The King smiled now. 'And how high would those ambitions soar?'

Locky cleared his throat, thinking of Herek and how much it had meant to meet him. 'Given the opportunity, sire, I would aim to be prime.'

Gyl gave little away in his expression, other than to lift an eyebrow. He knew what it felt like to have such a powerful sense of longing. He recalled how much he had treasured the chance to train under Herek as Under Prime. Knew the satisfaction and pleasure of anticipating becoming his King's first man – his father's champion, he thought sadly. Locky was still young enough to be able to learn about soldiering . . . and having someone so adept on board ship – and one with so many years ahead of him – would be a great boon.

'Oh, that lofty?' he replied.

'Yes, sire. Is that wrong?'

'Not at all. Well, lad. Settle your affairs in the north

and then come to Tal. We shall speak at length about your future.'

Locky looked fit to burst with pride. The weight of Eryn's, Quist's, and then Herek's, deaths — which had settled so heavily on his shoulders — seemed to lighten immeasurably and he smiled broadly for the first time in many days.

'I will, sire. I will make speed.'

The King held out his hand in the Tallinese way. 'Tallinor owes you much, Locklyn Gylbyt. You are most welcome at its royal court any time.'

Leaving the docks after the farewells to Locky and his crew, they felt a hollowness settle about them. Fear crept around the edge of their emptiness. The King dispatched his men to Kyrakavia with orders to leave a small company there and for the main group to return to Tal to await further orders. He was assuming full leadership of his men again . . . Prime and King.

'What now?' he said to Cyrus finally.

Before the soldier could answer, Cyrus felt the familiar cold slice of the Link opening, as did Rubyn, Lauryn, Adongo and Juno.

It was Solyana. *Where are you?* Her message was brief and urgent.

Rubyn answered. *Caradoon.*

Make haste. Use the trees without delay. Your father needs you.

She closed the Link permitting no further discussion.

Gyl suspected something was wrong by the sudden bleak expressions on his companions' faces. 'What happened?' he asked, turning to Lauryn.

'Trouble, I think,' she said, worriedly. 'Our father.'

Cyrus took command, hoping the King would forgive him any insult. 'Rubyn. Can you take us all?'

The young man nodded solemnly.

He looked back towards the King. 'Then we ride for Caremboche, sire.'

'And then what?' Gyl asked, perplexed.

'The most novel journey you'll ever experience in your own Kingdom, my lord,' Cyrus replied.

Dorgryl plotted. He was frustrated by Orlac, who was too thoughtful and closed to him. He had never been able to read his nephew's thoughts but his senses told him he was now navigating the dangerous waters he had known he would face. The time was right to take over Orlac completely. He must own his nephew by the time they reached the Heartwood. He felt it deep within his soul that Darganoth, King of the Host, would be there waiting for him and that he, Dorgryl, must have full possession of all his nephew's powers if he was to re-enter the land of the gods and deal with his weak brother.

How do we travel? he asked as his nephew brooded on the palace balcony, staring out over the beautiful royal gardens where he had strolled so often with Lauryn. *Surely not at the snail's pace of a clumsy ship?*

His host remained irritatingly silent.

Tell me. I'm intrigued, he persisted, his oily manner working hard to hide his annoyance.

When I'm sure they have arrived I will tell you. Until then, leave me in peace.

Dorgryl remained silent but had no intention of leaving his nephew in peace.

*   *   *

Rubyn noticed that his precious stone, his beloved and only personal possession – which had been quiet for years – had begun to gather heat. He could feel it burning through his thin shirt pocket. He felt curiously comforted by its sudden awakening as he led them from the great old oak into the Heartwood.

Gyl was too stunned initially to even comment on this unique method of transport. The King felt dizzy from the magic and from the realisation that just moments ago they had been standing on the edge of the Great Forest at one of its fingers which pointed to Caremboche. And now he noticed they were in the depths of the Forest where the air was cool and sunlight filtered through a thick canopy of leaves. He felt Lauryn squeeze his hand tightly in reassurance. Trust, he kept telling himself, hearing his mother's caution. Trust the magic. He felt relieved that he would be seeing her shortly; had not realised how much he had missed her presence in the strange blur of events since riding frantically out of Tal in chase of her daughter.

A huge silver wolf met them.

Come, was all she said, turning and loping away.

Although Gyl did not hear this he felt a heightened sense of fear wash over the small group of people as they moved forward. He looked at Lauryn, who clutched Pelyss close.

She shook her head briefly. 'We follow,' she whispered, feeling a comforting warmth begin to burn. It was the stone she had fiercely guarded throughout her imprisonment beginning to reawaken.

Solyana led them in silence until they emerged into a familiar clearing. Lauryn put Pelyss down and rushed

towards her father. He held her tight but there were no
bright words of welcome, no smiles or even tears of joy
to see her again. In her own relief at feeling his strong
arms wrap themselves about her, she did not sense his
grief. And even when she stood back she had no time to
consider his curious welcome because Gidyon descended
and swept her into another embrace.

He too was fighting tears. *Are you . . .* he began to say.

I'll be fine, she dismissed, reading his grief now. *Oh
Gidyon*, she whispered privately, *what's happening?* She
wanted to know why their mother was not there, but
Gidyon hugged her hard again. *Let our father explain.*

His stone suddenly began to burn urgently in his
pocket close to his chest. He felt strangely comforted by
it amidst the grief.

Cyrus had quickly ascertained something serious was amiss.
It did not take much to notice, despite Lauryn's initial squeals
of happiness to be reunited with her family, that others were
holding back – although his heart leapt at the sight of the
comical pair now emerging from another part of the Forest.
The giant and his companion, the dwarf, did not recognise
him. Of course, he looked very different these days. Instead
their eyes were shining with happiness to see Adongo again.
Suddenly Kyt Cyrus and Juno felt like strangers.

He cast only to Tor, who looked strangely devoid of
any emotion.

Thank you for bringing them back, he said before Cyrus
could say anything.

I always keep my promises. Tell me what occurs, Cyrus
pushed into Tor's mind.

Wait, came the softly spoken reply. *Make your saluta-
tions. It is important for the Paladin.*

Flames appeared and a chorus of chimes began.

Darmud Coril shimmered into view. 'Welcome back, brave souls of the Paladin,' he said, his delight quiet but obvious.

His few words seemed to open a valve within them. It was as though they had all been holding their breath and his welcome released it. Instantly the ten members of the Paladin were renewing age-old friendships; with smiles and tears offered freely to one another, especially when Cyrus's and Juno's identities were revealed.

It was a happy scene which Gyl drank in. The sight of Darmud Coril had made his jaw drop. He could not imagine he would ever behold such a vision again. He, a mortal, could feel the throb of a powerful magic as the Paladin were finally reunited beneath the canopy of the Heartwood.

Where was his mother?

He was desperate to see her again. He even leaned towards Torkyn Gynt to ask after her whereabouts, but pulled back for some reason. Something about the way the tall, dark man carried himself told him to wait. She would show herself soon enough. He imagined she was probably picking some flowers for Lauryn's welcome or, more likely, leaves for her herbals. He smiled, watching the Paladin embrace. Gyl suddenly felt he had so much to say to her. Well, with his father gone, she was all he had now. She and Lauryn. Precious Queens of Tallinor – that made him smile again. He was already thinking past the fear everyone else was feeling. He knew Tallinor would survive Orlac and he would see Lauryn on the throne at his side. He could not have said why, but Gyl did not doubt this picture which had come into his mind at the same moment Darmud Coril had appeared.

*   *   *

Tor was experiencing muddled emotions during the Paladin's reunion. He found himself standing so still, withdrawn, because it seemed the best method of handling this internal chaos . . . which was the only way he could describe what he was feeling. And all the while something insistent called to him. He was not sure what it was — but it was powerful, tapping away, trying to win his attention. Sparks of Colours came to mind, brilliant and dazzling. They spoke to him but he pushed them aside for now.

Alyssa. He could not bear to think on it. His heart would slowly bleed him to death at her loss but whilst he still had the strength, he must set his mind to Orlac. Alyssa and the bleeding would come later . . . if there was a later. He wanted to feel the same joy that the Paladin were experiencing but instead felt sadness. It was his fault — his fault that all of these fine souls had borne so much pain and grief. It was because his father, Darganoth, had delivered him up that all these people would now bravely sacrifice their own lives . . . for the second time.

He absently noted the golden puppy sniffing around the heels of Gidyon, who had introduced himself to Rubyn. Tor felt the keen cut of disappointment that he had let his own children down. Two brothers who had never set eyes on one another and now, awkwardly and urgently, would have to build the trust which would bind them. Who knew what they might face? Who knew what their purpose was? Lauryn, standing so close, had already paid a costly price on his behalf. In protecting him she had given the most precious and intimate part of herself over to a madman.

The anger arrived. He must not give in to it. Not yet.

Everyone needed to know the reason for his grief first.

He spoke for the first time. 'We have grave news.'

A hush fell over the Paladin. Tor spoke aloud so Gyl could also hear. He was frightened for the King. After all, Alyssa was his mother, in all but giving birth to him. He reached for Lauryn's hand. He was frightened for her too.

'My lord,' he said, turning and bowing reverently to his sovereign.

Gyl was taken by surprise at Gynt's courtesy. He had pushed aside all thoughts of royal protocol in such surrounds and under such strange circumstances. He gave a short nod in return to the man who had stolen his mother's heart.

'Thank you. May I ask where her majesty is?' He had not meant to reinforce her ties to himself but in regard to his mother he felt helpless – she was the former queen, married to his father, Lorys. They were his parents. He would not let her absence go unremarked without showing his own distress. Gyl sensed a nervous shifting amongst some of the people gathered before him at his enquiry. For his part, he noticed Torkyn Gynt's incredibly blue eyes held his fearlessly.

'It is that I wish to speak of, sire,' Tor admitted.

'Good,' Gyl replied, confused. 'Call her, then. Let us all be together. I keep being told that time is our enemy and yet we stand here amongst polite introductions and touching reunions. Surely plans need to be made?'

He was disturbed to see Gynt shake his head. 'No, sire. No plans. He will come and we will react.'

Lauryn took the King's hand again and flicked a glance towards Gidyon. Something was wrong with her mother.

She was sure of it now for there was no reason in the Land that Alyssa would not be here to see them back to safety within the Heartwood. She felt her stone burning whilst her heart thumped in her chest. What was the grave news?

All eyes now watched Torkyn Gynt take a steadying breath. Cloot had arrived to sit on a nearby branch.

Show courage, the bird whispered into his mind. *Like she did.*

Tor set his shoulders, pushed all other thoughts from his mind and began to tell his tale of grief.

34

Destiny

They await us, Orlac said suddenly.
  How do you know?
  I have my ways.
  Tell me.
  No. He stared again through the eyes of Pelyss towards Lauryn, watching her grieve.

Bad news, then. She has heard of her mother's courage. He saw that on one side of her stood the King, shocked and pale. If he listened carefully he could even hear the Tallinese sovereign's outrage at the news just received. Through the golden pup he noted another familiar person who stood on Lauryn's left. Saxon. The Kloek. The Sixth.

Pelyss sniffed amongst a circle of people and a wolf. Is the animal Cloot or Solyana he wondered? That was the final pair of Paladin he had not accounted for. He had checked off eight of the ten and for some inexplicable reason had felt his heart swell at the sight of them. Old Nanak, the Keeper, had once whispered that there was a fine line between love and hate. Orlac, in his rage, had never understood such a sentiment but increasingly he did now. He knew Lauryn hated him but perhaps she could not help but love him ever so slightly. And whilst he hated the Paladin — they had imprisoned him for centuries — he also loved them in a strange way.

He admired them for their courage and tenacity and respected them for going to their own deaths so resolutely. They had known only pain and despair at the end of the magics he wielded and still they were prepared to face him again. He felt a certain elation at their dedication to their cause and to those they protected. And so yes, he believed he loved them for that commitment. He wondered sadly what it would be like to be loved in return by anyone. He would never know, he decided.

Orlac noticed that Pelyss was scared of the wolf. He pondered this as he spied again the majestic falcon which was always close by. He dragged his mind back, searching for any clues as to why the pup would be scared. It was obvious this was no ordinary wolf. He knew if he considered it for long enough, it would come to him.

What are we waiting for? hissed his uncle.

Quiet! he roared. *Let me think!*

And he was right. It did come to him. Solyana, the Third. She had been a magical beast who had taken many forms over the centuries. He recalled a silver horse and later a silver-flecked bear. And now a wolf. The young dog would not like another beast as magically endowed as Solyana. Their senses would be familiar to each other. That would explain the puppy's obvious reluctance to go near her.

So Cloot was the falcon. When and why that had happened, he could only wonder, remembering the not-so-comely features of the man of Rork'yel.

His thoughts ranged further. The Ten. They were no match for him before and they would be no match for him now. So why did they think they could overpower him? He remembered Rubyn's words. He searched through the eyes of the animal and saw the young man. He sat nearby to the soldier he had once known as Cyruson and yet Rubyn seemed to sit apart from everyone. Remote, silent. The Three. *We will destroy you*, he had declared. How?

And now his attention came to rest finally on Torkyn Gynt. His brother. The man who had been sent to kill him. He had a kind face . . . a sad face. They both knew what it was to lose the woman they loved. His brother was his opposite in colouring. Where he was golden-haired and violet-eyed, his sibling was dark with an arresting pair of blue eyes. He too felt sad. In another lifetime, a different context, they might have been close brothers, good friends. A strong fraternal love might have existed. Instead they were pitted against one another. One must destroy the other in order to survive. He hoped his father would pay that visit and watch what he had contrived.

Next to his brother sat a younger version of Gynt. It was uncanny. Ah, Orlac thought, staring intently through the vision of Pelyss, this is the third child; Lauryn's other brother.

All accounted for. All waiting. He hadn't realised he had spoken the thought in his head.

What? Why are you staring out so intently? What do you see? Dorgryl exclaimed, his exasperation beating him.

Hush now, uncle, we are close.

* * *

Their initial shock had been replaced by tears. And when the weeping was done, the Friends of the Heartwood sat in an awkward pause. Solyana's usual suggestion to eat had failed to entice anyone towards the food laid out. Now they murmured quietly amongst themselves, wondering what might happen. At the back of each of their minds was the question of what would trigger the commencement of the final battle – for surely this was what they were facing? Orlac was coming – when and how no one knew – but they all understood this was it. This final confrontation within the Heartwood had been centuries in the making, during which time spirits had been broken and lives had been lost and won again. Orlac would die or they would. There was no turning back now; no escape.

Gradually their attention fell back upon Tor. The One. He alone would guide them now.

Tor looked up from his quiet thoughts. He had been experiencing the sensation for some time now that eyes were upon him; probing, searching. When he saw all of them staring in his direction he put it down to that and yet a vague sense of being 'touched' by someone else was still there – he could not shake the notion.

Can you feel it? he asked Cloot.

The eyes? Yes. Strange. What is it?

I don't know but listen to me now, no heroics.

What do you mean?

You know exactly what I'm saying. I want you to live, Cloot.

Not at your expense, my son. You forget. I am Paladin . . . and more, I am bonded to you alone. I would die before I would see you harmed.

Cloot, please I—

Hush, Tor. There is no more to be discussed. The moment has

*arrived. We face our destiny now. I have mine and you have
yours. Let's walk towards it bravely. Life or death change not
how I have loved you over these years or love you now. I feel your
grief. I also feel your anger. Don't let's allow her death to be in
vain. Don't let's allow our deaths – if that's what is asked –
to be in vain either. I am not afraid.*

Tears welled in Tor's eyes. Cloot's nobility was always
so potent and inspiring. *I am not afraid either.*

*Then guide those now who would follow you blindly and
faithfully no matter what stood before them. Don't waste their
precious blood in indecision. Be true to yourself. The answers lie
within you. Remember, Tor, you are the One.*

Tor looked around. 'Does anyone have anything to
share? Now perhaps will be our last chance.'

Faces still pinched from the shock of Alyssa's death
stared back at him. Tor felt their emptiness keenly.
Everyone, including himself, had worked towards this
time and yet now that they were here, none of them knew
what was expected of them; how to wield their magic
effectively. They were looking to him to show them and
he felt helpless.

All the Paladin were as still as statues – the only erratic
movement being from the dog, Pelyss, who scampered
around their feet – all, that is, except Solyana. Tor had not
noticed until now that the wolf had been restless for several
minutes. She had begun to sniff the air and pad silently
around the outside of the circle in which Pelyss played, the
circle the Paladin and the Trinity formed. A low rumble
had begun to issue from her throat – so soft at first as to
be hardly noticeable – but it built gradually in intensity
until they were all looking towards the wolf. Her lips had
begun to pull back to reveal long, menacing teeth.

This further disturbed everyone and the two soldiers amongst them instinctively reached for their swords. Somehow Cyrus knew it was useless but he liked the comforting feel of the blade in his hand. He noticed the King had even brought along a bow from amongst the weapons he had stocked on *The Raven*. Cyrus could see the beautifully fletched arrows in a quiver nearby. He loved to shoot with a bow. In his days as Prime, no one bar the King even came close to matching his skills. He could shoot down birds on the wing with such mastery that Lorys had good-naturedly proclaimed him a freak and refused to shoot against him. He wondered now, vaguely, amongst this fresh fear at Solyana's behaviour, whether Gyl was adept with the bow too. He promised himself that if they lived past this day, he would make a point of finding out.

Solyana was no longer just making noise. Her strange yellow eyes seemed to be riveted on the golden puppy playing happily amongst their feet.

'What is it?' Tor asked her. 'Is he coming?'

No, she growled — it was a chilling voice none of them had heard from her before. *He's already here*, and she sprang towards Pelyss, her large and powerful jaw clamping around the puppy's neck. Pelyss screamed in terror.

Orlac rocked backwards as his spell on Pelyss was broken.

It is time, he said quietly before taking one last long breath of the fragrance of the Ciprean royal gardens and casting out powerfully.

Dorgryl, caught unawares, felt the air around them sizzle. He knew he had but seconds now and with every last ounce of strength he could muster, forced the red mist to flow angrily through his host. Orlac, who was guiding them in a massively potent transporting magic, was momentarily weakened by his efforts. More importantly, he was diverted as he focused all of his energies on moving his body through the magical planes which would take him from Cipres to the Heartwood in moments.

He could not fight off the monstrous effort of Dorgryl *and* achieve the transportation.

He had to choose.

Panic gripped the Heartwood's own as Lauryn began to scream, terrified for her dog. However, the huge wolf released the pup almost as soon as she had struck because she felt the spirit of the god who used his eyes and ears disappear.

He's left the dog, Solyana said quietly across the Link.

Everyone began speaking at once. They were stunned by this news.

'Silence!' Cyrus ordered, the first to recover from the shock of Solyana's revelation. 'Form a circle and turn outwards.'

'Be vigilant,' Saxon said, his nervousness making him speak his thoughts aloud.

Silence gripped them as they waited. The old fear at facing Orlac came home to roost amongst the Paladin. It was a familiar feeling.

The falcon felt it too. *Be strong now*, Cloot whispered to his companions. *Our task is done now, Paladin. It is up to Tor and the Trinity – we must help them achieve what they were sent here to do. Hold the Link open, no matter what*. And then on a private Link to Tor he added: *This is your time, my son.*

Tor had no time to respond. He felt it first. *Orlac comes*, he said, looking at each one slowly in what felt like a farewell. *Brave Paladin, thank you*, he called gently. He glanced to each of the children he loved. *Trinity . . . you must do whatever it is you were meant to do. I know not what that is. But you will when the moment arrives. Trust yourselves. Avenge your mother.*

Tor felt the reassuring thump of Cloot landing on his shoulder. He sensed Gidyon, Lauryn and Rubyn moving towards each other. Meanwhile the nine other members of the Paladin gathered, fanning out instinctively in the shape of an arrow behind him. Gyl melted back into the bushes, directly behind Lauryn, his sword and his bow at the ready. He would save her; fight for her — die for her if it was asked.

Trees began to shudder about them and the soft sunlight which had filtered through seemed to dull, plunging them into a false darkness. Below them the land rumbled as if it might crack open. They held hands and opened their minds to each other.

The Light guide us, Cyrus said.

The air ahead began to spin, whipping up dust from the earth and leaves which had fallen from the trees in their mighty distress. It began to shimmer, ghostly pale at first but gathering in a golden intensity until they could make out the shape of a man. He was tall and broad . . . and possessed by madness.

His eyes glowed red.

It was Lauryn who screamed. *Dorgryl!*

The noise about him died down. The earth stopped its rumbling but the trees of the Heartwood still groaned softly. They did not like the beast amongst them.

'Greetings One and all,' Dorgryl said, smiling broadly with Orlac's mouth.

Tor seized control. 'I will not speak with you,' he said and watched the smile die on Orlac's face.

'Not speak with me?' the thing raged in its deep and ugly voice. 'Do you know who I am?'

'You are Dorgryl. Sad possessor of tragically fallen gods. You have no place amongst the Host and you have no place here. Begone beast!' Tor spoke angrily.

Enraging him is a clever tactic, Cloot offered sagely into Tor's mind only.

'I would speak only with Orlac,' Tor persisted.

'You will speak with me, fool, before I destroy you and all your pathetic protectors. Ah, Lauryn, my dear, have the bruises healed? I did not mean to push against you quite so hard when we lay together.'

Lauryn felt her bile rise but her brothers squeezed her hands so tight she could not move. No one had considered Gyl, who, hearing Lauryn so taunted, broke cover from the bushes, brandishing his sword. The bow and single arrow he had nocked dropped as he ran towards the god. They landed at the feet of Cyrus.

Orlac's hand twitched and the King of Tallinor was flung clear across their heads with such force there was little chance he could have survived the impact against one of the great oaks if that same tree had not deftly leaned down its branches to capture him in the air. The branches quickly lifted the limp body into their highest reaches and away from trouble. He was useless against Orlac. He was a liability amongst the Friends.

As Lauryn wept it was Rubyn's calm voice which helped her. *The trees will protect him. Fear not for him . . . only for us.*

It bewildered those around him to hear Tor sneer. It struck them as pointless to stoke the fury of this already-enraged god. Yet he persisted and they trusted.

'Is that it, Dorgryl? Is that the best you can achieve with all that power at your fingertips . . . and the King a mortal at that?'

'Time for you to die, Gynt,' Dorgryl announced.

'I'm ready. We all are, coward,' Tor shouted back. 'But let me look on my brother. Let me see with my own eyes this wretch you inhabit.'

They all felt Orlac's true presence pushing angrily against Dorgryl's.

'Clever you are, Gynt, playing us against one another,' the elder god said.

Tor ignored Dorgryl. 'Do you hear me, Orlac? Cast this demon out and face me – or is it that you fear me so much you hide?'

They watched the red mist of the eyes dull slightly and something else momentarily shone through.

'I see you cringe behind your uncle. So, all those centuries of struggle for this? You'll allow *him* the pleasure of defeating us? We go to our deaths knowing you are, and probably always were, a coward.'

Cloot no longer thought this wise. *Tor—*

Hush. Look.

The golden man's body began to shake. The face contorted horribly as an internal struggle began to take place. The Paladin and Trinity watched in a horrified fascination as two gods warred within one body for supremacy. A terrible guttural sound came from Orlac's mouth but they suspected the noise was Dorgryl's as he wrestled desperately to hang onto his possession.

Across the Link Tor heard the Paladin's frightened questions.

Trust me. Lys once told me it was Dorgryl's arrogance that won him his place in the Bleak. Arrogance will be his undoing again, she has counselled.

No one understood but their faith in Torkyn Gynt held strong.

What do you propose to do? Cloot asked privately.

Invite him out.

Where to?

Into me.

Have you gone mad as well?

It's the only way.

Why?

I'm strong enough to overcome him.

He heard Cloot click angrily in his head whilst they watched the monstrous battle taking place before their eyes. Orlac's body was sheened with the sweat of his exertions to oust his uncle. For the moment it looked as though he might be gaining the ascendancy, as the eyes now showed a definite violet hue.

What makes you so sure? the falcon demanded.

Because I'm smarter than my brother and . . .

And what, Tor? Cloot was shouting into his head now.

I have nothing more to lose.

Other than your children?

Other than my children, he echoed, before adding sadly, *and my friends.* He reached up and briefly patted his falcon. *You have to trust me.* He looked again to his brother as the trees around them creaked and groaned with sickening force.

'Welcome to the Heartwood, Orlac,' Tor called and the

golden god stared back, blazing fury through violet eyes. He was breathing deeply.

'I will show you no more mercy than Dorgryl,' Orlac's real voice said.

'I'm not interested in your mercy.'

The god nodded. 'Perhaps you are interested to learn that your Alyssa died bravely. She lured Xantia and Dorgryl away from your daughter for long enough to permit Lauryn's escape.'

Orlac watched Tor flinch at his wife's name. He knew he had hurt him.

Tor clamped his jaw hard. He would not allow his resolve to be undone so easily. He took a deep breath and pressed on. 'Dorgryl, I know you can hear me. I know what you want. All I want is to destroy my brother. I will give you my body, if you will help me.'

A Link opened in his mind and an ugly voice spoke. *Why?*

You have knowledge. You have power. Combine them with mine — we can defeat him. And then my body is yours to command.

I ask again, why?

Because I have already lost what I love.

Ah, Alyssa. She was very brave to her end, you know.

It took all his will to respond without showing despair. *So I hear.* Tor fought the urge to ask more. He bit back on the rush of questions and forced his manner to be calm. He watched Orlac raise his arms high and Tor immediately created a mighty shield about them so he could buy some time to ward off whatever was about to be hurled.

He tried one last time. *Come to me, Dorgryl.* He stepped forward. *I open myself to you. I am a god. I am what you want, surely? I can give you what you crave and in my body you can be all-powerful.*

The trees began to murmur their own despair and the Flames of the Firmament appeared, the normally sweet chimes discordant and angry. They rushed about Tor begging him not to do this. The Paladin intensified their Link, bonding themselves powerfully to one another. They had no idea what might happen but they did know they would need their combined strength to fight it. Pelyss began to bark and the three children called anxiously to their father.

Amongst this cacophony of sound, the people fell silent, transfixed as they watched a bloody red mist lift itself out of Orlac's body, and sway above him.

Are you ready? Cloot asked Cyrus privately. His voice had an urgency.

Cyrus bent and picked up the bow at his feet, resetting the arrow in position. *I can't do this.*

You will! the falcon commanded. *You may be the First. But I am First Paladin to the One. You will do exactly as I say.*

Cloot's voice was hard and angry. Cyrus did not like the plan one bit. But he nodded, frightened by what he had been told to do.

Orlac staggered, breathing deeply. The sense of freedom from the thing inside was intoxicating.

The burning of the stone in his pocket pulled Gidyon out of shock.

Rubyn! Lauryn! The stones. They're calling to us. Where are your stones?

They looked at him, stupefied, not having been sure whether they should tear their eyes from the red mist. Gidyon looked so intense they finally obeyed, digging deep into their pockets and lifting out their stones to match his. The trio of dull-coloured stones was blazing iridescent rainbow colours with such a fierce intensity, they were blinded.

The Stones of Ordolt were finally reunited but this time they were in the hands of gods. In these children ran the blood of King of the Host and the ancient blood of the Custodian. They alone had the power to command the Stones.

The red mist which was Dorgryl faltered, hanging in the air as he too felt this immense new power present itself amongst them, but it was Orlac who was transfixed by the blazing orbs.

What now? Lauryn asked as the Colours blazed so strongly about the trio it almost hummed.

We must wield its power, Gidyon said. *But I don't know what it is.*

Think! Lauryn yelled.

Their father spoke. *They were his flowers. You alone can command them.*

They looked towards Orlac. He was reaching his hand towards the Stones. 'They are mine!'

The flowers! They belong to the Glade. The Stones can summon the Glade! Rubyn suddenly yelled.

Join minds, Gidyon said and the Link immediately changed into something more intimate. It was as though he was Rubyn and he was Lauryn. His brother and sister felt likewise.

It frightened the Paladin to suddenly hear a strange and ancient language issuing from the three children. They began to murmur words of magic not uttered in countless centuries.

It was a language not of this world. It was the ancient language of the gods.

A vast power of a magnitude none present had ever felt before began to gather about them. The Flames of the Firmament intensified in brightness; no longer hundreds of them but now thousands, chiming in harmony but ferociously, now in a deafening chorus as the power continued to pull and centralise to a mighty shimmering by the great oak behind the three children.

But Cloot had eyes only for the red mist as Tor once again offered Dorgryl his body. The falcon took his chance while the mist hesitated as Ordolt, the Glade, suddenly winked into existence.

Leaping strongly into the air the majestic bird beat its wings angrily, covering the distance between itself and the mist in a blink and gathering up Dorgryl. Cloot lifted, higher and higher in what looked like an impossible ascent, his captive screaming into his mind and fighting violently. But Cloot's talons held on. He could hear the cries of his friends below and the soft encouragement of the trees.

He passed the gentle face of Darmud Coril who smiled his serene smile and whispered, *Fly bravely, precious Cloot.*

He went higher still, the thing writhing but still he dragged it with him. He could do this. Finally they were far enough away.

Now you must enter me, beast, he told it.

Cloot knew it had no other option. It could not survive outside a body for longer than moments. It had to use his body. As Cloot had anticipated the mist shimmered with rage as he felt the vile chill of it enter his bird's body.

*   *   *

Some had fallen to their knees. Tor gaped, distracted by the scene before him. Ordolt was here, summoned by the Trinity and their power over the Stones and their ability to speak Ordolt's ancient language. He glanced towards the children, blazing amongst the fantastical colours radiating from the orbs which held the Glade here in its return to claim back the three dried and hardened magical flowers which belonged to it.

Staring back out at him from the impossibly beautiful scene which Ordolt was wearing this day, stood two familiar figures amongst many others. He remembered them from his vision in the dreams which Lys had showed him.

They were Darganoth and Evagora. Orlac's parents. His parents.

Orlac too was mesmerised. He was back on his feet, his attention riveted on the tall dark man in the Glade who looked like his brother and the beautiful golden-haired woman at his side. The royal pair looked up towards Cloot who had now stooped into one of his dives.

It was only then that Tor realised Cloot had left his shoulder and understood what had happened. Darganoth was looking towards Cyrus now and nodding. Tor saw that Cyrus held a bow. He knew Cyrus was a deadly shot with an arrow.

And suddenly it all came together.

'No!' he yelled. *Cloot, no!* he screamed across their Link. *Farewell, Tor*, Cloot whispered. *I have loved you in my lives; I will love you in my death. Heartwood, I humbly ask that you accept me for the last time.*

Cloot began his steep dive, Dorgryl screaming angrily in his mind.

Cyrus let loose the arrow. It impaled the falcon through its breast, killing the man that was once Cloot of the Rork'yel. The First Paladin to the One died and the god, Dorgryl, trapped in a dead, falling body howled his despair as the trees of the Heartwood reached hungrily now to grab their own.

The falcon's corpse was still too high in the air for Dorgryl to escape to a new host. Between their hard fingers of wood, they crushed the fragile bones and feathers of the majestic Cloot until he was pulp. Finally the tallest of all the trees took the bird's remains and absorbed Cloot into itself, returning him to the sanctuary of the Heartwood and Dorgryl to a dark and desolate prison.

No one in the Heartwood that terrible day would ever forget the bleak expression on Torkyn Gynt's face when the Light died within and he knew his falcon, his bonded one . . . his beloved Cloot, was gone. He was bereft. Alyssa and Cloot. There was a hole too big now in his heart and the only thing he could fill it with at this moment was rage. He turned back towards Orlac and allowed all of his Colours to loose themselves. He was no longer thinking rationally.

Each of the Paladin and his children felt the bristling of another mighty power as the Colours of Torkyn Gynt combined into a pure white rage of throbbing magic.

Darganoth nodded and whispered out of the Glade into Tor's mind. *Use your anger, son. Destroy him. We will help you.*

The Paladin closed ranks behind Tor into a single line whilst Gidyon, Lauryn and Rubyn instinctively understood their part in this. They opened themselves up to the Host.

Orlac roared. 'Destroy me, then. Try. I will best all of you in your attempt and leave this place a smoking ruin. Let loose your power, Father, Mother, murdering brother!'

And Darganoth did. Using the Stones of Ordolt to channel not only his power but all the power of the gathered Host in the Glade, he cast with a frightening bolt of Quelling magic. As it touched the Stones the rainbow colours intensified and the Trinity allowed its linked powers to be tapped. Now it passed through the Stones becoming a silvery light as it touched the Paladin.

And as it passed through each of them harmlessly, they contributed their own powers, doubling and quadrupling its ferocity until it passed through Tor. Now it became a fierce, radiant white as all the Colours combined to produce the most pure of the gods' magics.

It was travelling so fast now and so savagely it created a hum.

It shot from Tor's fingertips, luminous white and angry, to hit Orlac in the chest. He tried to stand strong against it but this was like no other power he had experienced. Even the original Quelling had not felt like this. He staggered and bent beneath its brutality, trying to fight back but beaten down by wave after wave until his own powers were numbed.

Lauryn wept to see him pushed so violently and without even knowing she was going to do it, she linked to her father.

Does it have to be like this?

She heard her father groan; knew how much he detested killing with his power.

Orlac began to writhe on the ground, his death moments away.

Lauryn persisted. *Orlac did not kill my mother or Cloot. He did not rape me. He is your brother. Can we not save his soul?*

Something in her words touched the right chord. Tor faltered and the white light died. Orlac lay motionless and spent.

'Torkyn!' Darganoth called from the Glade. 'Finish it!'

'No!' Tor hurled back. 'Enough death. Enough killing!'

He walked to where his brother lay. The Paladin renewed their ancient skills, creating a field of imprisonment. Now, neither brother could depart without the sanction of the Paladin – or their own death.

Orlac. Tor could see he still breathed and whilst he still took breath there was a chance.

Come to gloat? Orlac whispered.

Tor shook his head. *Will you trust me?*

What for?

To save you.

Through his pain, the god actually laughed grimly. *You, save me?*

Tor said nothing. Everyone watching held their breath.

Orlac coughed weakly. *What do you have in mind?*

That you go back . . . back to where you came from. Back to Ordolt.

There was a long pause before Orlac gave a weak reply. *Will it accept me?*

It might. If we give it back its flowers which are what it seeks. Will you let me try?

Why would you do this after all the pain?

To end the pain.

Tor crouched down and placed his hands beneath his brother. *May I?*

Orlac nodded and grimaced as Tor lifted him into his arms. He was weaker than he had realised.

Brother, Orlac called softly.

Yes?

I may not make it to the Glade.

Please try.

Tallinor is claiming me, I fear. How ironic, Orlac said, a soft smile playing on his lips as his face began to slacken.

Orlac! Take my strength. Tor pushed, opening himself up, watching the horror move across the faces of the Paladin at this dangerous new suggestion. It was all Orlac needed to destroy Tor.

Do you trust . . . ? Orlac was so weak he could not even finish what he wanted to say.

Tor looked down into the blurring eyes of Orlac and nodded. *Take what you need. We are brothers.*

And Orlac took, drawing on Tor's strength.

The Paladin parted, dropping their imprisoning power at Cyrus's command and watched Tor walk slowly with his load towards a shocked Host.

He stopped in front of Ordolt, from where Darganoth watched him. Tor could see how he himself might look when he became older. It was an odd thought. He had no plan to live beyond this day without Alyssa or Cloot.

'Take him back,' he said.

Darganoth shook his head sadly. 'I'm not sure we can, son.'

Arriving behind the King of the Host was another familiar face. Lys. She smiled and Tor saw Alyssa echoed so strongly it made his heart begin its bleed. So be it. He welcomed death.

She bowed before Darganoth. 'My King. Tor is right.

Offer back the flowers to Ordolt. It is temperamental. We may just catch it in a forgiving mood, sire . . . please.'

They waited.

'Very well,' the King finally replied. 'We can try. Ask my grandchildren to make their offer to the Glade.'

Rubyn looked at his brother and sister. 'I'll do it.' He took their stones, still blazing, still holding Ordolt amongst the oaks. He walked to where he could see a soft tear in the shimmering, presuming it was the rent made by the scavengers who once stole an infant god.

He bowed solemnly to this magical place. 'Ordolt. Forgive us for holding onto three items which are precious and belong to you. They were taken in innocence by an infant. May we return them?'

The gorgeous scene shimmered brightly suddenly and although no one knew what it meant, Rubyn took a breath and hoped it was the answer they wanted. He reached in through the hole, feeling the instant warmth of the place beyond it. Reverently placing the three stones on the spongy, verdant grass of Ordolt he gently withdrew his hand and bowed again. They watched as the stones were absorbed into the ground and before their eyes three exquisitely beautiful flowers grew from where they had disappeared. Ordolt flashed this time, returning just as rapidly to its normal soft light.

It was Tor's turn to make a plea. 'Ordolt, may we return another who was stolen from you a long time ago? He is the innocent. He belongs amongst your forests and your beautiful gardens. He has known much sorrow. You would bring him great joy in granting us this. He is yours,' Tor beseeched.

Ordolt did not respond this time. Tor looked at his

mother. He felt nothing for her but he wished he had known her. Her smile for him was radiant.

'I shall chance it,' he said, stepping forward. 'I hope this does not create catastrophes for Tallinor.'

His mother shook her head gently. 'No, son. Because it is a returning, it is safe.'

He nodded, looking down at Orlac now. 'Fare well, brother,' he said, softly.

Orlac was spent, hanging onto life now courtesy of Tor. 'I'm sorry about Cloot. I liked him too.' They shared a sad smile. *The Light guide you, Tor*, he said privately. *Tell Lauryn . . . no. Tell her nothing. Ask her to take care of Pelyss.*

Tor looked towards his parents. 'I give you Orlac, Prince of Gods.'

His mother began to weep through her smile. 'His name is not Orlac, my child. That was the Tallinese name given to him by Merkhud. His name is Aeryn, Prince of Gods.'

Tor bent to kiss Aeryn on the forehead and as he handed his brother through Ordolt's shimmering presence, passing through its strange magics, he saw himself hand a sleeping infant into the arms of its mother.

It shocked everyone, including the Host. For Lys it was the sign she needed; had prayed for. Through her own grief she saw that perhaps, somehow, this all could be righted for two people.

'Tor, wait!' she called. 'Come through too. Ordolt will accept you.'

Tor was stunned. He paused, considering her suggestion.

She persisted. 'You have nothing left to do for Tallinor. Everything that is you is here.' Lys could hear the plea in her voice.

He glanced around the familiar faces of the Paladin. Saxon nodded. He understood, more than anyone, Tor's sense of desolation. He too had lost Alyssa, and a close friend in Cloot.

Go, boy, Cyrus said into his head. *Don't hesitate.*

Tor looked towards his children. Lauryn was nodding through her tears. *Find happiness there. Start again.*

He pulled his three children towards him. *Will you permit this?*

They all three nodded. *You've given enough*, Gidyon said, his eyes wet.

It was Rubyn who gave him the response he needed. It was a placation but it was what Tor needed to hear. *You may find her, Father.*

I don't suppose you three would consider it? Tor asked.

They shook their heads and he understood. They had reasons to stay in Tallinor.

Tor knew he must not linger. Lys was urging him to step through. Any further delay and the fractious Ordolt might reject him. He did not want to prolong an emotional farewell so he kissed his three children before grinning his unsaid thanks towards his friends in the Paladin.

'The Light guide you,' he said and stepped through the shimmering presence, taking both his father's hands and appearing on the other side as a newborn, returned to exactly how he had been before he was given over to save Tallinor.

The Host wept to have their princes returned.

And the Heartwood rejoiced.

Epilogue

'And we cannot persuade you to remain on our shores?' the King of Tallinor asked.

Kyt Cyrus shook his head. 'Rubyn and I have some unfinished business in Cipres, your majesty. But we shall return for the wedding in the spring.' He bowed to his King. 'Perhaps we might forge still closer ties between the two realms?'

Gyl smiled. His father had been right to choose Kyt Cyrus for Prime. And now Tallinor would have a powerful ally in Cipres. He watched the soldier turn and walk towards Lauryn, who was standing with her brothers.

She smiled warmly at the old soldier. 'You take care of my brother, Cyrus. Bring him back for my marriage.'

'It seems the Gynt children have a way with sovereigns,' he said, ignoring Rubyn's glare. 'Who knows, I may bring your brother with a new wife,' he risked. 'And you, Gidyon. Where are you headed?' Cyrus said, deciding it was time to change the subject.

'Back to a town in Brittelbury.'

'Ah yes, in the north. You have business there?'

The man who reminded him so keenly of the young Torkyn Gynt shrugged in the habitual way his father had at the same age. It nagged at Cyrus's heart.

'Unfinished, like your business in Cipres,' Gidyon replied with a wry grin. He turned to his companions nearby. 'Themesius and Figgis are coming with me . . . and after that I plan to return to the Rork'yel Mountains. There are people there we gave a promise to.'

Saxon strolled up. He alone could share none of the joy of this festive scene as the Friends of the Heartwood began their farewells.

'Sax. Care to join us on the road?' Gidyon asked.

'Well, I would jump at it if your cunning sister and her manipulative future husband hadn't already persuaded me to return to Tal and help a certain young lad out.'

Rubyn guessed. 'Locky?'

Saxon nodded. 'Yes. I think I owe it to him.' Then added sadly, 'I can lose myself in teaching him a few things, until I can sort out what to do next.'

Cyrus muttered agreement. 'And the others?' he said, turning to where the rest of their companions stood, saying their goodbyes.

'Adongo is headed back to the Ciprean islands where the Moruks roam. Sallementro, of course, is coming back to Tal — I think he's already dreaming up the wedding ballad.' They all smiled. 'Is it right, Lauryn, that Juno is going with you?'

She nodded. 'I've asked her to. She's thinking on it. I believe she will.'

'Which leaves our residents of the Heartwood,' Saxon continued. 'I don't imagine either Arabella or Solyana will ever leave here,' he admitted and the others agreed. 'I don't know where I'll end up – perhaps my birthplace in the southern islands. It's a bit early yet; wounds still too raw.'

Those listening nodded sombrely. They knew to whom he referred.

'Father refused to say goodbye to her, you know,' Gidyon suddenly blurted.

They looked at him, a mix of confusion and regret on their faces.

He explained himself. 'When our mother died and Darmud Coril wanted to take her into the trees, we all said goodbye – we kissed her.' He shrugged, remembering the moment of kissing that pale, cold cheek a little too clearly. 'But our father refused. He told me he would somehow see her again . . . in the Light – in another life, I think he meant.'

'And perhaps he will,' Cyrus said, echoing everyone's hopes.

A very young boy ran dizzying circles around his brother – a baby – cradled in a beautifully-woven basket. Their mother smiled in a radiant manner such as none had seen in centuries. These were no ordinary children – these were Princes of the Host. The eldest and heir to the throne was a sunny, happy child with golden hair and strangely violet eyes full of laughter. His brother was much darker in looks; a thick shock of black downy hair told his parents he might echo his father and if the presently-dark eyes turned into the brilliant blue they promised to be, then he might well be the image of Darganoth, the King of the Host.

As Aeryn played, singing an old rhyme to his baby

brother, Evagora was laughing with two other women.

'It turned out better than we could have ever hoped,' she admitted to her oldest and dearest friend.

Lys took the Queen's hand and smiled. She was still finding this happy scene hard to believe herself. 'Thank you for allowing me to bring her back.'

Evagora's eyes immediately brimmed but her voice was firm. 'They have suffered too much. All innocents. When you came to us with the plan, I knew if anyone could make it work, you could. It was an inspired move to bring her back through the Bleak.'

'I took a gamble, your majesty. I guessed that if I could force her spirit to lift free somehow whilst she still drew breath, then I could save her; claim back that spirit.'

'And did you know that Tor would return Aeryn?'

Lys shook her head. 'No, highness. That had not even occurred to me. He worked that out himself.'

The Queen noticed her other guest tentatively reach forward to stroke the baby's soft skin.

'May I hold him?' the woman asked.

'Of course, my dear,' the Queen said.

'Will he remember, do you think?'

'No, child. But it matters not,' her mother replied gently. 'There is no doubt that when he is grown, he will fall in love with you all over again,' Lys added.

Alyssa smiled and hugged the little boy close. She would wait.